NEQUA

or

The Problem of the Ages

by Jack Adams

Vol. 1

Originally published by
Equity Publishing Company
Topeka, Kansas
1900

Third edition published by
Green Snake Press
www.GreenSnakePress.com

Direct all inquiries or any information about the lives of any person mentioned in Nequa to Nequathebook@gmail.com

Library of Congress Control Number: 2014917668
International Standard Book Number: 978-0-9910895-0-5

Concept and Design
Jim L. Friesen

Printing by
Mennonite Press, Inc., Newton, Kansas
www.MennnonitePress.com

Dedication

TO ALL LOVERS OF HUMANITY, WHEREVER FOUND WHO BELIEVE THAT THE APPLICATION OF THE GOLDEN RULE IN HUMAN AFFAIRS WOULD REMOVE ALL THE BURDENS THAT IGNORANCE AND GREED HAVE IMPOSED UPON THE MASSES OF MANKIND, THIS VOLUME IS RESPECTFULLY DEDICATED BY THE AUTHOR.

Notice

EQUITY is a weekly paper devoted to the discussion of fundamental economics and the higher ethics of business published at Topeka, Kansas. Nequa is the first volume of Equity library series. Orders will be fulfilled at fifty cents in paper covers. One dollar in cloth: a liberal discount to the trade. Jack Adams, the author, will be a contributor to EQUITY and will answer correspondence addressed to the care of EDITOR EQUITY, Topeka, Kansas

Contents

Chapter IX

Chapter X

Chapter XI

Chapter XII

Chapter XIII

Chapter XIV

Chapter XV

Explanatory

The undersigned claims no credit for the concept of an "Inner World" in which the great economic problems which now confront the people had been solved in the interest of humanity and ideal conditions established for all.

This was the leading thought in a work by Dr. T. A. H. Lowe, deceased, which was placed in the hands of the writer by his widow, Mrs. Mary P. Lowe. It contains a glowing description of the ideal conditions which would prevail under the practical application of the principles of Freedom, Equality and Fraternity in human affairs, but the author died before he had an opportunity to work out a practical system by which the masses of the people, situated as they now are, without even a clear understanding as to just what is the matter, could commence with existing conditions, and peacefully, effectually and speedily establish the much to be desired system of absolute justice in distribution which he described. Hence it was determined to prepare a series of volumes, illustrating the operation of practical working methods by which this result could be secured, and then, publish Dr. Lowe's original volume, just as it was written as a fitting conclusion; and we now take pleasure in presenting to the reader the first volume of the series and respectfully ask a candid consideration of the principles which it is designed to elucidate.

JACK ADAMS.

Preface to the Third Edition

Nequa was originally serialized in the newspaper *EQUITY* which was published in Topeka from 1899 until September of 1901. Nequa was published in 1900, in book form, and appeared in both hard and soft bound editions. Those first editions exist today, in a dozen or so libraries. It appears that it was printed on paper with very little rag content so it does not age well. It's original existence is a testimony to the attempts in Kansas and throughout the midwest to find methods of refining the democracy and economics of the day to better protect the average person

The average person needed protection from the corporate giants as represented by the banks and the railroads.

The average person needed protection from the shyster, con man, and gun toting ruffian.

The average person needs protection from themselves as evidenced by the land schemers, day dreamers and eventual dust bowls.

Some educated guesses, well thought out projections, indicate that we as a people still need oversight of our hap hazardous attempts to "harness" the world. The majority of the population of the world still needs protection from the corporations who provide goods and services.

When Nequa was being written, a new day was trying to dawn. Women's right to vote, birth control knowledge, throwing off the oppression of that old time religion, living in an above ground dwelling, coupled with scientific agricultural practices that doubled yields; a lot of new ways were being written about in newspapers. Nequa was an attempt to put these ideas into combinations and explain how to get from where things were, to where they should be, so a new egalitarian society could come into existence.

The racial ideas of Eugenics had successfully sequestered themselves in peoples brains and so false conclusions about the "colored" races appeared even in the minds of those working for equality. Nequa's writers assumed that those with dark pigment preferred to be white.

One should read and compare the "hollow earth" novel "Mizora" by Mary E. Bradley Lane which appeared in 1880. It had only one race in the center of the earth. The people were blond white women, all men and all "colored" races had been removed.

As a defense for Nequa's poor racial attitude, please consider that Nequa's writers lived and worked in a highly integrated commercial section of Topeka. The Nequa people also started a business which stated that race would not be a consideration of service. Incorrect thoughts but not incorrect actions. The newspapers they published carried some articles about African-American people and it is very possible that the paper was printed by Nick Chiles, a black entrepreneur.

With the exception of the racial ideas many of the ideas Nequa presented are today accepted as gospel. Protection under the law has been extended to cover American citizens from coast to coast, even though many corporations are still oppressive and still out of the control of we the people. There are still a lot of bottom line companies with no input from those, who depend on a company for jobs. We have allowed our perceptions to over look the pain and suffering our materialistic existence costs the rest of the world. We like to send a few dollars for starving children rather than change the system to a more inclusive way of life. We have a hard time remembering the phrase "regardless of the race, religion, or national boundary". Nequa should remind us of other ways that could be tried again, with a lot better outcome.

While reading this book one might try to remember that the year this book was first published, Wyatt Earp was 51, Calamity Jane was 48, Buffalo Bill Cody was 54 and Frank James was still riding around on a horse.

It would be ten more years before Margaret Sanger's birth control rights campaign would start. Twenty years would have to go by before women could vote in a national election.

In three more years Orville and Wilber will finally get their aeroplane to fly. Oklahoma won't be a state for seven years. Marconi will send his first transatlantic wireless signal next year, in 1901.

Introduction

NEQUA is a dusty old book, it sat on my library shelf for fourty years. Why did I go to the trouble of reformating and republishing it? This publication is in your hands because of a whole series of very serendipitous situations. Situations where an object, a book would not leave me alone. We all have coincidences in our lives, but the truly serendipitous event is one where several situations, a series, seem to be placed together, not just in an observer's mind but also somehow in close proxmity in time.

Perhaps if we would try to look for or understand the possibility of a linkage through spirit only. Maybe we should try to accept the idea that events may be linked by non sensate connections. Our coincidences, those seemly acausal situations could be appreciated for what they really are. An attraction of our attention. A re-attraction of our attention. Our attention provides an entrance for a shift in our knowledge.

It seems that since starting to look for just a little info on the copy right holders I have been lead from book to book each with a snippet of information that seems in my mind to be relevant to understanding the times, and the people with ideas for a more magnanimous life style. My attention was caught by the message in Nequa, woven through personal family connections and some how attached to the original finding of Nequa, which has resulted in the republishing of this book.

Grigsby and Lowe had both been some where in the middle of the group of "socialist, populists, social justice Christians" that moved in and thru Kansas.

Financially they were failures, Mary and her husband are buried in unmarked graves in Topeka. Grigsby ended up in a soldier's home and then living with a niece. Slowly, but surely I became convinced that they were true believers and they-lived for the possibility of developing a better, more egalitarian tomorrow.

So I sort of feel that there has been some kind of guidance pushing me in the direction of finding and revealing a little about the lives behind the publishing of the book Nequa and the times they were trying to live in. Particularly today, when original copies are only found in a dozen libraries in the United States. Nequa is a good read and republishing it just might keep the thoughts moving that are covered on its pages. The fact that it is also credited with being one of the first feminist science fiction novels, should help it sell. It is also past the time that Nequa should take it's rightful place as a writing which, attempted to expand Social Justice in the United States. Those who were responsible for its original appearance should be credited with what they actually accomplished.

The republishing of this book with the accompanying story of its authors is my way of saying thank you. Thank You for not leaving me in peace , thank you for guiding me to other writings in an attempt to validate some basic tenets. Thank you for helping me roll sevens, time after time and allowing me the feelings and fascination of coincidences over and over and over. Thank you for helping the right person to show up at the right time, usually with just the right information I needed.

I am convinced of a truth ascribed to A. Merritt, editor of the American Sunday Magazine and a fantasy author. He said that, "occasionally he felt his ancestors looking out through his eyes." He is definitely correct, and sometimes they bring their friends along.

Mark Esping July 2014

Chapter I

BENEATH THE MIDNIGHT SUN — A STRANGE VISITOR COMES DOWN FROM ABOVE — AN OLD ACQUAINTANCE RECOGNIZED — STRANGE STORY BY AN OLD PHYSICIAN.

My private office was on the second floor of the sanitarium which I had fitted up in Kansas City to meet the demands of my large practice in the treatment of chronic diseases. The furniture consisted of a large book case, containing my library of standard works, and other publications useful in my practice; a writing desk, a few chairs, sofa and other conveniences usually found in such places. One door opened into the hall, and another connected with my bed chamber, bath room and laboratory in the rear.

In the front was a large bay window where I often sat, in a meditative mood, concealed by the heavy lace curtains, looking out upon the throngs of people and numerous vehicles passing to and fro on the street below. On the opposite side of the main hall, and separated from it by the wide stairway, was the parlor where I received visitors. In the rear of this were the consultation and operating rooms. I usually lunched in my private office, my meals being sent up to me on an elevator, from a restaurant connecting directly with the sanitarium.

As a rule, no one but the office boy, who occupied a small room over the stairway, was ever admitted to my private office. The boy attended the door, conducted visitors to the parlor, and then reported who was in waiting. If I cared to see them, I went around the head of the stairs to the parlor; otherwise I was "Not in."

Many of my patients came from a distance and had lodgings and board in the sanitarium. Others called at my reception rooms during my regular office hours, which were from 7 A.M. to 11 A. M. At other hours I was ordinarily occupied in my private office, reading, thinking and writing, or in my laboratory compounding medicines, etc. But it was generally understood that I frequently drove out, and hence people calling to see me, except during office hours, were not surprised to learn that I could not be seen.

This arrangement was an absolute necessity in order that I might have time to attend to my large correspondence and make my usual study of the diseases of patients who had placed themselves under my treatment as their last hope of regaining health. My success in treating these cases which had been given up as incurable, was such, that the sanitarium was always full, and it was a rare thing indeed, that I called upon patients at their homes.

One bright and unusually pleasant day in June 189-, after I had attended to my patients, I retired to my private office, feeling that a call even from my most intimate friends, would be very undesirable. I wanted to be alone. I had many letters to write, and other work that I could not well neglect, but I seemed in spite of myself to have lost my usual active interest in my business. I felt oppressed and dissatisfied with its restraints, and after worrying through with my most important correspondence, I got up and paced the floor to and fro.

What could it mean? Why was it I felt this restless longing for something that seemed just beyond my reach? My business was flourishing, my health was never better, my friends were numerous and all my surroundings pleasant. Then why was it that I could not compose myself to read or write? Whenever

I tried to do anything, my mind involuntarily reverted to the past, and especially to a voyage I had taken some years before in the capacity of ship surgeon. At last I despaired of being able to complete my work to my satisfaction, and determined to indulge this irresistible tendency to retrospection.

All the afternoon, whatever I did or attempted to do, my mind turned to Jack Adams, a beardless young man who shipped on the same vessel with me as supercargo. Turn which way I would, his image loomed up before my memory with a vividness that was startling. Why should I be continually thinking of him? True, we had been the closest of friends, and often spent hours together in the most enjoyable conversations.

However, notwithstanding our intimacy, there had ever hung around Jack an air of fathomless mystery. His character was faultless, his modesty, refinement and culture unexcelled. His perceptions were keen, his reasoning powers deep and comprehensive, and his innate truthfulness inspired every one with unlimited confidence who came in contact with him. In times of peril he was courageous as a lion and yet he was gentle as a woman.

He was of medium size and perfectly rounded form, too refined in his appearance to be masculine, but none the less active and efficient; and I must say that his face was the most handsome, and the most expressive of the finer emotions of the soul, I had ever met within man. We were the most congenial of associates, and I was more attached to his personality than I had ever before been to one of my own sex. Though young and beardless, his intellect was mature beyond his years, and by common consent the old and experienced soon came to honor his unusually remarkable judgment.

To me, he was a phenomenon that I was utterly unable to fathom. While he was not shy, he was always reserved and retiring. He never intruded where he had no business except in my cabin, where he often came to while away an hour discussing themes of lofty and far reaching import. He seemed not to live on the common plane of ordinary life, but soared far above it. Still he attended to all his duties in a prompt and energetic manner, often lending a helping hand to others when there was no necessity for him to move a muscle. He seemed to take real pleasure in lightening the burdens of others even at a sacrifice of his own comfort.

Such was Jack Adams, who had worked himself up from the most menial employments on shipboard to a position of responsibility. Such was my most valued friend, always reserved and reticent with others, but genial, sociable and confidential with me, notwithstanding the disparity in our ages. But why should he now be intruding upon my memory, and holding my thoughts to himself by a mystic chord which I had no power to break, much as I had striven to do so?

I had left the sea at the close of this voyage, the memory of which had haunted me all day. I had scarcely thought of Jack Adams for years, and now I found it impossible to keep from thinking of him all the time. I became almost superstitious, and began to speculate that perhaps he had just passed from earth, and that his spirit was now with me trying to force a recognition. As I was thus ruminating, my office boy announced that a gentleman wanted to see me.

I was just about to send back the word "Not in,"

when behind the boy, through the half open door, I beheld a tall, handsome and elegantly dressed man, of commanding personal appearance.

My rule had been never to permit anyone to enter my private apartments except on my personal invitation, and as the boy seemed entirely unconscious of his presence, I knew that some mistake had been made, and instinctively felt that the man was not an intruder; so all that remained for me was to recognize the requirements of common politeness and invite him in.

As he entered the room I mentally took his photograph. He was tall, symmetrical, powerful, with a high intellectual forehead, dark, deep-set eyes, dark hair and whiskers, and dark complexion. His countenance was very impressive, inspiring the beholder with a feeling of respect and confidence. As the door closed behind him he fixed his large, penetrating eyes upon me as if he were reading my inmost thoughts, and after a moment's scrutiny said: "Have I the honor of addressing Dr. Thomas H. Day, who was a surgeon some years ago on a vessel engaged in the East India Trade?"

"Yes," I replied, "that is my name, and I was surgeon on an East Indiaman."

"'Then," he continued, "may I further ask if you remember a young man on the vessel in the capacity of supercargo, who greatly trusted and confided in you?"

His words penetrated my inmost being like a shock and I exclaimed impulsively:

"You mean Jack Adams! I feel it! I know it! Is he still living?"

"He is alive and well," he said, "and your prompt recognition demonstrates that you are the man I am looking for. I bring you word from Jack Adams. He was also a trusted friend of mine, in whom I felt deeply interested, when he occupied the humble position of cabin boy on a steamer between New York and Liverpool."

His words came to me like a flash of sunlight, dispelling at once the clouds which had seemed to paralyze all my energies. I felt that any word from Jack Adams would be an inexpressible relief to my present agitated state of mind. I grasped my visitor's hand with a warmth I could not restrain, and with an enthusiasm that must have appeared to him effusive, I said :

"Thank God! Your words thrill me with delight. I will esteem any message from Jack Adams a blessing, and the messenger a benefactor. You are indeed a welcome visitor, and you have placed me under bonds of gratitude by removing a most oppressive burden from my mind."

He returned the pressure of my hand in a manner I had hardly expected, and handed me a card on which was traced a significant inscription in Jack's well known handwriting which, if any confirmation was necessary, would have removed every possible doubt. Shaking his hand again I asked:

"Will we ever have a world of truth such as has been the dream of every altruist?"

"Jack has found it," said my visitor, "and we must make it. That is the mission he sends me on. He has made it his life work to discover just how this may be accomplished with the greatest ease, and to convey the information to us."

"Then you are doubly welcome," I said."Be seated and make yourself at home. I hail you as a brother in a common cause, even if, as yet, I have no name by which to call you."

"Excuse me," he said, "I should have introduced myself' before, but I was so overjoyed at finding Dr. Day that I forgot he knew nothing about me. My name is Leo Vincennes. I have been in the public service in some capacity, ever since I came to years of maturity; as soldier, sailor, scout, and later, as civil engineer and explorer. I come now from Alaska, and my special business here is to see you and deliver a message, committed to my care by our esteemed brother and co-worker, Jack Adams."

I had moved my chair as near to him as decorum would permit, and said in reply:

"I am indeed happy to meet you, Mr. Vincennes. I have been thinking of Jack all day, and I want you to tell me all about him."

"I saw him last at Cape Lisburne, on the north western coast of Alaska, where I was on the lookout for a vessel that was to take me and my party to San Francisco. We were employed on the coast survey, and our allotted portion of the work included the cape, where we went into camp about the last of June. Our lookout was on top of the bluff, which at this point rises to a height of about eight hundred feet above the level of the sea. The other members of our party were out on a hunt while I remained at the lookout. Through my glass I had a clear view of the sea for leagues away, and I continued to sweep the horizon with my glass, as the unusually early breaking up of the ice led me to expect the appearance of a ship at any time. I casually turned my glass and espied a speck on the horizon, a little to the east of north, that at first gave me the impression of a· distant sail. Not thinking of a vessel from that direction, I observed it more closely, and soon saw that it was not on the surface of the water, but evidently in the air and coming directly toward me. It looked like some monstrous bird, of a magnitude such as I had never conceived.

"In my long experience as a soldier, sailor, scout and explorer of the polar regions, I had been accustomed to remarkable adventures, and had come to take pride in the fact that I could face danger of any kind without a tremor; but I do not hesitate to confess that as this gigantic, winged phenomenon of the heavens bore down toward me, I quivered in every vein and fiber of my being. It came with a rapidity that was startling, and ere I could recover my equanimity sufficiently to determine whether I should try to get out of the way or take my chances with the monster, it came to a halt directly over my head, and I could see that it was some kind of a mechanical contrivance for navigating the air, and that its movements were controlled by human intelligence. It remained stationary for a moment, as if the occupant were taking observations, and then dropped slowly down and alighted on the highest point of the cape, within twenty feet of where I was standing. As this strange vessel came to a rest, a door opened and out stepped a young man who said in the clearest of English:

"'Well, well, I declare! Here is the same Leo Vincennes who gave me my first lessons in navigation. How glad I am to see you so far north. I was heading due south for the mouth of the Yukon, when I discovered you scanning the horizon with your glass. I then changed my course a little to the west and came directly to you.' I recognized his features, but was dazed and stood rooted to the ground. Seeing my embarrassment, he advanced, extending his hand as he said: 'Surely you have not forgotten Jack Adams, the cabin-boy, who sailed on the same ship with you from New York to Liverpool, and asked you so many questions about ships and a seafaring life.'

"I grasped his hand, but for a moment my brain seemed benumbed, and my tongue, to use an oft quoted phrase, 'clave to the roof of my mouth.' I could only look at him in open eyed wonder the same smooth-faced lad that I had known and admired — nay loved, fifteen years ago. My temporary paralysis gave way to a flood of feeling such as I had never experienced before, and I convulsively shook his hand as I exclaimed:

"Yes! yes! My dear old Jack, I remember you, but never again did I expect to meet you and least of all on this barren rock, in the regions of eternal ice, beneath the midnight sun, and dropping from the heavens to this mundane sphere. Where did you come from and whither are you going? Have you put off this mortality with all its weakness and put on immortality in some far off clime of perpetual youth, beyond the utmost limit of our earthly vision?'

" 'Hold on Leo,' he exclaimed, with that mischievous twinkle in his eye that I remember so well, 'don't for Heaven's sake get superstitious. Remember that if the Kingdom of Heaven can be established in us, there evidently must be more in this mundane sphere than has ever been dreamed of in our philosophy. I am no visitant from another world, but I do come from another country, where man is master of his environments, instead of being their servile victim, just as you and I and all of the brothers and sisters on our plane of thought, believe that all of this glorious old world ought to be. We must continue to spread the light, and inspire our common humanity, in every stage of development, wherever found, with higher aspirations and brighter ideas of what is in store for them. We must give them hope and courage. The good time coming, so oft foretold, is almost here, and it will be realized just as soon as a respectable minority can be brought to fully comprehend the way out of all their miseries, as well as they now understand the crushing effects' of their present environments. It is for us to speak the word that will save them from all their miseries, pains, and woes, here and now, without waiting for some far off time, and wonderful change to be brought about in some mysterious and incomprehensible manner. No! No! Leo, this is no time for us to stop and simply wonder at something that is merely the birthright of every human being, while by a little well devised, intelligent and earnest effort on the part of the very few reformers who are not yet entirely submerged, we can secure to every human being every blessing he or she is capable of appreciating. There is nothing impossible about this, and if the world is not redeemed from its present low estate, it will be because the few altruists in the world do not make the necessary effort; --and they will surely make that effort when they comprehend how easy it is to quietly and peacefully remove the burdens that ignorance and greed have imposed, and thus rescue the toiler from the grasp of the selfish. How much are you willing to do toward this work of saving the world? Could you be persuaded to forget self for awhile and lend your services to the cause of humanity, by spreading the light that will save it, and save it too before even the older people of this generation shall have passed off the stage?'

"I was carried away by his earnest appeal, and promptly responded:

"'I am indeed willing to make any conceivable sacrifice in such a cause, my dear old Jack, but you must tell me what to do and how to do it.'

Jack asked, "Then, can you go into the interior of the United States — to the great Missouri Valley, and deliver a message from me to a dearly loved friend, which will secure his assistance?'

"'I certainly will,' I said. 'Personal matters require my presence in New York. I shall go from here to San Francisco, and thence across the continent by rail, and can stop off at any point you desire. I have been notified that, in the private papers of Richard Sage, who died some years ago, a document was found, clearly proving that I am one of the heirs to a large property, which was held in trust for minors, whose whereabouts were unknown to the testator, my grandfather. I am the representative of those heirs.'

"As I spoke, Jack's countenance became ashen pale and the expression hard and stony, and as I concluded he asked in tones that struck me with a chill like a polar wave:

"'And is Richard Sage dead?'

"'He died nearly fifteen years ago,' I said. 'Committed suicide, I believe. Did you know him?'

"'I think so,' he said. 'He was a friend of my father — But,' he added after a short pause, his face regaining its usual winning and kindly expression, 'we have no time to give to the discussion of the dead past. Come with me and take a look at our earth from the cozy cabin of the Eolus, while I tell you something of my adventures in the way of polar exploration, and explain what it is that I want you to do.'

"We stepped into a small but luxuriantly furnished car, which I shall not attempt to describe, and seated ourselves upon a soft cushioned divan. The walls were paneled on all sides with large transparent sections, through which we obtained a clear and seemingly magnified view of the surrounding scenery. There we were, poised on the highest point of this towering rock, overlooking the sea, the rolling waves of which dashed themselves into foam on the rocks below. Jack manipulated a delicately arranged keyboard at his side, and in a minute more we were flitting to and fro far above the earth at an almost inconceivable speed, and then loitering along or standing still to get a better view of objects of especial interest.

"Jack handed me what looked like a peculiarly constructed opera glass, and requested me to take a peep at Cape Lisburne through the transparent section at the bow. Though we were miles away, I felt that I could reach out and pick up a pebble anywhere along this rock-bound shore. This explained a mystery, and I turned to Jack and said: 'I can now understand how it was that you discovered me at such a great distance, for when I first saw you, your ship was but a speck, and several points to the east of north.'

"'Yes,' he said, 'I discovered you on the lookout when several leagues away. I had not expected to find civilized people so far north. As soon as I saw you, I put the Eolus to her greatest speed directly toward you, lest you should leave the lookout. As I came nearer I felt sure that I recognized your features, and I at once made up my mind that I had found one whom I could trust to assist me in the work I had undertaken to perform. This fortunate meeting enables me to return immediately, and relieve the painful anxiety of many loving hearts concerning my safety. They had a most exaggerated conception of he perils I would be compelled to encounter in attempting to traverse these frozen regions.'

"He told me a wonderful story of his trials, perils and adventures in getting past the great ice barriers, and his discovery of a World of Truth beyond.

"When we had circumnavigated the country for miles

around, we slowly descended to earth and alighted at the same spot from which we started, and as we separated, he to return to his new home beyond the ice barrier, I to come to you, he placed his portmanteau in my hands and said:

"'Go to Dr. Thomas H. Day, at Kansas City, and if he will agree to publish the manuscript contained in this portmanteau and scatter it broadcast over the world, place it in his hands and tell him to use the gold contained also therein, which was contributed by the crew of the Ice King for that purpose; for nothing but gold, the fetich of this benighted and money enslaved external world, can command labor; and yet it is labor and not gold, that is the sole producer of everything essential to the sustenance and comfort of humanity. If Dr. Day cannot be found, or is so situated that he cannot attend to this matter, use the gold yourself to find a publisher, and have eight printed volumes for me when I return with another manuscript of even more value, from the same fruitful field of discovery.'

"And now Dr. Day," continued my visitor, "will you undertake to discharge the trust committed to you by Jack Adams?"

"I will gladly do so" I replied, "for anything from Jack will surely be a blessing to humanity."

He placed the portmanteau in my hands and said:

"I must bid you adieu. Send the eight volumes for Jack to my address at Fort Yukon, Alaska, and as many more for myself, unless I should send you other directions. I shall be anxious to read the book as soon as it is published. Jack must have passed through some trying ordeals, and from what I saw, his discoveries have been wonderful. But I must go."

I tried to detain him, but with a cordial grasp of the hand he was gone.

I turned and opened the portmanteau with the key that was attached. It contained a package, securely enclosed in a wrapper of some water-proof material, and marked "MS," and below was a glittering array of gold eagles.

I examined the package of manuscript more closely. On either side it was addressed to Dr. Thomas H. Day, Kansas City, and below was written:

"In the name of civilization I ask that whoever may find this package shall place it in the hands of those who will publish the MS. contained therein and have it scattered broadcast over the world, so that the discoveries recorded shall not be lost to humanity.

Nequa"

This was repeated in French, German, Norwegian, Russian and Spanish.

And now dear reader, I shall give you the contents of this remarkable manuscript, from the pen of my sailor comrade of years ago, Jack Adams, but known in his new home as Nequa, the teacher. Ponder well the lessons taught in these wonderful discoveries.

Yours truly,
Thomas H. Day.

Chapter II

IN SAN FRANCISCO — WHERE SHALL I GO NEXT ? — A STARTLING ITEM OF NEWS ANSWERS THE QUESTION AND ENDS THE SEARCH — IN MALE ATTIRE — ENLISTS AS SCIENTIST ON THE ICE KING-OFF TO THE NORTH POLE — AN UNEXPECTED BLOW — THE DANGER SIGNAL — THE RACE FOR LIFE — THE EARTHQUAKE — "THE CHANNEL IS CLOSING! " — "THE SHIP IS LOST!"

I was in the parlor of the Palace Hotel in San Francisco. Since my last visit to the city, I had circumnavigated the globe. During the last three years, I had not only again visited the leading points of interest for tourists in Asia, Africa, Europe and Australia, but had extended my travels into the frozen regions of the far south, on a whaling voyage. Yet I had not found that for which I was searching.

My failure had brought a feeling of intense sadness and depression which I shall not attempt to describe. For fifteen years I had been a wanderer on the high seas. I had traversed every latitude from Greenland to the South frigid zone and was now mentally asking "Where shall I go next?" I had determined that I would not give up this long continued search until it was crowned with success, or death had intervened, as long as there was one spot on earth unexplored.

Thus pondering in my own mind what to do next, I picked up an evening paper and abstractedly glanced over its pages in the attempt to form an idea of its contents by reading the headlines. In the editorial columns my eye rested on the caption: OFF TO THE NORTH POLE.

This was travel into a region I had not penetrated. I was at once interested and glancing down the column I read the comments of the editor. "'The discovery of America," he said, "was the attempt to discover a more direct and consequently a nearer route to India by sailing westward. The object sought for was not found, but the search gave to the overcrowded and oppressed millions of Christendom a new world, where they might work out their destiny in conformity with the ideal of the founder of their religion, beyond the reach of the political and religious despotisms of the old world; and why may not this venture, even though it fails to reach the pole, ultimate in discoveries of inestimable value to mankind? We hope so, and hence we wish the most abundant success to the expedition now being organized in this city, by an experienced traveler and navigator, Capt. Raphael Ganoe."

The paper dropped from my hand; I was overcome; my senses were paralyzed; my heart almost ceased to beat; my brain for a moment was deprived of the power of thought. As the full import of this unexpected revelation dawned upon me, I arose and paced the floor.

"My God," I exclaimed, "this cannot be, it must not be, but how can I prevent it? All the arrangements are perfected. I cannot, I dare not, under the circumstances, speak the word that possibly might prevent this perilous undertaking." I was powerless. But I soliloquized, "If I cannot prevent it, I must join the expedition, for never again will I permit him to leave me."

My mind was made up. I was in the prime of life, about thirty-five years of age, and had traveled extensively. I was familiar with ocean navigation and versed in all the sciences taught in our higher institutions of learning. I would make application for the position of scientist, and failing in that would enlist before the mast as a common sailor, if nothing better offered.

I turned to the mirror and surveyed myself long and earnestly. I raised myself to my full height and critically viewed the womanly face and figure revealed to my vision. Though not masculine, my form was strong and muscular for one of my sex, and with the proper disguise it would do. For the first time in years I had donned the habiliments of woman. In masculine attire I had traveled without being discovered. Protected by this disguise, I had filled almost every position on shipboard and had succeeded in earning a competency, something I never could have accomplished as a woman. It was not an experiment. I had tried it successfully for years and would try it again.

I took up the paper and read the account of the expedition with more care. The ship was one of the staunchest that had ever been built and had been provided with all the modern appliances for the comfort and protection of the crew, during a cruise that was intended to be indefinitely extended. None but bold and experienced seamen had been enlisted. As time was no object it was intended to use the sails instead of steam whenever it was practicable. Hence the large space usually given to coal was mainly reserved for an unusual supply of carefully prepared provisions for a long sojourn in the Arctic regions. Every thing that human foresight could devise for the success of this expedition had been provided. The daring commander had determined to take all the time that was needed for making careful surveys of the shore lines of the frozen north, and sounding its seas.

My mind was made up. I retired at once to my rooms. The male attire that I had used so successfully, was in my trunks. I need not worry the reader at this time with the details of my hasty yet thorough preparation for concealing my identity from the keen observation of one who knew me so much better than the many with whom I had been associated in my wanderings. Suffice it to say that every arrangement was complete in my private apartments, without exciting the suspicion of any person. I dressed myself in a neat sailor suit, which was concealed from view beneath the ample folds of a fashionable wrapper. I packed my trunks, summoned a porter and ordered my goods removed to furnished rooms that I had previously engaged. When there, I removed every article that would indicate that I was a woman, and with valise in hand took my way to the dock, where the Ice King was being fitted up with the greatest care by the experienced navigator in whose services it was my intention to enlist.

It was in the early twilight of a glorious evening in May 189-. I lingered a few moments on the wharf to enjoy the scene and to collect my faculties for the trial that was to come. I was tall and slender and my appearance was youthful and refined. Yet I flattered myself that with my long experience in this disguise, I would be able to successfully act the part I had determined upon. As I stepped on board, I met an officer who accosted me with the familiar salutation: "Hello Jack, what will you have?"

"I want to see Captain Ganoe," I said. "Where can I find him?"

"He is in his cabin," he replied, and passed on.

I gained the deck. The calm waters of the bay reflected the full rounded moon and her stellar attendants. The harbor was almost deserted. Vessels here and there dotted the placid surface of the water. Music low, sweet and plaintive reached my ears. Its melancholy strains drew me forward. The soul of the performer seemed to float out upon the air through the tender caresses of the magic bow. The very waves, as they sparkled in the mellow moonbeams, seemed to dance to the sweet melody.

It came from the Captain's quarters. I passed in so quietly that I was not observed. As I suspected, the musician was Captain Ganoe. He was so absorbed in the plaintive notes of the violin, through which his soul was speaking, that he did not notice my intrusion. He was in thought, far away and oblivious to his surroundings.

I stood and carefully scanned the form before me. It was that of a man of mature years, broad shoulders and medium height, firmly knit, compactly built and fair complexion. His eyes were blue, his nose a combination of Grecian and Roman, his mouth firm, and his entire bearing indicative of courage and strength of character. His brow was broad and thoughtful; his expression kind and firm. Everything left the impression that, though comparatively young, he had drained the cup of bitter disappointment to its dregs. While I sympathized, his sadness brought a feeling of sweet relief. Oh, how my heart bounded, and for the moment I felt impelled to fall upon his bosom and sob out the story of my wrongs. But no, this would not do. I must be patient and first ascertain from his own lips, in just what light he would regard me when he learned the whole truth.

I aroused him from his reverie with the inquiry:

"Is this Captain Ganoe?"

He looked up quickly, surprised to see a stranger in his cabin, and responded:

"Yes, young man, I am Captain Ganoe, and let me ask to what I am indebted for the honor of this visit. Did you not meet an officer who could attend to your wants?"

"I did," I replied, "but I wanted to see and talk with Captain Ganoe."

The severity left his countenance, and he bade me be seated.

"Now young man," said he, "please state fully but briefly, what you want, for my time is entirely occupied."

I answered promptly, and without preliminary explanations I said:

"I have just learned from the papers that you are about to sail for the most thorough exploration of the Arctic regions that has yet been attempted, and I want to go with you."

He turned up the lamp which had been burning low, and looked me full in the face. I felt his searching gaze but withstood it, with no exhibition of the fears I felt for the success of my plans. But with inward tremor, I awaited his reply. After hesitating a moment, he said deliberately :

"You do not know what you ask. You are young and refined. This expedition must encounter dangers, known and unknown, and none but the strong and experienced should be permitted to make the venture. It would be wrong in me to take a young man like you from the bosom of his family, from society, and all the opportunities for a successful and useful life, to go with me on this perilous expedition. The fact is, you ought to return home and leave such hazardous adventures as this for those who have no hopes to be blasted , and who wish for reasons of their own, to hide themselves away from the world. Please tell me your name and where you come from."

"My name sir," I replied, "is Jack Adams, and I have just returned from a three years cruise, during which time I visited the leading seaports of the world. I have become familiar with a life on the high seas in all the medial latitudes, and now propose to explore the frozen north. As to family, I have none. I am an orphan, and all alone in the world. I graduated from school at the head of my class and then shipped as cabin boy and worked my way up to a position of supercargo. I have been a practical student of navigation never sailing twice on the same line of travel when I could avoid it. I now offer my services to you because I want to go with you into the unexplored regions of the north. I have had enough of the tropic and temperate zones. If I never return I leave no one to mourn my loss. "

He looked his astonishment and was visibly softened as he responded:

"We have no need of a supercargo and we have all the seamen we want. I have just formed a co-partnership with Captain Samuel Battell, who is not only an officer of ability and long experience in the Arctics, but an expert scientist and mathematician. Every place seems to be full."

"I am not," I replied, "seeking a position as supercargo, nor am I asking any position that requires pay or even board, if you can find room in your commissary for the supplies I stand ready to furnish. I can and will do any work that may be assigned me. All I want is to be permitted to go with this expedition, take my own chances and pay my own way . "

"You seem very much in earnest Mr. Adams, and I am frank to admit that I admire your courage even if I doubt your judgment in this matter. But what can you do, and what evidence have you to offer that you can render valuable service in an expedition of this character? As to pay, I would not have you infer that I regarded it as any object to one of your adventurous disposition. No one enlisted in this expedition is promised a salary but the common sailors, and that is paid by Captain Battell and myself . "

"As to what I can do," I responded, "1 am by education and experience, qualified. to navigate the vessel and make every necessary scientific observation and calculation. I am familiar with all that has been published on Arctic exploration and discovery. As to my ability, you can best ascertain that by inquiring into what I know. That is the best evidence of my training and experience on the high seas. I do not shrink from the necessary examination."

"You are right," said he, "and I will consult my partner. If it is agreeable to him, you may take charge of our library and scientific instruments, assist in our observations and keep a record of the expedition. I will summon Captain Battell."

He touched an electric button and in a moment a bell sounded at his side. He said to me:

"Captain Battell will be here in a moment, and I will leave this matter to him."

A moment later, the same officer I had met when I first came aboard the ship, entered and I was formally introduced. He cordially shook my hand and Captain Ganoe told him what I wanted, and, quite unexpectedly to me, said:

"Mr. Adams is admirably qualified, and I think we had better place him in charge of the scientific work of the expedition. We can assist him as occasion requires. This will enable us to give our entire attention to the exigencies of the situation in the dangerous waters of the Arctic regions, while Mr. Adams will keep a record of everything discovered that may be of value, and send out duplicates of the same by the balloons, as we intended, so that if the expedition should be lost, the winds may carry some account of our discoveries to the civilized portions of the globe. "Evidently in the mind of Captain Ganoe, I had already been appointed to the position which of all others I would have preferred, and one that would always keep me near his own quarters. And to this, Captain Battell assented, saying:

"I met Mr. Adams on his arrival, and was favorably impressed with his appearance and evident determination to see the senior officer of the Ice King." And turning to me he continued, "I will now take pleasure in showing you through the library, which will be your quarters during the voyage."

Captain Battell was the opposite of Captain Ganoe in his personal appearance. He was powerfully built, of medium height, dark complexion, dark hair, and steel grey eyes set beneath a broad and beetling brow. The general contour of his features indicated courage, firmness, and strength of character. He was just that type of a man who might be expected to appear to the best advantage in some great emergency that demanded qualities of a high order.

All the appointments for the scientific work were of the first quality. The library contained the leading scientific publications, together with encyclopedias, and historic and general literature, carefully catalogued for easy reference.

Every kind of scientific instruments, charts, maps, globes, cameras, etc., had been selected with the greatest care. Among the special supplies were the balloons to which Captain Ganoe had referred. These were small and could be inflated at short notice. They were designed to be sent up from time to time with accounts of the expedition, its progress, discoveries etc., hermetically sealed. It is well known that at the equinoxes, the heated air from the tropics ascends to the higher altitudes and flows toward the poles, while the cold air flows toward the equator to fill the vacuum, producing the equinoctial storms. These little balloons were expected to be carried south by the winds, and find a resting place on the land surface where they might be picked up by civilized people; or if they fell into the water, the bottles would preserve the dispatches and the ocean currents might carry them into civilized countries. Thus every precaution was taken to secure to the world the benefit of any discovery that might be made, even though the expedition should be lost.

I was well pleased with my quarters. All the surroundings would be, to me, most satisfactory, no matter what the trials and dangers that we might encounter. I was enlisted for the expedition, and in the position I preferred above all others, as it brought me into frequent consultation with the commander, and I should be able to acquaint myself with his present views and feelings and note what changes had taken place since I saw him last.

I lost no time in having my trunks brought on board and made ready for the voyage.

The Ice King was soon at sea. We stopped at one of the Aleutian Islands where we took on our dog teams, which were to be used for explorations on the ice. The sledges were so constructed that they might readily be converted into boats that would accommodate the whole crew and a good supply of provisions, in case we should be compelled to abandon the ship. We expected to be locked up in the ice during the winter, but with our sledges and dog teams, we could continue our explorations for long distances in every direction, with the ship for headquarters. Captain Battell was a whaler and familiar with all the methods of Arctic travel. His long experience on these northern waters enabled him to foresee many of the dangers we were likely to meet, and to make the needful preparations to over- come them. From this point our voyage northward through Behring Strait and into the Arctic Ocean, was without any incident worth recording. Our course after passing the strait, was a little east of north to avoid the ice, until we reached longitude 165 degrees West of Greenwich, and then north. Captain Ganoe often came into my cabin to while away an hour in conversation. His marked friendship seemed to increase with each visit. He always addressed me familiarly as Jack, and in these conversations he became more and more confidential, and revealed to me more and more of his inner life, his early hopes and subsequent disappointments.

One evening after we had been at sea about four months, he came into my cabin looking unusually gloomy. After the customary salutation he lighted a cigar and fell into a brown study, not speaking to me for several minutes, when suddenly he said:

"Jack, did you ever think what mere trifles sometimes change the whole course of a lifetime? I often wonder at myself for being out here on this wild goose chase, with the certainty of loss of property, business, comfort and possibly life itself, searching for something I have no use for, and which at best if discovered, will only gratify an idle curiosity. And yet, this has been brought about by what was only a trifling incident. Have you ever thought of these strange effects which flow from trivial causes?"

He spoke bitterly and I determined to take advantage of the opportunity to draw him out. I wanted to penetrate the inmost recesses of his being, and with this object in view I replied :

"Yes, Captain, I have often thought of it and have realized it in my own experience. It sometimes seems little short of a miracle, that after years of wandering, I am now here with you. In my case I was not influenced by a mere trifle, but a stern necessity. I had absolutely nothing to lose, and I thought I might find something which, under the circumstances, would amply repay me for all the hardships and dangers I might have to encounter. But you were differently situated. You were independent. You had wealth, business and influential friends, while I had been robbed of my patrimony, and was thrown upon the world with nothing but my hands and brain to work with. My course was a necessity, but it is a mystery why you should abandon a profitable business and organize this expedition at such an enormous expenditure of labor and money, while you regard its avowed objects as matters of such little importance. Your course seems to involve a self contradiction that I cannot comprehend."

"And thereby hangs a tale," said the Captain. "As a matter of fact, I never did attach any great importance to Arctic exploration. From my point of view, the discovery of the Pole would be of no especial value to mankind, as no practical use could be made of it. Even the discovery of a productive country, which may be possible, could not greatly benefit the world, as it would be inaccessible to the masses of humanity whose condition would be improved by the discovery of a new country and cheap homes. While such a successful culmination would be of small benefit to the world, it would be of still less interest to myself. I really care but little about what we may find at the end of this voyage."

"Then," I said, "if such be the estimate that you place upon the objects of this expedition, I am more than ever curious to learn what could have impelled you to undertake it. You must have had a reason of some kind. I cannot understand how men can act without a motive."

"Yes," said he, "I was impelled to organize this expedition by a power stronger than myself, but when I ask myself what I expect to accomplish by it, truth compels me to answer: 'Nothing.' As to the motive, I suppose that I have been actuated by an all-absorbing desire to forget the miseries of the past in the activities of the present."

"But this is not the tale that unlocks the mystery." I responded. "You have aroused my curiosity to a fever heat, and yet you fail to gratify it. It might be that I could pour oil on the troubled waters and possibly enable you to discover that you have been actuated by a mistaken conception, and that really there is nothing in the past that you should desire to forget. It would certainly do no harm to review the case, and it might reveal the fact that it was a source of misery, simply because all the circumstances were not fully understood."

"I have no desire," said the Captain, "to conceal the story of my life from you, if you care to hear it. But I fully understand it and it is of such a nature as to admit of no remedy."

"Do not be too sure of that," I said. "But until the story is told, of course I will not be able to form an intelligent opinion of the case. Yet, observation and experience have convinced me that there are always two sides to every question and that to get at the facts in all their bearings, we must closely examine both sides."

"Well," said the captain, "I see that you were cut out for a lawyer and the wonder is how you came to be a sailor. You certainly have a judicial cast of mind and to while away the monotony of the hour, I will submit the matter to you, reserving the right, however, to decide for myself . I have always exercised my natural right to examine every question from my own standpoint and decide it according to my own sense of right and wrong.

"It is the same old story of an all-absorbing love and a cruel disappointment, followed by long years of suppressed anguish, from which I am still striving to escape. I was an orphan, living with my bachelor uncle, Richard Sage, in one of the suburbs of New York City. He was my guardian and the executor of the estate left me by my father. My uncle was kind and indulgent, and my widowed aunt who presided over his home, was to me a loving mother, and so my childhood days were passed in happy contentment.

"One misty, dreary morning, my uncle announced at the breakfast table that he had been called to the bedside of his old friend, James VanNess, who was supposed to be dying. He said he would not return until his friend was much better or dead, and not to be disappointed if he was absent for several days, or possibly weeks.

"A week later I saw my uncle drive up to the gate and assist a very beautiful young girl from the carriage. He beckoned me to him, and introduced me, saying:

"Raphael, I have brought you a little sister. This is Miss Cassie Van Ness, whose father I was called to see. I have been made her guardian and this will be her future home. Both mother and father are dead and she has no near relatives. Remember this, and do everything in your power to make her home with us as happy as possible.'"

"We at once became great friends. Cassie was at that time about fourteen or fifteen years of age and I was eighteen. She proved to be the gayest, brightest, most winsome little lady I had ever seen. I must have fallen in love with her at first sight. I have often thought since," he added slowly, "that even his Satanic Majesty might look entrancingly beautiful, for to my intense sorrow, Cassie proved herself, it seems to me, a ten-fold greater hypocrite than Judas of old who betrayed with a kiss.

"But enough of this. Our school days, lasting some five years, were to me one ceaseless round of delightful experiences, which seemed to fill every vein and fiber of my being with unalloyed happiness. During our vacations Cassie and I were always together, either at home or traveling, and many were the excursions, romps and drives we enjoyed.

"I graduated at twenty-three and we laid our plans for the future. I had inherited an interest in a line of steamers running between Liverpool and New York, which enabled us to frequently cross the Atlantic during our vacations, and visit the leading points of interest in Great Britain and on the continent. I had acquired a taste for travel, and it was determined that I should visit the Orient, while Cassie returned to college to complete her study of the higher branches. I was to be gone about three years, during which time I would circumnavigate the globe, and on my return we were to be married.

"With these objects in view I secured, through the influence of my uncle, a lucrative position in the employ of a firm of importers, whose trade extended to all parts of the eastern continent and Australia. On the evening before my departure, I placed a brilliant diamond engagement ring on Cassie's finger and a gold chain and locket of peculiar workmanship around her neck.

"'These presents were made from special designs for this purpose and the patterns destroyed. I shall never forget the last night we spent together. 'The appearance of my affianced bride in her splendid evening dress, her diamond engagement ring sparkling on her lovely hand, the gold chain and diamond set locket and her luxuriant suit of golden hair handsomely ornamented, formed a picture of beauty, indelibly imprinted upon my memory.

"My ship sailed from one of the piers on the Hudson near the Battery. We contemplated the circumnavigation of the globe by way of Cape Horn, the Sandwich Islands, Japan, China, Australia, Africa, Europe, and thence returning to America, stopping at all the principal seaport cities and points of interest on our voyage. This would enable Cassie and me to keep up our correspondence with no very long interruptions.

"For the first year of my absence, at every port I received a package of letters from home, and this always contained letters from Cassie. We had agreed to write to each other at least once a week without waiting for replies, and it often occurred that I got a whole package of letters from her at one time, and the perusal of these affectionate missives was the one all-absorbing pleasure to which I looked forward when we came into port. Whatever else might be lacking, Cassie's loving letters never failed.

"At last, however, they ceased all at once. Letters from my uncle came regularly, and through them I heard of Cassie, but I could get no word from her. I wrote to her every week, but my letters brought no response. I was miserable, and urged my uncle to find out what was the matter and let me know if my letters came safely.

"My uncle's replies were at first evasive, but at last with an expression of the most cordial sympathy for me, he informed me that my letters came regularly, but that Cassie had changed her mind and they remained unopened. He enclosed a draft on London for the balance due on my estate, together with a complete statement of the account from the date of his taking charge, and the findings of the court as to all the property and investments that came to me from my father. Everything was complete and duly certified, so there was nothing that demanded my presence in New York. He advised me not to return home, but continue in my present position, as Cassie was to be married in a short time and my presence would be painful to her as well as to myself, and embarrassing to everyone concerned.

"I was thunderstruck. I did not, could not, would not believe that Cassie was false to our mutual and oft repeated pledges of love and fidelity to each other. I could get no satisfaction from my uncle. My aunt had been dead several years. I wrote to my lawyer to learn if possible, the truth of the reported engagement and approaching marriage. His reply was prompt, stating that it was not only true, but that the marriage had already taken place. He wrote that he had been called in by my uncle, who was in feeble health, to make out the papers in regard to the estate of Cassie Van Ness, which she was anxious to have settled satisfactorily to herself before her marriage. ' These financial matters being arranged,' wrote my lawyer, 'what was my surprise to be called upon to witness her marriage to Richard Sage.

Financially she did well, but it is hard for me to believe that it was a love match. Your uncle, however, is certainly much infatuated with her, and she is indeed beautiful.'

"This same letter contained a flattering offer from a firm of New York importers, for my interest in the steamship line, and I advised my attorney to close the deal at once and forward the proceeds to London and also to dispose of all my property in and about New York, lists of which were in his possession. I had made up my mind never to return home, as it would be distressing to me and certainly embarrassing to my uncle. After that my only New York correspondence was with my attorney.

"When I reached London, I found a letter from my attorney with drafts on the Bank of England for all my interests in America. This letter also contained the information that my uncle was in great trouble, his marriage with Cassie having resulted in much unhappiness. She had suddenly deserted him without giving any reason for her strange conduct. She merely left a note, stating that she would not live with him. This was the last that had been heard from her. 'Of course,' added my attorney, ' it would be next to impossible to find her in this large city if she desires to keep herself concealed.'

"Since that time I have been a wanderer, caring little whither I went, so that my mind was fully occupied. I purchased a staunch ship in which I cruised for years, avoiding as far as practicable the regular lines of trade and often sailing without a cargo, searching for a contentment never to be found. At last I conceived the idea of getting away from civilization altogether, joining in the work of Arctic exploration, and, if possible reaching the pole. With this end in view, I had the Ice King built according to special designs, and adapted, so far as human foresight and ingenuity could devise, for a long sojourn in the frozen north. And now here we are, in the Arctic Ocean, liable at any moment to be caught between the ice fields which appear on either side, and possibly crushed. What is to come next? God only knows.

"Such is a brief statement of the perfidy of the woman I loved, and its consequences. And this is why I am out here on this perilous expedition, searching for something that I care very little about. I think you will agree with me that it admits of no remedy."

"It does not look that way to me," I responded. "I would be unwilling to condemn your affianced bride until I had heard her side of the story. It may be that her marriage to your uncle was secured by unfair means, and that when she discovered the fraud, in her desperation she started out to find you. In that case, the remedy would be for you to find her and renew your plighted faith."

"Never!" said Captain Ganoe. "Even if your supposed case is correct, it could not set aside the facts. She knew that, in marrying my uncle, she was false to me, and when she deserted him with no legal cause for separation, she was false to her husband to whom she was bound in the holy bonds of matrimony. She acted from her own choice. She was not compelled to engage herself to me, and no law could have forced her to marry my uncle. Her conduct in both cases reveals an innate perfidy of character, and under no circumstances could I, as an honorable man, accept such a woman as my wife. Her tarnished reputation, if nothing else, would place an insurmountable barrier between us even if she were not legally the wife of another man."

I was paralyzed. I had indeed succeeded in getting from him an emphatic expression of sentiment covering my own case. I had penetrated the innermost recesses of his being, but had fanned to a flame the slumbering fires of a volcano, only to be submerged in the eruption of molten lava.

The blow was so unexpected and so sudden, that I was stupefied, and my astonishment left no room for grief, which gave me a moment for reflection. Here I was, in the ship with him, far within the Arctic Circle, at the beginning of the Arctic winter, and with the certainty of being locked up in the ice for months if not for years. I could not get away from him if I would, and from his own lips I had heard my conduct denounced as the acme of perfidy, and my love spurned as something treacherous and vile. Bitterly and in the most emphatic manner, had he declared that as an honorable man, he could never associate himself in the tender relations of marital love, with one of my tarnished reputation. In his own estimate, he had already assigned me a place among the most debased and abandoned characters, and all there was left for me to do was to preserve my disguise, in order to secure even respectful treatment from the man I loved.

As the full sense of the situation dawned upon me in all its crushing weight of humiliation and anguish, I must have fallen at his feet in a dead faint, but for the clangor of the great bell which had been agreed upon as the signal of immediate peril, to summon each one to the post that had been assigned him in case of sudden emergencies. The alarm came to me as a sweet relief from agony ten fold more difficult to endure than any possible hardships or dangers from an Arctic storm, amid towering mountains of ice.

There was no time for grief. The emergency demanding prompt action was upon us, and we hurried out upon deck. According to previous arrangements, Captain Ganoe seized the wheel and Captain Battell, as an experienced Arctic navigator, took command, while I, with glass and note book, stood by the wheel to make observations and to render any assistance to Captain Ganoe that might be required.

The cause of alarm at once became apparent. The stiff breeze that had been blowing all day from the southwest, had now increased to a gale, and the icebergs which for days were becoming more numerous on our starboard quarter, had formed a solid pack, which was evidently landlocked, as it remained stationary, while on the larboard, a solid field of ice of vast extent was approaching. It was only a question of a few hours at the utmost, when these two great ice walls must come together and it would be destruction for us to be caught in their deadly embrace.

Retreat was impossible. The only open channel was the one we were pursuing. The walls on either side were continuous, and with my glass I could see the channel behind us blocked with icebergs, urged on in our wake by wind and waves as if determined not to let us escape.Our only safety seemed to be in our being able to sail beyond these two continuous walls of ice before they came together. Captain Battell, with his glass kept up a rapid survey of the horizon, and gave orders through his trumpet as calmly as if scenes like this were matters of every day occurrence, and Captain Ganoe, at the wheel, responded as if he was part of the machinery, which he handled with rapidity and precision.

It was a scene never to be forgotten. The midnight sun hung just above the horizon. Off to our larboard, an unbroken wall of ice extending as far as the eye, assisted by a powerful glass could reach, was bearing down upon us. On our starboard another wall of ice against which the waves were dashing in all their fury, stood apparently as firm as the granite shores against which it rested. Behind us, the channel was filled with detached masses of ice, which if caught between these ice walls might hasten the closing of the channel before us. Could we escape? was the all pervading question that propounded itself to us.

Every sail was set and under the pressure of every pound of steam our boilers could carry, the Ice King leaped forward like a frightened deer, as if conscious of the doom that was impending. For hours we kept up this reckless speed. The foam flew in blinding spray from the ship's quarters, fretted along her sides and left a broad white line in her wake. The whistling of the wind in her rigging and the regular plunging of her engines, made pandemonium on board.

It was indeed a race for life, and in my perturbed state of mind I actually enjoyed the excitement, almost hoping that it might culminate in the destruction threatened. With the courage of despair I calmly surveyed the scene and took my notes, occasionally assisting Captain Ganoe at the wheel. This was the first real danger that we had encountered, and my interview with the Captain had given me a reckless daring to meet it without a tremor, that seems almost miraculous.

We still kept up this rapid flight, and as far as the eye could reach the two great ice walls still confronted each other and the channel of open water continued to grow more narrow. Soon we had to veer from side to side to avoid collisions with the jagged shorelines of ice, but nowhere was there any indication that when they came together an open space would be formed sufficient to protect the ship. We were compelled to reduce our speed, and still the ice-fields were coming closer together and at last we were forced to creep along a narrow, crooked channel between two great packs of ice-mountains which often towered far above the mainmast of the Ice King.

The outlook was desperate, but the ice on our larboard ceased to approach, and for a moment it seemed as if we might escape into open water. But not so. Our way was blocked. An ice-mountain loomed up before us, and we came to a full stop. It was this that had probably checked the advance of the moving icepack, and saved us from the cruel "nip" which has crushed so many hapless vessels in these dangerous waters.

The Ice King lay between two vast overhanging ice-mountains, which towered high above us. In the front was the huge iceberg, which had prevented the nearer approach of the wall of ice. The channel in which we lay could only be closed by the breaking up of the fields of ice behind us, and we could see no reason why this should occur. If the ice-fields remained intact until the freezing of the channel there would be no collision and we would be safe for the time being.

The weather had become intensely cold and we began to feel that the danger had passed by, when an ominous roar and the sharp reports of breaking ice, gave warning of the only thing we had to dread. A violent earthquake was lashing the ocean into fury, and the ice pack was broken into innumerable fragments, which were crashing against each other in the most violent commotion. Captain Battell shouted from the lookout where he had posted himself:

"Save yourselves if you can. The channel is closing and the ship is lost."

I looked up, and as I did so, the lofty ice-mountains between which we lay, seemed to be falling directly down upon us, and at the same time a violent shock threw me upon the deck with a force that must have rendered me unconscious for a few seconds.

Chapter III

IN THE DARK ALL IS STILL — CAPTAIN GANOE'S NARROW ESCAPE — IMPRISONED IN THE ICE — DISTRESSING SITUATION — HOW TO PRESERVE THE HEALTH AND EFFICIENCY OF THE CREW — A NEW DANGER — THE ICE IS MOVING — THE COMMON SAILOR TO THE RESCUE — LIEF AND ERIC SAVE THE SHIP — THE TUNNEL TO THE SURFACE — EXPLORING THE ICE-FIELD.

The first thing I remember after being thrown to the deck, was the profound quiet, and the consciousness that some mighty change had taken place in our surroundings. I opened my eyes. The deck was wrapped in semi-darkness, and instead of the thundering reverberations of the breaking ice and the waves dashing into foam upon their icy barriers, there was a gentle, swish, swish, of the sea as it lashed the sides of the ship. I felt dazed, and the memory of the awful scenes through which we had passed impressed me like the vivid imagery and fantastic pictures of some horrible dream.

At the moment of the shock, fully impressed with the conviction that all was lost, I was turning to grasp Raphael in my arms, so that we might die together, and on recovering consciousness, my first thought was of him. I sprang to my feet and in the dim light I saw something gliding away from me towards the edge of the deck, and I instinctively grasped it, as it was about to drop overboard. It was Captain Ganoe. He was living but unconscious. With my insecure footing, I feared for a moment that we should both go overboard together, when there was a flash of light and Battell seized my arm, exclaiming:

"Thank God, you are both alive! I called to you and as you did not reply, I feared that you were both killed by the falling ice. It was lucky that you were able to grasp the Captain just when you did, or he would surely have been lost."

I was holding Captain Ganoe in my arms, while Battell was briskly chafing his hands. In a moment he aroused, as if suddenly awaking out of a deep sleep, and straightening himself up in a dazed sort of way, he exclaimed:

"Good God, Jack , what is the matter?

Where are we? Have I been asleep?"

"Oh, we are only imprisoned in the ice," said Battell. "I feared that you were crushed by that huge block of ice which came so near carrying away the part of the deck where you were standing. If Jack had not caught you and drawn you back at the imminent risk of his own life, you would now be at the bottom of the sea."

Captain Ganoe, now fully aroused, took in the situation at a glance, and exclaimed as he grasped me by the hand :

"Jack, my savior! The last I remember was that you were turning as if to grasp me in your arms. It was indeed a close call. But why did you risk your life to save mine?"

I had scarcely spoken since the alarm had ended our conversation in my cabin, and I felt that to do so now, in answer to such a question, would betray my weakness and possibly my secret, which I had resolved to guard more closely than ever. Fortunately, however, he did not wait for a reply, but with his usual thoughtfulness for the crew and safety of the ship, he started below, saying:

"Come on, my bruises are not severe, and we must look out for the sailors and make a tour of inspection around the ship and ascertain as nearly as possible, in just what kind of a place we are."

Just as we reached the deck below, we met Paul Huston, the

engineer; Pat O'Brien, second mate; and Mike Gallagher, the cabin boy. They understood what had happened and feared we had been injured or killed by the shower of ice that had fallen upon the upper deck. They reported everything all right with the crew and that the vessel was apparently uninjured.

We passed entirely around the ship, narrowly scanning the walls of our ice prison, with a powerful reflector, which revealed every crevice. We lay in an enclosure which gave the vessel more than room enough to turn around if carefully handled. We ascertained that the great overhanging ice-mountains between which we lay, and that had threatened us with instant destruction, had actually been our salvation. When the earthquake shattered the two great ice-fields, these towering mountains had started to tumble over on the ship at the same time, and meeting far above had formed a massive arch which had prevented the closing of the channel at that point. Here and there were openings in the icy roof, but in the main, the colliding masses were closely joined together. The only injury to the ship was from the block of ice that had fallen so near to Captain Ganoe. From the number of fragments of from one to several pounds in weight, which were scattered over the upper deck, it seemed a marvel that we had escaped without serious injury.

When our tour of inspection was completed we repaired to the library to talk over the situation. Addressing Battell, Captain Ganoe asked:

"What do you think of the situation?"

"I apprehend no immediate danger," replied Captain Battell. "In a few hours with the present intense cold, this ice-pack will be frozen into one solid block. But if we are not crushed by the ice, God only knows when we will get out. As for the present, we are most fortunately situated. We could not find better winter quarters in the frigid zone. We are well protected from the cold, and the fishing will be good, as this will be a good breathing place where the fish will gather for air. We can lay in an ample supply of dog feed and I am inclined to believe that we might capture a whale and lay in a supply of oil for fuel."

"But how long do you think it will be," asked the Captain, "before we will have an opportunity to get the ship clear of the ice?"

"I would not venture a prediction," replied Battell. "One thing is certain. We are sealed up for the winter, and it may be that the entire summer will not be sufficient to produce a break up of the ice-field in which we are caught. So it may be that we will be cooped up for a year or two. There is no telling how long we will be prisoners."

"Well, I suppose then," said the Captain, "that all there is for us to do is to wait."

"Yes," said Battell, "that is all we can do, and," he added, smiling, "it will not take much effort. But," after a pause, "it will take some effort on our part to provide sufficient exercise and amusement to preserve the health and discipline of the crew, so that we will have a reasonable prospect of getting clear of the ice when the break up does take place."

"That is well thought of," said Captain Ganoe, "and I think it would be well to muster the crew and organize a regular system of employment and amusement. And," turning to me, he continued, "what do you have to say, Jack? I never knew you to be so silent. What is the matter? Have you no opinions to offer, and nothing to suggest?"

"I certainly have opinions and I might offer some suggestions," I remarked, "but before doing so, I want to familiarize myself with existing conditions. Only one thing seems certain, just at present, and that is, that we are locked up in the ice for several months and perhaps for years to come. This will give us ample time for careful reflection. There is no reason that we should be in a hurry to inaugurate a rigid system of any kind just now in order to preserve the discipline of the crew. There is no danger of their deserting the ship and we can well afford to wait until the novelty of our present surroundings has worn away."

"You are right," said the Captain. "There is certainly a novelty in our present surroundings, that will attract the attention of all and prevent ennui for the time being, but this will soon wear away, and the monotony of our imprisonment will become unbearable, except to the best disciplined minds. This will be particularly severe on our common sailors, who are uneducated, and thus deprived of the numberless sources of recreation and amusement to which we have ready access. When this time comes, what would you do?"

"So far as I am concerned," I said, "I have access to the library, and will really enjoy the association that it affords with the brightest intellects and noblest characters of earth, past and present. Now, if I should suggest anything for the relief of the common sailors, outside of such exercise and amusements as are essential to health, I would organize them into a school, and seek to bring these more exalted pleasures within their reach by increasing their knowledge, and giving them broader views of life and higher aspirations. This will also furnish us with needful and elevating employment and will certainly afford us a splendid opportunity to do good to others, and at the same time increase our own knowledge of human nature, and to trace the effects produced by environments, on the masses who have not enjoyed the advantages of a liberal education."

"Your suggestion" said the Captain, "is all right as far as the better educated are concerned, but it would be useless and probably hurtful to the common sailors. Remember the old adage that 'a little learning is a dangerous thing.' To the extent that we could succeed in giving them broader views of life and higher aspirations, we would only succeed in making them dissatisfied with their lot, and thus weaken the discipline on which the safety of all depends. All that we can do for the common sailors is to provide such healthful exercise of the muscles as will give them good appetites and enable them to enjoy rest and sleep. They would not appreciate the mental feast which you in your kindness of heart would set before them. Their training has been physical, and, hence, their enjoyments must be of the same nature. The same rules that apply to trained intellects will not apply to them."

"If that is your opinion," I said, "there is no use for any suggestions from me. You are the owner and senior officer of the Ice King, and, of course, good discipline demands that your will shall be law. You ought to understand the material of which your crew is composed, better than I. My duties have not brought me in contact with your sailors and, of course, I know practically nothing about them, except that I see they are courageous and efficient. But, nevertheless, on general principles, I believe that nature has planted the germs of all that is good and noble in every human soul, and if this is true, all that is good and noble can be developed in them by the proper influences, without detracting in any way from their usefulness as mere workers; besides, the effort to elevate them draws them nearer to us, and it seems to me, would tend to engender feelings of mutual love and confidence, that strengthen instead of weaken that perfect discipline which is of such inestimable importance to an expedition like this, when the safety and well being of every individual member is of vital importance to the safety and well being of the entire crew."

"I have always had the respect and confidence of my sailors," said the Captain, " not because I tried to lift them up to the same plane that I occupied, but because I provided them with good food, good quarters, never overtaxed their strength, and gave them ample time for rest and such amusements as they could appreciate. I have always had the goodwill and cheerful obedience of the common sailors, because I looked out for their physical needs and treated them kindly."

"I have no doubt of that," I said. "But your voyages in the past have been between civilized ports and all your sailors wanted was their pay, and in addition to this, you gave them better treatment than they could get elsewhere. Hence, their selfish impulses held them, to you. The relation between you and them was purely physical, and all that was needed to make them loyal to you, was to look out for their physical wants and treat them kindly. From their standpoint, this was an addition to their wages that they could not secure under more heartless employers. But you are now differently situated. You are not expected to come into a civilized port where sailors can spend their wages as sailors usually do. They have nothing to look forward to, and as mere workers they have no interests in common with you. But with the broader views of life to which association with the best intellects and the noblest characters gives access, they would take a more exalted view of the work in which they are engaged, and be true to you from a higher motive than their wages, which they cannot use in the supply of their physical wants. This is why I suggested the school."

"I recognize the force of your reasoning," said the Captain, "and if I regarded your premises as correct, I would come to the same conclusion that you do. But you make the mistake of overlooking the fact that a liberal education can only be secured by years of training in school, from the kindergarten to the college, and should be accompanied by the elevating influences of the home and cultured society, and followed by a life of study and experience in the higher walks of life, before the average man can be reasonably expected to rise above the plane of mere physical existence, and act from the high intellectual and moral impulses which impel the most cultivated and elevated character. And, you must still further take into consideration the fact, that even if we were imprisoned in the ice for a year or more, we would have time enough to give our sailors only a smattering of what they ought to know, in order to develop the high type of character that you propose, even if we could overcome the influence of their home lives and the low social status of the society in which they have always mingled. You do not realize, my dear Jack, the utter impossibility of the task you would have us undertake. They must still be sailors and perform the hard labor for which they were engaged, and we should be careful not to engender in their minds hopes and aspirations that would make them dissatisfied with their lot."

"I certainly would not do anything," I replied, "that would tend to make them discontented. This is something that should be most carefully avoided. But, nevertheless, I still think my suggestion, if carried out, would have just the opposite tendency. From my own experience, I regard my premises as stronger than my reasoning. I enjoyed all the advantages of a liberal education and the elevating influence of home and cultured society, and still, I have engaged in the most menial employments. Yet, I did not find that my education rendered me dissatisfied with my lot. On the contrary, it did much to enable me to adapt myself to the situation, and to find sources of enjoyment which were inaccessible to my uneducated associates. But, more than this, my experience among the lowly, convinces me that a collegiate education is not essential to the development of the noblest characteristics. I have met sailors before the mast, who had accumulated a vast fund of useful knowledge, and had the broadest and most comprehensive views of life, and its duties. The premises from which I reason, are the results of actual experience with the lowly."

"I fear," returned the Captain, "that in your enthusiastic love for humanity, you have made the very natural mistake of judging the uneducated by yourself. I do not desire to flatter, but you have certainly inherited qualities of a high order, and a temperament so well poised, that you could acquit yourself with credit in any capacity in which you might be placed. Your employers could not fail to discover your worth, and according to your own statement, you were rapidly promoted . This is the ordinary reward of those who have inherited exalted qualities. Real ability never remains very long in a menial position. The simple fact that our sailors, who are much above the average of their class, have, after years of experience, still remained in the same humble position, is a very good evidence that they are not qualified for anything higher. There are Lief and Eric, for instance. They have been with me for several years, and they have not even tried to master the language. As mere sailors, you could not find better men, but you would never select them for an emergency that required extraordinary quickness of perception, and the ability to lead."

I was about to reply, feeling myself master of the situation, so far as the argument was concerned, when a crashing sound from above, and a careening motion of the ship brought us to our feet. On gaining the deck the cause of the commotion was immediately apparent.

The ship was moving toward the starboard, and was being forced under the shelving ice. The crashing sound had been caused by the masts coming in contact with the sloping, icy roof. The masts were closely wedged under the roof and could go no farther, while the hull was still being carried forward by what seemed to be a strong ocean current. The situation was one of imminent peril, for if this motion continued, we were in immediate danger of being capsized. The ship was already careening toward the larboard.

The top could go no farther, while the hull was too far from the solid ice to admit of the use of pikes and spars to prop it back.

Battell was calling for axes to cut away the masts, when a shout from the larboard wall of our prison, attracted our attention. By the light of the reflectors we saw Lief, on a low lying bench of ice making a cable fast around an ice hummock, and at the same time we heard the voice of Eric calling for aid at the capstan on the lower deck. We saw instantly that this was the thing to do, and Captain Ganoe, Battell, Huston and myself were the first to take hold of the lever. Eric immediately motioned for the men who were coming forward with axes to man another capstan, while he seized a coil of small rope attached to a cable, sprang into the sea and swam rapidly to join Lief on the ice bench. The axmen hesitated for a moment and Captain Ganoe shouted; "Man the capstan! The Norwegians know what they are doing."

With remarkable celerity, the new cable was made fast and the men began turning the capstan. This was not a moment too soon, as the first cable, unable to stand the strain, showed unmistakable signs of breaking. The motion of the vessel toward the starboard and under the ice was stopped. But the Norwegians now called for a boat and more cables. Their orders were promptly obeyed. Captain Ganoe, Battell and myself were the first to respond. For the moment, our Norwegian sailors were in command, and all obeyed their orders with alacrity. The boat was manned and the Ice King was lashed to the larboard wall of our prison at a number of different points. The ship was saved from the impending disaster, but still was slightly careened and the masts were bent almost to the point of breaking.

Returning to the ship, Captain Ganoe and Battell began figuring on getting the masts clear of the ice and the ship righted.

The pressure of the water on the larboard side was immense, but the cables held her fast and there was no especial need of haste. The first thought suggested was to remove the upper splice of the mainmast, which would relieve the pressure, but the Norwegians had evolved a more simple plan. They motioned the engineer to set the screws in motion, slowly. As soon as the ship began to move forward the masts began to bend toward the stern, and the cables which held the ship firmly on the larboard, being relatively shortened by the forward motion, the vessel was drawn in that direction and righted herself. We now moved the vessel to the center of the enclosure in which she floated, and cables were made fast to the ice on every quarter, and thus secured from contact with it, the Ice King had the appearance of a huge spider with its web spread out in every direction.

The danger was past, the ship was safe, and we had time to inquire into the particulars concerning the important part that had been enacted by our two Norwegian sailors. We now learned that while the entire crew, except themselves, were resting from their recent fatigue in a feeling of security, Lief and Eric were far from believing that our winter quarters were entirely safe until the ship was securely tied up to the walls of our prison. Their especial charge was to keep the cables, capstans and anchors ready for use at a moment's notice, and they were satisfied that this was a time when they were needed. Hence, instead of retiring to their hammocks to sleep, they determined to carefully examine our surroundings for themselves. They observed that the larboard wall was nearly perpendicular to a point several feet above the top of the masts, while on the starboard, the sloping roof extended far out to the water's edge. They further observed that along the larboard was a low lying bench upon which the falling ice had formed a number of hummocks. This was a safe place to tie to.

Just as they had satisfied themselves on this point, they noticed that the ship was drifting toward the starboard, and that the masts were coming dangerously near the roof, and that in a few minutes we might be cap sized. There was not a moment to be lost. This motion toward the starboard must be arrested, and Lief, with one end of a coil of small rope, sprang into the water and swam to the bench along the larboard wall while Eric attached the other end of a cable. But before it could be made fast to the larboard wall the masts came in contact with the sloping roof on the starboard which gave the alarm that aroused the crew and brought the officers on deck with the results already mentioned.

Captain Ganoe was visibly affected when he learned how the ship and the lives of the crew had been saved by the quick perception and prompt action of the two sailors. He shook their hands and thanked them over and over again, declaring that such all-important service should not go unrewarded. They understood his allusion and declared in their very limited supply of English that they could not be induced to take pay from the Captain for saving the ship and at the same time saving themselves. That we must all stand together or we would all perish.

As soon as they had succeeded in making themselves understood, they withdrew. As a rule they kept to themselves, except when their services were needed. Yet they were not unsociable and often conversed with the engineer, Paul Huston, who understood their language. When they had an important communication to make, they secured his services as an interpreter. They seemed averse to the use of English.

When they were gone, Captain Ganoe said: " I little thought that Lief and Eric possessed ability of such a high order, and since I have discovered their true nobility of character, I am more than ever anxious that they should study English, as it would enable me to do so much more for them."

"You little understand the material of which these Norwegians are made," said Huston, who was standing by. "They do not want you to do any thing for them. They feel more than able to take care of themselves. They have not always been sailors, but that occupation suits their purpose best for the present. They are looking forward to great results that may be accomplished by this expedition, and they care more for its success than for anything you could do for them. As to the language, they already understand more than they care to use. They are proud of their native Norse."

"You astonish me!" exclaimed the Captain. "I must get better acquainted with them."

"Then," said Huston, "you must learn their language, and even then they may repel any familiarity. They preferred working for you because you did not understand their language. They do not care to be on confidential terms with anyone. When they found that I understood them, they became somewhat communicative but not confidential. Yet, I have learned enough to make me believe they have a history, and some well defined purpose in life. I would not think, however, of trying to draw from them anything that they did not care to give of their own accord. One thing is certain. You can place implicit confidence in their courage, ability, nobility of character and fidelity to the purposes of this expedition."

"Well, thanks to their watchfulness, quick perception and prompt action," said Captain Ganoe, "we can now have the much need rest we tried to enjoy before we had taken the precautions essential to our safety. I am surprised that we did not think of the possible dangers that might beset us from ocean currents. My only fear was that some disturbing cause might sunder the walls of our prison before they were frozen solid. And, even now, I have some fears on that score."

"No danger ot that kind," replied Battell. "Several hours have already elapsed, and the weather was intensely cold before the channel closed. Just listen how the storm still rages."

Through the rifts in our ice roof, we had been enabled to catch glimpses of the sky, but now it was all inky blackness. The gale that had brought the two great ice-fields together, had now grown to a terrific storm, and had changed its direction. The winds roared and raged like demons in mortal combat, and ever and anon the snow was driven in upon us like fine dust, indicating the intense cold. We, now that the ship was safe, had the best of reasons for congratulating ourselves on our snug winter quarters. Our icy prison was both our safety from the violence of the storm, and our protection from the intense cold.

We partook of a hearty lunch and retired to our rest with feelings of perfect security.

When I awoke everything was astir on board. The carpenters were busily engaged in repairing the broken deck, while the sailors were removing the ice and snow. Everything was being put in order as if we were preparing for a voyage. The storm had ceased to howl and we were in the grasp of an Arctic winter. Even in our secluded retreat, it was necessary for us to wrap up in furs and woolens when we went on the upper deck. But our cabins were warm and we had an abundance of everything to eat and wear to make us comfortable. The ice-field was frozen into a solid block, and there was no question as to our safety, but we had no means of making observations that would indicate our location. This to me, was the loss of an occupation that I really enjoyed and I felt the need of something that would take its place.

We were imprisoned in the ice on September 23d, and from my last observations I inferred that our location was about latitude 77° North and longitude 160° West. The sun made his appearance for a brief interval each day, and I calculated that the long Arctic night would be fully set in by the last of October. The rifts in the roof of our prison afforded us no opportunity for determining our location. Our recent danger had revealed the fact that we were moving. We tried the sounding line and found that we were in deep water, and that our motion was evidently due to the motion of the icefield. We were floating at the mercy of the winds and ocean currents. But whither would they carry us? None could tell. Assuming, however, that the currents were north bound, and reasoning from the fact that the motion of the earth was from west to east, the tendency being, as it were, to slip from under us, we concluded that as long as the ice was floating freely, our general motion would be toward the west and north.

For the present we were safe and comfortable with the ship securely fastened to the solid walls of our prison. But we knew summer would come, and the warm rays of the sun would beam down on us for months, melting and breaking up the frozen surface of the ocean which was now our security, but might then become the cause of our destruction. Our future safety, and the success of the expedition, demanded that we should have easy access to the surface, so that we could make the necessary observations, and, if possible, find some means of providing for the safety of the ship and crew when the ice went to pieces. This was the task before us, but we had no means of calculating the time it would take. All we knew was, that the two ice mountains by coming together had formed a roof over our heads, and towered many feet above the ship's masts, and if their other dimensions were in proportion, it might take a long time for us to tunnel through to the surface.

We felt that there was no time to lose. All needful arrangements were soon perfected under the direction of Battell, who took charge as engineer and manager. The ice-bench on our larboard was selected as the point of starting. The crew was divided into three reliefs, each with a foreman, and the work of excavation went on without intermission. This arrangement gave eight hours for work in the tunnel, and sixteen for rest and recreation.

I again suggested my "pet hobby" as it was called, of organizing the crew into a school and devoting a few hours each day to educational purposes. But I was alone in the recommendation, and it was not acted on, but the library was free to all who cared to read. I noticed, however, that Paul Huston, Pat O'Brien and Mike Gallagher, were the only ones who ever called for books, and Huston was the only one who seemed to know just what he wanted. Lief and Eric had some Norwegian books and writings which they often consulted, but all the others, when not at work, spent their time in playing games, spinning yarns and fishing.

As predicted by Battell, the enclosure in which the ship floated, seemed to attract the finny denizens of the deep, supplying fresh food for the crew and our dog teams, as well as oil which we used for fuel.

The library was the favorite resort of those who cared to read and discuss topics of general interest. Here we spent our leisure hours, reading, conversing upon subjects of every description and devising amusements that would enable us to pass the time pleasantly. When tired of these things we joined the working force in the tunnel and exercised our muscles. This was a work of necessity, as well as a healthful recreation, and we went into it with the utmost enthusiasm. We managed to get comfortably tired every day, and enjoyed excellent appetites and most refreshing sleep, in consequence. Altogether the winter passed very agreeably.

It was well on toward spring before the tunnel was completed. We now had access to the surface, up an easy incline, and beheld the uninterrupted beauties of an Arctic night. 'The scene which greeted us defies description. The sky was cloudless, and the Northern Lights, with their brilliant coruscation's, nature's compensation for the long polar night, presented a pyrotechnic display, the grandeur and beauty of which are indelibly impressed on my memory.

We took our bearings and found we were in latitude 84° N. longitude 170° W. We were seven degrees farther north than when we were caught in the ice, and ten degrees farther west. We were plainly in the grasp of north-bound currents, while our motion toward the west was uncertain. Subsequent observations revealed the fact that at times our longitude was stationary, or drifting somewhat toward the east. On the whole, our westerly motion exceeded any opposite tendency, but our progress northward was considerable though not regular, as if we were retarded by obstructions which were being overcome at intervals by the force of northerly currents.

It was now the 20th of Feb., and it was determined that the work of exploration should commence. The dog-team and sledges were brought out and provisioned for a journey to the eastward under the direction of Captain Battell. Captain Ganoe, Pat O'Brien, Mike Gallagher, Paul Huston, the two Norwegian sailors and myself remained on the ship. The sledge party was to be absent a month and possibly longer. Captain Battell wanted to make some thorough observations on the eastern borders of the ice field, and take soundings if he could reach open water.

We still had some weeks of Arctic night before us, but the full, round moon and the brilliant Aurora, made every object visible for a long distance. The weather was intensely cold, but the scenery was so attractive that I spent much of my time exploring the ice-field in the immediate vicinity of the ship. Many were the weird and fantastic scenes that I sketched, and many the strolls I took in a vain effort to find some prominent point from which with my glass I could get an unobstructed view of the horizon. But like our prison in the ice, all nature seemed cramped. The starry vault was contracted by the obscuration of stars which I thought should have been visible above the horizon. I kept searching for an elevated point of view, but this seemed always just a little ahead. These rambles often extended for miles and occupied hours.

Returning from one of them, I was met by Lief and Eric who pointed to the crest of the mountain of ice that formed the roof of our prison, and beckoned me to follow them. I did so and found that they had cut an inclined road around the icy mountain to the apex, where they had erected an observatory out of ice blocks. It was built over a rift in the roof of our prison that was directly above the ice bench on the larboard near the mouth of the tunnel. The wall at this point was almost perpendicular, and with but little labor they were able to put in an elevator, consisting simply of a platform secured by ropes, and attached to a pulley inside the observatory.

They showed me what they had done, and to convince me that it was entirely safe, they let themselves down on the elevator and raised themselves up again, much as a painter handles his swinging scaffold, but more rapidly. I was pleased with the contrivance, and more with the interest taken by Lief and Eric in making arrangements to facilitate my observations. I did not hesitate to take my place on the platform with them and return to the ship by this direct route.

I now learned that as soon as the tunnel was completed, Lief and Eric had found their way to the top of our prison, and seeing the advantages that this elevation offered as an outlook, they conceived the idea of an observatory on the top, to be connected with the ship by an elevator. They took no one into their confidence but Huston, and set to work immediately. In a little over two weeks they were ready to put in the elevator which connected directly with the ship, and saved a long walk by way of the tunnel. This work had just been completed and they were enabled to give me a very unexpected but agreeable surprise on my return from one of my usual rambles.

But it was no more of a surprise to me than it was to Captain Ganoe, who was just starting out to the surface through the tunnel, when Lief, Eric and myself came swinging down from the observatory on the platform which constituted the cage. Lief who was handling the rope stopped our descent just in time to prevent the platform from swinging against the Captain, who looking up exclaimed:

"Hello, Jack! Where did you come from, and what is all this rigging for?"

"Just ask Lief and Eric," I replied. "They have been looking out for a more direct route to the surface than by way of the tunnel. They have erected an observatory on the roof, and if you are going out for a walk, you had better take the elevator."

"All right," said the Captain stepping on the platform, "but I would suggest that you ought to have a light on board, to give warning in this gloom to all whom it may concern, to get out of the way of the engine."

"That can be provided for in the future," I said. "This is the first trial and we find that it works all right. Now we are ready for such improvements as you have to suggest. While the invention belongs to our Norwegian friend, we have no patent laws in this country and hence there can be no infringement. There is no restrictive legislation here to stand in the way of progress."

"I think in view of all the facts," said the Captain, "that this matter had better be left in the hands of the inventors. I have no doubt that they are fully equal to the task, and they have free access to the ship's stores for that purpose. It seems to me that the improvement most needed is some contrivance that will counteract the swinging motion, and no doubt Lief and Eric have a plan already that will accomplish that."

We were now in the observatory and the view in every direction was most satisfactory. This was by far the most elevated location anywhere in the region, and Captain Ganoe cordially concurred in my suggestion to fit it up in good shape for all the purposes of an observatory as well as a resting place when the weather became warm. We carefully explored the immediate vicinity and found that this towering mountain of ice could be made accessible from both the east and west. Towards the north and south it was easy to trace the seam where the ice walls had come together, and along this line were numerous depressions of great depth.

When we were ready to return to the ship we found that Lief and Eric had stretched ropes from the top to the bottom which passing through the platform held it steady while passing up and down. They had also devised a contrivance by which the elevator could be operated either from above or below as occasion might require; also a telephone connection between the observatory and the ship.

With this easy means of access to the surface, we seldom used the tunnel except for the sledges, or the transportation of some heavy burden. From this elevated point I watched with continually increasing interest, the roseate hues on the horizon which indicated the location of the rising sun. These grew brighter and brighter until the king of day made his appearance. This was the signal for inflating the balloons and sending up dispatches in the hope that they might be carried south into civilized portions of the globe by the equinoctial storms. It was also the time fixed for the return of Battell from his exploring expedition on the eastern portion of the ice field. His observations, in connection with my own, constituted our only means of accumulating that fund of information concerning these unknown regions which would make this expedition valuable to the world. Besides, our own safety depended to a very great extent upon the accuracy of the knowledge we could acquire concerning the forces which controlled the movements of this vast island of ice. My relation to the scientific work of the expedition, made me anxious to make the best possible use of our present favorable opportunity for investigation.

During our long incarceration in our ice prison I had kept

such notes and made such observations as our environments would permit. The movement of the ice field towards the west which at first had threatened to draw us under the ice and capsize the ship, had lost much of its force, and now that we were on the surface, and able to trace the seam which marked the channel in which we had been moving, we discovered that its general direction was from southeast to northwest, while at the time we had been caught between the colliding ice fields, we had according to my notes, been running northeast. This demonstrated, that the entire body of ice had turned one quarter around, while its general movement had been toward the west and north. And now my daily observations indicated that it was continually changing its position, and that while its motions were generally toward the west, they were by no means uniform. It seemed to have been at the mercy of contending forces ever since we had been held within its grasp, and it was one of the prime objects of the expedition to make a close study of just this kind of influences.

As soon as the sun began to show itself above the horizon, I kept a constant lookout for the return of Captain Battell and his sledge party. We knew that he had gone east, and that it was his intention to commence the exploration of the western portion of the ice-field before the sun was remaining above the horizon for the full twenty-four hours. But the weather during the early spring was unfavorable and I discovered nothing worthy of note. When the days became longer and with the sun in the west, I expected to make some important discoveries with my glass. And when I did get a clear view I was startled to observe what seemed to be a barren waste of sand and sand mountains. I called Captain Ganoe's attention to this appearance, and after a careful scrutiny with his glass he said :

"That looks very much like land. The surface is certainly neither snow nor ice. But where in the world did all that sand come from? I will telephone Huston to bring a larger telescope and we will make a closer examination."

In a few minutes Huston made his appearance and we placed the instrument in position. With the stronger glass, our first impressions as to the nature of the surface were confirmed but we discovered nothing that offered any explanation of the phenomenon. Here was a mystery and we were now more anxious than ever for the return of Captain Battell, who we felt assured had made some very interesting discoveries.

I continued to scan the horizon with the large telescope and my search was soon rewarded by the discovery of a man who seemed to have just reached the crest of what appeared to be a long sandy ridge running north and south, but a few miles distant. He seemed to be assisting others to reach the same position. Raising the instrument to its highest powers I was enabled to recognized Captain Battell and several sailors. They were hauling others up from the opposite side by means of a rope, who as soon as they reached the top, took hold and helped to raise others.

I described the scene and asked Captain Ganoe to look for himself. He took in the situation at a glance and said;

"We must go to their assistance. The sledges and dog teams are evidently on the opposite side and they must be lifted up as well as the men," and turning to Huston he said: "Return to the ship. Summon the entire crew. Explain the situation to the Norwegians, tell them to get out the sedges immediately and take such appliances as they deem necessary, and Jack and I will meet you at the foot of the mountains on the east side. Make all haste possible as we must hurry to the assistance of our comrades who are evidently nearly exhausted.

Chapter IV

A SINGULAR DISCOVERY — BATTELL CROSSING A SAND RIDGE ON THE ICE-FIELD — CAPTAIN GANOE LEADS A PARTY TO HIS ASSISTANCE — LIEF AND ERIC — BATTELL'S THEORY — A SECOND EXPEDITION — BATTELL'S LONG ABSENCE — IS DISCOVERED RETURNING ALONE, SCARCELY ABLE TO WALK — RELIEF PARTY FINDS HIM UNCONSCIOUS — CAPTAIN GANOE AS PHYSICIAN — BATTELL RELATES HOW HE WAS ABANDONED BY HIS MEN — PREPARING FOR THE BREAK.

Huston stepped upon the elevator and descended to the ship to carry out the instructions he had received, while Captain Ganoe and myself remained in the observatory to scan the surface more critically and map out the route we must travel. So far we could discover there seemed to be no serious obstacle in the way. The surface between us and the sand ridge which Battell must cross had the appearance of a level plain of snow or ice, with numerous hummocks scattered here and there. Beyond this, the ridge, with some lofty elevations, filled the outlines of the picture.

'The point which Battell had selected for crossing was a gap in this ridge. Directly below the gap the ridge was very steep but the top could be reached from this point by an easy incline towards the south. I made a hasty sketch of every prominent object on a direct line from the observatory to the gap which was the point we desired to reach as soon as possible, as we felt that our assistance was sorely needed. This work was completed to our satisfaction when we noticed the crew with the sledge coming around the north side, and we hastened down to meet them at the foot of the mountain on the east. We found everything in good shape for a rapid march. The sledge was lightly loaded with such appliances, ropes, pulleys, etc., as had been deemed necessary to enable us to render the most effectual assistance. The dogs were pulling on their harness as if anxious for a run, and the men were fresh, and feeling the need of exercise.

The thaw had scarcely commenced and the traveling was good. Every condition seemed favorable. Captain Ganoe and myself led off along the route which our observations had indicated as the most practicable. In less than two hours we had reached the foot of the ridge just below the gap where we had discovered Captain Battell. We found the surface covered with volcanic ashes and scoria, and our minds instantly reverted to the earth quake which broke up the ice-field, and our narrow escape from destruction. However, this was no time for speculation. Our business was to reach the top as soon as possible.

We found that a direct ascent would be exceedingly difficult, but that the inclining shelf along the face of the ridge would enable us to reach the top at a point about a half mile south of the gap. This shelf, or bench, was several yards in width and its appearance, covered as it was with ashes, gave the impression that it had been a level shore line that in some great convulsion of nature had been tilted up from the south at an angle of about twenty-five degrees, and that the general surface had been leveled up by a subsequent deposit over the lower part.

We at once began our ascent along this comparatively easy route. Yet it was a tedious and toilsome effort to get the sledge with its load of necessary appliances to the top. However, within less than an hour, notwithstanding numerous resting spells, we reached the top and found ourselves on a level plateau, several hundred feet wide, and about one half mile south of where we expected to find Captain Battell and his comrades.

While our party halted in order to give the dog-team a rest, Captain Ganoe and myself hurried on to the gap. On reaching the edge we discovered that the men were taking a rest, after having lifted most of the contents of the sledge to the top. We could see that they had been compelled to cut a road through some hundreds of feet of frozen ashes, in order to reach their present position, and we did not need to be told that they had been having a very hard time.

Most of the party were asleep and no one observed our approach until we had descended into the gap, and Captain Ganoe had called out in regular sailor style the familiar: "Ship Ahoy!" This unexpected greeting brought Captain Battell to his feet, but for a moment he was too much surprised to make any response. Recovering himself, he advanced and grasped Captain Ganoe by the hand exclaiming:

"How did you get here? I was just thinking how fortunate it would be if you knew the predicament we are in and would come to our relief with a capstan and some more ropes and pulleys."

"That is just what we have done," said Captain Ganoe. "Jack was on the lookout for you from his observatory on top of the mountain of ice that covers the resting place of the Ice King. As soon as we discovered you, we started to your relief with a sledge load of such appliances as it seemed you most needed."

"This is indeed fortunate," said Battell. "We are almost exhausted with the efforts we have been compelled to make in order to reach this gap, and now that we are here, we find that our difficulties are by no means ended, and it is most important that we should get well over the ridge and commence our exploration of the western portion of this vast island of ashes and ice."

As he was speaking, our sledge appeared at the top of the gap and the men joined us at once. Huston acting as spokesman for our Norwegian sailors, said: "Lief and Eric request that they be permitted to complete the work of transferring the sledges and their loads to the west side."

"Tell them," said the Captain, "to go ahead in their own way and accept our thanks for their most welcome services."

In a few minutes they had their ropes, pulleys and capstan in place and gave us to understand that the dogs would furnish all the power that was needed. They soon had one of the sledges slowly but surely gliding up the steep incline to the top.

We watched them a few minutes, when Captain Ganoe said:

"I think we can safely leave this matter to the Norwegians and we may start on our return to the ship. "

"I am willing to trust them," said Battell, "and it is important that we begin at once to compare notes and lay our plans for the future. I feel that there is no time to be lost." And giving some instructions to Brown who had been selected as foreman in the work of road making, to give such assistance as might be needed, we started on foot for the ship, a distance of between five and six miles.

On our way back, Battell gave us a concise account of his observations and the conclusions at which he had arrived.

"When we left the ship," he said, "we took a southeasterly direction. The cold was intense, but with our ample preparations we did not suffer so much as might have been expected. We reached open water within three days, but the shore line was so precipitous that we could not launch our sledge boats and sail around as I had intended. So, we continued our journey around the icefield toward the north, as we had begun it. The general direction of the shoreline at this point was from the south west toward the northeast. The traveling was fairly good and we made good time for about a week, and then our trouble commenced. The entire surface was covered to an unknown depth with volcanic ashes.

"The surface formation was evidently new, but careful examination revealed the fact, that this covered an older formation of very considerable thickness. Our soundings, owing to the precipitous character of the coast line, were not satisfactory, but taken in connection with my observations as to the motions of the ice-field, I came to the conclusion that it was frequently grounding on the tops of submarine mountains. If this is true, it will probably hasten the breaking up when the ice becomes rotten under the influence of continuous sunshine.

"Having satisfied myself on these points we started on our return trip, and but for the difficult nature of the surface, and the frequent necessity for road making, we would have been with you by the time the sun made his appearance."

Before we reached the ship, it had been definitely settled that after a short rest, Battell should continue his explorations toward the western borders of the ice-field, and time the expedition, so as to return to the ship before there was any immediate danger from the thaw. We had come to the conclusion that we were floating in an open sea, and it was our intention to press on for the north when the ice went to pieces; and some phenomena, that we, in common with other explorers had observed, led to the opinion that we would find land and not unlikely a habitable country around the pole.

Since the sun had made his appearance, flocks of ducks, brants and geese, coming from the north were quite numerous. When killed we found them fat and juicy and their crops were often filled with a species of grain resembling rice, which seemed to indicate that they came from a temperate climate. We now began to confidently expect that when the ice-field went to pieces we would find the country which produced this grain — the northern home of these flocks of birds.

"We argued that the six months and more of continued sunshine at the pole, would necessarily produce a. mild, if not a warm climate, for the greater portion of the year. We held that refraction would secure perhaps as much as seven months of sunshine at the pole, and add to this the long twilights and the Aurora, preventing absolute darkness, the immediate vicinity of the pole might be in many respects, a most desirable climate. Of one thing we felt sure, and that was, that those flocks of ducks and geese that came from the north had been well fed with grain that must have grown in a productive country.

When we came to the ice mountain that covered the ship, Captain Battell turned to the north, saying:

"I believe that this is the route to the mouth of the tunnel."

"Yes, that is true," replied Captain Ganoe, "but let us go by the way of Jack's observatory, which is directly over the ship."

"All right," said Battell. 'Lead on. I want to see the observatory any way, and it is probably no further over the mountain than it is around it, even if the traveling may be a little more laborious."

We offered no explanation as to our elevator, and in a few minutes we were in the observatory, under the canopy of sail cloth which protected it from the rays of the sun.

"Well, this is a cozy place," said Battell, as he seated himself upon one of the extemporized cushioned seats with which it was furnished.

"It is," said I, "but I am more interested in seeing how Lief and Eric are getting along in their coveted task of transferring the sledges to this side of the ridge."

So saying, I went directly to the large telescope which we had left bearing upon the gap Battell had chosen for a crossing place. A glance was enough, and in reply to a questioning look from Battell I said: "Both sledges are on top and they are preparing to let them down on this side. Come and see for yourself. I believe that our Norwegian sailors are equal to anything they are willing to undertake."

"I believe you are right," said Battell, as he took his place at the telescope. "There," he continued, "they are letting the sledges down the steep incline fully loaded. From the progress they are making, they will be here in a few hours, with everything in ship shape for the expedition toward the west. That rests me so, that I will not mind clambering down to the mouth of the tunnel."

"Why go by way of the tunnel?" asked Captain Ganoe. "Just take your seat on that divan and there need be no clambering down."

"Yes," I said, "and just let me share the seat with you, and let the Captain act as chief of transportation and take command of the expedition, down to the ship." He did as he was directed with a puzzled look. Captain Ganoe took hold of the rope while I turned on the light and we began to drop down toward the ship.

"Well you have got things fixed up in grand style," said Battell. "Who would have expected a few weeks ago, that we would now be descending into the interior of an iceberg on a grandly upholstered elevator, with the stern Captain of the Ice King as our elevator boy? Is not this putting on a little too much style for these regions of eternal ice?"

"Not at all," I responded. "I hold, you know, that every human being is justly entitled to the very best that his own labor can produce. But this arrangement for facilitating our access to the outer world is the product of the labor and skill of our Norwegian sailors. They had the observatory almost completed before they revealed their designs to any one but Huston."

"'Then," said Battell "if that is the sort of men they are, I think they had better remain with the ship. I had thought of proposing to take them out with me on our western expedition and leave some of the other men to take their place here."

"I could hardly consent to part with our Norwegians even for a few days," said Captain Ganoe. "Since I have discovered their ability, I want them on the ship in case of emergencies. I would not hesitate, if it was necessary, to place them in command. The quickness of perception and general reliability they have shown, almost persuade me that Jack is right and that under some circumstances the highest qualities may be developed among the most lowly."

"And it may be," said Battell, "that as Huston intimated, Lief and Eric have some great purpose in life, and under such influences as Jack would like to place around the common sailors, many of them might develop qualities of a high order. I have thought much of Jack's 'pet hobby.' On this last expedition, I have realized more than ever, the importance of having men of lofty characters in the capacity of common sailors, if such a thing is possible."

"And it is possible," I added. "And whether it is possible or not, it is our duty to ourselves and to humanity to do everything in our power to inspire all with whom we come in contact, with broader views of life, and nobler aspirations for the future."

"Well," said Captain Ganoe, "it is certainly not my intention to antagonize your exalted idea of our duty toward our fellow beings. It is an ennobling thought to dwell upon, but whether it will ever be possible for us to do much for our sailors in this way or not, it is clearly impossible to do anything immediately, and surely Captain Battell wants one good sleep in his own bed before he starts on another expedition. So I propose that we now retire to our quarters for rest. We certainly need it, and there is no duty pressing upon us to prevent it."

We acted upon the Captain's suggestion as soon as we could reach our cabins. In a few minutes I was sleeping soundly, and did not awake until the gong gave notice that breakfast was ready. The crew had returned with the sledges, and after a nap were now ready for the first meal on shipboard that they had taken for over a month. Captain Battell had completed preparations for his expedition toward the west, and once more the officer's mess was complete, and while we enjoyed our repast we discussed plans for the future. As we arose from the table, Battell took me by the hand and said:

"You may keep a sharp lookout for me after the First of July. By that time we ought to be able to reach open water on the west and return. If we can launch the sledges, it is my intention to sail around the ice to the north and if possible return along the seam which marks the channel through which we were moving when we were entombed beneath these 'bergs.' I have already made use of your observatory to make a sketch of the most prominent objects toward the west and north. I apprehend no trouble. Of course we will have channels of water to contend with before we return, but as our sledges make excellent boats, they are as likely to expedite as to obstruct our movements. I need not caution you to keep up your observations, and note everything that has a bearing on our situation. I will do the same and together we cannot fail to secure a fund of valuable information."

He bade us good-bye, and at once departed. I repaired to the observatory, and through my glass watched the sledges until they disappeared from view in the distance.

It was now the 20th of April, and it would be two months and a half before we expected the return of the exploring party, and if it met with no mishap, there was ample time for an extended tour around the icefield. I anticipated great results from the observations that might be made.

Captain Battell had left with us three of his party who seemed the least able to bear the fatigue of the long journey over the ice which he contemplated. This was a valuable addition to the force left with the ship, and at the same time relatively strengthened the exploring party, as it relieved them of the prospective danger of being compelled to take care of disabled comrades.

The weather was favorable, and soon the rays of the sun began to slowly but surely change the surface of the ice. I watched the process with constantly increasing interest. If we were ever to escape from our imprisonment, our release must come as a result of the thaw. Hence, I came to regard the little rivulets that were forming in every direction, and usually disappearing in a short distance through some crevice, as our saviors. If the process kept on with sufficient vigor, the ice-field was sure to break up before we were again locked in the embrace of an Arctic winter, and we would have an opportunity to escape.

At last the sun had reached his highest altitude, and the time had come when we might expect the return of Battell. The thaw had progressed rapidly and the ice was becoming rotten, and with the first storm would probably go to pieces. But the weather was serene and there was no immediate danger. The 1st of July had come and gone and Battell was still absent. The thaw, under the continuous rays of the sun was accelerated, and I began to fear the break up would come before his return with the larger part of the crew. This might prove to be fatal to all our hopes. I felt that we sorely needed Captain Battell with his experience in the navigation of these frozen seas.

I now began to dread the thaw as much as I had been inclined to welcome it two months before. I continued my observations with more interest, if possible, than ever. The motions of the ice-field puzzled me. We seemed to be slightly oscillating from one side to the other of longitude 180°, but with a frequent motion toward the north.

I spent most of my time in the observatory, more on the lookout for some indication of the return of Captain Battell than for any other purpose. This interest was shared by every member of the crew, and we established regular watches for this one purpose, so that there was always some one at the telescope. Captain Ganoe and myself took the first watch, Pat O'Brien and Huston, the second, and Lief and Eric the third. So the entire twenty-four hours were occupied in the lookout for Battell. In addition to this, we made several expeditions to the north and west for many miles. While we learned that the traveling was very toilsome, we discovered no reason why the exploring party should not be able to return as long as the ice-field remained unbroken. It was true that the expedition might have reached a section where the thaw had destroyed the solidity of the ice, but it was well equipped for such a contingency, as the sledges could readily be converted into boats.

We tried in vain to figure out the cause of Captain Battell's delay. The ice was becoming more rotten every day and our suspense became more and more painful. We had almost despaired of his return, when through my glass, I observed what seemed to be a human being, directly west of us, slowly struggling along over the rotten, slushy surface of the ice.

I called the attention of Captain Ganoe to my discovery and after a careful scrutiny of the object he exclaimed:

"That is certainly a man. It must be Battell or one of his men returning alone. And," he paused, and then added hastily: "He is scarcely able to walk and falls down from sheer exhaustion. We must go to his relief at once." And turning to Mike Gallagher, who was present, he said:

"Hurry down to the ship and tell O'Brien to summon a relief party with a stretcher. Bring my medicine case with restoratives for an exhausted man. Tell Huston to explain the situation to Lief and Eric. Make all the haste possible and meet us at the mouth of the tunnel."

Mike started down on the elevator at once to deliver these orders, while Captain Ganoe and myself went down the winding way on the west side. At the mouth of the tunnel we were joined by the relief party. Lief and Eric carried the stretcher, while Pat O'Brien, Paul Huston and Mike Gallagher, each had a parcel containing something intended for the relief of an exhausted man. The medicine case and some warm blankets were on the stretcher.

The ice-field in this direction spread out before us into a vast plain, but the exact spot where we had observed the approaching man was hidden from view by a number of hummocks and we took these for our guide.

As soon as we reached the nearest and highest of these elevations, I climbed to the top and carefully scanned the plain beyond. Several minutes elapsed without discovering any indication of the object of our search, when not more than a mile away, I saw through my glass the head and shoulders of a man, arise above the surface. For a moment he seemed to support himself on his hands and then dropped back out of sight. I carefully noted the location and we then hurried on.

In a few minutes we came to a channel in the ice that had been worn out by a stream of water. A little to one side a man was lying on the bottom as if dead. We called to him, but he did not move. Lief and Eric sprang into the channel and lifted him out.

It was Captain Battell and he was entirely unconscious. We could now see that he had been trying with all his strength to lift himself out of the channel which was not over four and a half feet in depth by six or seven in width. When I saw him from the summit of the ice hummock he was doubtless making the last effort to climb out, that his exhausted energies would permit. We had arrived just in time to rescue him from certain death.

As he lay upon the stretcher unconscious and scarcely breathing, in fancy, I pictured the trials through which he must have passed. His worn out boots and tattered clothing; his sunken eyes and pinched features, all indicated more than words could express his terrible struggle for life against the combined forces of cold and hunger. True, it was not freezing weather, but the water through which he had been compelled to wade was ice cold, and the bed upon which he rested, must have been a melting ice hummock. All these things were evident from the environments and did not need to be stated in words in order to be understood and appreciated. While he alone could give us the particulars, we were already familiar in a general way with his experiences, traveling on foot over the fast melting ice and almost without food for weeks and possibly months.

While no physician had been engaged for this expedition, it was because Captain Ganoe was well qualified by education and experience to fill the place as occasion might require, and among the stores of the Ice King, there was an ample supply of medicines, surgical instruments and appliances of all kinds. The Captain was very averse to being classed as a physician, and yet his knowledge of medicine, surgery and practice would have enabled him to aspire to the highest rank in the profession. Hence he at once took charge of the patient with the readiness and skill of an experienced practitioner, and soon he had him as comfortable as dry clothing, a warm bed and appropriate restoratives could make him.

The patient did not regain consciousness, but he was soon breathing naturally and apparently enjoying a sound and refreshing sleep.

When all was ready for us to start on our return to the ship, Captain Ganoe said:

"As it is evident that I must turn doctor for a few days I will place Jack Adams in command. That will leave just six of us to carry Captain Battell to his cabin in the Ice King. For this purpose we will divide into three reliefs. Huston and I will take the first; Pat and Mike the second, and Lief and Eric the third. This seems to be about the proper order, as our Norwegian comrades carried the camp bed and medicine case all the way from the ship."

"But what if I object to the arrangement?" I asked. "While I am willing," I continued, "to render any service in my power, I am not disposed to usurp your place as commander. You lead the way and I will take my place at the handles of the stretcher. I enlisted to obey orders and take any place assigned me, but not to usurp the prerogatives of commander."

"Then I have only to insist upon the terms of the contract as you understand it," said the Captain. "You say that you enlisted to obey orders and take any place assigned you, and hence as the captain of the Ice King, I order you to take the place of commander until I choose to resume the duties of that position. This is just as it should be. It was you who discovered Captain Battell and then led us to the spot where we found him, and now you are appointed to lead us back to the ship by the most direct and practicable route. It is fortunate for us that you have spent so much of your time in the study of the topography of this country, if that is the proper word to apply to a dreary waste of ice. It is your first duty as commander to divide the distance to the ship into easy stages and see that each relief does its part of the work with all possible care for the comfort of our comrade. This is 'orders,' if you prefer to look at it in that light. I shall certainly take my place at the stretcher until in your judgment, the second relief, Pat and Mike, ought to take hold."

"All right,"I said. "If I am to be commander-in-chief, whether I will or not, my first order is, 'Follow me.'"

We returned to the ship without any particular haste, frequently stopping to rest and to administer restoratives to the lips of our exhausted comrade. He was conveyed to his own quarters and everything was, by the direction of Captain Ganoe, placed as nearly as possible, in the same shape that he left it.

He was still sleeping, and the Captain assured us that he was doing well, and that if fever could be avoided, he would soon recover. He cautioned us to keep quiet and not ask him any questions in case he should awake to consciousness.

Captain Ganoe took his place at the side of the patient and from time to time touched his lips with water. After several hours he partially aroused from his lethargy, and the Captain administered a few spoonfuls of broth, which were swallowed with avidity, and he again relapsed into a profound slumber.

The Captain now directed us to leave him entirely alone with the patient but to hold ourselves in readiness to come at a moment's notice. He told us that all the patient now needed was profound silence, and a little nourishment whenever he was sufficiently aroused to partake of it. "I want Mike" he said, "to remain with me so as to be ready at any moment to execute my orders. Captain Battell's restoration to health and vigor is of more importance to us now than any other consideration. I need Mike more than you do, and you must get along with cold lunches, or, do your own cooking. If I need any of you, Mike will let you know."

Through Mike, we heard from the sick room from time to time, but the word was always the same; that the patient was doing well, but still sleeping. Mike said that whenever Battell showed signs of awaking, the Captain would administer a spoonful of soup and he would drop off to sleep again without ever being fully aroused to consciousness.

I was keenly alive to the fact that the death, or even the great disability of Captain Battell would be an irreparable loss to all of us. He was the only experienced Arctic navigator and explorer among us, and notwithstanding the cheering news from the sick room, I felt the most intense anxiety, and remained in the library all the time, so as to be ready to respond at once to any call from Captain Ganoe.

After forty-eight hours of this anxious waiting had gone by, I was surprised at a personal call from Captain Ganoe, who greeted me in his usual cordial manner, while his face fairly glowed with happiness. Without waiting for me to ply him with questions, he exclaimed:

"Well, Jack, the danger has passed. Captain Battell has come to himself. He is still very weak, but there are no signs of fever. I admonished him not to talk until he had taken another nap, to which he consented on the condition that I would call you. He wants a conference at once."

"I am delighted to hear such good news!" I exclaimed. "But what did he say when he realized that he was in his own cabin, and you sitting by his side in the capacity of attendant. I have all of a woman's curiosity in regard to this matter, and insist upon your giving me all the particulars."

"Certainly," he replied. "Your interest is but natural, and shall be gratified as nearly as my memory will permit. In his treatment, I sought to keep him asleep until he had gained strength for mental and physical effort. When he showed signs of waking up, I knew that it was from the gnawings of hunger, and would administer a small quantity of beef tea or some strengthening cordial, and then he would again relapse into a profound slumber. These spells of semiconsciousness became more and more frequent as he gained strength, and at last he opened his eyes and looked me full in the face. He closed them again, and seemed to reflect and then looking at me, he said in his usual calm and deliberate manner:

"'The last thing I remember, is, that I was trying to climb out of a channel that had been worn in the ice by a small stream of water. The bank only came up to my chin, but I was so weak that I could not succeed. After that, I seem to have dream-memories of delicious feasting, and reclining on luxurious couches. I want you to tell me at once how I got here, into my own quarters.'

"I told him to be careful and not permit himself to become the least excited until he had gained more strength, but to content himself with the simple statement that Jack had noticed his approach from his observatory; and that we went immediately to his relief. 'Now,' said I, 'drink this cup of beef tea and turn over and take another nap.'

He drank the tea and said, 'I will do as you say, if you will agree to have Jack here when I wake up. It is a matter of the greatest importance that we have a conference immediately. We must be ready for the break up and I have much to tell you.'

"So saying he turned over and was soon sleeping soundly, and I am here to request you to come to his quarters. As he is not likely to sleep very long we had better go at once. Nature will soon be demanding exercise for mind and body as strenuously as she has demanded rest. Let us go."

Some ten or fifteen minutes after we entered Captain Battell's cabin he awoke, and immediately got up and shook hands with me most cordially. He was naturally a man of few words, and never very demonstrative of either joy or grief, affection or anger, and usually preserved the most perfect equilibrium, but he was visibly affected when he said:

"My dear Jack! How fortunate it has been for Captain Ganoe and myself that you joined this expedition. But for your watchful care we would both have been dead, and in all probability, the Ice King and the entire crew would have been lost. You have certainly been our guardian angel, and must ever hold the very highest place in our esteem and affection."

"I deserve no especial thanks for anything I have done," I responded. "We are out here all alone, imprisoned in the ice and our only hope of escape depends upon our standing together and helping each other, at all times and under all circumstances. The safety of every individual depends upon the safety of every other individual. Common sense and our common interests, dictate that we should be a unit and realize that 'an injury to one is the concern of all.' Our rule of action toward each other should be, 'each for all and all for each.' This is the only principle that a truly intelligent people anywhere would ever adopt, but here on this waste of floating ice, situated as we are, the most stupid ought to be able to comprehend the necessity for its application. So, I repeat that I deserve no especial credit, for in looking out for the safety of others I do the only thing that can be done for my own safety. This thing of caring for self, regardless of the interests of others, indicates a deficiency in intellectual development as much as it does hardness of heart; and a careful regard for the comfort and interest of others, is indicative of intellectual development as much as it is of kindness of heart and love for our fellow creatures."

"Your philosophy," said Captain Battell, "is always right; but what is still better you practice what you preach. Would to God that our misguided crew had understood the self evident truths to which you so frequently give expression. They might have saved themselves from a terrible fate, and we would not have been short handed, now that the ice is liable to go to pieces at any time. And as this matter is referred to, I suppose I had better tell you at once what became of them and why I was stranded on the ice in such a woebegone plight."

"And that is just what we are most anxious to hear," said Captain Ganoe, "but I have resolutely suppressed this anxiety because I feared fever and a possible fatal culmination, as the result of your exposure and privations. We certainly do want to hear all about your expedition, your crew and what you discovered. But do not relate it even now, if it is going to excite you in the least. The fact is, that you must be very careful for several days until your strength is fully restored."

"Do not be alarmed about me," said Battell. "It is not the first time that I have been stranded on the ice and so I was to some extent prepared for this by past experience; besides you know that I am much inclined to be a stoic and never permit my feelings to very seriously disturb my equilibrium."

"Then go ahead," said the Captain. "We want to hear what is uppermost in your own mind, and we will listen. If we have any questions to ask, or other matters to discuss, we will do that when you are through."

"Just speak when the spirit moves," said Battell. "It will not disturb me. As you doubtless remember, when we started on this last expedition, I was anxious to reach open water on the west and if possible launch the boats and circumnavigate this island of ice around toward the north as far as practicable, so as to be able to return early in July, keeping a close watch of the movements and condition of the ice, and noting any signs of its breaking up. We found the traveling exceedingly difficult, and it was late in June before we reached open water, about one hundred and fifty miles west of this. We found the ice sloughing off in great sections and floating away from the main body, demonstrating that the ice-field was comparatively stationary so far as any westerly motion was concerned. By careful observation I satisfied myself that it had grounded somewhere to the north, probably against an island and was oscillating on that point."

"This made me more anxious than ever to launch our boats and make observations along the shore of the ice-field which sloped off towards the northeast. We would therefore during the exploration of its shoreline be getting nearer to the ship, and I thought that we would be able to reach the obstruction against which it had grounded, which I found reasons for believing was not so very far north of the ship, and probably near the seam where the two original ice-fields had come together. I reasoned that it was held against an island under the influence of north bound currents, and that the entire field might be expected to part along this line as soon as the ice became sufficiently rotten, which would give us a chance to keep on our way. If such a break came along the line of this seam, the ice-field urged forward by the northernly currents, would spread apart and we would only have the fissure as it formed, to come either to land, or out into an open polar sea. In either case we would be safe for the coming winter. Our greatest danger will be from the falling of the ice when these 'bergs' part company, and that, to a great extent, can be provided for."

"After careful investigation we selected a spot where by cutting a short road down to the water's edge we could easily launch our boats. When I gave the word, the men sprang to their work with the greatest alacrity and in good time we had an inclined way admirably cut out and arranged for launching the boats. We first unloaded everything of importance, as our stores were too precious to run any risk of loss or damage. Our boats were very soon riding the waves without any mishap, and the dogs and baggage placed on board. While all this was going on, I noticed frequent consultations among the men, but it seemed that it was because they were taking unusual care in their work. As soon as the last of our baggage was on board, the men took their places at the oars with a promptitude which I regarded as highly commendable. Then came the climax that I had least of all things expected. Tom Brown halted me at the plank and asked a word with me. He said that the men had determined to return to civilization and that they would prefer I should go with them and retain the command."

"I was astounded at such an unreasonable, as well as infamous, proposition to abandon the ship, and I told him I did not believe that any body of sane men would contemplate such a suicidal undertaking. He replied very emphatically:

"'Then, if you do not take my word for it, you may speak to the men. I have only spoken at their request.'

"And so saying, he stepped quickly into the boat and drew the plank in after him. The men in the boats pushed out into the water and halted as if to listen to what I had to say."

"I expostulated with them, and explained how it would be utterly impossible for them to reach civilization in such frail boats, and that their provisions, at the farthest, would not last them more than four or five weeks, and then, they must look starvation in the face. Brown, who acted as spokesman, replied:

"'We have decided upon this thing deliberately, and we have closely calculated how long the provisions will last. Besides, we have plenty of ammunition and can certainly kill some game, and if the game is not abundant, we will kill the dogs and salt them down."

"l then tried them on another tack, and called their attention to the comrades whom we had left behind, and the imminent danger of their being lost, as well as ourselves, if we did not all stand together, and make good use of the observations we had made.'

"'They have the ship and must take their own chances,' said Brown. 'We know that there is no hope of the ship being able to get out of the ice, and we propose to save ourselves while we have an opportunity, and you had better go with us. Let Captain Ganoe and his shipmates take care of themselves. We cannot afford to take any chances, in a case like this, to save them. We are determined to look out for ourselves, and let them do the same.'

"I was so exasperated at this cold-blooded speech, revealing, as it did, such a depth of perfidy, that I felt that I could scarcely refrain from opening fire on them, and evidently they feared something of the kind, for as I turned to take hold of my gun, which was leaning against a block of ice, Brown gave the order, 'Ready!' and instantly twenty rifles were aimed at me, and he "said:

"'We do not want to hurt you, but if you do not let your gun remain where it is until we are out of range, I will give the order to fire and you will be filled with bullets, and you will not have even the poor satisfaction of dying with your friends at the ship, whom you seem to think are worth more to you than the entire crew.'

"'Have your own way,' I said. 'I certainly shall not stain my hands with your blood, neither will I be responsible for the miserable fate that awaits you as the result of this infamous and rash undertaking. I have given you fair warning.'

"I watched them until they were out of range, and then started on my return to the ship. All the food I had, was the hardtack and bacon which I always carry in my haversack, for emergencies. I had, however, my cartridge-box with some ammunition, and I could kill game, but considering the long journey before me, and the slow progress I could make, the supply was indeed very small.

"The traveling was terrible, through water and slushy ice, often for miles at a stretch. I often had to make long detours around chasms and inaccessible elevations. When I slept it was on a melting hummock of ice. I could have killed a large number of brants for food, but I felt that it would be suicidal for me to waste my ammunition on such small game. Hence, I took my chances of finding something larger. I killed a goose occasionally, but was compelled to eat it raw, as I had no means of making a fire. But I did not fear starvation as long as my ammunition lasted.'

"I had reason, however, to fear that the ice would break between me and the ship, and this came near being the case when I first started on my return. When I was only a few hundred yards from the place where the boats were launched, a large strip of the shoreline broke away behind me. But, I now think this rapid breaking up on the western border was due to a strong ocean current, that did not extend very far east. However, I was very apprehensive that I might be sent adrift into an unknown ocean on a cake of ice, and probably, for this reason, I exerted myself more than I should have done for the first few days."

"I got along tolerably well until my boots gave out, and then the ice cold water seemed to paralyze my limbs, and my progress was correspondingly impeded."

"I often felt that I must drop in my tracks, and never make another effort to move. But I was buoyed up by the thought that every step brought me nearer the ship. At last I could catch glimpses of this ice mountain, and the sight gave me renewed strength and courage. But my ammunition had given out, and

I was famishing for food. I would often fall from sheer exhaustion, but would rally again, and stagger on toward the goal of my hopes. When I came to the channel where you found me, I made an effort to spring across, but landed on the bottom. I repeatedly attempted to climb out on this side, but failed. You know the rest. "

"I thank God," said Captain Ganoe, "that Jack discovered your approach so that we could come to your assistance. The loss of so many of our crew is much to be regretted, but your loss would have been much worse, as your experience is indispensable to the safety of all. And now you must take some refreshments and another nap and then I think you will be all right."

"I will take the refreshments," said Battell, "but we have no time to waste on sleep until work has commenced in earnest on the necessary preparations for our escape. How long have I been here?"

"A little over forty-eight hours."

"Then we cannot afford to delay another two days before we commence work."

"Do you think the danger so pressing as that?" asked the Captain.

"I do," said Battell emphatically. "We are at the close of an Arctic summer and we may look for storms and a breaking up at any time. The ice is very rotten, and the ocean currents, which are holding this ice-field against some point of land or sub-marine mountain, may part it in twain at any time, and then we will be compelled to run for our lives."

"And what preparation do you advise?" asked the Captain. "Tell us just what to do and I will see that work is commenced at once and pushed to completion as rapidly as our small force will permit."

"The first thing to be done," said Battell, "is to see that the boilers are free from all sediment, and that the furnaces are filled with the most combustible material we have, so the application of a match will produce a fierce heat and get up steam in the shortest time possible. If we had plenty of coal, I would get up steam at once and keep up a moderate pressure until the ice had gone to pieces, or we were securely frozen up for the winter. But with our small supply of coal we cannot afford to do this, and I am quite sure that we cannot afford to wait for the break to commence, or the coming of a storm. In either case we will have a few minute's warning. Of course in such an emergency we must use steam, as with our small force the sails might be a positive detriment."

"Secondly, when the break comes, there will be a fall of ice from over head that might prove fatal to those who must remain on the upper deck. This must be provided for by the erection of substantial structures to protect those who direct the course of the ship."

"Thirdly, cut all the cables that hold the ship but four, so that our diminutive force can cut us loose with one blow of their axes.

"This is all the work that our small force can possibly get through with before the breaking up of the ice, if that is to occur at all, this season."

"Then," said the Captain, "I will go at once and commence work, and if the necessity is as pressing as you think, you had better take all the rest you can, so that you can lend a hand when the emergency comes."

"I will rest and eat," said Battell, "but I will not be idle. To gain strength, I must take exercise, so Jack and I will make some observations along the seam in the ice which marks the old channel, as the break will in all probability be along that line."

Captain Ganoe, commenced the work of preparation immediately, and Battell and myself engaged in the work that he had proposed. Our observations, made with the greatest care, seemed to confirm, more decidedly than ever, the theory that the ice-field had lodged against some obstruction, not very far north of us.

Since we had reached longitude 180°, we had been oscillating from one side to the other but had made. considerable progress toward the north, indicating that the ice was sloughing away in that direction while the main body was held against some obstruction, by the force of the currents. My own observations all the time had shown that we were oscillating, and these compared with observations made by Battell, one-hundred and fifty miles west, where this movement was much more apparent, gave us reliable data on which to make calculations. At the present time, the sloughing off of the ice was evidently much more rapid on the west and hence our position was tending more than ever toward the east of the longitudinal line on which we lay. From the observations we had made we calculated that the obstruction against which the ice-field had lodged, was about one degree due north of our present position.

We closely examined the seam in which we lay and found numerous indications of its weakness. In many places, where the walls of the closing channel had not come into close contact, we found open water for considerable distances, where the fish were making their appearance. On the theory which Captain Battell had evolved, it did not seem difficult to prognosticate just where the break would first make its appearance, and some of the contingencies which would confront us when that time came.

Within a few days, notwithstanding our very small force, everything was ready for the emergency we anticipated and now we anxiously awaited the storm that would sunder the ice-field and release us from our long imprisonment. But the weather remained calm while it was steadily growing colder and we began to fear that we would be locked in the ice for another winter. At last, however, a stiff breeze set in from the southwest and the barometer began to fall, indicating an approaching storm. Immediately every man was at his post, but hours passed away and the wind did not increase. The order was given for every man to remain at his post and be ready to act as soon as the alarm should be sounded.

As no special duty had been assigned to me, I retired to my quarters in the library to take a much needed rest and was soon asleep.

Chapter V

THE BREAK — A RACE FOR LIFE — THE ISLAND — STRANGE TOWER — A SAFE HARBOR — CROSSING — THE OPEN POLAR SEA — STRANGE PHENOMENA — SAILING SOUTH-- HORIZON OBSCURES FAMILIAR CONSTELLATIONS — RETURN TO THE TOWER — NO EXPLANATION — OFF FOR THE POLE AGAIN — A WONDERFUL DISCOVERY.

I was startled from my slumbers by the alarm and sprang to my feet. The strong breeze that had been blowing from the southwest had increased to a gale and the hissing of the steam revealed the fact that sufficient warning had been given to enable the engineer to be ready to start the machinery as soon as the parting of the ice gave us an opening through which we could move. The time for action had come and I heard Battell give the order to cut the cables.

As I hastened on deck, the two great ice mountains between which we lay were lifted by the waves, and a moment later parted, and a shower of ice fragments from the sundered roof fell upon the upper deck with an awful crash; but thanks to the wise precautions that had been taken, no one was hurt, and the injuries to the vessel were but slight. The ice-field had parted along the line that had been predicted by Captain Battell, and the Ice King was at once subjected to the full force of the winds and waves which urged us forward with an irresistible force. But under the influence of the same power the ice continued to part before us, and all we had to do was to keep in the channel that was forming.

While the waves behind us were driving the ship to seeming destruction, they were at the same time rending the ice-field asunder in the direction we were moving, creating a narrow, but constantly widening channel between the walls of ice on either side. Captain Battell, as usual in cases of emergency, was in command. Captain Ganoe was at the wheel, while I took my place at his side to take notes and render assistance as occasion might require.

Captain Battell was right when he said we might be compelled to run for our lives. The gale continued to increase in its fury, and as we followed the channel that was forming before us, the wind was closing up the channel behind, by huge masses of ice in wild commotion. A halt would have invited destruction, and if we missed the channel that was being opened before us, we might be dashed to pieces against the ice.

While the general direction of the channel being formed was toward the north, the ice did not break along a straight line, but was often zigzag, and it took the closest kind of attention to keep the ship from dashing against one side or the other and being disabled. The ice pack that was always forming behind us, urged forward by the wind and probably a strong ocean current made retreat impossible, even if we had so desired. There was but one thing that could be done, which was to move forward regardless of the continual danger of a collision that might prove fatal.

This strain was kept up for several hours, when to our great delight we could discern what seemed to be a small island toward the northeast and an open sea beyond. A minute later, what appeared to be a mighty watch tower, at least two hundred feet in height, loomed up before our astonished vision just a little off from our starboard quarter. It stood at the edge of the water and the waves were dashing against its base.

This island was evidently the obstruction against which

the ice-field had been lodged. The tower was built of dressed stones accurately piled upon each other; and at one time had apparently been surrounded by a spiral staircase which led to an observatory on top. This conclusion was the logical deduction from the existence of a spiral ledge from the base to the summit, plainly indicating that it had been used as a support for an external structure.

We were now running under a full head of steam through a channel that had been formed between the ice and the island, which led into an open sea beyond. This channel brought us close to the strange tower, and as we came even with it, Captain Battell gave the word: "Starboard your helm! hard up!" " Aye, aye, sir," came the response, and the wheel fairly spun in Captain Ganoe's hands. The Ice King lurched, trembled, and in the next instant shot around the tower, and into comparatively still water, under the cover of the island, which we now discovered, extended from west to east, about two miles, in the form of a crescent, constituting a safe harbor from all storms except from the north. We determined to cast anchor until the wind had subsided and give our small crew a much needed rest. This gave me an opportunity to make sketches of the tower and island at my leisure.

The rest was most welcome to officers and men after the unusual fatigues of the last few days, culminating in the excitement and extraordinary efforts of the last few hours. While we slept, the winds ceased to howl, the skies became clear, and I sketched the tower and the island while they were bathed in the glorious hues of an Arctic sunset.

I applied the camera to every prominent object in sight. The island had the appearance of a segment of the top of a circular mountain which might have been, in geologic ages, the crater of a vast volcano, since which time the land had been depressed, or the water level elevated, perhaps several hundred feet. The shoreline was a granite precipice, rising to the height of about one hundred feet. Over this was a lofty covering of ice, cut into the most fantastic shapes by streams of water which come with summer and depart with winter. In places where the surface had been laid bare I could discover traces of man's handiwork, which for the present I had no opportunity to investigate, owing to the precipitous nature of the shoreline.

But the object of the greatest interest was the tower. As I made my sketch, the last rays of the sun illuminated this strange guardian of these unexplored waters with a luster which impressed the beholder with a feeling of awe. We examined it closely with our glasses and speculated as to its origin. It had evidently been erected to serve some important purpose, by a people who were skilled in architecture. From its location, it might have served the purpose of a lighthouse in some far off time, before these regions were covered with their present mantle of ice.

As this mighty column loomed up above its icy background, its presence was thought-provoking as well as awe-inspiring. It seemed like some sentinel placed here to guard the gateway to this unknown northern sea. But when was it built? and for what purpose? were questions that were continually forced upon our minds. As to the time: it must have been before the great ice age, when tropical plants as well as animals, flourished in the far north, and a tropical, or semi-tropical climate extended from the equator to the poles. But this did not indicate the purpose for which it was erected. Was it an observatory for astronomical purposes, or a lighthouse for the guidance of the prehistoric navigators of these waters, now locked in the embrace of almost impassable ice barriers? Who could tell? All we could do for the present was to record our observations. The tower was there, two hundred feet in height, and its latitude was 85° north, and longitude 180° west. This was all that we could learn for the present.

As had been the experience of all other navigators in high northern latitudes, the dipping of the needle rendered the compass useless, and we had to depend on the sun, moon and stars for our guidance. But the skies were clear and the sea open, so that we apprehended no further trouble, notwithstanding this was the beginning of winter. Accounts of the expedition were sealed in bottles and sent up in balloons, as was our custom, and as there was no ice in sight, we determined to sail due north from the tower.

After holding our course for a few days, we found that the needle had again assumed the horizontal position and that we were sailing due south. We knew we had started north and had not consciously changed our course. Here was a mystery we could not fathom. But this was not all. The horizon seemed to be rising up and obscuring stars that ought to have been in full view.

The pole star, which had been near the zenith was sinking toward the horizon behind us. The whole face of the celestial vault was changing. As the northern lights, which were dropping to the rear grew less brilliant, the southern horizon beamed with a halo of light, which continued to grow brighter. Without having changed our course we were now sailing away from the constellations by which we had so long been guided in our progress toward the pole. What could it mean?

These strange phenomena upset all of our calculations. Everything seemed weird and unnatural. The engines were stopped and we lay to, in order to make observations and study the situation. Accounts of these strange phenomena were securely sealed in bottles and committed to the care of the winds.

Captains Ganoe and Battell held a council in the library and made a careful study of the best authorities, but could find no solution to the problem, as to why we should be going south. It was determined to change our course to the northeast. Continuing in this direction, we found the cold increasing, while the northern lights grew brighter, and stars that had been obscured, again made their appearance above the horizon.

At the end of this run, the ice-pack, now frozen solid, made its appearance. We changed our course toward the east, keeping the ice on our starboard quarter until we were again at the great tower from which we had started. We had discovered no opening in the ice-barriers and no solution to the problem we had started out to investigate.

We found ourselves in an open sea, but encompassed by an impassable barrier of ice. We again determined to sail directly north, and, if possible, cross this wide expanse of ocean around which we had been sailing.

In a few days we again found ourselves running south and leaving the pole star behind us. Star after star began to disappear behind the horizon. Again the light in the south appeared and began to grow brighter.

Again, Captains Ganoe and Battell held a conference. After carefully comparing notes and going over all the facts revealed by our observations, Captain Ganoe asked me to hand him a magazine which he selected from the catalogue. I complied, and he looked through it for a minute and handed it to me saying:

"There is the solution of the problem."

I found the article which he had marked, to be a review of the "THEORY OF CONCENTRIC SPHERES," by Captain John Cleves Symms. "According to this theory," says the reviewer, "the earth is a hollow globe and open at the poles. The diameter of the northern opening, is about 2,000 miles, or 4,000 miles from outside to outside. The south opening is somewhat larger. 'The planes of these openings are parallel with each other, and form an angle of twelve degrees with the equator. The shell of the earth is about 1,000 miles thick, and the edges of the shell at the openings are called verges, and measure from the regular convexity without to the regular concavity within, about 1,500 miles."

I turned and read the passage again, which he had marked for my careful perusal. I had never heard of this "Theory of Concentric Spheres." Could this earth be a hollow shell with an outer and inner surface? At first thought, I felt like rejecting the idea as utterly absurd, but in view of the strange and inexplicable phenomena which we had encountered, and my confidence in the judgment of Captain Ganoe, I only requested him to tell me just what he thought about this "Hollow Globe Theory."

"I believe," he said, "that this theory offers the only logical solution of the phenomena which have upset all of our calculations. "'We found the open polar sea, just as we expected, but when we tried to sail across it, we found ourselves sailing away from it. We also found that constellations which ought, according to the popular astronomy, to have been seen above the horizon were entirely obscured. You will remember that you remarked the cramped appearance, as you expressed it, of the celestial vault, when we were imprisoned in the ice.

"This 'Theory of Concentric Spheres' offers a ready and complete explanation of all these phenomena by which we have been so much puzzled. It now begins to look as if this theory had been rejected by scientists with the same unreasoning haste that every other new idea has encountered. Many things that explorers have met with in the polar regions, seem inexplicable, unless we admit the truth of this theory."

The last remark aroused the interest of Captain Battell, who was ordinarily more inclined to listen, than to join in conversation. Taking up the subject where Captain Ganoe seemed disposed to drop it, he continued:

"In my long experience as a whaler and explorer, I have often found tropical vegetation, and evidences of man's handiwork, on the northern shores of Iceland, Spitzbetgen and the borders of Siberia; trees, vines and flowers. The position where these were found, on the northern shores, precludes the idea of their having been brought by ocean currents, from our own temperate and tropical countries. Besides this, we find that after we pass 80° north latitude, the cold never increases. We further observe flocks of birds coming from, and returning to, the north. When we kill them for food, we often find their crops filled with grain and seeds which must be the product of a mild climate. All these things have come under my personal observation, and this 'Theory of Concentric Spheres' offers the most complete explanation that I have met with."

"Then, do you believe this theory?" I asked, somewhat surprised at the unusual interest taken by Captain Battell.

"Why not?" he responded. "I have always been among the few who treated every new thought with fairness and consideration, no matter what might be my own preconceived opinions. While not accepting every new fangled theory that comes along, I do not condemn, but investigate, with a view to ascertaining the exact truth. I will not knowingly twist and misrepresent facts and logical deductions therefrom, for the purpose of proving a pre adopted creed. Hence I have given this theory an impartial hearing and justice compels me to admit that the arguments in its favor are well worthy of careful consideration. Scientists have all agreed that the earth is not a cold, solid body, and to account for its lack of density they assume that the center is expanded and diffused by heat. They further assume that it was originally a nebulous body entirely destitute of a solid surface. If this is true, then the centrifugal force generated by its rapid revolution on its axis would certainly throw its constituent elements outward toward the surface, thus tending to produce a hollow shell, the very thing claimed in this 'Theory of Concentric Spheres.' The operation of this mechanical law, which governs revolving matter, can be readily illustrated by placing a quantity of oil in alcohol of the same density. The oil at once assumes the globular form by virtue of the law of molecular attraction. Then insert a disk through the center of the globule and begin to turn it around. The oil at once begins to rotate on its axis and becomes depressed at the poles and bulged at the equator, just the form which the earth is conceived to be. Increase the rapidity of the revolution up to a certain point and the oil separates from the disk and becomes a revolving ring. Reasoning from these well-known mechanical laws, we are forced to the conclusion, that if the earth was ever a soft revolving body it must be hollow at the center, and it is not at all unlikely that there may be openings at the poles into this hollow space. So, we see that there is some logical foundation for this "Hollow Globe Theory."

"It is true," I replied, "that the motion of a soft revolving body, such as the earth is supposed to have been, may be so accelerated, that the mass will separate from the line of its axis, but in such a case it would become a revolving ring, and not a hollow shell, as required by this theory of concentric spheres. Have you any theory as to how a revolving ring could under the operation of known mechanical laws, be converted into a hollow shell, with convex and concave surfaces?"

" Yes," responded Battell," "I can very easily formulate such a theory. I can assume that the earth was at one time a revolving ring of meteors, or minute planetary bodies, which by the mutual attraction of its parts became solid. This ring, besides the motion on its own axis, was revolving around the sun, or common center of the solar nebula, through space filled with meteors, and by its attraction it gathered other rings of meteors exterior to itself, thus forming a series of concentric rings revolving around the first, or present ring. 'The materials composing these external rings could not reach the parent ring at its equator because of the centrifugal force generated by its revolution around its axis, but under the operation of well-known mechanical laws, they might be drawn toward the pole where the attraction was the greatest and the centrifugal force the least. Under the influence of these contending forces, these external rings, thus acted upon, would one by one spread out and form, first a canopy over the central ring, and then it would part at the equator, and be drawn to the poles where it would ultimately find a resting place upon its polar edges. Such a process kept up long enough would convert the original revolving ring, or infant earth, into a hollow shell. Of course all this is mere speculation, but the same thing may be said of the nebular hypothesis, the supposed igneous condition of the earth's center, and in fact of nearly all the teachings of science when it attempts to go beyond the domain of undisputed facts."

"I am much interested in your reasoning," I said. "This is a new thought to me and I would like to follow it a little further. How does this Hollow Globe theory account for volcanoes and other evidences of internal heat, that have led scientists to the conclusion that the center of the earth is an igneous mass ? "

"To my mind," said Battell, "these evidences of intense internal heat do not conflict with the Hollow Globe Theory. Assuming that the shell is one thousand miles thick; at the center, between the outer and inner crust, there would be a pressure of five hundred miles of solid matter, more than sufficient to generate a heat that would melt every known rock, and this of itself will account for every evidence of internal heat. Scientists have taught us that heat is a form of motion, or rather that it is the result of motion when arrested. Now pressure is only arrested motion, or in other words heat. Hence it has been estimated that the weight of a column of steel blocks, sixty-five thousand feet in height, would generate sufficient heat to melt the lower tier of blocks. These well-known laws, to my mind, offer a more plausible explanation of the existence of intense heat at great depths, than the assumption that this heat is the residue, that was left over from the heat of an original planetary nebula. Well known laws of physics, force us to the conclusion that this earth can never become a cold body and that the igneous condition at great depths, will continue as long as the centripetal and centrifugal forces continue to press the outer and inner surfaces toward each other. Or in other words, as long as the surface continues to press down upon the materials below, as they do now, there will be intense heat at great depths."

"Your theory," I replied, "if true, will force scientists to abandon the wonderful history of creation which they have evolved from long and persistent research."

"Nothing but their opinions will need to be revised," said Battell. "Every fact they have discovered will continue to be a fact. We are here on this expedition to discover facts of scientific importance, and it now looks as if we are making a most wonderful discovery that will force scientists to abandon some of their long cherished opinions and revise others. If we find that this earth is actually a hollow shell, it will be a fact, that must in the very nature of things harmonize with every other fact that has been, or will be discovered. Facts are facts, and while they may not be understood, they cannot be set aside. It was to discover facts that might benefit the entire human race by increasing their knowledge that I sacrificed a whaling business that was paying a handsome profit, to join Captain Ganoe on this expedition, in which I might lose the accumulations of years, and possibly life itself. I certainly did not join this expedition in order to either confirm, or disprove, any of the theories which scientists have given to the world."

"Then it seems," I responded, "that you joined the expedition with a view to making discoveries by which mankind would be benefited, by adding to the sum total of human knowledge, rather than from any hope of personal advantage."

"Possibly," he said. "But I cannot draw the line that your

remark would seem to suggest. I cannot see how I could help mankind, without helping myself, at least so far as it would give me satisfaction, and that after all is the one great object that makes life worth the living. As to just what I expected to discover, I have only to say that I am not surprised at present appearances. There now seem to be as many indications of the existence of a habitable country on an inner surface of the globe, as there were of a western hemisphere, before the discovery of America. Columbus gave to mankind a new world, and should we be the means of discovering an inner world, and of opening a line of communication between that and the outer world, it would not be so much a matter of astonishment as it would be of actual advantage." Then turning to Captain Ganoe he asked: "What do you think of our prospect of success?"

"The present indications," replied the Captain, "are certainly most encouraging. From the observations which we have already made, I believe that we have passed over the verge into the gateway of an inner world. You remember," he continued, turning to me, "that when we made our escape from the ice, we sailed directly north and soon made the discovery that something interposed between us and certain stars that ought to have been visible just above the horizon."

"Yes," I replied, "I remember. But what do you infer from that?"

"I infer," he said, "that it was the opposite side of the verge that interposed between us and the stars which we calculated ought to have been visible. And now, I propose to sail south until we find land, or failing in that, run out at the south opening, if we find one. We have circumnavigated the north pole and yet when we tried to sail across the open polar sea we found ourselves sailing away from it, assisted by a powerful ocean current. Now, the water which comes from this impassable polar sea, is going somewhere, and it is our business to follow it up and find out all we can about its destination."

As he spoke, a large flock of birds passed over our heads.

"There," said the captain, " go our oracles that will lead us to land, and as they are going in our direction I propose to follow them," and going to the wheel, he placed the ship directly in their track.

"How is it," I asked, "that you now take the birds for our guide, something you have never done before?" "Because," said the Captain, "we want to find land and these birds are evidently on their way to find feeding grounds. I wonder that it did not occur to me sooner to follow them."

The light we had observed in the southern horizon grew brighter, and soon we saw the sun emerge as if from behind a cloud and disappear again near the same point, when we saw the full moon and a few stars shining through the northern verge. It was indeed a strange sight to visitors from the outer world. It never became actually dark, as light from the sun either direct or reflected, reached us at all times. We had therefore reached a country of which it might be truly said: "There is no night there."

Some two days after the first appearance of the sun shining through the opening at the southern pole, we sighted a small island with a high, rocky shoreline, and a deep inlet, which formed a natural harbor, well protected from storms if any ever came to these placid waters.

We steamed into the inlet, cast anchor and went ashore. This was the first time in over eighteen months that we had the opportunity to set our feet upon land. As there seemed to be an abundance of game birds, Captain Ganoe gave orders that all who desired might take their guns and enjoy a day's shooting. Notwithstanding the general desolation of the island it was a most welcome diversion for our small and overworked crew.

The first thing that attracted our notice, was the stump of a tree that bad been cut down with an axe. Though the stump was much decayed, the marks of the axe were plainly visible. On examination, we found plenty of evidence that the island had been inhabited at no very distant day, as everything in the shape of timber had been cut down. This we regretted, as we would gladly have availed ourselves of an opportunity to take on a supply of wood, our coal being well nigh exhausted.

On one side of the narrow inlet in which the ship was

anchored, was a wall of stone which was covered with figures of men, animals and hieroglyphics. Captain Ganoe said that he had seen similar sculptured stones in New Mexico, and from this, he inferred that the time had been when the same people had visited both localities, and that time had been before the great ice caps had enveloped the poles. On the other side of the inlet was found a rude hut constructed of rough stones, and from the inscriptions on the walls we learned that it had been occupied by an English speaking people, whose vessel had been wrecked on this lonely island.

The powerful current which had been the chief factor in liberating us from the ice, and sweeping us out into the open polar sea, touched at this lonely island and it was not unlikely that it was this current, which had stranded some disabled whaler and its crew, the vestiges of which were now attracting our attention .

This would also account for the destruction of the few trees which had grown upon this stony waste. So near the icy verge, fire was a necessity. The scant growth of timber had been needed for fuel, by these shipwrecked mariners.

But what had become of the crew? They had evidently burned up all the fuel, but they had not been frozen, as their skeletons would have revealed their fate. The supply of ducks, geese and fish seemed inexhaustible, and hence they had not starved. We searched diligently, but could find no indications of death in their ranks, except one lone grave, on the most elevated point in the island, marked by a rough stone on which was inscribed the one word : "Father."

With my camera I took views of the most prominent objects. We spent two days on this island to the great relief of all. The sailors enjoyed the hunt, and a goodly supply of ducks, geese, etc., rewarded their efforts.

Chapter VI

SAILING SOUTH — THE WIND CEASES — OUR COAL EXHAUSTED — DRIFTING ON AN UNKNOWN OCEAN — IN THE GRASP OF SOUTHBOUND CURRENTS -DESCENDING — VISITED BY AN AIR SHIP -THEN A WHOLE FLEET — AMONG FRIENDS — A MOST HIGHLY CULTIVATED PEOPLE — WE EMBARK FOR ALTRURIA — AN AIR VOYAGE.

As we again proceeded south, the weather became more and more spring-like and the air more invigorating. The climate seemed to have opposite effects on different temperaments. The more delicate and refined were stimulated to greater vigor and endurance, while the most powerful physically were stricken with a fever, attended by acute pains.

This reduced our small crew to a point where we were helpless. Our coal was also exhausted. The light breezes which had enabled us to utilize the sails, now ceased entirely and we lay becalmed.

For weeks the Ice King lay idly on the bosom of this most placid ocean. So monotonous it became that even an Arctic gale would have been a most agreeable diversion, by enabling us to move. With a supply of fuel our chances of finding land would have been increased manifold. We could have made some headway, notwithstanding the fact that we had at this time only five persons able to render any efficient service. These were Captain Ganoe, Battell, Huston, Mike Gallagher and myself. Pat O'Brien and the two Norwegians, Lief and Eric, were scarcely able to move around and the three sailors that had been left with us by Battell while exploring the ice-field because they were not able to stand the exposure, were now utterly helpless, and not expected to live from hour to hour.

We had plenty of provisions for an indefinite period, and when these were exhausted, the sea would furnish an unlimited supply of fish. Our vessel was seaworthy and there was seemingly no possible danger of a storm. And yet our condition was most depressing. The ocean currents were drifting us slowly along towards the south and might eventually bring us to land. But this hope, at best, was only a bare possibility. These same currents might carry us into the ice-fields at the south pole which in our present disabled condition, meant almost certain destruction.

We dropped bottles into the sea containing dispatches, stating our condition, and describing our location as nearly as possible. But the chances were that these would never reach a people who would understand their purport, and be able and willing to offer us any assistance. All these considerations, added to the sickness of our most sturdy seamen, had a most depressing effect, and every hour the outlook became more hopeless.

With these gloomy forebodings, I had become discouraged indeed. I am naturally hopeful, but now all hope seemed to be gone. As I look back to this period I regard it as certainly the darkest of my life. Early one morning I had gone upon the upper deck, hoping that the fresh air might brace me up and revive my drooping energies. In my mind, with my note book before me, I mentally reviewed the leading incidents of our voyage on this unknown ocean. According to my reckoning we had escaped from the ice on the 23d of September, sketched the island and tower on the 24th, and on the 25th set sail as we supposed for the north pole. Without having consciously changed our course, five days later we found ourselves sailing south. We then under a full head of steam changed our course to the northeast, and circumnavigated a large expanse of sea surrounding the pole.

When we again attempted to cross this open sea we again found ourselves sailing south. We landed on a barren island on the first of November. In a few days we were becalmed, but in the grasp of a powerful current which carried us steadily southward, and now on the 25th of December, when Christmas festivities were the order of the day throughout the Christian world, here we were on a broad ocean, drifting we knew not whither. I never felt so utterly devoid of hope, but I was determined to keep up courage.

We were in a most agreeable climate. The air was sweet and refreshing and I thought if we could only find land, what a glorious discovery we had made, and if we could convey the news to our own country, how it would stimulate the latent energies of the whole people to find some ready means of access to this inner world, and thus our perils and privations might ultimately prove a blessing to mankind. But why speculate ? We were lost on an unknown ocean which seemed to be boundless, and utterly unable to direct our movements. The thought struck me with a chill.

Suddenly in the midst of my cogitations I was startled by a loud, "Halloo!" It was certainly near at hand. I sprang to my feet and looked around over the placid surface of the ocean. I could see for leagues away in every direction, yet could not discover any living thing. I then started to go below, thinking that perhaps Captain Ganoe had called me. As I disappeared, the "Halloo!" was repeated in a somewhat louder tone.

I met the Captain coming in search of me, and I told him what I had heard. With an incredulous look on his face, he placed his hand on my head and said:

"I fear my dear Jack that your brain has played a trick on you."

"That may be so," I said, "but let us go above and investigate before we jump to conclusions."

He assented, and as we reached the deck, the "Halloo!" was repeated in a much louder tone than before and this time, apparently directly over our heads. We looked up and about one hundred feet above our starboard quarter we beheld what, at first sight, appeared to be some monster bird, with outspread wings slowly moving as if to maintain its position. But a second glance revealed it to be some kind of an aerial conveyance, with transparent sides, through which we could plainly see two persons on board, who were watching us with intense interest.

"Well Jack, what do you think of it?" asked the Captain.

"I hardly know," I replied, "but this seeming monster bird is some kind of a contrivance for navigating the air, and it has passengers on board who evidently want to communicate with us."

Our colloquy was brought to a summary conclusion by one of our aerial visitors addressing us in a strangely musical but unknown tongue. We were astonished at the salutation, but we had had so many strange experiences lately, that we did not lose our self possession, and Captain Ganoe responded at once by inviting them to " Come on board. " They did not seem to understand, and after a moment's pause he beckoned to them. They understood the gesture and after a short consultation, their strange vessel began to circle around in a spiral and came to a rest on deck, when a side door opened, and two of the finest looking people I had ever seen stepped out and shook hands with us. They were large, very fair and looked almost exactly alike.

One of them who seemed to be the leader, presented a paper which I recognized as one of the dispatches which we had committed to the care of the winds a few days after our escape from the ice. I was surprised to see written below it, in strange characters, what seemed to be a translation, and this was signed, "Mac," in a plain round hand. We examined it closely, and handing it back, Captain Ganoe turned to me and exclaimed: "Thank God! English is understood by some people in this inner world. This removes our greatest difficulty. We can get acquainted."

Our visitors seemed pleased when they saw that we recognized the dispatch and the leader at once stepped to the larboard side of the ship and waved a handkerchief. I now noticed for the first time that two other airships hovered near, and one of them immediately responded to the signal and came alongside. After a brief consultation with the occupants, it began to circle around and ascend until it had attained a great height, when it darted off at an amazing speed toward the west. I had noticed that the aerial conveyances both ascended and descended, by circling around in a spiral.

While this was going on, I took especial notice of our visitors. They wore soft felt hats, slightly turned up at the side, with broad silver bands. Their hair was parted in the middle and hung in ringlets to their shoulders. They wore embroidered slippers, with silk stockings. and pants that fastened just below the knee, attached to a loose waist with a short skirt. Around the waist was a broad silken girdle, fastened in front by a silver buckle, and tied behind in a bow, the ends deeply fringed and hanging even with the bottom of the skirt. Their necks were bare but encircled by a golden chain to which was attached what seemed to be diamond set lockets and at the girdles they wore watches of magnificent workmanship.

While they were conferring with the occupants of the other airship, Captain Canoe said to me:

"These persons are surely women."

"And, " added Battell, who had come on deck, "What beauties! Where did they come from?"

"They came through the air in yonder little vessel," said the Captain, and they seem to have been looking for us, as they have one of the dispatches we sent out after we escaped from the ice; and more than that, it has been translated into an unknown tongue, by some one who signs the name 'Mac'"

Then they are our saviors," said Battell.

"I certainly feel so," said the Captain, "and they have evidently made up their minds to stay awhile, for some purpose."

"No doubt, " replied Battell. "See! They are sending the other bird off for help. They understand what they are about. "

As the airship disappeared from view, our strange visitors returned to where we were standing, and seeing Captain Battell, the leader advanced and gracefully extended her hand. Her unaffected and cordial manner at once placed us at ease.

They now manifested a disposition to examine the ship, and seemed by motions to confer with each other about it, pointing to the smoke stacks, the sails and the steering apparatus as if they were discussing the motor power.

Observing their evident interest in these things, Captain Ganoe suggested that Battell and myself would conduct them over the ship, while he would attend to having a breakfast prepared that would be a credit to the Ice King. Thus prompted, we motioned our visitors to accompany us below, which they seemed pleased to do.

We took then through the engine room and pointed out such portions of the machinery as we felt would interest them the most. We showed them our liberal supply of scientific instruments, maps, charts, etc. I was astonished at the keen interest they manifested in our large library.

We then led them into the presence of our sick sailors. Sympathy was plainly depicted on their countenances as they passed from one to another and cordially grasped their hands, frequently conferring with each other in low tones, as if planning for their relief.

In the meantime. Mike Gallagher, who in our disabled condition was nurse, cook and general factotum, had prepared an ample repast, in which our guests participated with evident relish. While we were enjoying our meal, I noticed that our visitors were observing me closely, and then looking at the others, as if making a comparison and mentally taking notes. When we had arisen from the table the one who had presented the dispatch came up and pointed to the signature as if to ask if it was mine.

I nodded assent, and she took me by the hand and drawing it through her arm, led off toward the deck and conducted me directly to her airship.

I noticed now, for the first time, that the entrance was about thirty inches above the deck, where it rested, and was approached by steps so constructed that they dropped to their place when the door was opened.

We entered, and I found it to be a splendidly upholstered car, about six feet wide by sixteen in length, coming to a sharp point at the bow, while the stern was oval. I could see by a glance at its proportions, that it was designed to dart through the air at a great speed. But I had no time to take many notes of this small, but elaborately finished vessel. The proprietor, so to speak, at once opened a little bookcase, and handed me a small volume with a knowing smile on her face. To my surprise, I found it to be a school history of the United States in English, with a translation, presumably into her own language, printed in parallel columns. She handed me several other volumes printed in the same manner in both languages. Among these I noticed a grammar, dictionary, small geography, a New Testament, hymn book and several introductory works on the natural sciences.

She showed me a card on which was printed the English alphabet, that had evidently never been used, and opposite each letter, a varying number of characters, corresponding with the number of sounds which we assign to each. I understood from this, that the people of this country used phonetic characters.

I at once realized that she had the means of acquiring a knowledge of our language, history, geography and science as taught in our common schools. I surmised that this collection of school books, had been brought to this country on the vessel that was lost near the barren island on which we had stopped. It was just such a collection as might be expected among sailors who were trying to obtain the rudiments of an education, while employed on a whaler.

She had doubtless shown me these books as a means of letting me know that our country and its language were not entirely unknown in her country, and that she had contemplated making a study of these things.

We were soon joined by her comrade, Battell and Huston, and this unique library of outer world school books was again exhibited, and while we could not exchange a word, we soon felt that we were old acquaintances.

Our visitors were evidently highly cultured people, and while not speaking our language, they certainly knew considerable about our country, while we knew nothing about theirs.

I was a little surprised at the active interest taken in our guests by Captain Battell, who was usually so reticent and retiring, and this interest was plainly mutual. Although they were not able to converse, they could understand each other, and spent their time strolling about the ship and peering out over the calm waters of the ocean.

After the airship had been gone about eight hours, our guests began to consult their watches and look intently toward the west. Soon a whole fleet of airships came into view. In a few minutes the foremost one separated from the others, circled around, and alighted upon our deck, and one of the occupants stepped out, and as he did so exclaimed in good English:

"Thank God, you are safe! How happy I am to welcome so many of my countrymen into this world of Truth, Justice and Fraternity."

"And how happy are we," said Captain Ganoe." to be welcomed by a fellow countryman after our long voyage in these unknown waters. We have not looked in the face of a fellow being for nearly two years, and we welcome you to the deck of the Ice King, as the saviors of all that is left of its once numerous crew."

The new comer threw his arms around the Captain's neck, and embraced him as a mother would her long lost child, sobbing with sudden emotion until we were all shedding tears in sympathy. Then leaving Captain Ganoe he embraced each of us in turn.

"I never was so happy in my life," he exclaimed. "I hope you will excuse me for thus giving way to my feelings. I had thought I would never again look into the face of a single human being from my own native land , and this meeting with so many overcomes me."

"No apologies are necessary," said Captain Ganoe. "We appreciate the man who has feelings and is not ashamed to show them, while we could not have any respect for the man who is destitute of feeling."

"Thank you," said the newcomer, " and now permit me to introduce myself. My name is, or rather was, James MacNair, an American born Scotchman.

Captain Ganoe then introduced himself, Battell, Huston and myself. MacNair in turn introduced our visitors as the twin sisters, Polaris and Dione, of the Life Saving Service, and then continued:

"Ever since they discovered me, almost starved, on a desolate island far to the north, these self devoted saviors of humanity, have kept an especial lookout for stranded mariners from the frozen north. And since they captured your little balloon with the dispatch I translated for them, they have known that an entire crew had passed the ice barriers, and they have been more than ever on the alert for an opportunity to render assistance, and conduct you into a safe harbor. They feared that you would be disabled by the almost perpetual calms on these waters, and be carried to the southern verge by these ocean currents which seem to carefully avoid the land. You see with all their watchfulness you have been carried nearly to the equator without being discovered, and you are now fully one thousand miles from land."

"It was indeed fortunate," said Captain Ganoe "that we continued to commit dispatches to the care of the winds."

"That is true," said MacNair, "but it is more fortunate that you sent up dispatches just when you did, for at that time, the sun begins to heat the air at the southern verge and it rises to higher altitudes and the air in the vicinity flows in to fill the vacuum. This produces a current of air that flows south from the northern verge. It was this breeze which occurs but once a year that brought your balloons south. Had they been sent up at the beginning of the northern summer they would have been carried south on the outside by your equinoctial storms. This is my theory. It may not be a correct one but it satisfies me."

"Whether correct or not," said Captain Ganoe, " "we know by experience that we had a northerly breeze for several days, which enabled us to use our sails to some advantage. But this breeze soon ceased and as we had no coal we were at the mercy of the ocean currents."

"Yes," said MacNair, "there is but little use for sails in this inner world. But with plenty of coal you would have had no difficulty in finding a safe harbor among a highly civilized people, in a country where extremes of heat and cold, and violent storms are unknown."

MacNair's remarks were cut short by the appearance on the scene of another magnificent woman who had evidently remained on the airship which had brought him to our deck, and he added:

"And now permit me to introduce to you my wife, Iola, who wished to be among the first to welcome you to this inner world."

"Glad to meet you," said Captain Ganoe, extending his hand, "and I hope that you will have no reason to regret this addition to your circle of so many of your husband's fellow countrymen."

"Thank you," said lola, in good English, but with a peculiar accent. "On behalf of our people, I take pleasure in extending to you a cordial welcome to our home in Altruria, where we are making a special study of everything we can get concerning the outer world."

"And happy are we;" rejoined the Captain, "to be welcomed by a people where our language is not entirely unknown. It will be so much easier for us to get acquainted, and adapt ourselves to our new surroundings."

"In our district," said lola, "you will find quite a number of people who can converse in English. We are teaching it in our schools."

While this conversation was going on, Polaris had stepped to the side of the ship and commenced signaling with a yellow silken flag to the fleet of airships which hovered over us. Soon one of the largest, and seemingly the most elaborately furnished, swerved around and alighted upon the deck of the Ice King.

Seeing that our attention was attracted to this new movement started by Polaris, MacNair 'said:

"That is our hospital or relief ship. Polaris has called them to the assistance of your sick sailors."

"Thank God!" ejaculated Captain Ganoe, "for indeed the poor fellows need the most careful attention. She and her comrades have placed us under obligations for their kindness, that can never be repaid. I am indeed most thankful to our new found friends."

"Why feel under such obligations to anyone?" asked lola. Polaris is only doing her duty and so are her comrades. This is a duty which we owe to each other, and you and your sailors will only receive that which justly belongs to you."

"But are we not under obligations to those who assist us when in trouble?" asked Captain Ganoe, "and should we not repay them for the burdens we impose on them?"

"I do not quite understand you," said lola. "You certainly are under obligations to yourself to entertain feelings of grateful appreciation toward those who assist you in getting out of a difficult and distressing situation, as this feeling tends to make us all better men and women, and hence more desirable members of the community. But as to repaying others for their assistance, I cannot see how we could do so unless we were to place them under similar environments, and we certainly would not do that, simply for the purpose of securing an opportunity to do for them what they did for us."

"And I do not understand you at all," said the Captain. "When people help us, we are certainly under obligations to compensate them for their assistance, with something more substantial than mere thanks."

"Then I will try to make my meaning clear," she said. "We all seek happiness, but a well ordered mind cannot enjoy real happiness while others are miserable. So in helping others into a condition where they may be happy, we are working to establish and perpetuate conditions that are essential to our own happiness. The act itself brings its own reward. In order for a people to be happy, it is necessary for them to do to others as they would have others do to them. This is one of the most simple and obvious laws that govern our relations to each other. It cannot be ignored without establishing conditions, under the operations of which, misery would become the normal condition of mankind, ourselves included."

"I begin to get a glimpse of your meaning," replied the Captain. "The founder of our religion, inculcated the same principles in his teachings which we call the 'Golden Rule,' but I have never before met with such a practical, matter-of-fact application of it to all the relations existing between the individual members of the human family. It may be that among our people a few small circles, to some extent, apply this rule of action to a chosen few, but it is never applied to the people in general, except by some cranky individual, who in popular esteem, is regarded as a fit subject for a lunatic asylum."

"It seems strange to us," said lola, "that your people do not universally apply this fundamental law, upon which human happiness depends, in all their relations with each other. They must certainly desire happiness and the most ordinary intelligence ought to incline them to use the means by which they could secure happiness. But I know from history that this law was entirely ignored by our ancestors thousands of years ago. It was first taught as a religious tenet, but for ages it has been accepted as a fundamental principle in our civilization, and as a teacher of moral philosophy in our schools it becomes my duty to inculcate these principles into the minds of the children. The civilization which we have now, carries out in practice, the fundamental, humanitarian principles to which the founders of our old religious system gave expression. These teachings were in many respects identical, even in language, with the teachings of Jesus and the apostles as I find them recorded, in the copy of the New Testament which was among the books that my husband, then a small boy, saved from his father's ship which went to the bottom near the barren island where he was discovered."

"This is indeed remarkable," said the Captain. "I had thought from the tenor of your remarks that the apostles must have penetrated this inner world and taught these doctrines, and that they had taken a better hold on the minds of the people than they have in the outer world. I see, however, that you claim an independent origin for your religious system, yet you have the same fundamental doctrines. How is this?"

"Nothing strange about it," said lola. "Truth is truth no matter where it is found. All people, no matter where they live, have the same faculties, and the same sources of knowledge are open to all alike. All the religions of the world have had their origin in some form of inspiration, and these religions have, in turn, left their impress upon the civilizations of the world. Jesus, of the outer world, and Krystus of the inner world, both inculcated the same fundamental truths, which we have incorporated into our civilization, and now teach in our schools as the fundamental natural laws which must regulate human relations, before the race can attain to the one great object of existence, — Happiness."

While this most interesting conversation was going on, Polaris, Dione and MacNair were busy fitting up the Hospital ship and giving directions by signals, to the fleet which hovered above us. Ropes were attached to the bow of the Ice King, which connected with a number of the largest airships. The design was apparent, by the preparations. They intended to tow us to shore. But this was not all. Electrical apparatus was placed on board and they evidently intended to use electric motor power to set the machinery in motion. As soon as the preparations were well on the way, MacNair broke in upon the discussion by saying:

"Captain Ganoe, we are now ready to look after your afflicted sailors. We want to attend to them, just as we would like to be attended to, if, unfortunately, we were compelled to change places with them, and with your permission we will take charge of them at once."

"You not only have my permission, but my heart felt thanks for the interest you take in them. So now let us go below," and suiting the action to the word, Captain Ganoe led the way and we all followed.

We found the ever active Mike, busy ministering to the wants of the sick and keeping up the spirits of all by his inimitable Irish wit, in which Pat O'Brien, notwithstanding his acute rheumatic pains joined with a hearty good will. This buoyant Irish lad and the herculean Irish sailor, had been the life of the expedition, when we were imprisoned in the ice, and but for these typical sons of Erin, our environments would have been much more gloomy. No matter how serious the outlook might be, they brought out the comic and laughable side of the picture by their mirth-provoking comments.

A half dozen persons from the Relief ship at once began their examination into the condition of the sick, and Captain Ganoe, turning to MacNair, asked: "Are these persons all physicians?"

"Well, yes, and no," replied he. "In the outer world you would call them doctors but here they all nurses. These skilled hospital attendants, understand all that has been discovered in regard to the treatment of both mind and body."

"But what do they use?" asked the Captain. "I see no sign of medicines and the usual hospital appliances."

"They need none," replied MacNair. "But this is something that must be learned further on."

"Yes," interposed lola. "You will doubtless find a very different system of treating human weakness from that which I understand is adopted in the outer world by the medical practitioners. In their system of healing they depend exclusively upon external appliances and ingredients, while we depend mainly upon arousing the internal powers of mind and spirit, which alone can exercise any absolute control over the human organism. Your system of treating the body is from without, while ours is from within, directly opposite to it."

I did not at that time comprehend her meaning, neither did any of our crew. Its depth was beyond our grasp and we found that indeed this was something to be learned further on. But as she ceased speaking, Polaris called her to one side, and after a brief consultation with the nurses she said to Captain Ganoe:

"The nurses report that it will require an hour or more to get the patients in proper condition for removal and that they want to be left alone with them, and will let us know when they are ready."

With this, we all returned to the upper deck to await the pleasure of the nurses. Captain Battell, who had been an intensely interested listener, notwithstanding his retiring disposition, now moved to renew the conversation by turning to MacNair and saying:

"My dear sir, did I understand you to say that the special

business of Polaris and Dione is to look out for those who may be lost at sea and render assistance as occasion may require, and especially for such as may drift in from the outer world? Where are your men, that women are permitted to engage in these hazardous enterprises?"

"Nothing strange about that," said MacNair. "As you well know, the women of the outer world take the lead in all humanitarian work, because they are naturally more sensitive and sympathetic than men. The women of this inner world are even more inclined to extend a helping hand to the distressed, and they are not handicapped by usages which restrict the influence of the woman of the outer world. Here, both sexes are placed upon terms of absolute equality, and every individual has an opportunity to find the place that is best suited to his or her inclinations. Men are also engaged in this work, but the women here, as in the outer world, are more sympathetic, and as there is nothing to prevent it, they have carried their humanitarian work to such perfection, that all the oppressive conditions which afflict humanity have been wellnigh removed. To this, more than to all other causes combined, do we attribute the existence of the ideal conditions which you will find throughout this inner world. You certainly cannot think that women are out of place when they are protecting their own offspring?"

"Not that," said Battell. "I certainly esteem it most fortunate that we have fallen into the hands of these humanity loving women, but it all seems so strange. You have women commanding fleets in the air, and if so, why not have them navigating the ocean and commanding your armies and navies?"

"We have no armies and navies to destroy our offspring," interrupted lola. "We know nothing of these things except from our ancient histories. When woman secured her true position in the world she put an end to war by removing the vicious commercial, financial and governmental systems that enabled one class of people to oppress another. When greedy and domineering classes could no longer have soldiers to do their bidding, poverty was abolished by securing to the whole people equal access to the unlimited productive power of the earth.

The women demanded peace because it prevented the slaughter of their offspring in useless wars, and in order to have peace it was necessary to secure to all an equal opportunity to create wealth by their labor."

"But I do not see," said Battell, "how equal rights to women would prevent governmental injustice, with its consequent wars and bloodshed. In the outer world, some of the most bloodthirsty rulers in the annals of history have been women."

"And the same thing was true in the inner world, said lola,"until all women had secured their personal freedom from the domination of man-made laws and prerogatives. When that time came, Mother-love completed the work of human redemption. In time the women became a unit for peace, and this thought was impressed upon their offspring and these grew into maturity without any inclination to rule by violence, and war was abolished. And the same love of offspring which put an end to war and all its horrors, demanded the removal of the discriminations which enabled the offspring of one woman to defraud and oppress the offspring of another woman. It was the inspiration of Mother-love which set the women to investigating the systems which enriched the few at the expense of the many; and in defense of their children, they united their efforts along peaceful lines to establish equitable relations in all the affairs of life. The women of that day, were not more intelligent than the men, but love for their offspring gave them a deeper and more abiding sympathy for the oppressed, and this feeling, if not crushed out by the iron heel of military power, will ultimately save the people of any country from the consequences of inequitable conditions."

"I believe you are right," said Battell, "but this does not explain to me why women should lead in such a hazardous business as this in which Polaris and Dione are engaged."

"It is because they desire to do so," said MacNair. "Polaris is a sincere lover of humanity. She is a true womanly woman, and as such takes pleasure in rendering assistance to all who are afflicted or distressed. Besides, she is by education, inclination and long experience, an expert in aerial navigation, and holds her position as head of the Life Saving Service by virtue of her superior qualities."

"But," said Battell, "as head of a department, she might send her subordinates and not take the hardest work on herself. It seems to me, that she personally superintends everything, doing as much work as a half dozen others ought to do. "

"Polaris always leads," said MacNair. "Besides, in your case there were especial reasons why she should personally lead the search. You were exposed to peculiar dangers, and it was uncertain whether you had been carried into the Oscan or Umbrian oceans, by the ocean currents. So, to guard against possible failure, she did not trust entirely to the patrols, but continued to circumnavigate the concave herself.

"But few persons could have kept up the incessant activity and watchfulness that she and Dione have done ever since they captured your dispatches. They were determined that you should not be carried into the stormy waters of the south if persistent vigilance could prevent it."

"Well, thank God, they were successful!" said Battell. "If we should live a thousand years we could not pay them for their efforts in our behalf."

"No thanks are required," again interrupted lola. "Polaris has only done her duty, and as to pay, she could hardly comprehend what you mean by it. She doubtless felt that she was amply rewarded for all her efforts when she succeeded in finding you. Success, in a praiseworthy undertaking, is the only reward that any man or woman can afford to work for. She has found you and therefore has her reward, while we can enjoy the pleasure of providing you with the comforts of a home and freedom from anxiety, toil and danger. You will only get what our common mother nature has prepared alike for all her children, while we have been especially benefited by the opportunity it has given us of helping a brother in distress. If there is any difference, we have more reasons to be thankful than you have, as we take pleasure in contributing to the happiness of others. It is in very truth 'more blessed to give than to receive.'"

"I am not an enthusiast," responded Battell, "but I am frank to admit that I am carried away by the transcendent character of the sentiments you express, in regard to our duties toward each other.

But it seems to me, that your grand ideal as to what human character ought to be, is so far above our fallen human nature, that it can never be realized in this life. Such a character was Jesus, the Savior of mankind as painted by our religious teachers. But this character is so very much above the human plane of development, that it would be regarded as sacrilegious for anyone to attempt to be as pure, as noble and as holy as he is said to have been."

"The great mass of our people," said lola, "would not understand your allusion to fallen human nature, and the Savior of mankind, but I have read a number of your religious books, and from comparisons with our own ancient history, have concluded that the Fall of Man and his Redemption through the Cross are allegories which were intended to teach a wonderful truth. But, be this as it may, the character of Jesus, I regard as the only truly human character that I have met with in the few outer world books that we have. The wonder is, that this magnificent character has not been incorporated into all of his professed followers. After two thousand years of preaching and discipline, it is strange that you have not developed many of these characters; even surpassing his exalted standard, especially as he told his disciples that they might do greater things than he did."

"But," said Battell, "we are told that he was more than man. He was the Son of God, sent upon earth from his Father's home in heaven, to save fallen man."

"l am willing," was lola's reply, "to admit all this, as I understand it. We had similar characters in the olden time, who tried to save their fellow beings from the low estate in which they lived. But a time came when the effect of their teachings was to produce a multitude of such characters, and then the entire people made one great bound upward, and now we are all saviors whenever and wherever we find a demand for our services in that capacity."

Battell looked his astonishment as he asked: "Is this heaven? Am I to be brought into the presence of not one, but a world full of these God-like characters?"

lola smiled as she said in response:

"Yes, this is heaven provided you have heaven in you, the only place where you will ever find it. And this God-like character whom you call a Savior, is also in you, as it is in every other human being, just as soon as you permit it to be developed. This spark of Divinity --this Son of God -- is latent in the human soul, and its efforts to make itself felt, is the source of every noble, pure and holy impulse to elevate our common humanity. Give the God that is in you a chance to develop, and you will become like unto Jesus, a 'God manifest in the flesh.' "

"But how am I to develop this God-like character?" asked Battell.

"By becoming a savior of the race to the best of your ability," answered lola. "You were taught that it was the mission of Jesus to save the world. It is also your mission. He did his duty in his age and generation, to elevate humanity, and it is your duty to make just as much of an effort in your age and generation, to make the world better for your having lived in it.

"You cannot afford to sit down as if you had nothing to do and 'cast all your cares on Jesus.' You have no right to impose, even if it were possible, any more burdens upon the 'meek and lowly carpenter of Judea.' He did his duty, well and truly, and you ought to do yours. You, in common with every other human being owe a debt to humanity, and you must pay it by your efforts to save humanity —

From all its sin, its aches and pains
From all its multitude of woes,

You cannot be released from your share of the obligation to save the world, by singing:

'Jesus paid it all, all the debt I owe.'"

"I acknowledge," said Battell, "the justice of your criticism as applied to the churches of the outer world, but I am, or rather, I was, a whaler, and they do not fit me. As a sailor, and as a whaler, I never shirked any duty or danger, and I expected every other man to do his duty. I think if I had been called upon to do the work of every other man on shipboard, I would have objected to it most strenuously. On the same principle, Jesus certainly has a clear case against every one of his followers for neglect of duty."

"I did not expect you to take my criticism to yourself," said lola, "notwithstanding the fact that you referred to the religious system of your country, as if it was your standard of faith and practice. I only sought to impress upon your mind, the truths that, it seems to me, the founder of your religion intended to teach. 'Those who took up the work after him, seem to have entirely lost sight of the purpose and spirit of his teachings. But here comes Polaris. She has something to communicate."

Polaris came forward, and after a brief conference with lola and MacNair, she signaled the fleet, which began to maneuver, as if aligning itself under orders, according to some well-defined plan, while MacNair, addressing himself to Captain Ganoe, said:

"Polaris reports that the nurses are ready, and to guard against any excitement that might disturb the patients, they want everyone to embark on the airships except Mike, who will stay with the patients on the Relief ship. Polaris will take Battell and Huston in the ship with herself and sister, while Jack and yourself will take passage with lola and your humble servant. The rest of the fleet will tow the Ice King into port, where you can remove your baggage at your leisure. She will be taken up the Cocytas to Lake Byblis, where all will be safe and under the charge of Pat O'Brien and Mike Gallagher. It will be a convenient distance from the home we have prepared for you until you have become familiar with the language, customs of the country, and so forth."

"How far will it be?" asked the Captain.

"Only about 150 miles," replied MacNair, "which can easily be reached by airship or electric car in half an hour."

" So quickly as that ! " exclaimed Ganoe.

"Certainly 300 miles an hour is nothing extraordinary.

Chapter VII

CARING FOR THE SICK—NEW METHODS OF TREATMENT-NOT PHYSICIANS BUT NURSES — A VOYAGE THROUGH THE AIR — WONDERFUL OPTICAL INSTRUMENTS WHICH REVEAL A PANORAMA OF THE WORLD — ARRIVAL IN ALTRURIA — MARVELOUS IMPROVEMENTS — DRUDGERY AND POVERTY BOTH ABOLISHED.

Captain Ganoe and myself took passage with MacNair and Iola. For the first time, we had embarked upon an airship. I had witnessed many balloon ascensions and had read much in regard to various contrivances for navigating the air, all of which had been failures. But here was a success, and I was on the alert to learn everything possible, in regard to the mechanical principles involved.

We found ourselves in an elegantly furnished cabin, but we saw no signs of machinery. Everything in sight seemed to be arranged for the especial comfort and convenience of the passengers. The view in all directions, through transparent sections, was unobstructed, but the sections could be readily shaded, or the light shut out entirely as the occupants might desire.

In the center was a table of exquisite design and workmanship, on which were various optical instruments for the use of the occupants, and also an electric keyboard connected with the hull which was elevated about thirty inches above the floor upon which it rested.

The shape of the hull in which I concluded that the motor power was placed seemed to be adapted to the navigation of the water as well as the air and in answer to our inquiries MacNair informed us that it could readily be converted into either a water craft or land carriage. The ordinary propelling power consisted of an ingenious combination of wings shaped like those of an insect, but when extraordinary speed was required there was a rudder-like appendage, similar to the tail of a fish, that was shot out from the hull. These were operated by electricity and appropriate mechanical contrivances. He further explained that the power of levitation, or rising in the air, did not depend entirely upon the wings, but, that by a discovery in magnetism, the vessel was rendered positive to the earth so that they mutually repelled each other.

When all was ready, MacNair touched a button on the keyboard, and at once our aerial conveyance became instinct with life. Its broad wings that had been neatly folded, as it alighted upon the deck, now extended out like the pinions of some mighty bird, there was a slight whirring noise beneath our feet, and we began to ascend, moving as it were forward, around a spiral incline.

As we circled around and arose to a place among the fleet which had hovered over us, we had a full view of the ample preparations which our deliverers had made for our rescue. On some of the ships we noticed cables and powerful dynamos. These vessels were as unlike the light and airy passenger boat on which we were embarked, as the ponderous freight train is unlike the lightning express. They had evidently come prepared to take charge of the Ice King as well as the crew. Polaris, Dione, Battell and Huston had embarked,and ascended a short distance, as if to be in a good position to give directions. The hospital attendants were carrying the afflicted sailors on board the Relief ship, on stretchers, with the exception of Pat O'Brien, who was getting around as lively as if there never had been anything the matter with him, and Mike seemed to be trying to keep him still. We were surprised at what seemed to be such a wonderful recovery; and MacNair, noticing the intense interest we were taking in what was transpiring on the Ice King, asked:

"What is the matter? Anything going wrong?"

"Nothing wrong," replied Captain Ganoe, "but something strange. Do you see that herculean sailor rushing around down there and evidently making himself useful in caring for his comrades?"

"Well, what of that?" asked MacNair.

"Only this," said the Captain, " a few hours ago he was confined to his bed with a severe attack of rheumatism and now he seems the personification of health and vigor. Can you explain the change in his case while the others are still helpless?"

"Perhaps his rheumatic attack had actually run its course, but still remained to trouble him as the result of the impression that had been made upon his mind. If that is the case, then he only needed a mental suggestion, to remove the rheumatic impression which had fastened itself upon him."

"That is a queer view to take of the matter," said the Captain, "yet there may be something in it. But, why are the others still helpless? Why would not mental suggestion have the same effect on them?"

"I do not understand the particulars in regard to their condition, and hence, am not qualified to offer an opinion. It may be that the disease in them had worked some organic change that was not so easy to overcome, or, it may be that the suggestion that removed the pain put them to sleep. I see they are apparently sleeping soundly."

"I hope their sleep may be a favorable indication," said the Captain. "I do not," he continued, "understand this strange disease which seems to single out the most robust and powerful. Can you explain it to me?"

"The atmosphere of this inner world," interposed lola, "is highly stimulating, and it requires much active exercise to provide an outlet for the surplus energy that is generated. You were becalmed. Your sailors had nothing to do but to rest when they were not tired. The energy was created and it must be expended. Mental activity would have accomplished this, and their health would have been improved. But failing in this, it took the form of fever and acute pains. The best, in fact, the only efficient safeguard from disease, situated as you were, is to be found in mental activity."

"You certainly do not mean to say that mentally active people are not liable to get sick in this inner world?" remarked the Captain.

"Nothing of the kind," said lola. "But I will say this, that all other conditions being equal, mentally active people are not in as much danger, provided they think healthy thoughts. If they think disease and fear the worst, they will be even more liable than others to get just what they think. But if the active mind is trained to exercise its power to preserve the health of the body, there is no danger from disease."

"This is a strange doctrine," said the Captain, "and one that I am anxious to know more about, but that must be learned further on, I suppose, as MacNair says."

We had been rising slowly until we had now attained a great height and MacNair interrupted the discussion of mental suggestion by saying:

"We have designedly ascended to a greater height than usual, so as to be above the more humid atmosphere. This will give you a better opportunity to make observations."

"But what observations can we make," I asked, "that could not be made from the surface? When I became satisfied from seeing the sun shining through the southern verge, that we had passed into an inner world, I expected with the telescope, to be able to scan every part of the surface, but I found that I was seemingly as far from being able to do so, as when I was in the outer world. Can you explain to me why I cannot turn my glass to the zenith and see the opposite side of the concave?"

"There can be but one reason," said MacNair, with a merry twinkle in his eyes. "The gaseous contents of the concave must be opaque to your vision."

"Well, well," I said laughing, "I found that out without your assistance, and I am not going to let you dodge the question by a play on words. What I want to know is, why these gaseous contents at the center, are opaque while the air at the surface is not?"

"Well I see," said MacNair, "that you are determined to compel me to reveal how little I know. The scientists of the early ages evolved the theory that the center of the concave is a gaseous globe composed of the very lightest materials which they knew by actual experience to be opaque to their vision. "

"But why," I asked, "is it that this concave sphere does not shut off the light from the sun?"

"Because," said MacNair, "this opaque sphere is above our line of vision, --our position on the surface, being twelve degrees below the verges. Besides this, the central opaque sphere is conceived to be flattened at the poles and bulged at the equator, and some have contended that it is also hollow like the earth. But for this opaque sphere our nights would be as light as day by the reflection from the hemisphere above."

"I have thought of that," I replied, "and still I have so much wished that the opposite hemisphere could be seen with the telescope."

"Well, that is precisely what you will be able to do from this airship," said MacNair.

"How so?" I asked. "We certainly cannot rise above the opaque sphere, and if we could, and got a clear view of the opposite hemisphere, that would not be seeing from one side of the concave to the other."

"Not that surely," said MacNair, "but scientists knowing that magnetic currents often pass more readily through opaque than transparent substances, began to search for rays of this kind that would pass through dark bodies and be reflected by substances beyond. At last they succeeded in securing a photograph through wood and metal, and then, all that was required in order to enable us to see through opaque matter, was an optical instrument that would cast the reflection on the retina of the eye. This, in the course of time, was accomplished. And now, these wonderful discoveries are used by the medical profession, in order to enable them to look into the bodies of their patients and examine the internal organs. And, these electromagnetic optical instruments have been so improved that they are in general use, in observations where opaque bodies obstruct the view."

"And do you tell me this as sober truth?" I asked.

"Certainly," responded MacNair, "I propose to give you a practical demonstration. You discovered that the space between us and the zenith was opaque to your vision. Now, take these glasses and adjust them to your eyes and look through those semi-transparent sections, which are like a lace-work of tubes. The penetrating power of these glasses, you see, can be increased or decreased by moving this slide. They enable you to use the magnetic rays which pass through all substances for the purpose of vision."

We followed his directions and the first glance gave us an ocular demonstration that the surface was concave. "Now," continued MacNair, " in order to get the best idea of the leading geographical outlines of this inner world, I want you to examine with your glasses a zone from the horizon in front of us, through the zenith to the horizon behind us. We are now moving on an airline for your future home in Altruria. Our course is a little south of west and the distance about one thousand miles. We are now very near the center of the Oscan ocean. East of us is the continent of Atlan. So, a zone, extending through the zenith along the line on which we are moving will pass through the equatorial belt, and give you a clear concept of the great centers of population and material improvement. This is the most important part of the world for you to study for the present, and until you learn the language and mingle with the people, you must depend upon your eyes as the chief source of information.

We were now moving at great speed and the sensations were most exhilarating. Looking out over the bow we beheld the horizon of water and raising our glasses as we had been directed, at an elevation of about twenty degrees, the coast line of a continent came into view. And still elevating our glasses, we rapidly passed in review a wonderful panorama of flowing rivers, cultivated fields, tangled wildwood, and lofty mountain chains until at an elevation of about forty-five degrees, we beheld the western coast line of the Altrurian continent. At the zenith, we saw the Umbrian ocean, and further down, and directly opposite to Altruria, the · continent of Atlan, suspended, as it were, in the eastern sky like a map. Looking toward the north, and some ten or twelve degrees above the horizon, was the barren island on which we had landed.

We were so engrossed with our observations in a world where we could take a bird's eye view of any part of it, that we did not care to continue the conversation in which we had become so intensely interested. The continent which we were approaching, looked through our glasses like a vast concave picture of a most lovely country suspended above the horizon, and covering almost the entire western sky. But when we looked through our ordinary glasses, the general appearance was not materially different from what it would have been in the outer world. I could but wonder at this marvelous discovery, which had enabled the inventor to construct instruments that converted opaque rays into rays of light, and I could not help thinking, what a restraint the general use of such wonderful optical instruments would be upon evil doers. Nothing could be hidden from those who cared to investigate.

While my thoughts wandered into other channels, my gaze was riveted upon the wonderful panorama presented to our view. I noted that the divisions between land and water were strikingly similar to the physical geography of the outer world, except in this, that the land surface of the inner world on the line of the equator seemed to correspond very closely with the water surface of the outer world, though on a much smaller scale. The clear weather prevailing in the western hemisphere gave us a splendid view of the continent of Altruria. In a few localities dense masses of clouds obscured, but did not entirely shut out the view; and on the whole we got a clear concept of the topography of the country.

A lofty mountain chain extended from the north to the south, and many long rivers flowed from the mountains into the ocean on either side. Large areas of the surface seemed to be highly cultivated, and even in the mountains, palatial buildings were brought into view by the higher powers of our telescopes. Boats plowed along the rivers and on the lakes, and the entire country seemed to be a network of railroads, while airships appeared like specks in the field of our vision, flitting here and there and speeding in every direction.

But the most singular feature which attracted our attention, was, that notwithstanding all the evidences of a highly cultivated country and the most active traffic and trade between the different sections, we nowhere discovered any indications of great cities; and while what appeared to be extensive manufacturing establishments existed in numerous localities, and the harbors along the shore lines were filled with shipping, nowhere did we see vast clouds of smoke such as vitiate the atmosphere in the large cities and manufacturing districts of the outer world.

We were so taken up with what we could see, that we had no inclination to withdraw our attention from this wonderful panorama, to ask for many explanations of minor details. We now had a view of an entire continent and were disposed to make the most of the opportunity. It was doubtless highly civilized, and had its libraries filled with historical, scientific sociological and ethical works that would, in time, reveal to us all that was worth knowing. As MacNair had said, we must use our eyes as our chief source of information, until we had acquired the language and familiarized ourselves with the daily life and usages of the people.

We were now nearing the continent and MacNair reduced our speed so as to give us time to make our observations more in detail. The general direction of the coast was north and south for some hundreds of miles. Along the mainland, capes and promontories were numerous, while running parallel therewith was a chain of islands, forming a continuous series of bays which in the outer world would have been of inestimable value as harbors.

One long island, lying parallel with the coast immediately before us, particularly attracted our attention. It seemed to be some twenty-five or thirty miles in length, and lay like an elevated ridge, between two promontories which extended out from the mainland at either extremity, from which it was separated by narrow channels. This formed a magnificent bay which contained a number of smaller islands that divided the bay into a series of landlocked harbors.

The Cocytas river, to which our attention had been called, flowing from the mountains in the northwest, entered this bay at its northern extremity, through two outlets about five miles apart. Between these outlets was a triangular island about fifteen miles in length. The north bank of the northern outlet was a promontory which extended out from the mainland, to within a few hundred feet of the northern extremity of the island which separated the waters of the bay from the ocean.

As we neared the coast, what had seemed to be a huge smokestack on the point of the promontory that constituted the southern shoreline of the bay, was revealed to our vision as a colossal tower, that in its general appearance, was an exact duplicate of the strange tower we had passed at the northern verge, at the point where we had escaped from the ice. The material used, the style of architecture, and everything about it indicated that it was erected by the same people and for the same purpose.

We had now been speeding forward in a straight line for five hours. We had covered fully 1000 miles, and MacNair assured us that we had been traveling slowly, in order to give us an opportunity to study the topography of the country, as a whole, from an advantageous position, at an average height of about four miles, though at times we had ascended to higher altitudes, as Iola suggested, to so train our lungs to an attenuated atmosphere, that we would experience less discomfort from the lofty aerial flights we were destined to make.

MacNair now called our especial attention to the region of country we were approaching. It was an agricultural district, and, evidently, in a high state of cultivation. It looked like a vast prairie farm, regularly laid out, in the shape of a parallelogram, extending from east to west about thirty miles, and from south to north about fifteen miles. Magnificent buildings appeared at regular intervals, surrounded by beautiful grounds, and connected by broad boulevards, reaching from one end to the other, and crossed by elevated roads at regular intervals. On these magnificent highways, splendid carriages were rolling, but no horses were in sight.Electric cars were continuously moving both ways between these houses, the north and south lines being elevated.

Airships of all sizes and designs, seemed to be ubiquitous, and were moving in every direction. Children amused themselves on the shaded lawns that bordered the boulevards, and in the flower gardens of the highly ornamented grounds around the palatial buildings which appeared in every direction. While this district seemed to be distinctively agricultural, much of the surface was given up to parks, shaded driveways, miniature rivers, artificial lakes, fountains, ornamental gardens and orchards.

The lands devoted to cultivation, were laid off into rectilinear fields running the entire length of the district, thus securing a saving of labor that could not have been accomplished in any other manner. From one end to the other of these long fields, monster machines were moving, operated by electricity, and completing their work as they went. One machine to which MacNair directed our especial attention, was a combined breaking plow, seeder and roller. It was moving at a rapid rate, and leaving behind it a strip, fifty feet in width, thoroughly pulverized, seeded and rolled. The operator occupied a comfortably furnished cab, and directed the progress of the machine by what we were told was a delicately arranged electric keyboard on a table before him.

Everywhere within the range of our vision was presented a scene of industrial activity, and yet comparatively few appeared to be engaged in actual labor. The major portion of the population seemed to be out enjoying a holiday. So impressed was Captain Ganoe with this appearance, that he asked if it was some special festival occasion.

"Not at all," said MacNair. "This scene of recreation and enjoyment is of every day occurrence. The people of this inner world have learned that it takes very little physical labor to provide an abundance of every article of necessity, comfort and luxury for the whole people. They have discovered how to control the great forces of nature and the machine has taken the place of human muscle."

"But," said the Captain, "does not that throw the great masses of the people out of employment, and place them at the mercy of the people who own the machines and the land?"

"It certainly does," answered MacNair. "It deprives all persons of toilsome drudgery, and places them absolutely at the mercy of the people who own the machines and the land. But this is just what they want, because these same people who are deprived of employment, own both the land and the machinery of production and distribution. Hence, they are enabled to enjoy a perpetual holiday. The amount of work to be done, is a much coveted task, as it provides necessary exercise, and from the fact that it is useful and contributes to the commonweal, it is ennobling. The people of this country are too wise to permit the private ownership of land and the means of production, and thus deprive themselves of the abundance, that can be provided for all by the intelligent application of human labor to those natural resources which exceed in productiveness all the demand that can be made upon them.

"But here we are," continued MacNair, "over the land, and now we will loiter along, so you can study the immediate neighborhood in which you will have your home until you want to make a change. These magnificent buildings are communal homes, and this is a communal agricultural district. I am engaged here as a teacher of English, and it has been thought best to bring you here, because quite a number of people are learning to speak our language. It will therefore be more agreeable to you until you have learned to speak the language of Altruria, which has long been universal throughout the inner world. But this will not take you long, and then your services will be in demand as a teacher. The people are anxious to learn all that can be discovered concerning the outer world.

This country is divided into numerous districts which are numbered from north to south. This is District No. 1, Range

No. 1, west. This range line corresponds with longitude 180°. These longitudinal lines are numbered east and west just as they are in the outer world, but as the circle is smaller, the distance between the lines is proportionally less.

"The tower which you were examining so closely as we came to land, is the point from which longitude is calculated. It stands on the equator, and the north and south verges are said to have been marked on the same longitude by similar towers, in ancient times, before communication between the inner and outer worlds was closed by the great ice age, and floods which are said to have submerged all the lower lands. Some regard these traditions as mythical, but many of the ablest scholars accept them as the fragments of authentic history which were saved from some great cataclysm."

"Then," said Captain Ganoe, "it will doubtless be interesting to these people to learn, that our log book confirms the truth of these traditions. At the point where we escaped from the ice was a stupendous tower situated on a point of land, and it was in latitude 85° north, longitude 180° west. So from this it seems that we are now situated directly under the Pacific ocean."

"This indeed will be welcome news to the people of the inner world," said MacNair. "Numerous expeditions have been sent to discover these towers, but thus far, they have either perished, or have been driven back by the cold and storms of the icy verges. Our ancient histories record, that, from the top of these towers, the philosophers made note of some wonderful appearances in the heavens which threatened the race with destruction. Oqua, who is at the head of our district schools will indeed be glad to converse with you on this subject. She has been an enthusiastic patron of polar expeditions, believing that the discovery of these towers would confirm much in the history of the world that has been regarded as mythical. It was the first of these expeditions to use the airship, that rescued me. The only important discovery made was that while the airships are all the most enthusiastic expected in these medial latitudes where storms are unknown, they are not equal to the task of penetrating the icy verges."

Chapter VIII.

ARRIVAL IN ALTURIA — COLOSSAL COMMUNAL HOME — DISTRICT 1, RANGE I — UNDER THE PACIFIC OCEAN -BATTELL AT THE TELEPHONE—STARTLING APPARITION IN A MIRROR — ENROLLED IN SCHOOL — STUDY OF THE LANGUAGE — PHONOGRAPHIC ENUNCIATOR — A COMMUNAL AGRICULTURAL DISTRICT -THE FIRST REVOLT AGAINST LANDLORDISM—FREEDOM THE RULE — A NEW WORLD — STRIKINGLY SIMILAR TO AMERICA.

While MacNair was speaking our airship had alighted upon the top of one of the monster houses. We found that a portion of the roof constituted the boat yard for the airships which were kept for the use of the community. In the center of this roof and elevated far above it, was a circular structure which was slowly revolving, and we could see that it was occupied by people who seemed to be enjoying a siesta. MacNair informed us that this was the reclining room where the members of the community retired to rest and enjoy the scenery in every direction, as well as a place for conferences in its many private apartments.

From this roof, elevators connected at various points with the floors below. This was by far the largest residence building I had ever seen. It consisted of one main building, twelve stories in height and 600 feet in length by 200 wide. On either side were three wings, of the same height, 200 feet long by 100 feet in width. The building was constructed of semi-transparent material which admitted a mellowed light. At the points occupied by the elevator cages were awnings of the same material as that which constituted the roof. We took our seats in one of these elevators, MacNair touched a button and the cage descended, leaving its covering as part of the main roof.

We landed in an extensive dining hall where a magnificent repast had been provided for us. The tables were loaded with the finest soups, bread, vegetables, honey, fruits and nuts in the greatest variety. MacNair informed us that any person had the right to eat at any communal home or public dining hall in the world provided that he had performed his share of productive labor in any part of the world.

No matter where the labor is applied, the product is added to the world's supply and it does not signify where its equivalent is consumed. The evidences of useful service rendered to society, which are issued by the proper authorities in every part of the world, entitle the holder to food, shelter and raiment in any other part of the world. These evidences of labor performed, procure the right of way upon any public conveyance on land or water, or through the air.

To us, this had indeed been a most eventful day. We had been discovered in our forlorn condition early in the morning and at 4 o'clock in the afternoon we had embarked for a voyage of 1000 miles through the air, during which time we had been permitted to enjoy a bird's eye view of the mighty oceans and vast continents of the world. By the time we were through with our suppers it was 11 p. m., and MacNair's announcement that we would now be conducted to our rooms, was indeed most welcome. He explained that they were in the visitor's department which we would occupy until our own apartments were ready.

I was introduced into a magnificent bed chamber but was so sleepy that I scarcely noticed its contents. It was late next morning when I awoke, and when I went out into the hall, I found it full of people passing to and fro, and wondered how it was that I could sleep so soundly. But the mystery was soon explained. I met MacNair in the dining hall and in his usual cheerful manner he asked:

"Well, Jack, how did you rest?"

"All right," I said, "but I seem to have lost my ability to waken up. I am usually aroused by the least noise, but all the passing to and fro in the hall had no effect on me."

"Of course not," said he. " We wanted you to sleep all you could, and so cut off the sounds from your rooms. These walls are all upholstered so that no sound can enter when the sound conductors are disconnected.

"Now," he continued, "just make yourself at home and look around for a day or two. Go wherever your inclinations seem to direct, and make good use of your eyes. Remember that transportation is free. I am now going to register your arrival. Your other comrades have gone to Lake Byblis. Polaris will take care of them and the Ice King."

I took him at his word, and roamed at will over the grounds and through the public offices, Library, Museum, Lecture Room, Music Hall, etc. I found that the heads of the departments and many others understood some English, and all treated me with the utmost courtesy. The second morning lola informed us that Battell wanted to communicate with us and conducted us to the telephone room. On entering I was surprised to see Battell standing before me, and he greeted me in his usual cordial manner:

"Well, good morning, Jack. How do you like this enchanted land?"

"I am delighted to meet you," I replied, and extended my hand. Imagine my surprise when it touched the smooth surface of a mirror, and Battell broke into a hearty laugh, saying:

"I would indeed like to shake, but we are not yet able to reach 150 miles."

I was astonished. Indeed I was so taken aback by the unexpected and lifelike apparition, that for once I was completely dumbfounded. lola, seeing my confusion came to my rescue, saying:

"l ought to have prepared you for this by some explanation of our system of inter-communication, but I thought that the use of our electro-magnetic optical instruments, by which we are enabled to see through opaque substances had prepared you for this. The reflection of Captain Battell on the mirror, is only another method of applying the same principle. The rays from him, converted into rays of light, are reflected upon the mirror, on the same principle that the rays from the eastern hemisphere are reflected on the retina of the eye."

"I ought to have anticipated such an application of this wonderful discovery, " I replied, "but it was nevertheless so unexpected, that I was entirely unprepared for it."

"Well Jack," came from the phonograph, "you are not alone in your astonishment. I would have been quite as much surprised to see you, had I not been apprised of what I might expect. I called you up in order to let you know that we have just arrived at Lake Byblis. The Ice King is coming. The hospital boat is here. Pat and Mike are well. Lief and Eric have gone on to the hospital and the other three sailors are dead. We are all well pleased with the possible exception of Mike, who thinks we are bewitched. Pat got well so soon that Mike thinks he must be crazy . But what shall be done with your baggage when it arrives?"

After consulting with Captain Ganoe, who was present, I replied:

"Send our trunks to Headquarters, District No. 1, Range 1, Continent of Altruria."

"Well, well, Jack," responded Battell, "I am glad you know where you are. I am not so sure about myself. We are treated royally. This is a lovely lake with the most magnificent surroundings I ever beheld. I take it, that this is a great pleasure resort, for a people who seem to have nothing to do but to enjoy themselves. We are taking lessons in the language, and find it very easy. I have taken the liberty to authorize the Department of Education to translate our library, and they were so anxious about it, that they went out on airships to meet the Ice King, and commence the work."

"That is right," said Captain Ganoe, who now came forward and took up the conversation. "Tell them the Ice King, and all we have so far as I am concerned, is at their service."

"They have no use for the ship," responded Battell, "but would highly appreciate it, as a specimen of American ship building. They will place Pat and Mike in charge as soon as the ship comes in. Polaris informs me that the whole world will give us a reception at Lake Byblis when some great council meets here. By that time she thinks we will have become masters of the language and learned in all the wisdom of the Altrurians."

We frequently conferred with Battell, and he kept us advised in regard to everything of interest relating to the Ice King, and other matters in which we felt especially interested. Acting upon MacNair's suggestion, I gave my entire time to the study of our immediate surroundings. I found that this magnificent home contained over 2000 people, men, women, and children, and still there was no crowding. The main building contained all the offices and store rooms, public halls, school rooms, library, museum, dining hall, kitchen and laundry. Powerful storage batteries furnished electricity for heating and lighting, and motor power for manufacturing, which formed a part of the educational system in every home. The wings were given up entirely to apartments, so that the members of this immense family could be just as secluded and exclusive as they desired. Each one had a private apartment furnished to his or her taste.

Each room was numbered and connected by telephone with the library, storerooms and business offices, and could be placed in communication with the occupants of any other apartment, or with the District Exchange which could place them in communication with any part of the world. If a book was wanted from the library or any article from the storeroom, it was ordered by telephone, and delivered at once, by pneumatic tube. Every apartment could be connected by phonograph with the lecture room or music hall, and the occupant could listen to the lecture or music, without leaving his or her room. There was also a universal distribution of news by the same means to any person who desired such service.

In each of these communal homes was a publishing department, and all the facilities for manufacturing furniture, clothing and almost any utensil needed, equal to the supply of the community, if it was found to be necessary. While the district was devoted mostly to agriculture, in its educational system, every member was trained in the mechanic arts and general business methods.

This training began with the children and continued for life as occasion might require. People never imagined that they would become too old to learn. 'They were taught that the most important service they could render to themselves and to society was to educate themselves, physically, mentally and morally, and that for this kind of service society could well afford to give them access to all that was required for their sustenance and comfort.

Hence all facilities for improvement, books, papers, scientific instruments and instruction were not only free, but the use of them was regarded as a valuable service to society. The pupil attended school, got his or her evidence of labor performed, which entitled the holder to food, shelter, clothing, etc., the same as the teacher, ---as both were alike serving society. The pupils, in training themselves for lives of usefulness, were regarded as benefiting the community as well as themselves, and hence the community was in duty bound to provide them with all the essentials for their highest development of body and mind, in harmony with the demands of an advanced or advancing civilization.

These lessons concerning this inner world civilization, derived from conversations with MacNair, lola and others who could converse in English, and confirmed by our own observations as far as they had gone were intensely interesting, and we never tired of asking questions, which were always answered courteously and in a satisfactory manner. But I soon reached the point where I began to feel the need of more comprehensive sources of information. I wanted to be able to speak the language of the country, converse with all the people, attend lectures and make the fullest use practicable of the extensive libraries and numerous publications which contained the current literature of the times, so that I could enter into the spirit and purpose of this wonderful civilization, which seemed to be far more attractive than the most entrancing picture of Utopia.

Feeling thus, I was prepared for what was to follow.

One morning after we had somewhat familiarized ourselves with our new surroundings, and we felt inclined to rest and think, rather than to roam around, MacNair asked:

"How do you like your new home since you have had time to look around and get acquainted?"

"So far as I am concerned," I replied, "I am delighted with the country and the treatment I receive wherever I go. But there is so much to learn, that I feel overwhelmed. If I were able to converse with the people, and enter into the spirit of their daily life, I would be more at home. I want to be able to utilize all the sources of learning which are contained in your literature and I think that the time has come when the best thing we can do is to settle down in earnest to the study of the language."

"I knew that you would soon come to that conclusion," said MacNair, "but what you have seen is a necessary step in your education. We must soon go to our classes and you can go with us and take your first lesson. In order to facilitate your studies, you have been assigned apartments adjoining the Library and Lecture room."

We assented and were at once conducted to our apartments. lola presented each of us with just such a bookcase and library as Polaris had shown us, on her airship. As she opened one of these cases and displayed the contents, she said:

"You will find here everything needed in order to acquire an accurate understanding of our language. It has been prepared under the direction of MacNair and myself by the publishing department, particularly for the use of English speaking people who might succeed in getting through the ice barriers. These cards contain the English alphabet with our corresponding characters printed on the right. The only difference is that we have a character for each sound while you have a number of sounds to one character. When you have learned our alphabet you will be able to read our language. If there should be any difficulty with the pronunciation all you have to do is to formulate the word by pressing the characters on this keyboard and you will hear every sound clearly enunciated. Every word thus formed is inscribed on a cylinder and after the sounds have been recorded all you have to do is to increase the speed of the clock work in order to have the word pronounced just as it is spoken in ordinary conversation. This instrument is called a Phonographic Enunciator and it records the sound of every character by means of a simple but most delicately constructed mechanical contrivance which has been carefully adjusted to the tones of the human voice. The sounds thus recorded by the use of the sound characters on the keyboard are then pronounced audibly on the principle of our old fashioned phonograph."

"You will find that the definition of the words and the grammatical structure of our language are very easy to learn. This small dictionary of root words, defined in English, contains the key to the definition of every word in our language. When you have committed these definitions to memory you will not find it difficult, even without a teacher, or lexicon, to define every word compounded from them. The grammar, as you will see, is not essentially different from your own, except that we have simplified its treatment. We recognize but four parts of speech; nouns, verbs, modifiers and connectives. The study of our language is further facilitated from the fact, that when its fundamental principles are fully understood, you will naturally have a word for every meaning, instead of a variety of meanings for one word. Our Altrurian language has been repeatedly revised by carefully selected committees of eminent scholars, with a view to making it so easy to learn that it would become universal, a result that was accomplished several hundred years ago."

"Polaris showed me a school library something like this," said I, "but it was adapted to pupils who wanted to study English."

"Yes," remarked lola, "we have been urging her for a long time to study English, but we never could induce her to make the effort. But," she added, smiling, "no doubt she now regrets it. I predict that it will not be long before she is speaking English as glibly as she does her mother tongue. But I must go now. If you need any help, just touch that button and I will come at once."

She bade us adieu, and we went to work to master the language. As lola and MacNair had informed us, we found it remarkably easy. We had been well trained from childhood in distinguishing all these sounds, and our eyes soon became familiar with the characters by which they were represented, and before we retired to rest after our first day's study, we were practicing the pronunciation of words, and committing definitions to memory.

We soon had quite a vocabulary of words at our command, which we introduced into our ordinary conversation. This could be the more readily done, because of the grammatical construction of the language being so similar to the English. Associated as we were, with a number of highly educated people, who understood both languages, our progress was very rapid, and in a short time we could express all of our wants in the language of the country, and when we did not have the right word we substituted English, knowing it would be understood, and also, that some one would supply the right word. We determined from the beginning, to use no language but the Altrurian, just as rapidly as we could acquire it. We used it in reading, writing and conversation, and soon we scarcely thought of our mother tongue, except when we heard it spoken.

MacNair and lola were engaged with their classes an average of two hours a day, and we ordinarily spent our leisure and recreation time together. Our home was also District Headquarters, and here we were continually meeting with representatives from every home in the district, and our acquaintance was rapidly extended. We often visited other homes, sometimes by electric carriage or airship, and sometimes we would walk for miles. When tired, we could always hail a car or carriage. Thus, we were by our associations continually improving in the use of the language, while we were adding to our fund of knowledge concerning the country, by observation and conversation with the people.

I carefully studied the economy of the home in which we lived, being assured that this was a sample of a multitude of others. The same thing was true of the district. So in a general way, we were making a study of the entire concave by having a sample submitted to our inspection. At least, I could get a very clear idea of agriculture, the great basic industry that sustains the race, and hence, I am condensing into this chapter the results of a long and careful investigation under exceptionally favorable conditions.

During our attendance at school, lola and MacNair frequently took us for a sail in their airship. This gave us an opportunity to study its mechanism, and at the same time obtain a bird's eye view of the country, and if anything especially attracted our attention, all we had to do was to ask for an explanation. As we had first approached the continent we were struck by the large residences, storage buildings, and the long rectilinear fields, but now that we examined the scene at leisure we began to take in the details, and were impressed by the general sameness of the picture.

These magnificent buildings were strikingly similar to each other and the same thing was true of the long rectilinear fields and the arrangement of the crops. The residence buildings were apparently situated at alternate section corners and hence about two miles apart each way. Midway between these were large warehouses, elevators, mills, factories, etc. To the east and west these long rows of buildings were connected by surface, electric roads, and north and south by elevated roads. These roads, both passenger and freight, all passed through these buildings. This general arrangement of everything into squares, gave the entire district, from the cabin of the airships, the appearance of an immense checkerboard.

This district which may be taken as a sample of many others, had a complete system of waterworks, a continuous pressure being secured by a series of standpipes, from three to five hundred feet in height, which forced the water to every point where it was needed. This system also provided water for irrigation purposes as the season seemed to require. This with a complete system of drainage, constituted a method of keeping the most perfect condition for producing the greatest abundance. In addition to this, all the waste products were converted into fertilizer and returned to the soil. These wise, economic, scientific methods and intense cultivation, explain how this small district, sustained a population of 200,000 and yet gave up fully one half of its lands to boulevards, lawns, parks, drive-ways and ornamented grounds.

Electricity was the universal motor power, as well as a stimulant to the growth of crops. The soil was pulverized, seeded and rolled by vast machines. The grain was harvested, threshed and placed in sacks by huge combined reapers and threshers, and dried by passing through evaporators on an endless belt which conveyed it to elevators, from which it reached the mills by force of gravity, if that is the right word to apply to the centrifugal force which in this moral world held everything to the surface.

The standard day's labor was but two hours; and yet with the aid of machinery, ten persons harvested a strip of grain one hundred feet wide and thirty miles in length, delivering the same at the elevators in sacks, while another ten prepared the soil and put in another crop. All the other work was carried on in the same labor saving manner, and this two hours of labor was deprived of every feature of drudgery and became only agreeable exercise.

One thing I noticed particularly; domestic animals seemed to be raised more as pets than for use. The only animal diet ordinarily used consisted of eggs, milk, butter and cheese. Sheep and goats were raised for the fleece which was manufactured into the finest fabrics. Fruits and nuts were produced in the greatest abundance and constituted a very large part of the diet of the people.

The district was in fact a stupendous farm and in its original design the prime object had evidently been utility rather than ornament. The work of the landscape gardener had been utilized to the largest extent, but it had not been permitted to encroach upon the useful. The economy in the uniformity in which the lands were laid out, the houses constructed and the work of production carried on, gave to the whole country such an artificial appearance, especially from the airships which we used most generally in our observations, that Captain Ganoe could no longer refrain from commenting upon it. One day as we were soaring above this magnificent farming district, he asked MacNair if the entire inner world had been cut out according to the same pattern.

"Not at all," replied MacNair. "You will find plenty of variety. Every person has an opportunity to gratify his or her tastes, provided that by so doing they do not deprive others of the same privilege. There is nothing compulsory about it. People who do not desire to dwell together can find plenty of opportunities to be by themselves. The rule here is freedom. People live together in communities because it secures so many advantages, but they often take an outing and find variety, and solitude if they want it, in comparatively wild and uninhabited parts of the country.

"But," I said, "I am curious to learn how it was that the communal system came to be established. In the outer world I am inclined to believe that it would be impossible to find so many people who would live together in harmony."

"That is doubtless true," said MacNair. "But as I now understand it, influences are at work, which will ultimately compel the producing masses to come together as one family, in order to enable them to preserve any semblance of personal liberty and economic independence."

"And was it," I asked, "necessity that compelled the founders of this district to organize this system of community life?"

"It certainly was, "interrupted lola. "This district was founded by a few of the more intelligent laborers in the great city which at that time existed at the mouth of the Cocytas. A time had come when the laboring masses were forced to get together in colonies and cooperate with each other in order to live. This represents the first organized revolt of the masses against landlordism and the spirit of commercial and financial cannibalism, which had reached its apex in the large cities existing in the olden time along this eastern coast. The few owned all the land, all the machinery and all the facilities for distribution while the many were often famishing for food, and always begging for an opportunity to serve some master who would feed them."

"If they were indeed so poor," I asked, "how was it possible for them to break the chains by which they were bound?"

"That is a long story," said lola, "and cannot be recorded in a word. Volumes are filled with the futile efforts of the working classes to protect themselves by organization, and their education had to come through their repeated failures. But all these futile efforts at organization were on the competitive plan, and actually placed one class of workers in competition with another class. At first the skilled artisans, seemingly secured some advantages by the trade unions, but it was only a question of time when the improvement in machinery and a division of labor, placed the skilled workman, to a very large extent, in competition with the common laborer for the privilege of running the machines, which did the work better than the most skillful mechanic, and with a speed that had never before been dreamed of. From that time on to the end, the employed in every branch of production were placed in a bitter and destructive contest with the unemployed for the privilege of working for a master.

"It was not until they had reached this condition by bitter experience that they began to learn just what was the matter. Among the first things that occurred to them, was, that they were at the mercy of the landlord until they had access to the soil, but how could they obtain access to the soil in their penniless condition? This was the question that racked their brains."

"But conditions, which neither they, nor their oppressors could control, were forcing a solution. It had been recognized in the civilization of that time, that the poor and the physically infirm, had a just claim on society for food, shelter and raiment which must not be disregarded. All that they needed, was the fruits of their labor applied to the soil, and the money kings had to a very great extent monopolized the soil. It was worthless to them unless it was cultivated. Its possession still gave them power to oppress the landless, but not the opportunity to speculate, as no one was able to buy. So to save the expense of feeding their victims they were willing that the land should be used, by these objects of charity, to produce their food by their labor.

"Thus was provided the opportunity that enabled far sighted reformers to introduce a new system of organization among the poor, which placed all their relations to each other on an ethical, instead of a selfish basis. They began by organizing exchanges among themselves, and what they saved to themselves in this way was invested in land for which there were no other purchasers. For a time this enabled the land owners to sell the lands which were useless to themselves, as a source of profit. The colonists continued to cultivate the land, sell the surplus in the cities, and buy more land, but they never sold an acre. In the course of time, the lands of this district were socialized and rent abolished.

"Thus, by using the profit, which under the old competitive system left the hands of the producers, never to return, they were able to abolish landlordism, as far as they were concerned, and their wealthy oppressors congratulated themselves that they had gotten rid of a dangerous class. But the same causes continued to impoverish others, and thus create other dangerous classes, and the only way to get rid of them, was to give them an opportunity to dig their living out of the soil. It became a common thing for cities to organize movements which enabled the poor to secure subsistence by cultivating vacant lots. Indeed, this was one of the first signs that marked the decline, and presaged the early abolition of the then existing system of commercial and financial cannibalism that impoverished the people.

"This community demonstrated that labor could, even under the most adverse circumstances, by cooperating in production and distribution, get control of land and the means of production, and abolish tribute to nonproducers in all its forms. You will find the history of these movements most intensely interesting, and I should think from what I have learned, of inestimable value in your native land."

"Since MacNair gave us the benefit of his knowledge of the economic system which exists in the outer world, our scholars have studied our own ancient histories as they never did before. Situated as we are, it is hard to believe that any people, no matter how ignorant they may be, would permit a few to take possession of the earth and starve the many, but such was the situation here in the olden times; hence, it is not strange that these conditions exist in the outer world."

"Well," I remarked, "since I think of it, I am not surprised that you can hardly believe such conditions could exist in any country claiming to be civilized. But why is it that the people of this inner world, understood the nature of this evil and removed it so long ago, while the masses of the people of the outer world seem to be utterly oblivious to the fact that there is anything wrong?"

"On this question I can only theorize," said lola. "I have thought that it may have been the long continued ice age, that with its rigors, held the people of the outer world back and retarded their development until long after the inner world had made a very considerable progress toward civilization. But MacNair has a theory that may have something in it. He believes that the psychic conditions in a concave world, tend directly toward concentrated effort and co-operation, because the heads of the people all point toward each other and converge at a common center, while in the outer world they point outward, each in a direction of its own, tending directly toward individualism and the development of every selfish instinct."

"Well," said Captain Ganoe, who had been an attentive listener, "I am glad, for the honor of my own country, that a fellow countryman of mine has evolved a theory that has not been previously thought out and demonstrated by this most progressive people. I think, Jack, that we had better go to work and evolve an improvement on these airships that will enable us to carry the news of these wonderful discoveries to our own people."

"I have been thinking of the same thing," I replied, "and that is why I have always been insisting that we should use these airships for our short journeys that did not require speed. It is when we go slowly that I can study them best, and in my mind I have partially solved the problem of constructing a ship that would be proof against both cold and storms."

"Just like my luck," said the Captain. "I always succeed in getting an idea in my head after someone else has worked it out. But still I think that I am something of a mechanic and you can depend upon me to do my best to assist you."

"Thank you," I replied, "I shall certainly call upon you for assistance."

"I have reason," said MacNair, "for believing that Battell and Polaris contemplate something of the same kind, and I am sure that they will call upon both of you for your co-operation."

"Why," I asked, "have you had any intimation of the kind?"

"Not directly from them," said MacNair, "but I, have heard this, that Battell and Polaris spend much of their time in the airship factory at Lake Byblis and that they are experimenting with their private airship every day, and that they have succeeded in making some changes in the gearing that enable them to reverse the wings and run backward; also in moving the steering apparatus so they can ascend or descend without the usual spiral motion."

"That is good news," I said, "but I thought that Captain Battell was giving most of his time to the study of the language and customs of the country."

"So he is," said MacNair. "Polaris told me so by telephone, and what is more, she spoke in good clear English. She further said that the work 'Of translating the library was progressing rapidly and that several volumes had been completed and furnished to Norrena, the Continental Commissioner of Education at Orbitello, for distribution to the commissioners of all the grand divisions of the Concave."

"Orbitello! What is Orbitello? A country or a city?" asked Captain Ganoe.

"We have no cities," said MacNair, "but Orbitello is what you would probably call the seat of government. It is the center of business for this continent, the headquarters of all the departments of the public service. The Altrurian Council meets at Orbitello every year, and the World's Parliament every four years. Here the Continental Executive Committee meets every day to transact business in which the whole people are interested. It is located on the Cocytas at the foot of the mountains."

"I would indeed be pleased to visit this center of business and learning," said the Captain.

"We have thought of that," said MacNair, "and as soon as Oqua returns, I think that we had better go. She is our District Commissioner of education and I am deputy and must officiate in her absence. She is attending the Quadrennial Congress of Educators in the mountains of Atlan at Lake Minerva. The sessions seldom last more than thirty days and that time has passed, so we may expect her return from the old world almost any day."

"What's that? The old world!" ejaculated Captain Ganoe. "Am I to understand that you have an old world here, and is this the new, just as we have it in the outer world? "

"Yes, very much the same," said MacNair. "Altruria is often spoken of as the new world because it was originally settled by colonists from the other side of the Ocean. The early history of this country is in a general way very similar to the early history of America. This similarity holds good even to the almost total destruction of a warlike race of red men. The original colonies achieved their independence of kingly rule and established a republican form of government, just as was done by our thirteen original colonies. But here the similarity ends. Altruria now extends all over the continent, and has carried out to their logical sequence, the principles set forth in our own Declaration of Independence; and more than this, these principles have extended over all parts of the inner world. This is why I often speak of the concave as the World of Truth."

As MacNair ceased speaking, our airship alighted on the roof of our home, and we were informed that Battell wanted to meet us at the telephone. We went at once to the telephone room and again met Battell, but I was not dumfounded at the sight. He addressed me in his usual familiar style, saying:

"Well, Jack, we have a boat factory here and I have conceived the idea of becoming an inventor of airship attachments and I want you and Captain Ganoe to join me. I want the Captain for his mechanical skill and I want you to test our inventions, make observations and report such changes in the mechanism as you deem advisable. Polaris cannot stand the cold at the verges and I will not have time. Can you undertake the work?"

"Certainly," I replied. "Just notify me whenever you are ready. I have been contemplating the same thing myself, and Captain Ganoe has offered his services as a skilled mechanic."

Chapter IX

A HAPPY SCENE — TWO CIVILIZATIONS COMPARED — ARRIVAL OF OQUA — DISGUISE PENETRATED — HUMAN RIGHTS — "GLITTERING GENERALITIES" REDUCED TO PRACTICE — A STRANGE CUSTOM — NUMBERED, LABELED AND REGISTERED AS CITIZENS — EXIT JACK ADAMS -A NEW NAME — NEQUA — BITTER MEMORIES — OQUA'S SYMPATHY.

The proposed improvement of the airship, so that it could withstand the storms of the polar regions, and MacNair's report of the progress that Battell had made in that direction inspired me with the determination to prosecute my studies with more energy than ever. I saw at a glance,that if we should be able to open up a channel of communication with the outer world, the knowledge that could be acquired here would be of incalculable value to the people on the outside of the sphere, and especially to my own native America, on whose virgin soil the new and improved thought was the most likely to germinate and grow to perfection. Before this trip to the outer world was made, I felt that it was my imperative duty to glean the wisdom of the ages from these vast libraries, and from the oral lessons of these ripe scholars. My one, all-absorbing thought, was to trace the progressive evolution of these people and discover the fundamental principles and practical business methods that had enabled them to reach their present ideal civilization. Hence I determined to apply myself to study, with an earnestness of application that I had never before attempted.

When I needed rest or desired to be alone, my favorite resort was the large observatory or reclining room on the top of the building. This room is octagonal in form and is detached from the roof on which it rests, and is placed upon small wheels which run around on a circular track whenever the occupants turn on the electric power. In order to enjoy a most beautiful panorama, all I had to do was to seat myself at one of the windows, with or without my glass, and set the room to revolving slowly. I never tired of the scenes thus presented to my view from this elevated position.

This room is furnished in the most superb style. Its elaborate upholstery is of the finest and softest materials, of the most exquisite designs. It is large and airy. The walls are adorned with many magnificent paintings and ornamented with festoons of trailing vines and flowers, while the windows are garlanded with green and fragrant foliage. Around the circumference of this luxurious retreat, are small, well furnished alcoves at each window, which can be cut off from observation by sliding doors which are upholstered with some soft material that excludes every sound that might disturb the occupant.

One day, about a week after the interview with Battell in regard to the improvement of the airships, MacNair, Iola, Captain Ganoe and myself had descended to the observatory for our usual after dinner rest. I was in a meditative mood, and not caring to take part in the conversation, I had retired to one of the little alcoves, closed the doors, set the room in motion and brought my window around to a point overlooking the great boulevard, with the pleasure grounds, shrubbery, flower gardens and giant forest trees just beyond. From my lofty perch I looked down upon the scene before me. Bright, happy faces, and kind, cheerful voices, greeted eye and ear through the open window.

I felt entranced by the wonderful scenes around me. I could not help but compare this great communal home, where all was abundance, elegant leisure, fascinating social enjoyment, health and happiness, with the crowded, filthy and ill-ventilated tenement houses of New York, London and other large cities of the outer world, which are pre-eminently the abodes of destitution, misery and woe. How often has my heart ached when I have found families of ten and twelve persons, huddled into one or two diminutive rooms, poorly lighted, ill-ventilated and disgustingly filthy.

In the living hells of the outer world, I had witnessed every manner of deformity, degradation and filth. Children in rags, just from the arms of their mothers, creeping like cowardly wharf rats about the slums and alley ways, picking up pieces of mouldy bread or fishing in slop barrels and sewers for bits of meat, were scenes of human misery that often made my heart bleed.

Then, add to this picture of the conditions into which the children are born, the abject misery of their decrepit grandsires and grandmothers. How often have I seen them, dressed in tatters and exposed to the wintry winds as they tottered off to some alley, or some rich man's ash heap, to scratch out with naked and almost freezing fingers, the little bits of unconsumed coal, so that they might have a little fire to warm their half-famished bodies, while they dined upon the garbage gathered up by the children.

Such were the scenes that I had often witnessed in the poverty stricken districts of the large cities of the outer world, and with them I compared the happy scene before me. Not one deaf, dumb, blind, lame, deformed or disfigured individual among the multitudes which often gathered upon the grounds I was now contemplating. Not one ragged, barefooted and bareheaded urchin, nor one snowy-haired, tottering and infirm old man or woman among them.

What a contrast! A heaven was opening up before me, in comparison with the living hells that had been so indelibly impressed upon my memory. Why such a contrast between humanity here in this great communal home, and humanity in the tenement houses in the large cities of the outer world? There must be some cause for this extraordinary difference in the physical makeup and personal appearance of the people. Why were the people in this communal home more robust, more beautiful and more kind and cheerful than the people of the outer world? And why had the usual decrepit appearance of age disappeared from view? Here was the evidence that a physical regeneration of the race had taken place. I did not doubt that this was the logical result of improved social and economic conditions and I was determined to find if possible the scientific explanation.

But here my meditations were broken in upon by the sight of an airship crossing my line of vision, in the direction of that portion of the roof used as a boat yard. I opened the sliding doors and looking out toward the landing, I saw the vessel alight and a splendid looking person step out, just as MacNair opened the door upon that side, saying: "There is Oqua!" and motioned for her to come into the reclining room.

MacNair and lola had so often spoken of this person in such eulogistic terms as a ripe scholar and experienced educator, prominent throughout the world, that I had pictured her as aged, sedate and probably careworn from the discharge of her onerous duties, showing the wear of years of careful study and attention to public affairs. But what was my surprise, as she came up to the observatory, to see a most beautiful woman, showing no signs of age or care. I could but stand spellbound, and admire her form and features which were simply perfect. Any attempt at description would be presumptuous and I will not attempt it.

As she came in and was introduced by MacNair, I noticed that she understood our language and customs, for stepping forward and extending her hand to Captain Ganoe she said in a most musical voice:

"I am indeed most happy to make your acquaintance and offer you a most cordial welcome to our country and a place in our esteem. Your arrival has been heralded all over the world, and it is regarded as an event that may be pregnant with the most important results to the entire human race. The Congress of Educators at Lake Minerva passed a resolution requesting that the next meeting of the World's Parliament, shall be held at the Auditorium of the Transportation Pavilion at Lake Byblis, and that this shall be the occasion of giving a world's reception to the crew of the Ice King. But Captain, how many do you have with you?"

"Only one," said the Captain. "The others are at Lake Byblis. But here is Jack Adams, the scholarly artist and scientist of the expedition, and as such I have no doubt that you and he will become fast friends."

She turned to me and placing one hand on my shoulder grasped my extended hand with the other. She scanned me from head to foot with an expression of amazement and inquiry playing over her smiling countenance; then with a light, musical laugh she bent forward and kissed me on the forehead, saying:

"Yes, I am sure that we will become fast friends." The action was so sudden and unexpected, that I blushed, stepped back and stammered. I instinctively knew that her keen eye had penetrated my disguise, and the recognition tested my nerves. Yet it was so cordial, that I felt that my secret was safe, and my reply was a laugh, a lifting of the eyebrows and a closer pressure of her soft, warm palm as I merely responded, "Yes, I am quite sure," and from that moment I knew that she was indeed a friend. A chord of sympathy and affection had been touched, that enraptured while it bound me in bonds of friendship to this grand woman, a relationship of the most enjoyable character, as well as of incalculable value, in opening up for me a life work, as agreeable to myself as I hope to make it profitable to others.

For some time we joined in general conversation when Oqua asked MacNair if we had yet been registered and enrolled as citizens.

"In part," said MacNair. "'They have been given numbers on the schedule of the school, but have not yet been called upon to select the names by which they desire to be known. In fact I have not yet explained this matter to them. Iola has been giving them language lessons in their room, and instructions concerning such matters as they desired to understand more fully in regard to the country, its history, customs, etc. But as they can now read and speak the language understandingly, their selection of names and registration as citizens ought not to be put off any longer, as at present their numbers only rank them as minors."

We were more than a little mystified at the turn the conversation had taken and as it related to us Captain Ganoe asked:

"What does this mean? It seems from your remarks that we have been numbered and that we are now to be labeled. I would be pleased to have an explanation. We highly appreciate the interest you have taken in our welfare, and anticipate much pleasure and profit to be derived from a knowledge· of your language, as it will give us access to the boundless stores of wisdom which are contained in your literature. But is it really necessary for us to be numbered and labeled? I take it for granted that it is all right, but I do not understand it."

"Perhaps," said MacNair, "this should have been explained to you sooner; but I was guided by my own experience when I found myself among these people.'

'There was so much to be learned and it could not all be acquired at once. I deemed it best to give you as nearly as possible just what you asked for, and let you get somewhat acquainted with the customs of the country before asking you to take the steps necessary to become citizens of Altruria, which also makes you citizens of the inner world, entitled to all the rights of citizenship, no matter where you go. In America, you require a foreigner to declare his intentions to become a citizen, and then, after five years you permit him to be sworn in as a full-fledged citizen. We have no regulations but such as apply to all alike. The child has no choice of birthplace, but it has a natural right to food, shelter, clothing, education, etc. Hence, children are numbered, so we may know how many are to be provided for. When they reach maturity and graduate from school, they are requested to select the names by which they desire to be known. This entitles them to a voice in public affairs and makes them eligible to any public trust. When I gave you a number, the right to food, clothing and education was conferred upon you. When you select names you will be registered as citizens and will be entitled to a voice in public affairs and eligible to any public trust for which you may be selected."

"Then," said the Captain, "it seems that we have no reason to be dissatisfied with either the number or the label, as the first gives us free access to wealth that we did not create, and the second confers upon us the sovereign right to be consulted as to how our benefactors should conduct their business. We seem to be the beneficiaries in all these regulations, 'reaping where we have not sown.' What right have we to the fruits of the labor of others to whom, as yet, we have been of no benefit whatever?"

"The same right," said Oqua, "that you have to live. Your right to life cannot be questioned, and you cannot live unless you have access to the fruits of the earth, which are garnered by the labor of the people. The primary object of human society is to secure to each individual member the right to live and be happy, and to this end, each must be secure in the possession of the means of subsistence and the liberty to enjoy the healthy exercise of every function of mind and body. This, being the primary object for which our social organism was created, our first duty is to humanity, and all of our rules and regulations have this one object in view."

"But does not this endanger the perpetuity of the social organism," asked the Captain, "by opening the door to those who would take advantage of this broad definition of rights to impose grievous burdens upon those who confer these rights?"

"Not at all," responded Oqua. "When all the people enter into an organization of society, the primary object of which is to provide the best possible conditions for each of its members, the personal interests of each, will, to say nothing of the moral obligations, impel them to perpetuate such organization, by doing everything in their power to promote the best interests of all. Hence, just as soon as all have been made secure in their natural rights to life, liberty and those equitable conditions which place happiness within the reach of all, sound policy, as well as equal liberty and evenhanded justice demands that all should have an equal voice in the conduct of public affairs in which all are equally interested. It would be manifestly unjust and oppressive, to ask the people to submit to regulations to which they never consented."

"I admit the force of your reasoning," said the Captain. "The same ideas, expressed in different language, were adopted in my own country and have served to embellish platform utterances and sensational newspaper appeals, but in practice, they have been treated as mere 'glittering generalities.' Here, you seem to regard them in a far different light, as something to be reduced to practice in every day life; and with a people as well educated as yours this seems to be easy, but, with an ignorant and brutal populace the case would be very different."

"Not so," said Oqua. "There is more good than evil in the human soul. The populace might be made ignorant and brutal by the violation of these principles, and if so, the application of these principles in all the transactions of life would inevitably produce an intellectual and refined populace. This is no 'glittering generality,' but a sober truth, and this is the lesson that your people must learn before they can ever reach their ideal of what they ought to be. When the leading minds among any people realize that there is absolutely but one way by which the masses of mankind can ever be elevated to higher and better conditions mentally and morally, and that way is, by placing them under better conditions physically, it will be found that the whole people can be lifted up to a higher plane of being as if by magic. It is on this line that the people of this country have been moving for centuries and it is to this that we desire to call your attention. We give you a number, which signifies that because you have an existence, you are entitled to the blessings of our civilization. But now we want you to register your name, as a co-worker. When you take this step, you will have given us your permission to ask your co-operation whenever it is needed. Are you willing to register and assume the duties incumbent upon citizenship?"

"Certainly," said the Captain. "You have a right to command our services and all we want is to know what is required of us."

"Then you will register," said Oqua. " This will make you one of us and equally responsible with us for the exalted trust which is committed to our hands of preserving intact the blessings of a humane civilization. So if you are ready we will attend to this preliminary work at once."

We assented, and stepping on the elevator passed down to the lower story and into the Registry office which was made a part of the Department of Education. For school purposes it was of course necessary to register the children and as all adults were supposed to be graduates of the schools, the same department kept a registry of the entire people, so that at any time, the population of any community, district or continent could be ascertained at short notice."

Oqua opened an immense volume and turning to the proper letter said:

"You see here the name of your countryman, James MacNair. Just opposite, on the left, is a number. Of course his introduction to our schools was that of a child, as he had everything to learn concerning the language and people of our country while we knew nothing of his language or his country. As a pupil he was known by a number; as a citizen he is known by a name; and according to our customs that name must be one of his own choosing. There could be no objection to his taking the same name by which he was known in the outer world, and you can of course suit yourselves in the selection of names, but it must be your own signature and when recorded it becomes permanent. All that we care for is, that it shall be your own choice."

"As to that," said the Captain, "I prefer to retain my original name. However, I rather like this custom of permitting people to select names to suit themselves. In the outer world, the name is selected for you, and you are not permitted to change it, except by application to the courts or the lawmaking power. But as I have no reason to change my name you may record it as Raphael Ganoe."

"But let me suggest," interposed MacNair, "that you retain the prefix of Captain as it is familiar to your crew and also designates your relation to what I doubt not is destined to take its place in the minds of the people of the world as the only polar expedition that brought blessings to humanity. Of course the title signifies nothing here, but it does in the outer world which is to receive the greatest benefits from it, and there is no reason here that you should not retain it as part of your name:"

"Then so be it; Captain Raphael Ganoe will give me the regulation three names of the outer world, for the edification of a people who seem to be, as a rule, contented with only one."

My turn to select a name came next, and Oqua toying with her fan between her fingers, and with a smile she could not suppress, said to me:

"Well, Jack, why is it that you take no part in this discussion? You seem to have no interest in the matter of selecting names. Is it because you deem it of no importance, or do you disapprove of our custom of requiring every person to select a name in order to become a citizen?"

"Oh, as for that," I replied, "I approve your custom, but as yet I have not given any thought to the name I should select for myself. But as I have always been rather indifferent in regard to names, I hardly know how to give myself a cognomen which seems to be so much more important than I have been accustomed to think it."

"Oh then," interposed MacNair, "there is no hurry. You have an unquestioned right to take all the time for reflection that you require, provided that you are willing to remain a minor."

"I am not trying to evade the responsibility," I replied. "This matter may just as well be attended to now as at some future time."

Oqua then raising her eyes with a mischievous twinkle, asked with a comical expression of countenance:

"Shall it be Jack Adams?"

I pressed my finger on my lips and with a side glance at Captain Ganoe, replied: "No, not Jack Adams, if you please."

MacNair caught the silent message but could not interpret its purport, and looking first at me and then at Oqua, said:

"What kind of a sideshow is this being exhibited under our very eyes and we left in the dark? What have you against Jack Adams, that you should thus take the very first opportunity to put an end to his existence, so that he will not have even the poor tribute to his memory of an inscription on a marble slab?"

"No mystery at all," I replied. "Jack Adams is all right for a sailor but too commonplace for this land of romance and sublimity . I intend to exercise my right to select a more euphonious title, more in harmony with the part I hope to play," and turning to Oqua I asked: "Will you please to suggest some appropriate name? Something short and significant." After a moment's reflection she said:

"I have a name for you, Jack, that I think will be most appropriate. I have been told that you are a student, and our people greatly desire to obtain all the knowledge that is within reach of the outer world, its geography, history, manners and customs, and as you are inclined to be studious, we will doubtless want you as an instructor in our schools; and for that reason I select for you the name, Nequa, which signifies teacher."

I was much pleased with the name and even Captain Ganoe who was quite a stickler for established usages intimated that he regarded it as much more appropriate than commonplace Jack Adams. Of course I assented and Nequa became the name by which I am known in the inner world.

I was now a citizen of Altruria and had been assigned a position in the public service as a teacher which gave me the opportunities I so much coveted, to gather gems of wisdom for the benefit of my own country, which was grappling with great problems that had here been solved. I retired to my apartments to think. It had been just two months since we arrived at this great communal home, and I had recovered from the long strain to which I had been subjected for two years on the Ice King.

I now discovered that it was this strain brought on by the dangers which continually beset us, that had held me up. But now that all the dangers were past and the future bright with hope, a flood of bitter memories swept in upon me like a mighty avalanche. For the first time in years I gave way to uncontrollable emotions, as I buried my face in the soft silk cushioned sofa on which I reclined and wept as seldom mortals are doomed to weep.

How long I had remained thus I do not know, when I felt a gentle hand tenderly stroking my head and a voice I could not mistake said, in the most soothing tones:

"Nequa, Nequa child, what troubles you? Listen to me dear. It did not take me long to discover that under the smiling exterior of Jack Adams, you carried the aching heart of a stricken woman. Do not start. I am your friend. Confide in me. I know that there is some deep secret gnawing at your heartstrings, and that it relates to Captain Ganoe, and of which he is entirely unconscious. And I know that there must have been some great wrong in days gone by from which you suffer." I could stand no more and throwing both arms around Oqua's neck and drawing her down to me as the suffering child would its affectionate, sympathetic mother, I kissed her repeatedly between my sobs as I replied:

"Yes, my dear Oqua, you read me aright. But the crushing wrongs of the hideous past are irreparable and the future promises no healing balm for the wounds that have been inflicted. I must meet my fate alone. It would be wrong for me to burden you with my troubles. No! Let me bear them alone, on, on, to the bitter end. I must drain the cup of misery to its dregs absolutely alone."

Here I again broke down and gave way to another flood of tears. I wept until my brain seemed a livid flame and my heart bursting with despair while Oqua sat silently by my side stroking my head until the storm of contending emotions had time to subside when she said:

"Nequa, I am glad to find you in tears. They will give you relief as nothing else can. I knew you needed a friend, and I have come to constitute myself that friend. Now listen to me. I knew from the first that you were a woman and that Captain Ganoe did not suspect anything of the kind. I further discerned that there was a hidden chord which drew you to him and yet for some reason you dare not reveal yourself to him. This secret is wearing your life away. You must tell me all about it and I can, and I will, help you to bear it. When we look at things philosophically and see them on all sides, just as they are, there is no wound of body, mind or spirit that may not be healed. There is no wrong that is not too limited in its scope to effect any permanent injury. Our bounteous mother nature, has provided a healing balm for every wound if we will but search for it with the right spirit."

I could not be mistaken as to the spirit and purposes of this noble woman, nor resist her entreaties. She had penetrated my disguise and read my secret and I had every reason to respect her judgment. For years I had carried my burdens alone. Under the weight of the wrongs imposed upon me I had sought relief from the burden of grief in the exercise of an indomitable will, in a vain effort to force my heart to become, if need be, as cold as ice, and as hard as adamant. But it could not be. I was forced to realize that

"There can be no philosophy
Which steels the heart 'gainst ev'ry bitter woe;
'Tis not in nature, and it cannot be;
We cannot rend the heart, and not a throe
Of agony, tell how it feels a blow."

And now this agony, which I had carried so long, concealed under the smiling countenance of an assumed character, had forced a recognition. This was nature's demand for human sympathy, and the kind and loving heart of Oqua was here to respond. Much as I had desired to keep my sorrows deep buried in my own bosom, I could not repel this noble woman whose keen intuition had already divined my secret. I felt the need of just such sympathy as hers, and why should I spurn it from me? My soul went out to her and I felt impelled by some irresistible impulse to clasp her to my bosom and tell her all.

My heart was breaking with the silent misery that it had carried for years, unshared by a single human being, and which I resolved should be carried unobserved to the grave. Again I resolved anew that I would not even share it with this noble, sympathizing woman, but nature's floodgates, once opened for the outpouring of long suppressed sorrow, close no more to force it back upon the surcharged heart, and before I knew what I was doing I was folded to her bosom and weeping out the long pent up load of grief that had been gnawing at my heartstrings.

As I looked up into her face, I could see the cordial, heartfelt sympathy reflected from her beautiful countenance as she whispered:

"Go on, dear Nequa, and tell me all about it. Do not distrust a friend who is able to help you as I can. Remember what I told you that our bounteous Mother Nature, has provided a balm for every wound. This is no fanciful exaggeration, but a well ascertained truth."

"I do not distrust you," I replied, "and when I am more composed I will tell you all. I have done nothing to be ashamed of, but I cannot talk now. I am too much agitated. Call this evening and I will tell you all."

"So be it," said Oqua, "and I will be here early this evening. Do not be discouraged. Compose yourself and be of good cheer and all will be well," and imprinting a kiss on my forehead, she left me to my meditations, which now began to assume a more roseate hue. Some of the blackness of despair which had overwhelmed me had begun to depart, and I felt more hopeful and became more composed.

Chapter X

OQUA'S VISIT --THE REVELATION — A STORY OF PERFIDY AND WRONG — CASSIE VANNESS — RAPHAEL GANOE -RICHARD SAGE — A DESIGNING GUARDIAN — FALSE CHARGES AGAINST GANOE — A FRAUDULENT MARRIAGE — HOME ABANDONED — ON THE HIGH SEAS — JACK ADAMS — GANOE FOUND — EFFECTS OF A FALSE EDUCATION — LEGAL WRONGS VS. NATURAL JUSTICE — OQUA HOPEFUL.

As the sun disappeared behind the western edge of the verge, I was reclining upon my sofa awaiting the promised visit to Oqua. I was now as anxious to tell the story of my sorrows to a sympathizing friend as I had formerly been to conceal it from all the world. Since my conversation with Oqua, a longing sensation had come over me to confide to her the story of my life. The hour had arrived for my meeting with her, and a minute later she was by my side. Laying her hand on my head, she said:

"Nequa, I have come at the time designated, and in order to be able to assist you, I must not be left to surmise what is the matter. By the very act of telling me your troubles, you will to a certain extent obtain control over your own feelings, and thus take the first step toward finding a remedy."

"Then you shall know all, from my earliest recollection," said I. "My name is Cassie VanNess. I was born and raised near

New York City. My mother died when I was an infant, and I was cared for by my devoted old father, James VanNess, and a kind motherly colored woman who had been a servant in the family. My father died when I was fifteen years old, and I went to live with my guardian, Richard Sage, who was also the uncle and guardian of Raphael Ganoe, whom he had taken to raise when an infant. At this time Raphael was eighteen years of age. Our school days, of about five years, were the happiest, nay, I may say the **ONLY** really happy days of my life. When I was twenty and Raphael twenty-three years of age, he was offered a lucrative position on a ship engaged in the Chinese trade. During our vacations we had crossed the ocean together, and he desired to travel in the Orient. While on this voyage he expected to circumnavigate the globe, stopping at all the leading ports. On his return we were to be married.

"He promised to write to me at every available opportunity, and for the first few months his letters came regularly, always couched in the most affectionate terms and often referring to our coming marriage as the beacon light of all his fondest hopes. Then his letters ceased altogether, and though I wrote repeatedly to him, I never heard from him again.

"As the months rolled by, often at noontime, when the music of birds filled the air, and all was life and light, or at eventide, when the mellow twilight was over hill and dale, and the activities and light of day were giving place to the stillness and shadows of night; when the perfume of the flowers filled the air, or the yellow leaves of autumn fell about my feet, I, the forsaken, and perhaps forgotten, could have been seen seated beneath some broad-spreading tree, where we used to read and converse together. I would sit thus for hours in silent meditation, recalling the tender words and caresses of my absent lover. Then arising sad and disconsolate, I would leave the lonely spot and try to bravely wait and hope for the word that never came.

"My guardian professed great sympathy, and with seemingly the most poignant grief informed me that his nephew had committed some desperate crime in foreign lands for which he had been tried, convicted and sent to prison for a long term of years. Yet, with this black shadow resting upon him, the truth of which was vouched for by his uncle, I continued to write as it had been agreed between us and many were the tear stained missives I addressed to him, hoping that comrades on the ship would see that they reached him. Though he might be a criminal and an outcast from his kind, my affection for him never wavered for a single moment.

"My guardian, in order to make his deception more complete, pretended to deplore the actions of his nephew, and even his own unthoughtfulness, in telling me of them, and thus causing me so much suffering. He seemed to be aging very fast, and I feared that he, the only friend to whom I had never looked in vain for kindly counsel and advice, was falling into a decline from the crushing weight of what I believed to be our common sorrow, and consequently, my woman's sympathy and pity went out to him in what I regarded his disconsolate lot. "

"He fully realized the sincere and all pervading character of my sympathy for him, and took advantage of every opportunity to impress me with the dangerous state of his health. He intimated that the chief cause of his suffering, aside from the grief caused by the wayward and criminal course of his nephew, was the agony that it gave him to leave me all alone in the world, with no one to guard and protect me from the manifold dangers that threatened an inexperienced girl when thrown upon her own resources in this cold and unfeeling world. He did not ask my affection, except as a daughter, but suggested that under the circumstances, I had better become his wife, and then my position in the world, as his widow, would be secure. I would be protected against the intrusion of society and would be alone, as he felt sure I so much desired.

"'You are already in mourning,' he said, 'and yet, your grief is so indefinable that no one will be disposed to respect it as I do. Besides, situated as you now are, with no female companion, you are in some sense at the mercy of the evil-minded who never lose an opportunity to asperse the character of the good and pure, while as my wife, you would be safe, and your position honorable in the eyes of the world. I could then, even more than now, console you, and sympathize with you in your affliction.'

"I told him that I had never thought of my position as being in the least compromising, in the home of my lawful guardian, and if it was so, I would go away at once, but I could not be his wife. He besought me again and again, and I continued to give him the same answer. In the meantime, I was greatly troubled by what he had intimated regarding my compromising position in his house without a female companion. I had all faith and confidence in his unselfish and paternal regard for my welfare. For years, he had treated me with marked kindness and consideration, such as a loved daughter might expect from a kind and loving father. For this, I regarded him with the filial affection of a devoted and trusting nature. To leave him now, when stricken with sorrow and apparently with one foot in the grave, was repugnant to my feelings, as it seemed to me that it would be an act of base ingratitude, and yet, it was brought to my ears that people were beginning to make flippant and disrespectful remarks concerning my position. Yet I felt that I could not be so cruel as to forsake him now. The situation was a most trying one to me, as I never for a moment suspicioned that it had been made up for the occasion to influence my feelings.

"He continued his importunities under the guise of paternal counsel for my own good as a loved daughter. One day he brought me a newspaper clipping which stated that Raphael Ganoe had died in prison. He seemed to be so grief stricken and depressed, that for many days I feared that he would drop off at any moment, and he seemed so entirely dependent upon me that I dared not leave him for a moment, and yet my position was such that I must necessarily often give place to others, who had no such regard for him as I had. If I were his wife in the eyes of the world, I might do much more for him, and believing that my affianced husband was dead, I at last consented to become his legal wife and the ceremony was performed while he lay as I believed, on his dying bed. Two hours later, feeling lonely and disconsolate, I had gone into the library and taken a seat in one of the deep windows behind the curtains, where I was hidden from view."

"He seemed to have fallen asleep and my long watch was wearing upon me. I was exhausted and took this opportunity for rest and communion with my own thoughts. I soon fell into a reverie, in which the past came up before me like a panorama, and again the fancy I was with my handsome, happy lover when suddenly I heard voices in the adjoining room where I had left my guardian asleep. A strange voice asked :

"'Where is your young wife?'

"'Gone to her room to rest,' said my guardian. 'She thinks I am very sick and she has watched by my side, to minister to my pains until she is worn out. I got easy and told her that she might go and rest herself, as I would, now that the pains had ceased for the time, be able to take a long nap. She remained until I was seemingly fast asleep and then she tiptoed out of the room as softly as a cat for fear she would awaken me.'

"'You worked it well,' said the stranger, 'but what shall I write to Ganoe? He has written me a long letter engaging my services as his attorney to find out all about Cassie. What shall I say to him?'

"'Here,' said my guardian, 'are the letters I have written to him in regard to Cassie's change of mind. You can take your cue from these and be governed accordingly.'

"'But,' asked the attorney, 'what if she should suspicion something and drop a letter to Ganoe into some street box? It might prove to be a serious matter for us if she should learn the truth.'

"'I have provided for that,' said my guardian. 'There is a round million in the deal for us, after all the expenses are paid, and no mail can reach him on the ship, without being inspected by a man who has as much interest as we have in preventing him from hearing from Cassie. If a letter should not be intercepted by my agent in the post office, which is not likely, it would be intercepted at the ship. So rest easy in regard to this matter. There is no danger; besides she is now my wife, and I have all the legal rights of a husband. But as we want to avoid everything like friction, it is best to prevent Ganoe from returning to America, which will not be difficult if it is managed well.'

"'All right, said the lawyer, 'provided you deal squarely with me. I am the only one who could defeat the plan and of course I will not lose a million to do that.'

"'Of course not,' said my guardian, 'and you know that I have even more to lose than you have ----a life long reputation for integrity and purity of character, which to a man in my position is worth more than money. It would cut off my income as a favorite administrator on large estates.'

"'Well, we are both in the same boat, 'laughed the lawyer, 'and we can well afford to trust each other. I guess that now you have recovered from your very serious illness we may expect to hold our conferences at the proper place.'

"'Oh certainly, 'laughed my guardian, 'and my lovely bride will not object to my being away, as she is in widow's weeds, mourning the untimely death of her first and only love. So, good day. I must rest and take a long and very refreshing nap to account for my unexpected recovery.'

"'Just so,' laughed the lawyer, and I heard the door close behind him.

"The conversation that I had overheard froze the very blood in my veins. I learned that I had been deliberately deceived and not only robbed of a large fortune, but had been robbed of my affianced husband. Worse than this, I had been induced to take a step that made me false to him and at the same time precluded the possibility of our ever consummating our plighted faith without violating the marriage laws, as under the law I was his aunt and marriage with him would have been a crime, for which under the law I could be imprisoned for a long term of years.'

"My whole nature arose in revolt against the iniquity that had been perpetrated against me. I determined to find Raphael and explain the whole matter to him. I hastily wrote a note to my guardian and left it where he would be sure to find it, denouncing his treachery and informing him that under no circumstances would I ever enter his door again."

"I made my way into the city and disguising myself in male attire I succeeded in finding a position as cabin boy on a steamer bound for Liverpool. I was determined to find Raphael. I kept up the search for nearly fifteen long years, visiting almost every part of the known world, and at last found him at San Francisco, on the eve of starting on an expedition to the north polar regions. Before revealing myself to him I wanted to ascertain beyond any doubt whatever, from his own lips, in just what light he would regard my marriage to his uncle and my subsequent long career on the high seas in male attire. So I applied for a place on the Ice King and succeeded in getting the position of scientist. I cultivated the acquaintance of the Captain, secured his confidence so far that he related to me the story of his life, which gave me the opportunity I wanted to draw him out, and soon learned, what I had come to dread, that the prejudices engendered by social usages were stronger than his sense of natural justice, and I heard my own conduct denounced as perfidious and vile. But for the sudden sounding of the alarm I must have fallen at his feet and thus have in all probability revealed my identity."

"But I was saved that bitter humiliation and now, after a long and perilous voyage, locked up with him on the same ship, I am at last permitted to pour my tale of woe into sympathetic ears, far away from the land where legal wrongs are honored while natural rights are regarded as disreputable."

Oqua had listened to my story without a single interruption, and with a sympathetic interest which drew me closer to her than ever. When I ceased speaking, she looked at me with a puzzled curiosity, which I shall never forget as she remarked:

"Your guardian certainly committed a great wrong against you, and under the operation of an awakened conscience, I can well understand that his remorse would be most excruciatingly painful, but you have not committed any wrong, and I do not understand what it is that you are feeling so badly about. The blame all rested with your guardian and the fact that you discovered his perfidy so soon, and at the same time discovered that the man to whom you were the betrothed wife, only awaiting the time set for the consummation, was still living, ought, it seems to me, to have been a source of rejoicing. While the deception practiced upon you was painful to contemplate, it brought with it a certain measure of compensation. Had you failed to make this discovery, you might have unwittingly violated the most sacred obligation, that to your betrothed husband. The wrong might have been much worse."

"You have mistaken my meaning," I said. "I was not under that obligation to Raphael that you seem to think. I had only promised to become his wife but I was actually married to another man. Under the circumstances I do not see how the wrong could have been worse, and I, as its innocent victim, was certainly excusable for feeling badly about it. The wonder is how I could bear it at all."

"If I was mistaken," said Oqua, "in regard to your relations to Raphael Ganoe, I fear that your explanation of the situation only makes the matter more difficult to understand. I certainly understood you to say that you loved Ganoe and that he loved you, and that you had both agreed to go through life as husband and wife. This you had a perfect right to do, and this agreement constitutes a marriage bond that cannot be set aside without sufficient cause, as long as you both live, and hence you could not become the wife of another man, without violating the most sacred of all obligations. And if by misrepresentation you were induced to enter into any such relation while Ganoe was living and true to you, such relation would be on the face of it, null and void."

"But I was married to my guardian," I said. "Actually married. The clerk of the court had issued the license which was a legal permit for us to marry, and the minister pronounced us man and wife according to the solemn rites of the church. My guardian took an obligation to love, cherish and protect and I, an obligation to love, honor and obey; and then the minister invoked the blessing of heaven upon our union and pronounced the solemn warning to all who might object: 'Whom God hath joined together, let no man put asunder.' Yes, I was actually married to Richard Sage, according to law and the sacred rites of the church."

"The more you explain, my dear Nequa, the more incomprehensible your ideas of marriage become. You say that you were actually married to Richard Sage. That God joined you together, but before He could do so,· a permit had to be granted by the clerk of the court. Yet, in your own soul you repudiated this fraudulent marriage, and for nearly fifteen years you searched for your betrothed husband, to whom you felt bound by the laws which God had implanted in your own soul. To me it seems that this first engagement to Raphael Ganoe was the only true marriage, in which God had joined you together and that the court and the minister united to put you asunder. Your own inner consciousness, the spark of divinity that is in you, forced you to take this view of the transaction. From all the facts, just as you relate them, I must still insist that you were not married to Richard Sage. That the ceremony was a fraud and could not annul your obligations to Raphael Ganoe. Your actions demonstrate, that your own true self, took the same view of the matter, and that when you found your betrothed husband you loyally stood by his side in the hazardous effort to reach the pole, and now you are here with him in this inner world where we regard it as our first duty to accept the true and discard the false in all of our relations to each other, and to the universal system of which we form a part."

"I agree with you," I replied, "that my marriage to Richard Sage was false, and that in order to be true to myself and my higher convictions of duty to my absent lover, when I learned that he was still living, I was forced to rend these legal bonds regardless of the consequences; but still, in the eyes of the law, of society and the church, I was the wife of my guardian, the uncle of Raphael Ganoe, and hence his aunt, and as such could never become his wife. Yet I realized that I was united to Raphael in bonds of affection that never could and never should be broken. But all the powers of law, religion, and society were united to hold me to a union secured by deception, which I loathed and abhorred. It was the environments established by this world wide power that held me incarcerated, as it were, in a prison, from which there was no escape but the grave."

"Thank you," said Oqua, "for the light which you have thrown on the present state of your outer world civilization. It seems almost incomprehensible that the laws and usages of any people would seek to make right wrong and wrong right, but I can readily turn to a corresponding period in our own history and trace the evolutionary forces which must now be at work among your people. The old institutional life is ever striving to preserve its forms and ceremonies while the advancing spirit of freedom is continually protesting. At first the advocates of the old order, persecute all who protest against its dictum, and this protest in the name of liberty, often only means license. Both extremes are essentially wrong. But the friction between these two elements, in the end will lead to the discovery of the truth upon which both extremes can unite, and this truth will make them indeed free. The manifest progress of the race is in the direction of the truth, and its logical culmination must be the establishment of altruistic conditions in all the relations which exist between individual members of the human family."

"Well, I am glad that you have at last penetrated my meaning," I said. "The misunderstanding grew out of my inability to formulate my own thought, so as to adapt it to your Altruistic conceptions. I like the word altruism, but the thought that it expresses is so little understood in the outer world, that the word is, as far as I know, generally excluded from our common school dictionaries, while in this country I find that it forms a necessary part of your every day vocabulary. I realize that all of my troubles grew out of environments which were the legitimate product of the false premises from which we drew our conclusions. In speaking of myself as actually the wife of my guardian I only used the popular phraseology to express the conceptions of the people among whom I was raised. They regarded the license and the ceremony as the actual marriage without reference to the plighted troth of devoted lovers. I only used their language to express their conceptions, while my own were expressed by my actions."

"Thank you," said Oqua. "I surmised that you spoke the language of your environments rather than your honest convictions, but I wanted you to say it yourself. You know that I insisted that you should say just what you mean and leave nothing for me to surmise. In all that you have to say, I want you to draw the line clearly between the true and the false, in thought and action, just as you understand the terms, and then we can ascertain where the trouble is and take steps to remove it.'

"You are now in a country where truth alone is recognized as a standard for the regulation of human conduct, and it seems that there ought to be much in the way of mutual explanations between you and Captain Ganoe, and then all will be well."

"I dare not risk it," I said. " I thought just as you do when I secured a position on the Ice King, but I deemed it advisable to conceal my identity until I had ascertained in just what light he would regard the course I had taken. The opportunity came as I have already told you and as yet I have discovered no indications that he has in any way modified his views in regard to such matters. I have ascertained beyond a doubt from two years' association with him, that in him all the prejudices of the popular education of the outer world, its laws, usages and religious notions have crystallized. If he knew that I had spent years, associated with men, in the character of Jack Adams, the sailor, his sense of propriety would be shocked, and I should forfeit his respect, which would be something that I could not bear."

"I cannot see," said Oqua, "how he could cease to respect you. I know that as the scientist of the Ice King, he entertains the most exalted opinion of your ability, courage and refinement of character."

"Yes, Oqua, I doubt not that he respects me as Jack Adams, the sailor. He has given me numerous proofs of that. But as Cassie VanNess in that garb he would regard me as unwomanly and immodest, much below the standard of propriety and respectability of the women of the outer world, with whom he would be willing to associate on terms of equality. Remember that his education, like my own was as far removed as possible from the spirit of altruism. When I left my guardian's home I was penniless, except for an allowance known as 'pin money.' By the marriage ceremony, my fortune had been transferred to Richard Sage. As a woman, I stood no show of being able to acquire a competency, besides I was liable to pursuit and arrest.

I had no legal grounds for divorce, and if I had been discovered as the absconding wife of Richard Sage, the multimillionaire, the courts would have declared me insane, and I would have been incarcerated, most likely for life, in some lunatic asylum. Hence it was from necessity, rather than choice, that I donned male attire and sought employment as a cabin boy. My education, tact and close attention to business led to more lucrative positions which required ability as well as a strict integrity and close application. By rigid economy, I succeeded in accumulating a moderate competence. As a woman I could not have even procured a comfortable subsistence; but I was in male attire, associated with men in all my relations to society, and hence in the eyes of the world my womanly character was under a cloud. For this reason I did not care to reveal my identity to Captain Ganoe until I knew that he would approve the course I had taken. As for myself I was prepared for altruistic principles. My association with the working classes gave me a knowledge of their condition, and I familiarized myself with the best thought of their leaders. But Captain Ganoe had been differently situated. He had continued to move in the narrow circle in which he was born. I had hoped that experience with the world had broadened his views. But I found that I was mistaken. I have studied his feelings and hence have resolved never to give him the opportunity to reproach me for my unwomanly disguise and associations."

"How could he reproach you, Nequa, when he realized that it was all for love of him?"

"You cannot, my dear Oqua, educated as you were in the most advanced thought of this altruistic civilization, realize the almost irresistible power of prejudices when they have been incorporated into the education of a people for thousands of years. They constitute a race belief; the correctness of which the people seldom, if ever, heard questioned. 'When I assumed male attire and associated myself with men in the ranks of labor, I knew that I invited not only social ostracism, but laid myself liable to arrest and imprisonment, if my disguise was discovered. And Captain Ganoe as a high spirited gentleman of the old school, could not unite his destinies with such a social outcast."

"But surely," said Oqua, "he will not entertain such mistaken conceptions of honor when he learns that the people of this inner world with out an exception, would honor you for your heroic devotion to your bridal troth and regard Captain Ganoe as the most fortunate of men in having such a companion."

"That may indeed be true, sometime," I said, "but before I reveal myself to him, I must hear from his own lips such expressions of opinion as will demonstrate that he would not regard the career of Jack Adams, under the circumstances, as unworthy, immodest and unwomanly. There is a deep seated prejudice in the outer world against 'mannish women,' and the donning of male attire is prohibited by law, and what is even worse, it is regarded as positively disgraceful. Hence I must know that he of his own option has abandoned all these prejudices, before I will consent to be known to him as Cassie Van Ness. "

"I believe," said Oqua, "that his association with Altrurians will certainly give him a higher regard for truth and correspondingly weaken the influence of time honored errors. We can very easily ascertain his views and if we should find them adverse, do not be discouraged, for the atmosphere of truth which surrounds him is creative in its influence and will surely establish itself in his mind. An error is powerless to hold anyone in thrall very long where truth is cultivated and free to express itself in thought and action. Truth is eternal and cannot be destroyed, while error is transitory and disappears with the ignorance on which it is based."

"I will leave this matter to you," I said, "with this understanding, that to Captain Ganoe I must remain simply Jack Adams, or Nequa, until I know that he approves and appreciates the sacrifices made by Cassie VanNess. I love him too well to be willing to face his disapproval, but knowing the purity of my own purposes, I will never put myself in a position that will imply even in the remotest degree that I was wrong. My self respect forbids this. My heart tells me that I was right and I will never apologize to any human being for the course I have taken, and least of all to Captain Ganoe, for love of whom I have braved the danger of social ostracism as well as the dangers incident to the life of a sailor, from the blistering heat of the tropics to the intense cold of the frigid zones. I certainly could never ask him to forgive me for loving him so well."

Oqua threw her arms around my neck and kissed me most affectionately, saying :

"My dear Nequa, I knew that I was not mistaken in the estimate that I had placed on your mental and spiritual character. You have a great work to do, not only in the education of our people, but a work for your own people. Intercourse between the inner and outer worlds must be re-opened. In this work much depends upon the crew of the Ice King, as you are the only people among us from the educated classes who have ever penetrated the frozen regions which surround the verges. Our people will of course assist in every way possible. But my dear Nequa, a still greater work depends upon you, more than upon any of the others, in which we can be of but little assistance."

"And what is that greater work?" I asked. "And how could I get along without assistance? No matter what I undertake I want you as a tutor. To me it seems, that in this inner world, I have everything to learn, and I must have a teacher at every step."

"And I, too," said Oqua, "have much to learn from you. All that I have learned of the outer world came from MacNair and the few books which he saved from the sinking ship. With the Ice King comes a well selected library of standard works and three scholarly, well read people, and from this, I anticipate a most valuable addition to our knowledge, especially of a scientific, geographical and historical character, which has been hidden from the people of the inner world. We have, it seems, made more progress along lines of a social, economic and ethical nature and in mechanical inventions. So while we need that knowledge which can be more readily acquired in the outer world, your people need the lessons taught by our progress along other lines. Our libraries are filled with these lessons and the work evidently marked out for you is to gather this knowledge for the benefit of your own people. In this you will have the cordial co-operation of the scholars of the inner world."

"This," I said, "is certainly a work in which I am most anxious to engage, just as soon as I can qualify myself for the task, and l will certainly need all the help I can get. I do indeed want the people of America, the great republic of the outer world, to learn that the highest ideals of their revolutionary sires, are not mere 'glittering generalities,' but realities, and have been carried out to their logical culmination in this country with the most beneficent results to humanity. To this end, that they should not only learn this most significant fact, but that they should have laid before them a clear and concise statement of the methods that have been used so successfully to produce these results and evolve this wonderful Altrurian civilization. I most keenly realize that it is my duty to accomplish this work for humanity, but when I think of the vast libraries, written in a strange tongue, that must not only be read but studied, in order to trace the operation of the evolutionary forces which have produced these grand results, I am overwhelmed at the contemplation of the magnitude of the task set before me."

"Do not be alarmed," said Oqua, "at the multitudinous array of ponderous volumes. These records are only preserved for reference. The scholars of every age have been over them, with the special object in view of condensing and simplifying their lessons, for the benefit of students who could not afford to neglect other studies of the most pressing importance, in order to familiarize themselves with the details of so many thousands of years of history. Hence the lessons of permanent value, such for instance as relate to the social, economic and ethical progress of the people, have been carefully arranged in the form of attractive condensations, with marginal references to the authorities. With these lessons from History, designed for the use of the pupils in our schools, the students can rapidly trace every step in our progress, from the original half-civilized condition down to the present time, and if there is any matter which they wish to examine more closely, the marginal references will direct them to volume and page. So, my dear Nequa, you will find that the greater part of your work which looks so overwhelming, is ready made for you, in our School Concordances. Another thing will help you; these lessons of progress have all been treated in the shape of allegories and historical romances, in order to make them attractive. Perhaps you could not transmit them to your own people in a better shape, than by translating some of the works that bear directly upon what they need to understand. These works trace in a most attractive form the operation of every evolutionary force which has contributed to our Altrurian civilization as you find it today."

"This, indeed, my dear Oqua, relieves my mind of a load of doubt and apprehension, which amounted almost to a dread, whenever I thought of reading so many ponderous volumes in order to get a clear idea of the forces which have contributed to your present ideal conditions. It also explains to me how it is, that your entire people have such a clear understanding Of every economic, social and ethical problem. These things are taught to the children in your primary schools."

"Yes," said Oqua, " the blessings of a high state of civilization can only be preserved by educating the children of a country into a comprehensive understanding of the laws of progress, by which these blessings are secured. While a very few can set the machinery in motion by which the masses may be relieved of any burdens that can be imposed upon them, yet unless the children are universally educated in regard to these matters, a few will be able to reenslave them. These so-called 'great problems' which you inform me are puzzling the brains of your statesmen, ought to be thoroughly understood by the children. Hence we teach these things to children while the mind is the most receptive and the most capable of acquiring knowledge rapidly."

"But," I remarked, "it sounds so strange to hear you speak of children thoroughly understanding these questions of worldwide importance, with which the great statesmen of the outer world have grappled for ages, without finding a solution."

"Nothing strange about it," said Oqua. "The mind of the child is plastic and is remarkable for the facility with which it receives and retains impressions. When it reaches the adult stage these impressions become crystallized and are hard to change. Hence the importance of starting the child rightly, with correct habits of thought on these vital matters, upon which its future weal, and that of every other human being depends. If the impressions on the mind of the child are erroneous, they are liable to crystallize and be retained through life, no matter how absurd they may be. As an apt illustration of this tendency, I have only to refer to some of the notions which were popular in this country at the time when the old economic system had run its course and was producing widespread poverty and suffering among the people. At that period all of the exchanges among the people were on a money basis, and the few had control of the money while the many were not able to utilize their labor to produce the wealth they needed because they could not get the money to effect the necessary exchanges. The reformers of that time were loud in the demand for more money, while the controlling minds among the majority insisted that the one thing needed was less money so that the money they had would purchase more; and others were equally sure that more tax on products of foreign countries was just the thing to relieve the industrial depression by holding the home market for the products of our own labor. Keep foreign products out by a high tariff and protect home industry, was the doctrine. But we cannot help smiling as we read that these same people who wanted to exclude foreign products from our markets in order to protect our own labor, expected to get revenues from a tax on foreign goods to run the government. It is difficult to imagine at this time that any sane people ever entertained such absurd and self contradictory opinions, but it is nevertheless a fact, as demonstrated by the history of that time. These absurd notions could not have found lodgement in the human mind, if as children, the people had been trained to correct habits of reasoning."

"And such," I said, "are the notions which predominate at this time in my own country and the result is, that a few are very rich while the many are hard pressed and poor. The few who protest against this system are denounced as cranks, agitators and dangerous characters."

"This is just what might be expected," said Oqua. "Like causes produce like effects. The masses of mankind are always prone to deride and persecute isolated individuals who know more than the mass, which is physically so much more powerful. This is the protest of brute force against mental, moral and spiritual superiority. This was why your Jesus was crucified and this is why your reformers of the present day are denounced as cranks, agitators and dangerous characters. It is an invariable trait of human nature in a certain stage of development."

"I have long entertained these same views," I replied, "but the object lessons which can be drawn from your history will cover all these questions and they ought to reach our people with the first announcement of the discovery of this inner world where all the great problems of human development have been solved. I have found your language remarkably easy to learn and from what you say, I expect to find lessons from your history equally easy, but still I need your assistance. I want to make the very best possible use of my opportunities, and to that end, I want the benefit of your experience, observation and knowledge of Altrurian civilization as it is today ."

"Then, to begin," said Oqua, "my work as counsellor, I would advise you to complete your account of the expedition which brought you into this inner world; a brief description of your reception; the civilization you found as it appeared to you at first sight, and the information that you gathered from intercourse with the people in regard to the progressive development of the country from the semi-barbarous conditions which existed in early times. This ought to be sent to the people of the outer world just as soon as possible. It will make an excellent introduction to a series of works consisting of your own observations in regard to the existing educational system, customs of the people and business methods, together with translations from our literature that will be of use to your people. In the preparation of the account of your expedition and your discoveries, you will need no assistance and when it comes to translations from our libraries and travel over the five grand divisions, you will have the help of ripe scholars wherever you go."

"Concerning the work here in this inner world," I said, "among such a people, I have no doubt that it will be well done, but how are we to transmit the information across the ice barriers at the verge? I at first had great hopes from your airships, but I find that while they are all right in this serene climate, they would be worse than useless in the stormy atmosphere of the outer world and as at present constructed the occupants could not live an hour in the intense cold of the Frigid Zones."

"I do not," said Oqua, "apprehend any insurmountable difficulty from this source. The inventors of the airship know nothing about storms and cold and hence made no provisions for guarding against them. The case is different with arctic explorers. Our inventors have learned how to navigate the atmosphere, with ease and safety. This is the main point. Now you people of the outer world can take up the work where our inventors left off, and construct ships which can ride the storm. I have learned since my return from the Minerva congress, that Captain Battell is working on this problem with good prospects of success. I do not believe that there is anything impossible to the human mind when it acts in harmony with nature's laws. The airship factory at Lake Byblis is at your service, with every facility of material, machinery and mechanical skill. All that is needed is a comprehensive understanding of outer world atmospheric conditions, and you brought that knowledge with you. This is all that our inventors needed in order to enable them to construct an airship that would be equal to every emergency."

"You give me great encouragement," I said. "Captain Battell has asked me to assist in this work by making experimental voyages to the verges, in order to test the proposed improvements and make observations."

"Then all seems to be gong well," said Oqua, "but there is no time to lose. You must be gathering materials for your first volume as rapidly as possible for I feel that it will soon be needed. To this end, I want you and Captain Ganoe to go with me tomorrow to Orbitello, to see how business is carried on. What do you think of it?"

"Think of it!" I said. "I have been very anxious to take this trip and have only been awaiting your return so that we might have company, who could assist us in our observations."

"Then," said Oqua, "we will start early, and I will telephone Polaris and Dione to meet us and bring Battell and Huston. I know that Norrena will be most happy to meet you. He is a walking encyclopedia of knowledge and I know that you will enjoy his acquaintance. "But," she added after a moment's hesitation, "you need rest and I will go. Be of good cheer. All is well, and do not forget that there is a wonderful power in truth when it is left free, to remove errors from the pathway of human progress,"---and kissing me goodnight, she was gone.

Chapter XI

AN AIR VOYAGE — CHANGE OF SCENERY — HOMES FOR MOTHERS — EVOLUTION FROM COMPETITIVE INDIVIDUALISM — THE MOUNTAINS — BATTELL JOINS US — ORBITELLO — A PERPETUAL WORLD'S FAIR — DEPARTMENT OF EXCHANGE — THE BUSINESS OF A CONTINENT — NORRENA — PUBLIC PRINTING — THE COUNCIL — ALL MATTERS SUBMITTED TO THE PEOPLE — LIBRARY OF UNIVERSAL KNOWLEDGE.

Every preparation had been made for our proposed voyage into the interior and as the sun appeared from behind the eastern edge of the southern verge we were embarking on the airship. Our party consisted of MacNair, lola, Oqua, Captain Ganoe and myself. I took my place at the helm with MacNair and told him that I wanted to take lessons in aerial navigation. He kindly explained the use of the electric keyboard which controlled the machinery, and I found it so simple that I felt no need of an instructor. In this placid atmosphere all I had to do was to set the ship in the direction we wanted to go and turn on the power until we reached the speed at which we desired to travel. All the motions of the vessel were under absolute control. I found that the steering apparatus could be readily adjusted to overcome a light wind, and reasoned that the same principles would enable us to ride the storm. This first practical experience in aerial navigation gave me confidence.

Our course was a little north of west, and we were soon leaving the great communal agricultural district which we now regarded as our home. According to our reckoning it was now the lst of February and I had begun to figure whether it would be possible for us to be ready to attempt the proposed journey to the outer world during the northern summer. If we did, it would certainly require intense application. These thoughts were continually running through my mind, and they spurred me up to gather all the information possible for the book that I was preparing.

The country over which we were passing was still agricultural, but the surface was more broken and the general arrangements were changed accordingly, presenting to our vision an agreeable variety. We still saw the magnificent communal homes with correspondingly large areas of cultivated lands, but we also saw cottages gathered into groups, with large public buildings which MacNair informed us were schools, public halls, homes for the aged, hospitals, and especially homes for prospective mothers who felt that the ideal conditions which these homes afforded would secure the best possible development of their offspring.

I was forcibly struck by the number and grandeur of these homes for mothers. I had noticed that every communal home had its department for the care of mothers, and now I found that the grandest structures that I had ever seen were devoted exclusively to this purpose. In reply to my inquiries I was informed that this care for motherhood was a universal feature throughout the inner world. But in this, as in everything else liberty prevails. The mother is always free to select her own conditions. Many prefer these large public homes which are exclusively under the control of women, while others, with different temperaments, prefer greater exclusiveness in their own apartments, but all alike make this period of prospective motherhood, one in which all the environments are calculated to produce the best possible pre-natal influences upon the unborn child.

For this purpose, different temperaments require different surroundings. The impressions produced by beautiful scenery and social enjoyments on one, may be more readily produced by reading, lectures, music and intellectual entertainments on another. The unperverted taste of the mother is always accepted as a sure guide to what is best in each case, and the best is always provided.

While the country over which we were passing did not have the same artificial appearance as if laid out by one uniform pattern, like that where we had been located since our arrival in Altruria, I still noticed the general tendency of the people to get together in large communities. We passed over large districts of wild lands which afforded ample opportunities for isolated homes but nowhere did we see anything of the kind. This induced Captain Ganoe to ask if there was any law against people getting out by themselves and cultivating these wild lands.

"Nothing but the natural law," said Oqua, "which impels people to do that which is the most conducive to their happiness. The people of this country do not like drudgery and they have learned by experience that in order to avoid drudgery, they must work together on a large scale, as one family, each for all and all for each. In the olden time, people in their ignorance scattered into single families consisting of a man and wife and their children. They wasted their energies in their isolated efforts, and were at the mercy of the few who had the intelligence to work together. When the masses became more intelligent they gathered into communities and co-operated with each other to make the most out of their labor and to avoid the payment of tribute to speculators who did not work at all. They soon found that they could not possibly consume all that they were able to produce and they began to work less and enjoy more."

"But," asked the Captain, "have you no arrangement by which a man and his wife could get out on these wild lands and make a home for themselves?"

"We certainly have no arrangement," said Oqua, "that would prevent their doing so. But if they should try such an experiment it would not last long. As soon as they found themselves toiling incessantly to procure a bare subsistence, while the great masses in the communities were spending eleven twelfths of their time in the enjoyment of rest and pleasurable recreations, they would seek admission into a large communal home, where all who are willing to perform their share of the labor are welcome."

"But," said the Captain, "you say that the people of this country once lived in isolated homes. The people in the outer world do so now, and they feel that to be the best possible condition for the development of the highest qualities. How were the individualists of this country persuaded to give up their individual holdings and accept in lieu thereof a community interest in the products of their own labor?"

"They outgrew their preconceived opinions," said Oqua.

"Among the reformers of the olden time none were more earnest than a large and very intelligent class of individualists, who believed that the people ought to own the land, and that the individual holder ought to pay the community for its use, in proportion to its value as land, not counting the value of the improvements. These reformers agreed to the abolition of land titles, and in accordance with the doctrines which they had promulgated long and earnestly, they took their lands in severalty and paid the community a tax for its use. As individualists, they could not object to other people forming communities and having all things in common. But when they discovered how much more they had to work than their neighbors, they were true to their own interests and joined the communities where their labor became so much more effective. They found that instead of sacrificing any of their individual rights by so doing, they actually made those rights more valuable by being relieved of drudgery. The land tax to the community was abolished in the course of time, and then any individual might take a homestead and cultivate it in his own way without being taxed for the privilege of doing so, but this right is never exercised, as it would deprive the individuals thus setting up for themselves, of free access to the common wealth of the community, and the common advantages which belong to community life. They could only enter the communal homes as guests and strangers, and while free entertainment is never refused, proud spirited individualists would never think of securing a subsistence by visiting around. They would naturally prefer doing their share of the work to create the common stock. And hence our individualists are all in our communal homes and have no desire for individual holdings of any kind. Their community interest in the common wealth is worth vastly more to them than all the wealth that they could create by individual effort."

"But," asked the Captain, "do you permit no private ownership of property at all in these communities?"

"Yes, we do," said Oqua. "All persons may accumulate property which they create by personal labor, if they wish to burden themselves with the care of it. But as there is an abundance in the common stores to supply every want, there is no motive for the private ownership of anything but personal belongings which are ordinarily of no value to anyone else. Members of the community may have anything they need out of the common stock and intelligent people would not encumber themselves with the care of more than they have a use for. The greed for the accumulation of property which I am informed is so prevalent in the outer world, if manifested here would be taken as an evidence of insanity and would be treated accordingly. It is very difficult for the average Altrurian to realize that people should ever desire to hoard up wealth which is impossible for them to consume But when we scan the pages of our early history at the time when legal money was the medium of exchange and the standard of value, the people made a mad scramble for money, in which they disregarded every interest of humanity."

We were now approaching a region where art and nature seemed to have united in one mighty and persistent effort to excel each other in the entrancing beauty and rugged grandeur that could be added to the picture. On either side was a broad expanse of cultivated lands, interspersed with parks, lawns and ornamental grounds, which revealed the work of the most artistic landscape gardeners. Beneath us the Cocytas meandered its way toward the distant ocean, between its wooded shores, like a shining pathway of silver, while before us the great continental divide with its towering mountain peaks piercing the clouds, closed our view towards the west. At one moment we were admiring the rugged grandeur of this lovely mountain chain and at another entranced by the beauty of the highly ornamented landscape, where art had improved upon nature. Take it all in all, the scenery presented to our view from the cabin of our airship, sailing at a height of several thousand feet, was sublime, beyond the power of words to describe.

As we neared the mountains, MacNair took charge of the ship and made a detour toward the south, which brought into view the mighty canon through which the Cocytas reaches the plain. On either side were mountain torrents dashing over the rocks on their way to join the waters of the deep flowing river. Here, nature in all her majesty revealed her titanic powers. But suddenly another scene opened upon our vision, which art revealed itself as master of all the forces of nature. It was more like a city than anything we had seen since leaving San Francisco. And yet it was very much unlike any city I have ever seen. I was bewildered by its sudden appearance upon this wonderful panorama of nature and art which seemed to hold us spell bound.

Palatial buildings in white and silver appeared in every direction, surrounded by highly ornamented grounds. No smoke, no dust and no miserable shanties to remind us of the poverty and misery which characterized the cities of the outer world. In the distance, it presented a panorama of beauty and grandeur, more like the paintings of a gorgeous midsummer dream, than any real achievement of human skill and human taste. It was more like the fancied abode of the gods than the dwelling place of men.

This was Orbitello, and as it lay spread out before us, it presented a scene beyond my powers of description. It was located on an elevated plateau and almost enclosed within a bend of the river, which flows around it on three sides, the west, south and east, like a silver highway, over which electric yachts of almost every size and description were gliding. It was a dream of beauty that once seen, could never be erased from the memory.

"This," said MacNair, "is our continental headquarters. Here, was at one time a large city, but every remnant of the old structures was removed long ago. The location, however, is so central that it was selected as our chief center of business for all the departments of the public service. It is a favorite gathering place for large numbers of people from all parts of the world. Hence the number of buildings for the accommodation of visitors. It is in fact a perpetual World's Fair, a miniature picture of the world as it is today. There is no better place to study the civilization of the inner world in all its phases."

MacNair was interrupted by a familiar voice with the well remembered "Ship Ahoy!" and as we turned around to see from whence it came, another airship came alongside, and we exchanged greetings with our old shipmates, Battell and Huston, and our saviors, as we called them, Polaris and Dione, who both addressed us in English.

"Please speak Altrurian," I said. "I have abandoned English except in cases of emergency, as I am anxious to perfect myself in the use of your native tongue. Remember that I have become a citizen of Altruria, and have no desire to perpetuate the use of a foreign language."

"And we," replied Polaris," want to perfect our selves in the use of English, as we want to visit America and talk like natives, just as soon as a ship can be constructed that will enable us to navigate the frozen regions without being frozen ourselves."

"And one," I responded, "that can hold to its course with a side wind of a velocity from fifty to one hundred miles an hour."

"Have no fears on that score," interposed Battell. "We have the principal parts of the machinery completed, and all that remains to be done, is for you to take a trial trip to the southern verge and see how it will work in a storm, and in the meantime we will try our hands at constructing one that will be proof against the cold of a polar winter. Better go to the southern verge now, while it is comparatively temperate and test our improvements in a gale."

"All right," I said. "I am willing. But who will go with me? I ought to have the assistance of someone who could not only stand the exposure, but be able to make observations. It will keep one person busy to manage the ship during a storm, no matter how perfect your machinery may be."

"I suggest," said Battell, "that you take Lief and Eric, who are first-class mechanics as well as scientists. This is their request, and it ought to be granted. We need both Huston and Captain Ganoe, to assist in the construction of a cold proof vessel. This is the plan of work that I suggest. How will it suit you?"

"Anything suits me that looks toward success," I said. "Since you have already completed the inventions that I had contemplated, it is but fair that you dictate how they should be used until we can improve on your improvements, which, by the way I hope may not be necessary."

"Oh yes, it will," said Battell. "Just as soon as there is no room for improvement, everything will be perfect, and with nothing to do, nothing to live for and no improvements to make, constituted as we are now, we would very likely be just as unhappy, as we are now anxious to improve the airship or to accomplish any other object that is dear to us. This is a working world and we are workers, and when there is no work to do, there will be no use for us on our present plane of development."

"You talk like a philosopher," I said. "One would think you had graduated from an Altrurian university."

"So I have," said Battell. "Were you not talking Altrurian philosophy all the time we were together on the Ice King? So I was to some extent prepared for what we have found in this highly developed country."

"But what's the matter?" I asked, as Battell's airship came to a full halt, and seemingly began to fall. Before I recovered from my surprise, it had settled lightly on the top of a stupendous structure, and MacNair was evidently aiming for the same place, as he set our ship to circling around in the way I have often described. I had seen the practical workings of one of Battell's improvements, and could not help seeing that it was an undoubted success. The mechanism that would control the vessel while dropping toward the earth, seemed to me, more difficult of construction than that which would hold it on its course against contrary side winds.

A minute later and we had reached the surface. Polaris, and her crew, so to speak, had disembarked and we had a cordial handshaking, and then took a stroll around the roof of this immense building. Everything about it seemed to indicate that it was especially designed for the accommodation of business on a gigantic scale. It was built of the semi-transparent material which we had found so common in the district where we had made our homes. The cornice, windows and doors were trimmed with aluminum, which gave it a peculiar grandeur of appearance.

MacNair, who was ever ready to make explanation , informed us that this was the Continental Department of Exchange through which all the commercial transactions between the various districts throughout the continent were carried on. This was the chief center of distribution, and bore the same relation to the continent, that the District Exchange bore to the several communities of which it was composed. The community stores made the actual distribution of products to the people. These larger exchanges, District and Continental, did not really handle the products at all, but collected the orders from the consumers and sent them direct to the communities where the goods were wanted, in this way saving very much unnecessary labor in handling and transportation. The actual exchange of commodities was always direct between the producers and the consumers.

I did not quite comprehend all this, but it prepared me for the object lesson which was to come. I was keenly alert to everything that was to be seen and heard, as it was valuable material for the book which I now felt sure I would be able to lay before the people of the outer world.

It was now noon, and MacNair suggested that it was about time for dinner. "No doubt," he said, "your fifteen hundred miles of travel has given you an appetite." And suiting the· action to the suggestion, we all stepped upon an elevator, and descended to the largest dining hall I had ever seen. It seemed that thousands of people were seated at the tables, quietly conversing and enjoying their midday meal. We seated ourselves at a vacant table and Oqua said:

"I shall order for all, as our American visitors are not yet perfectly familiar with our customs." And manipulating a button at her side, I was surprised to see the center of the table disappear, but it reappeared before I had sufficiently recovered my equilibrium to ask questions, and it was loaded with the most tempting viands. Oqua explained that these central tables which carried the food stood on the top of an elevator that connected with the kitchen below. That when an order was received, a table was already prepared to take the place of the one which the elevator brought down. Everything moved with quiet celerity; no bustling waiters, and no waiting for orders to be filled.

After dinner we passed into a large sitting room, elegantly furnished with chairs, divans, sofas, etc., splendidly upholstered. I noticed chairs and divans on wheels and asked MacNair for an explanation, and he replied:

"These chairs are moved by electricity, supplied by storage batteries just under the seats. You apply the power by pressing a button on the arm by your side, and guide them with your feet. You will often find them in use, particularly in large places like Orbitello, where travelers coming in fatigued, and people on business with the various departments, having many places to go, need some easy means of locomotion. In the olden time, waiters used to push these chairs around by hand, but with the advent of electricity, electric motors were substituted, and now the people who use these chairs need no such assistance, and all the chairmen have to do is to see that the chairs are returned to their proper place."

After a little instruction we found no difficulty in going where we pleased in our chairs, and regulating their direction and speed with perfect ease. This novel experience was so agreeable that we decided to visit the leading points of interest in these electric chairs.

The first place to visit was the business offices of this great Continental Exchange. We took our places in a large elevator room and passed down to the office of the Commissioner of Exchange. On either side of the great hall were shelves containing large books in which we were informed, were statistics of production that are sent in from every district twice a year, at the close of each crop season. These records show just how much surplus each district has for exchange, and of what it consists.

This information is for the Order and Supply Department which is on the same floor, toward which we were directing our chairs.

Here we entered a long hall, on either side of which were arranged desks and electrical instruments. The clerks in attendance, each represented a district, and were selected by the districts to fill these positions because of their intimate knowledge of the wants of their several localities and of the surplus they had for exchange.

The District ·commissioners sent their orders to their own clerk which was written out by telautograph on his own desk. The order was at once transmitted by the same method, to the district having the surplus, through its own clerk, and a duplicate of these orders to the Record Department. These orders when received from the District Commissioners were transmitted to the communities having the surplus. The Community Department of Exchange then shipped it directly to the place where it was needed.

Under this system of distribution, products passed directly from the producer to the consumer and were never handled but once. The producers held their surplus in their own possession until they had orders from consumers by whom it was needed. The Commissioner of Exchange at Orbitello had a tabulated report of the surplus held by each district, and each district had its clerks in the Order and Supply Department of the Continental Exchange. When an agricultural district wanted machinery, musical instruments, furniture, clothing, etc., the order for the same was transmitted to its own clerk in the Department of Exchange and it was at once sent to the district, or districts, having a surplus of the products needed. And when a Manufacturing District needed food supplies the orders were sent to the clerk in the Continental Exchange and the order was transmitted to the nearest agricultural district that had a surplus for exchange.

Under this system of organized exchange, if any district found that it had a surplus accumulating in its warehouses for which there was no demand, this was all the notice required that a time had come to curtail production in that particular line.

From what we could see of the workings of this system, by going through this department, we could readily see how the law of supply and demand, if permitted to act freely with no artificial restrictions, would be a perfect regulator in the world of commerce. Neither would there ever be, under this Altrurian system of exchange, a glut in the market at one place while there was a scarcity at another.

"You see here," said MacNair, "a business house which handles the trade of a continent, containing over two hundred millions of people. All the products of the soil, the shop, the factory and the mine, are practically bought and sold in this establishment, and yet without any of the excitement and bustle, hard work and worry, which characterize the comparatively diminutive business houses of New York and London."

"I see evidences," I remarked, "of a most admirable business system on a stupendous scale. But the question that will be asked in the outer world will be, How are these goods paid for and how are the prices fixed and the accounts adjusted without money? This is what the people of the outer world will want to understand. I am asking more for them than for myself."

"Nothing difficult about it,"said McNair. "Product pays for product here just as it actually does in the outer world, but under co-operation, the elements of interest, profit and rent have been eliminated. The price of an article is fixed by the amount of labor expended in its production and distribution. This of course only applies to such commodities as are in demand. A great deal of labor might be expended in the production of something that no one wanted. Such labor would be wasted here as it would be anywhere else."

"I had thought of this contingency," I replied, "but was not seeking a difficulty. I referred only to such articles of necessity, comfort and luxury as the consumers wish to secure. How are the prices fixed, what is the standard and how are balances settled?"

"These questions," said MacNair, "are well put, to draw out a concise, as well as a comprehensive statement of our business methods. We readily ascertain by statistics, the average number of minutes, hours and days of labor invested in the production of every commodity which enters into common use. This includes the labor invested in the necessary transportation, superintendence and distribution. Hence in our accounts, the value of products of all kinds are credited and debited as given amounts of labor. This is what in the outer world would be called the price. A given number of hours of labor in one branch of useful service to society is worth just the same number of hours of labor in some other branch, and the exchange is made on that basis. The one primary object of this system of exchange is to secure equal and exact justice to all."

"But how are all these numerous employes on your railroads, in your stores and the various departments of industry paid?" asked Captain Ganoe.

"Very easily," said MacNair. "The people produce all the supplies and render all the service, and the people enjoy all the benefits. This is about all there is of it. We produce what we consume, and consume what we produce, without paying tribute to anyone else for the privilege of exercising these natural rights, as the people in the outer world are forced to do."

"But," said the Captain, "would you have me infer that all these expert clerks and accountants, and the commissioner who superintends all this business do not receive any more than the laborers on the farms and in the shops, factories and mines?"

"Why should they get more than people who are engaged in laborious occupations?" asked lola. "They get all they can consume. If they should use a little more or less no one cares. They can have all they want without working any more hours than other people and I cannot understand how they could use any more food or clothing without ruining their health or making themselves very uncomfortable. I cannot conceive of any person wanting to eat more food or wear more clothes, because he or she is employed in some position of trust. Can you, Captain Ganoe?"

"I admit," replied the Captain, "that your question is a poser. And this is not the first time that I have been puzzled by your remarks. I do not say that you are wrong; but I never heard questions handled in this way until I drifted into this inner world. I can only say that I am bewildered and while I do not comprehend your philosophy I do admire your civilization."

"And," responded lola, "I cannot comprehend how anyone can admire our civilization without accepting our philosophy . The civilization of a people is only reducing to practice, the mental and moral concepts of the people. Our civilization is the logical outcome of our philosophy. People always think first and act afterward. Our philosophy is what we think, and our civilization is the result of what it induces us to do."

"Well," said the Captain, "it has certainly induced your people to do many things that would look very strange in the outer world, but which seem to work rightly here."

Oqua, who had quietly dropped out of our party without being observed, now joined us, accompanied by a man of commanding appearance. He was about six feet, four inches in height, brown hair, full beard, blue eyes, fair complexion and a high intellectual forehead. Oqua introduced him as Norrena, Chief of the Continental Department of Education. His address was most gentle, pleasing and kind, but firm and decided. Turning to me he said:

"I had hoped to have an opportunity to make the acquaintance of Jack Adams, the scientist of the Ice King, but Oqua tells me that I must be content with Nequa, the teacher. She informs me that you are preparing a book to be published in your own country, and to that end you are making a close study of our civilization."

"That is true," I said, " and she has spoken to me of you as one who could render me great assistance, in gathering the lessons that would be of the most value, in our transition from competition to co-operation."

"I shall gladly render you any assistance in my power," he said, "but what you can see here of our completed system of co-operation in every department of human endeavor, will be indispensable to a clear comprehension of the lessons to be drawn from the history of our own Transition Period."

"Thank you," I said. "And I would be pleased to have you show me through the departments, and call my attention to such features as will be of the greatest advantage for me to understand just at this time."

"That is the same request that was made by Oqua, as it would take a long time for you to find just what you want without the assistance of someone who is familiar with all the departments and who also understands the nature of the work in which you are engaged. To begin, we will now visit the Department of Public Printing and News Distribution."

We now dispensed with our electric chairs, as we felt the need of exercise. As we emerged from the Exchange building, Norrena took the lead, and conducted us into another stupendous structure, devoted to the Public Printing and the Distribution of News to all parts of the world. The upper story was an immense auditorium, where public meetings of unusual proportions could meet and have ample room, and where the acoustic properties were so scientifically adjusted, that all could hear the speaker in ordinary tones of voice.

Norrena conducted us first into the press room, where printed sheets were being turned out with a rapidity I had never before witnessed. These passed on an endless belt into the binding department and from thence in completed form to the mailing rooms for distribution. Everything seemed to move with the same quiet celerity that we had noticed in the Exchange Department.

From the press rooms we ascended in an elevator to the composing department, where we found a number of machines turning out stereotype plates, but no operators were anywhere in sight. Norrena informed me that the machines were operated on the same principle as the telautograph, or writing telegraph, and with the multi plex system of transmission, an expert could operate a number of these machines in different parts of the world at the same time. The matter for publication, was thus delivered in the composing room in the shape of plates ready for the presses.

But the most interesting and important feature of this great publishing house is the manner of collecting and distributing news. The News Department is connected by telegraph with news offices throughout the world and is continually receiving items of general interest, which are classified and distributed by the same means to the people in every home throughout the continent. 'The printed pages are of matter of a more permanent character, which is regarded as worthy of preservation. Copies of new books are sent to similar establishments in the other grand divisions and by them reproduced and placed in their local libraries where all have access to them. This free distribution of intelligence to the whole people is under the direct control of the Department of Education.

During the meetings of the Altrurian Council, this department has another important duty to perform. The council, through this department, is practically, at all times, in communication with the majority of the people. When a matter of public interest has been carefully discussed pro and con, it is formulated and transmitted to every community where the people are interested, a vote is then taken at once, and the result transmitted to the council. By this means, a majority of the people can be heard from in regard to any matter of importance in a few hours. The people are at all times familiar with the matters which are being considered by the council, and are prepared to respond promptly. The communities ordinarily have decided any important question in their minds before it is submitted to them and reply at once. I could readily see how, under an advanced state of civilization, direct government by the people is not only practicable, but remarkable· for its simplicity and promptness of execution.

The council acts upon all matters in which two or more districts are interested and the matter is formulated and submitted at once to the people of such districts for their approval or disapproval. But in any matter of great importance the people are not compelled to wait for the regular meeting of the council, but may by the action of the communities place the matter before the executive committee which meets every day, and it becomes their duty to submit the question to a vote of the people. In this way, under this system, the people can always secure prompt action, as it is the duty of their officials to serve, but not to govern, as they do in the outer world.

If a public improvement is agreed upon, the districts and communities interested, make an appropriation of necessary material and labor, and the work is pushed forward. In all things this great council is advisory in its character and the executive committee only takes such action as the people have agreed upon, and when any matter has been agreed upon the executive power acts at once without question. The will of the people is the law which no one ever assumes to question.

We passed rapidly through a large number of magnificent structures, filled with exhibits of all kinds. In Machinery Hall were samples of every conceivable mechanical device. Another vast building was devoted to textile fabrics of all kinds. Every industry had its exhibit. All the great Grand Divisions had similar buildings. Everywhere, accommodating attendants were ready to show us anything and give us any information we wished. And one remarkable thing was, that while every one seemed anxious to display the goods on exhibition, no one ever tried to sell us anything, as would have been the case in the outer world.

Here, as MacNair said, was indeed a miniature picture of a world. I could write a volume on each one of these great buildings without exhausting the subject. But for the present I had seen enough and requested Norrena to conduct us next to the Library of Universal Knowledge which was the most highly finished and imposing of all these palatial structures. It was built of the usual semi-transparent material which shut out the direct rays of the sun while it admitted a mellow radiance rendering artificial light as a rule unnecessary.

We took an elevator to the top where we began our survey of the contents. Elevators at frequent intervals connected every story. A description of one story would in a general way apply to all the others. Each floor is divided longitudinally into three halls or suites of rooms. The central division is ordinarily a single hall fifty feet in width by six hundred in length, and in these central halls are stored all the books, papers and relics of the past. Also specimens of ores, metals, alloys and compounds of everything that goes to make a complete museum of natural history, and scientific methods in chemistry and the mechanic arts. Different stories are given to Archaeology, Ethnology, Geology, Chemistry, Electricity, etc., and constitute a most instructive feature of this Library of Universal Knowledge.

The divisions on either side are given up to reading rooms, lecture halls and schools for culture in technical branches that can be studied to better advantage here in this vast library than elsewhere. In the reading rooms, which are always open to the public, full catalogues are always kept for visitors, and courteous attendants are ever ready to give any information and procure any book that may be needed. Books are all numbered and catalogued, so the visitor has but to press the number on an electric keyboard, and it is delivered at once by a pneumatic tube. The attendants return the books to their proper places in the same rapid and quiet manner. No noise, bluster, or confusion anywhere. Everything is reduced to system, and moves along like clock work.

Instruction is free in any of the technical schools, to all who apply and submit to the rules. These schools embrace every specific branch of study, and are usually patronized by graduates from the public schools who desire to perfect their knowledge of some specific branch in order to be better qualified for a special calling. Here, can be studied under the most favorable conditions, the progressive development of a world, illustrated at every step by the relics indicative of its status which are carefully preserved in the museums, thus tracing in the most instructive and satisfactory manner, the progress of the people from their primitive condition of barbarians to their present high state of culture.

I saw at a glance that this was the place where my contemplated work of investigation, into the practical methods which had enabled the people of this country to develop such ideals, could be prosecuted under the most favorable conditions. I determined to make good use of these facilities for gathering the ripened sheaves of human thought in every age and condition of life, for the benefit of the people of my own native land.

In the lower story, we passed into the department where new publications are received and catalogued. The first thing that attracted my attention was the translations from the library of the Ice King, which seemed to have the right of way over everything else. Among these translations, I noticed the American Cyclopedia, Ridpath's History of the World, the Decline and Fall of the Roman Empire, histories of the United States and the leading countries of the world, together with a selection of works on polar exploration, and a number of scientific works. I was astonished at the progress that had been made, but Norrena informed me that, under their system, a work could be translated almost as fast as it could be read, and that the work had been divided between the scholars of all the grand divisions.

I asked Norrena if there was much demand for these translations of outer world literature, and he replied:

"Yes, the orders from each grand division, amount to millions, and they can be translated in all parts of the concave as rapidly as the presses can turn them out. This is especially true of everything pertaining to America, whose history up to date is so similar to the early stages of our own."

"But," I said, "with the usual large attendance at the reading rooms, one volume will do for a number of persons, and I should think that would greatly decrease the demand."

"That is true," said Norrena, "but all have an equal right to be served, and this addition to our knowledge of the outer world is in such great demand, that all want to be supplied at the same time."

"Of course that is impossible," I said, "and so I suppose that with all your improved methods many will be compelled to wait."

"Not so very many," said Norrena. "All may not be able to get books, but all who desire to do so can hear them read."

"How," I asked, "can that be, when millions are asking to hear them read all at once ?"

"Not so very difficult," he replied, "when we use the multiplex phonograph. One reader can be heard all over the concave. A vast number would rather listen to a good reader, than to read themselves, and as the voice of this reader can be connected with a large number of phonograph reading rooms at the same time, in each such room, as many can listen as can be seated. "

"You astonish me," I said." Will you please explain how this is done?"

"I will do more than that," he said. " I will show you how it is done. Come with me. "

I followed him into a large room, where I found, I should think, from two to three hundred people, composedly sitting in chairs, or reclining on sofas and divans, with phonographic attachments in their ears.

"These," said Norrena, "are all listening to readers at Lake Byblis who are assisting in the translation of these works. They are using these attachments in the ears because they are not all listening to the same matter. This is a fair sample of what is going on in every room of this character, throughout the concave. A large number of professional readers are employed who are connected by telephone and phonograph with every home and reading room in all parts of the country. By such means you see that we can disseminate knowledge almost simultaneously, to all who are most anxious for it. The demand for printed books is mainly from libraries and reading rooms, public and private. The masses of the people at this time are spending much of their ample leisure, in listening to the reading of this new addition to our literature. It will not be long, before the most industrious, intellectually, have absorbed, to a considerable extent this most valuable addition to our knowledge, and then a very large number will apply themselves to the study of the English language, so that they may be able to judge for themselves as to the accuracy of the translations."

"I see from your admirable system of distributing knowledge that there must be an extraordinary demand to be supplied."

"Nothing extraordinary for us," said Norrena. "The demand is steady with a tendency to increase. Our people are all workers who have enough physical exercise to keep their bodies in good condition, and this stimulates the mind to demand food, which it is our duty to provide."

"Do you not often find this difficult?" I asked.

"Not at all," he replied. "In this, as in the supply of food for the body, the quantity is always ample where the operations of natural law are not antagonized in the administration of public business. We have ample facilities for gathering news, and everyone who has a thought to express finds an opportunity to do so. There is a steady supply which we distribute alike to all. This demand for mental food is even more pressing than the demand for physical nourishment. The real man and the real woman are not their physical bodies, but the living souls which occupy these bodies, and it is the duty of this department of the public service to provide these souls with the staff of life, which is knowledge."

Before leaving the library, Norrena requested us to record our names on the visitor's book. We complied, and then continued our rambles until I, for one, was utterly exhausted, and asked to be excused from further exercise.

"Then," said Norrena, "we will retire to the Department of Public Comfort, where I have my private rooms, and while you are resting, we can talk over plans for the future, or other matters that may demand attention. I am much interested in this move to improve the airships with a view to opening up a line of communication with the outer world."

"And," I remarked, "I am, if possible, more interested in the completion of my book in time for it to go to the United States by the first airship, for publication. And I want it to contain every lesson of importance to our people that can be gleaned from the present condition and the past history of the people of this country."

As we were speaking, Norrena hailed a passing electric carriage, and in a few minutes we were landed at the grandest hotel I had ever entered in my life. I could see at a glance why it was called the Department of Public Comfort. Every facility for the comfort and enjoyment of guests was provided. But the dimensions assigned to this volume will not permit a description. I need only say that all its' appointments were complete, for the accommodation of thousands of guests.

While each of the department buildings had its own arrangements for accommodating its own force of employes and its own guests, this Department of Public Comfort was designed more especially for guests from other Grand Divisions. Here, the heads of departments of all the Grand Divisions held their conferences; and here the continental heads of departments very appropriately had their headquarters.

After supper, Norrena informed me that on the morrow, he would devote an hour to oral lessons at the institute of district school superintendents and that his subject would be the History of the Transition Period.

"This," he explained, "covers that period in the history of Altruria which marks the decline and fall of the old system of competition and the introduction of cooperative methods. It may be just what you want in the way of lessons from history. If you think that you do not yet understand our language well enough to fully comprehend all the points, I will provide you with a translation into English."

I thanked him for his interest in my work and assured him that while I wanted to hear him in his own tongue, if he could provide me with the same matter in English, it would help me to a better understanding of the language of the country, and that certainly I did not want to miss any point of real value in the subject matter.

Chapter XII

THE INSTITUTE OF SCHOOL SUPERINTENDENTS -NORRENA'S ADDRESS ON THE TRANSITION PERIOD — FROM COMPETITION TO CO-OPERATION — THE CLOSING DECADES OF MONEY SUPREMACY — THE POWER OF GOLD — ITS CONQUEST OF THE WORLD — POLITICAL GOVERNMENTS ITS TOOLS — THE PEOPLE HELPLESS — A HINT AT THE WAY OUT.

At an early hour we were up and had our breakfast. I felt that my journey to Orbitello and the hasty glance through the leading departments had been the most instructive day I had ever experienced. But I was not surfeited, and looked forward with interest to the meeting of the Institute of School Superintendents and especially to Norrena's oral lessons from the Transition Period of the great Industrial Commonwealth of Altruria.

We met in the Auditorium over the Department of Public Printing. Many had already arrived and were gathered into groups in various portions of the vast hall conversing with each other. I took a seat on one side by myself to contemplate the scene before me. I was by nature a student, and here I was among, as it were, a nation of competent instructors, and in a country where everything demonstrated the power to control the great potent forces which govern the external world, and the innate force of our higher moral and spiritual concepts of what should be our relations toward each other in order to convert this earth into a heaven of blissful, happy contentment. I was among a people who universally regarded "an injury to one as the concern of all," and hence health, happiness and abundance for all was their normal condition.

I could hardly realize that this country had once been the abode of poverty and all of its consequences of ignorance, vice and crime; that here where equal rights, equal opportunities and an equal share in the unlimited abundance which nature places within the easy reach of intelligent labor were the universal and unquestioned law of being, there had once been a grasping and cruel financial and commercial power that condemned the wealth-producing millions to lives of unrequited toil. But such, I was repeatedly told, had been the fact, and Norrena, at this meeting was to give an oral lesson from that period and describe the power that had oppressed and degraded the people in those early ages.

But a short time had gone by since my first meeting with these people and yet I had become thoroughly absorbed in their mental, moral and spiritual life. I felt myself to be to all intents and purposes one of them. What was it that had so entirely taken possession of my consciousness? In all my life I had never felt so completely at home, and at peace with myself and all the world. I was fully satisfied.

Norrena broke in upon my reverie by asking:

"What is it Nequa, that so absorbs your attention that you seem to be utterly oblivious of the presence of this large assemblage of teachers from all parts of the country to talk over the history of the olden time when **'wealth accumulated and men decayed**?' Have you forgotten what I told you last evening? Oqua will report the lesson from the Transition Period in English for you and you can afford to give some attention to your old friends, lola, MacNair, Polaris, Dione and your comrades of the Ice King."

I looked around and found that while I had been musing, our party had all gathered near me without attracting my attention and I said apologetically: "l must have been dreaming."

"Then you were dreaming with your eyes wide open," said Oqua. "I noticed that you seemed to be unusually absorbed. What were you thinking about?"

"I was pondering," I replied, "how it was possible that this country could ever have been cursed with poverty as the normal condition of the masses of the people while the few were rich beyond the dreams of avarice, and held those masses bound by fetters that they could not break."

"It is now time for the exercises to commence," said Norrena. "I will explain the mystery in my address, at least so far as the leading factors are concerned, for in its entirety it is indeed a long and ghastly picture of human ignorance on one side and human greed directed by a morally perverted human intelligence on the other."

The chairman called the meeting to order and stated that the first thing on the program would be an address on the Transition Period, by Norrena, the Continental Commissioner of Education. Without extended preliminary remarks, the speaker opened the discussion of the question under consideration from which I condense the following from Oqua's report in English. Yet notwithstanding my short residence in the country I believe that I could have given the gist of the address myself without any assistance.

"l need not," said the speaker, "enter into any lengthy explanation before an institute of teachers, as to how our ancestors under the old civilization exchanged the products created by their labor for products created by the labor of others, by the use of a law-created medium of exchange called money. Neither need we trace the history of many kinds of products and devices which were used in different ages as a medium of exchange, such as cattle, slaves, shells, tobacco, the skins of animals and certain stones and metals. These things are only of interest to the antiquarian. It is enough to know for our present purpose that money had originally been devised as a substitute for barter, and marked the first step towards the establishment of a system of exchanging products which required the exercise of a higher order of mental faculties. During the early part of the Transition Period, gold and silver were the exclusive materials from which money was coined, except for sums of only a few cents, when the so-called baser metals were used. As the supply of gold and silver was not equal to the demands of business, banks were established to issue notes to circulate as money with the consent of both parties to the exchange. These notes were made redeemable in gold and silver on the demand of the holders, and at frequent intervals the banks failed and the people lost the wealth which they had exchanged for the notes. This was a transfer without compensation, of the actual values created by the labor of the people, to the note issuing power, and this process, oft repeated, laid the foundations for many colossal fortunes."

"In this connection, it may be well to note that in times of great public danger when the metal coins disappeared from circulation, the government exercised the right to issue a legal tender paper money to meet the deficiency. It served all the purposes of gold, and often in the midst of adversity and disaster brought great industrial prosperity to the people. But when the danger had gone by, strange as it may appear, the government funded this legal tender paper into government bonds, payable, interest and principal, in coin. This process of converting the debt paying medium of the country into an interest bearing debt that must be paid in another kind of money which had been hidden away by the more wealthy in times of danger, was the foundation of the great bonded debt of this country which was established during the Transition Period. This bonded debt was made the basis of a national bank currency for the redemption of which, at first in legal tender paper and coin, and later in gold, the people as debtors to the banks were in the last analysis responsible. In other words the national bank currency derived its sole value as a reliable medium of exchange from the fact that it was based on the public credit, and this public credit belonged to the people, but the private banking associations got the benefit for the private gain of their stockholders, and the service rendered, cost the people many times its worth."

"During the Transition Period in this country the people

had three kinds of legal tender money, gold, silver, and paper, together with the national bank notes which were a legal tender as between the people and the government. At the close of this period, silver coin, and legal tender paper were made redeemable by the government in gold, on the demand of the holder; and all deferred payments were made payable in gold on the demand of the creditor. The great bulk of the business of the country among the people was transacted by the use of silver, paper and bank notes but the holders of these forms of currency could demand gold in exchange, and if for any cause the government failed to collect enough gold from the people to meet the demand it became the duty of the Secretary of the Treasury to sell interest bearing gold bonds to meet the deficiency."

"Such in brief, was the complicated, cumbersome and unscientific system of exchanging, or distributing wealth, which existed under the old civilization. The means of production being fixed by natural law were the same then as now. Wealth always was and must always continue to be, the product of human labor and skill applied to natural resources, facilitated by such mechanical contrivances and business methods as human skill may devise. But the system of distribution being entirely under human control is continually changing as affected by human impulses, whether they be selfish, as in the olden time, or altruistic as they are now."

"We now exchange a product for a product of equal value, for the convenience and benefit of all, without any charge except for the necessary labor expended in the production and distribution. But under the old civilization the product was first exchanged for money and the money was then exchanged with some one else for the product that was wanted in return. As a method of exchanging one value for another, this was a very awkward and unscientific process, but in and of itself it was not necessarily unjust and oppressive; yet the system such as it was, could be used by the greedy few who controlled the financial and commercial affairs of the country, for the purpose of exacting such exorbitant tribute from the many as would, and did, condemn the millions to poverty. The few, with their superior business sagacity took advantage of this semibarbarous idea of a perpetual money token which was supposed to contain within itself an actual value, equal to the values which it was used to exchange, and they organized banking as the chief factor in the mechanism of exchange among themselves, which in its operations also gave them control of the perpetual money tokens which the people must have to carry on their ordinary business transactions with each other."

"These shrewd financiers had no use for money except to pay balances, and at the time of the end, ninety-seven per cent. of the great business transactions of the country were carried on by means of organized credit through banks and clearing houses. This system of minimizing the use of legal money through banking methods, as a matter of course left a large surplus in the hands of the great operators, which was loaned to the people, who in their unorganized condition were compelled to pay cash. These loans bore various rates of interest, but always much above the average increase of wealth, and very often so exorbitant that the states for very shame's sake were compelled to establish certain arbitrary rates beyond which the money lender dare not go."

"It will be seen at a glance that this system of transacting the business of the country on a cash basis by the people and by organized credit through banks by large operators who controlled finance and commerce could not fail to give to the latter an enormous advantage in the aggregate business of the country. The great masses of wealth producers naturally became a debtor class. As all wealth was the product of their labor, they must necessarily create the means of paying all indebtedness, interest and principal. Hence they constituted the interest paying masses while the comparatively small number of large operators constituted a powerful creditor class who were continually receiving interest, and hence always had money to loan or invest in such a manner as to be able to receive more interest. And the larger the interest-charge against the people, the more they needed money and the more inclined they were to borrow. Cities and towns often voted a bonded debt upon themselves for improvements, for the express purpose of providing employment for the workers, so that business might derive some temporary advantage by having the wages expended in their midst. The great masses of the people did not realize that a part of the same dollars they borrowed must go back to the lender to pay interest, and that the consequent deficiency in the means of payment could only be met by transferring to the creditor a portion of the wealth created by their labor equal to the interest. And the larger the aggregate indebtedness in proportion to the volume of money available for debt paying purposes, the larger must be the deficiency to be met out of their savings, or what should have been their net income from the exercise of their producing power.'

"But the interest on loans, public and private was only a small fraction of the burden of usury imposed upon the wealth producing masses. All the large industrial, financial and commercial enterprises of the country were on a debt-creating basis. Stock companies. owned the railroads of the country; the streetcars, waterworks, gasworks and electric light and power plants of the cities; all the great manufacturing, mining and commercial enterprises; the steamship lines, and even vast bonanza farms and stock ranches. All these interests were operated with a view to paying dividends on the stock in addition to the operating expenses, and were therefore equivalent to a perpetual interest bearing debt, the principal of which never could be paid."

"This constructive indebtedness was intended to be perpetual, and its volume was not limited to the actual cost of the various enterprises that were incorporated. The railroads, for instance, sold stock to many times the cost of the roads, or as it was called, 'watered their stock,' and then they ordinarily bonded the roads for vast sums besides. These bonded debts however, were very often created for the purpose of bankrupting the companies for the enrichment of an 'inside ring.' This process was known as 'freezing out the stockholders,' and by thus reducing capitalization it was not necessary for the roads to exact so much tribute from their patrons in order to pay dividends. Other corporate enterprises also 'watered' their stock, and some of them got such a hold upon the people that they continued to pay exorbitant dividends on their fictitious valuation until they were absorbed into the larger combination of the whole people."

"At the close of the Transition Period the volume of interest bearing indebtedness and dividend earning investments .was estimated at fifty thousand millions, and the average cost to the people six per cent per annum, or. an aggregate of three thousand millions every year to be taken out of the wealth produced by the people. The bulk of these obligations, public, corporate and private was held by the great banking institutions which had been established by the corporation and. trust magnates, who practically owned the lands and all the machinery of production and distribution. They owned not only the indebtedness against the people but they controlled the medium by which it must be paid, and on their demand under the law, this medium of final payment was gold."

"As this great creditor class was the principal employer of labor and controlled both the buying and selling of products which the people must have for the purposes of consumption, thus fixing both the income and the expenses of the producer, it was not difficult to collect their tribute. A pro rata of the great annual charge of interest, dividends and profits against the people was collected from the producer in the shape of a discount on what he had to sell, whether it was his labor or its products. The remainder was charged up to consumption and constituted a part of the price that was paid for every article that was purchased. The cost to the consumer of every commodity purchased, consisted of five distinct elements :

First, interest on the money supposed to be invested in its production and distribution;

Second, rent upon all the buildings in which it had been stored, which would include cars or vessels used in transportation;

Third, profit to all who had handled the product; Fourth, its pro rata of taxation and Fifth, the wages paid to the labor expended in its production, transportation, superintendence and distribution.

This fifth element in the cost was all that went to useful labor, while the other elements went to the great financial, industrial and commercial combines which held the masses of the people in their grasp.

"Of course under the operation of this system, where both· the income and the expenses of the producer were determined by this great creditor class for its own selfish purposes, it is not strange that the condition of the average toiler was one of poverty, nor is it strange that a widespread spirit of unrest, and often of angry and violent discontent threatened the peace of society and the perpetuity of established institutions and a stable government. But to us, it does indeed look strange that the brawny millions whose strong arms and undaunted courage had conquered the untamed forces of nature and made the wilderness a fit dwelling place for a refined and cultured people, could have been bound, hand and foot, by such a gossamer thread as the puny power of a few owners of gold. But when we take into consideration the fundamental truth that mind controls matter, and that the few who were at the top had cultivated brains while the many who were at the bottom had only cultivated muscles, the mystery is solved. The toiling masses had no conception of their power, and on their plane of intelligence were utterly unable to hold their own against the wily schemes of the more intelligent few."

"At the time of which we speak, **four-fifths of the aggregate wealth of the country had passed into the hands of a small fraction of the people,** and millions were landless, homeless and dependent for subsistence upon the crumbs, so to speak, that fell from the tables of their lordly masters who controlled every avenue to employment and dictated the terms upon which they were permitted to live. Being few in numbers, they could and did cooperate with each other for their mutual advantage. All they had to do in order to keep wages at a minimum was to leave a large number of applicants unemployed, and hence very poor, who at all times, would be ready to take the place of workmen who demanded more liberal wages. The self-employed farmers were but little better off than the wage workers, as they were forced to sell their products and purchase their supplies at prices fixed by the great financial, industrial and commercial combines which controlled the business of the country. Under the inequitable methods of exchange which existed at that time, the masses of the people were powerless to help themselves. The fortunate few who controlled money, dictated how much they might receive for their labor or its products and how much of the products created by the labor of others they could purchase with the proceeds."

"To us the natural remedy for discriminations of this kind, so unjust and oppressive to the masses of the people seems so self-evident and easy of application that it is not strange that many have been inclined to doubt the correctness of much that is recorded in the history of the economic conditions which existed under the old civilization, when human selfishness ruled supreme in business affairs. But when we take into consideration the fact, that at that time, the world had never had a single object lesson large enough to be seen by the great masses of mankind, as to what would constitute an equitable system of distribution, we are forced to the conclusion that the adverse conditions existing during the Transition Period were just what might have been expected under the circumstances. The few who had the ability to conduct the business of the world did not understand that the productive power of the earth is practically unlimited so that under an equitable system of exchange there is absolutely no possibility of any person being reduced to poverty. Then, too, the great masses were but a few generations removed from a condition of absolute serfdom, and were just what ages of drudgery had made them, and could not be expected to take broad and comprehensive views of the great economic problems by which they were confronted. The world had never known anything but the private ownership of all the means of production and distribution and the desire to lay up treasures was universally regarded as laudable and praiseworthy. Under these circumstances neither the few who had monopolized the earth nor the many who were disinherited could have been reasonably expected to be other than they were. Both alike were the product of long ages of growth. The wheat and the tares must necessarily grow up together, nurtured by the same soil, until the harvest is ready, and then the separation takes place strictly in accordance with natural law."

"The gold power which established itself in this country during the Transition Period was an exotic, that had been imported from the old world. Its object was to control every nation on earth, for its own gain, without being the loyal supporter of any. It had secured absolute control over the nations of the Old World before it succeeded in financially conquering the New. Whenever it succeeded in establishing the gold standard in any country, it established its local branch for controlling that country's finances. Its first object was to promote the creation of national bonded debts, payable, principal and interest, in gold. For this purpose, it was always ready to loan money to carry on wars, and each country could negotiate its loans through its own local branch, but the creditor in every case, as a matter of fact, was the international Gold Power of the world, which had no preferences between nations but sought to impose a bonded debt alike upon all. There was absolutely nothing patriotic about it. All it wanted, was a lien upon the industries of the world, that would produce a steady income in the shape of interest."

"In this country, we had a Republican form of government and with our vast area of public lands the people were more independent by far than the people of any other country ever had been, notwithstanding the fact that they were robbed unmercifully by the private banks which issued notes and then suspended so that the notes which the people had accepted for their property became worthless. At frequent intervals, these bank panics reduced thousands of people to bankruptcy. But the country was new and land could be had. for the asking, so when pressed to the wall, as it were, in the more populous districts along the eastern border, they came west on the public lands, made new homes and soon accumulated another competency. It is not strange that this international Gold Power of the world cast longing eyes upon a country that was so productive, and could recover so rapidly from industrial depressions and financial disasters."

"For nearly one hundred years after the establishment of our Republic, notwithstanding the prevalent 'wild cat' banking system as it was called and the absurd reverence for the so-called precious metals, the people of this country were practically independent of the great Gold Power which had its headquarters in Atlan. While the founders of the Republic had made gold and silver coin the standard money of the country, they reserved the right to issue treasury notes and also to make them a legal tender, and as there was no great debt, and land could be had for the asking, the economic independence of the people could not be entirely crushed out, and therefore Altruria offered an effectual barrier to the encroachments of the gold power. Before the people could be actually subjugated financially, a vast bonded debt must be created, and in order to induce the people to agree to such a debt, the life of the Republic must be placed in jeopardy. A foreign war was not to be thought of, as it would arouse to fever heat all of the innate democratic hatred against aristocratic rule of every name and description, but a war between the states would serve the same purpose."

"The conditions that made such an interstate struggle possible, had unintentionally been provided for by the founders of the Republic. At the time when the Republic was established, the colored people were held as slaves in nearly all of the original colonies. This institution was regarded by the founders of the Republic, as inconsistent with the spirit of its institutions, and it was unsparingly denounced as the 'sum of all villainies' by a large number; and one state after another emancipated its slaves, and new free states were admitted, until the country was practically half slave and half free."

"In the manufacturing states uncultured slave labor was not profitable and hence there was but little objection to its abolition. But in the agricultural states such labor was valuable, as the old world furnished an unfailing market for all the surplus products. The gold power of Atlan took advantage of the situation to sow the seeds of discord between the two sections."

"Missionaries were sent into the manufacturing states, papers established and literature distributed appealing to the sympathies of the people in behalf of the slaves. and creating a public sentiment against the slaveholding states. These anti-slavery missionaries came in the name of religion and humanity and it cannot be denied that ample grounds existed for all that could be said against chattel slavery, but the PURPOSES for which the anti-slavery agitation was used by the Gold Power were, if possible, to destroy the Republic, or failing in this, involve the country in an interstate war and induce the patriotic lovers of liberty to consent to the establishment of a vast bonded debt."

"Another class of missionaries were sent into the slaveholding states and another class of literature circulated, proclaiming that 'cotton is king' and that if Free Trade with all the world was established, the planters would be the wealthiest and happiest people on earth. That all that stood in the way was the union with the anti-slavery states, which sought to abolish the 'peculiar institution' that enabled the planters to produce such a magnificent surplus, which the Old World stood ready to take in unlimited quantities, at high prices in gold, just as soon as Free Trade could be established. To secure this grand victory for agriculture, all that was needed was to dissolve the union with the anti-slavery states and their pet hobby of tariff duties on imported goods."

"Both sections of the country were flooded with literature, all of which contained enough of truth to make it attractive to honest people, and enough of misrepresentation to engender the most bitter and antagonistic feelings between them. The institution of slavery was wrong, in and of itself, but the anti-slavery agitators ignored the fact that the masses of the slaves were not qualified for self-government, and that the perpetuity of free institutions depended upon the intelligence of the voters. They did not try to convert the slaveholding states to the policy of educating their slaves and preparing them for freedom, but they went to the non-slave holding states and demanded the immediate and unconditional abolition of slavery in the other section. This was, as a matter of course, most exasperating to the people of the slave states who in their capacity as independent states felt themselves amply competent to attend to their own affairs."

"In the political discussions of that time, half truths served all the purposes of full grown falsehoods as a means of deluding the people. The Free Trade agitators of the slave states were unqualifiedly right when they called attention to the fact that all import duties were a tax upon the people in proportion to their expenses instead of their incomes and were therefore unjust and oppressive to the great masses of the people; but they ignored the fact that the absolute Free Trade that did exist between all sections of the country was of vastly more importance to the slaveholding states, than Free Trade with any foreign country could possibly be. The manufacturing states of their own country were over two thousand miles nearer to them than the manufacturing countries of the Old World, and that fact, with a fair compensation to labor would have given them an assured market for their surplus products without paying transportation charges both ways across the ocean."

"But the leading object of these Free Trade agitators, was to appeal to the selfish impulses of the few who owned slaves, and to the race prejudices of the masses of non-slave holders, by telling them that the abolitionists proposed to place them on terms of political and social equality with the slaves. They were taught to believe that under the prevailing tariff regulations, they were taxed for the special benefit of the 'mudsills' of the manufacturing states, who being low down in the social scale themselves wanted to bring the proud, chivalrous people of the slave states down to the level of their chattel slaves."

"As a matter of fact, neither the producing masses of the Free States or the non-slave holders of the slave states had the remotest conception that the international gold power of Atlan was taking advantage of the discussion of slavery and free trade through its paid agents, to sow the seeds of discord between the two sections of the Great Republic of the New World. And they permitted their resentments for fancied wrongs to be fanned into a flame of fierce indignation, which, as was intended, culminated in a bloody strife and the creation of a vast bonded debt.

"This fratricidal struggle lasted nearly five years, and when it ended, the people found themselves in debt, billions of dollars, to a class of people who had speculated on their necessities. The unsuspecting masses on both sides had bared their breasts to the storm of battle, endured all the privations and suffered all the losses, and were in debt for all the expenses of the war, INCLUDING THEIR OWN SERVICES, to an international money power which ruled the world."

"In order to carry on the war, paper money was issued and paid out to the soldiers, sailors and citizens for their services. This money performed all the functions of gold and notwithstanding the fact that the people were engaged in a most destructive war, it stimulated all branches of business and brought on an era of great industrial prosperity. But after the war was over this same paper money which had been paid to the people as the original creditors of the government, and for which they had signed receipts in full for their services, was converted into interest bearing bonds, and these same soldiers, sailors and citizens were taxed to pay to those who speculated on their necessities in the hour of danger, the same debt that had originally been due to themselves, and for which they had received legal tender paper money."

"But had the process of funding the legal tender debt paying medium of the country into bonds ceased at this point, the international gold power of the world would never have been able . to financially subjugate the people of this country, as under the law creating the bonds, the debt was payable in legal tender paper money. So another step must be taken. The debt had been created and a large portion of the money had been burned, but the bonds did not call for gold, except for interest. Hence a law was enacted resuming specie payments, and the bonds were made payable in coin, and now the people who had taken paper dollars for their services in saving the union, were taxed to pay gold dollars to the money kings for the paper dollars they had received."

"We can scarcely conceive at this distant day, how it was possible for our ancestors to have been so stupid, as not to see through this outrage that was perpetrated for thirty odd years after this bare faced legalized robbery had been committed, a vast majority of men were voting their approval, which was proclaimed throughout the world as the triumph of patriotic statesmanship."

"As the direct result of this kind of financial legerdemain, which converted the DEBT-PAYING medium of the country into an INTEREST-BEARING DEBT, the wages of labor and the prices of products steadily declined, business enterprises were wound up in bankruptcy at the rate of more than one thousand per month and millions of workmen were forced into idleness and thronged the highways in all parts of the country, demoralized, degraded and becoming a sure menace to civilization."

"As a result of the war between the states, chattel slavery had been abolished, but another form of industrial servitude, the wage system, had fallen heir to all of its worst features. The owners of the chattel slaves had the power to be oppressive and cruel, but personal interest demanded that the slave should always be provided with food, shelter and raiment, while the wage slave could be turned out to starve when from sickness, age or any other cause it was more profitable to dispense with his services. The wage slave, who must work or starve was serving a much more exacting and cruel master than the most heartless owner of chattel slaves ever could have been. In the great sphere of human servitude the tables had been completely turned. While the slave owner had always been very careful not to give his chattel slaves an opportunity to run away, the wage slave very often lived in a perpetual dread that his master would pay him off and tell him to go."

"Conditions such as these could not fail to arouse a widespread feeling of dissatisfaction and as every man had a vote, political agitation was the logical result of the situation and politicians were kept busy in defending old policies and proposing new ones, all for the professed purpose of securing better conditions for the great masses of the people. A slight glance at a few of the popular economic and political ideas of that time indicates the average status of popular intelligence, and is therefore useful in tracing the evolutionary forces which were operating at that time for the elimination of selfishness and the establishment of equity in human affairs."

"As the times grew harder, the politicians of the old school told the people that the over production of wealth was the cause of all their poverty and distress, and for a time the great masses seemed to be satisfied with this explanation. They did not pause to inquire how it was possible for them to produce so much food and clothing and build so many houses, and for that reason be compelled to go hungry, dress in rags and be without shelter."

"Further on, this same class of politicians told the people that what they needed was to make their silver and paper money redeemable in gold and then they would have a dollar that would purchase more, and a majority of the people decided in favor of the gold standard. They did not reflect, that the larger the purchasing power of the dollar might be, the more of their labor it would require in order to get the dollar, and so without understanding what they were doing, the laboring masses of the country actually voted to decrease the money earning power of their own labor. But had they decided in favor of more money, while their wages would have gone up, their cost of living would have increased and they would not have been materially benefited except incidentally, as a part of the great debtor class, which was required to pay interest as part of the price of everything purchased for consumption. And we may add, that but for the fact that the great masses who produced wealth by their labor, constituted a debtor class, the advantages and disadvantages between a larger or smaller volume of money, would have formed a perfect equation, and the condition of the masses would neither have been better nor worse, as in either case, the banks would have determined the amount that was permitted to circulate among the people, by making or withholding loans as might at the time, best promote their own interests."

"While the Gold Power was international in its character, and not loyal to any country, it always took an active interest in moulding the opinions of the dominant political parties of all countries. It was necessary for it to have at least two favorites among the dominant parties, so that by turns they might spring reforms, so-called, based on half truths, to attract the constantly increasing number of dissatisfied voters. The demand for an increased volume of money in order to raise the wages of labor and the price of farm products was a question of this character, and it was sufficient to sidetrack and head off a more searching investigation as to the real causes of poverty. This was met by the demand for a better quality of money that would purchase more goods. The arguments in favor of both, contained half truths which were dwelt upon with great force, but the success of either, still left the gold power, directly or indirectly, in a position to control the situation."

"The same thing was true in regard to the tariff question which the gold power made a dominant issue between its favorite parties. The question itself could be used to call attention away from the question of finance, which had a more direct bearing upon the vital matter of EXCHANGE and was therefore more likely to educate the people to a point where they could no longer be deluded by an ingenious discussion of half truths. This question, in order to be made available for the purposes of the gold power, must necessarily have two SEEMINGLY antagonistic political parties to go before the people. One party advocated a tariff-for-revenue, with Free Trade arguments, while the other advocated a tariff-for-protection, and appealed to the laboring classes to maintain liberal wages for themselves by voting for a high tariff that would exclude foreign goods."

"The positions taken by these parties were about equally delusive and neither would have in the least delayed the dangerous encroachments of the gold power. A tariff-for-revenue could in no sense be a Free Trade party, but it did propose to raise revenue by duties on imports. This duty would of course be paid by the people as part of the price of the goods which they consumed, and hence the tax would be in proportion to their expenses without any reference to their incomes. Those who expended their entire incomes in consumption would be taxed upon the whole, while those who expended only a small fraction, would be taxed only on the fraction so expended. As a system of taxation it is difficult to conceive of one that would be more unequal in its bearings, and more oppressive to people of small incomes."

"On the other hand the tariff-for-protection party, proposed to make the duties on imports so high that foreign productions would be kept out, and the home market secured to the employers of home labor. This, it was claimed, would enable the employers of labor to pay higher wages, which was true; but the selfishness of the heartless employer, was always in favor of keeping wages at a minimum and the noble, generous, employer could not afford to pay any more. If he did, his heartless· competitor would undersell him in the market and destroy his business. Hence we are not surprised that statistics proved the tendency of wages to be toward a minimum under both parties ----that is, a sum barely sufficient to provide food, clothing and shelter, and to enable the workman to raise other toilers to take his place when he was no longer able to work."

"Under this tariff-for-protection policy, the revenues raised were just as oppressive and unjust to people of small incomes as under the policy of 'a tariff for revenue only,' but with this additional burden, that the increased price of home products was assessed upon the people in the same unequal manner. But on the other side, more home labor could be employed, which benefited the workmen in protected industries at the expense of the classes which were not protected. Of course, even the tariff-for-protection party which had so much to say in favor of holding the home market for home products, never seriously intended to exclude foreign products, as that would have put an end to all revenue."

"These delusive theories of a tariff for revenue and a tariff for protection, served the purposes of the Gold Power, by calling the attention of the people away from the real difficulty which stood in the way of wealth producers. All that the people needed was an opportunity to apply their labor to natural resources, and be able to exchange their products for products of equal value, produced by the labor of others. The foreign trade of the country was a matter of small importance compared with the home trade. If at almost any time during the latter part of the Transition Period, the people of this country had been guaranteed just such rations as were provided for soldiers, or even convicts, there would have been no surplus for exportation; and had the whole people been provided with all the clothing that was needed to keep them well clad, it would have taken the entire product of wool, flax, cotton and leather. But the press of that day, religious as well as secular, was to such a large extent under the control of the Gold Power, that facts such as these were kept away from the masses of the people. And it may be added *in* this connection, that the educational system of the country was controlled by this same power to suppress the truth on economic questions, and many eminent scholars were removed from professorships in the higher institutions of learning, because they refused to teach such sophistries as suited the purposes of the Gold Power."

"In our very brief mention of the political agitations of that time we have only referred to the leading measures advocated by the dominant political parties. It is due however to even that benighted age to state, that at every step taken by the international Gold Power to financially conquer the world, a few of the more enlightened and self-sacrificing spirits, boldly exposed the financial wrongs which were being perpetrated against the people for the still further enrichment of the money kings of the Old World and their agents and co-workers in the great centers of wealth in this country. But these courageous, clear headed and humanity loving pioneers of a higher civilization were frowned down as dangerous agitators and enemies of law and order, and every foul epithet was applied to them. If in business, they were boycotted, and if belonging to the ranks of labor, they were black-listed and in many cases imprisoned on false charges, and some were even executed for crimes which they did not commit. And yet the measures of reform they advocated along political lines were usually of such a nature that had they been enacted into law they would only have prolonged, for a few decades perhaps, the false system which pauperized and degraded the toiling millions."

"So much for the political agitations which had for their ostensible object the improvement of the economic condition of the great masses of the people. Yet they did much good as a means of educating the more intelligent into a better understanding of the situation, and revealed the apparently utter hopelessness of ever being able to secure necessary reforms by political action, as no matter how pure at first might be the objects of a political party, just as soon as it was successful, and offices were in sight, the work of corruption set in and its principles became subordinate in the minds of its leaders, to the more profitable occupation of office seeking."

"But other more potent factors than political agitation, were at work among the masses in the shape of great industrial organizations of farmers and wageworkers. These organizations as a rule were strictly nonpolitical. The farmers sought to secure higher prices for the products of the farm without any regard for the interests of the millions of wage workers and others upon whom they depended for a market. Another object of the farmers was to reduce their cost of living by securing lower prices on their implements and other supplies. By concentrating their trade and taking advantage of the competition between dealers they often succeeded in securing very much reduced prices on goods, and this furnished what was regarded as a legitimate excuse for reducing the wages of the employes engaged in their manufacture. This reduction of wages crippled the market for farm products and offended both the employer and the workmen, so in the end the farmers defeated themselves and succeeded in arraying all other classes of people against them."

"But it was the wageworkers who suffered the most from the great oligarchy of wealth which had been established in the name of the people for the express purpose of exacting profits from the industrial classes. They organized Trade Unions which ultimately federated into one great national organization with a view to securing higher wages and fewer hours of labor without any regard to the interests of the consumers of their products. The number of workmen in these Trade Unions were at all times but a small fraction of the multitude which depended upon wages. As a rule the purposes and methods of these labor organizations were in practice, if not in theory, based upon the same false principles that characterized the industrial despotism against which they were protesting. Selfishness was a distinguishing characteristic and a fatal defect. The skilled workman who had employment, cared but little for the nonunion workman of his own craft except as a possible competitor for his job, and nothing whatever for the great masses of common laborers who were so numerous and so poor that organization could do them no good as a means of maintaining wages. The union workman recognized no interest in common with the unemployed outside of his own fraternity."

"Instead of banding together to devise ways and means by which all could find employment, the Trade Unions sought only to secure work and maintain wages for the comparatively small number who were members in good standing. Hence in case of strikes and lockouts the unemployed workmen were actuated by the same selfish motives and did not hesitate to take their places whenever they could be protected from violence. And whenever they did so, the union workmen made war upon them. While they recognized the relation of master and servant as one that was to be perpetuated, they denied the right of the 'scabs' as they were called, to accept employment from THEIR masters, no matter how destitute they might be."

"Neither did they question the right of employers, who in the days of the old civilization were principally powerful corporations, to control the enactment and the enforcement of the laws. As a rule, the workmen divided their voting power between the political parties which were controlled by their masters. With such evident inability to grasp the situation in which they were placed, it is not strange that the employers were enabled to obtain absolute control of every branch of government, state and national, legislative, executive and judicial, notwithstanding the fact that every laborer had a vote which counted just as much as that of the most wealthy corporation magnate. Conspiracy laws were enacted which could be used for their suppression as occasion required. The right of trial by jury was denied by the courts, and the champions of labor were imprisoned for long terms for disobeying the mandates of the courts. Finally the Supreme Court, in the case of a sailor who had refused to serve for the period for which he had hired, decided that his employer had a right to hold him in bondage until the expiration of the contract; that the ownership over himself had ceased for the time specified, and that the constitutional provision which prohibited involuntary servitude did not apply to such as him. One of the labor papers of that time characterized this opinion of the Court as the 'FUGITIVE SAILOR DECISION,' a name by which it is known in the history of those dark days of the Transition Period."

"But unfriendly legislation and one-sided court decisions, were not the only factors in crushing the hopes of labor. This was a period of wonderful scientific discoveries of natural forces and mechanical inventions by which they could be utilized in saving labor. The grandmothers who boasted that they could spin three miles of thread in one day, from sunrise to sunset, lived to see their little granddaughters spin three thousand miles in ten hours with the aid of machinery. Similar improvements were introduced into every branch of industry. The machinery belonged to the employer and he added the saving to his profit. He did not need so many workmen to produce all that the people were able to purchase, and the workmen were dismissed to join the mighty army of the unemployed. For a time certain skilled workmen were enabled to maintain living wages by means of organization, but continued improvements in machinery ultimately enabled common laborers to take their places, and reduced the number of experts required, to such a degree, that their condition was but little better than that of the unskilled. Among the best paid organizations of the olden time was the Locomotive Engineers, but ultimately, electricity took the place of steam, and a motor-man from the ranks of common labor took the places of both an engineer and a fireman. The machine displaced three-fourths of the printers at first, and later a still larger number of what remained, by introducing the principles of multiplex telegraphy, which enabled one expert to operate machines at the same time in a number of separate offices in different parts of the world whenever the copy was the same."

"Labor economists called attention to this displacement of labor by machinery, but the press and the politicians in the service of the corporations claimed, that this cheapening of production was of great benefit to the people by securing a corresponding reduction in prices. Finally, after a persistent agitation for years, the national Commissioner of Labor was required to make a careful examination, and in his report, among a multitude of similar items, we find that the labor cost of a five-dollar hat was only thirty-four cents, a ten-dollar plow, seventy-nine cents and so on to the end of a long catalogue of commodities which the people always needed. The question was, Who got the difference between the amount received by the actual producer and the price paid by the consumer? The answer was self-evident; outside of clerk hire, it must have gone to pay profits in some form to non-producers. But after this official demonstration that the 'lion's share' of the wealth created by productive labor went to nonproducing speculators, the great masses of the people still continued to use their influence to perpetuate this inequitable system which practically confiscated the wealth created by their labor to pay profits on speculative investments."

"The mass of the small dealers of that time were no better off, in many respects, than the wealth producing laborers, but being in some sense a part of the profit-exacting system, they held to it longer, in the vain hope that a time might come when by some fortuitous turn in business, or lucky speculation, they could amass millions. As a class they had never devoted themselves to an earnest and careful study of economic questions, but as long as the people came and purchased goods and left a profit in their hands, they were satisfied, and paid no attention to the far reaching influences which were surely paving the way to their ultimate failure in business. Hence it was not until just before the end of the old civilization that they began to realize that something was the matter. Sharp competition among the large number of small dealers reduced the average profits below a fair compensation for the labor expended, and large combines with unlimited money capital, were able to meet the universal demand for cheap goods. The dealers were finding themselves crowded out of business. They blamed their customers for not giving them the preference, even if the large department stores could afford to sell for less. They demanded legislation against the large stores and took an active interest in the Anti-Trust agitation of the time."

"This opposition to Trusts and Department stores, like the farmer's organizations and trade unions, took a very narrow view of the situation. They saw their profits decreasing and their sole object was to prevent this, without any reference to the interests of the people who as purchasers of goods must pay all the profits. The masses of the people understood their motives and did not hesitate to patronise Department stores and purchase Trust products, provided they could get them for less. They might have been able to protect themselves from the inordinate greed of the trusts and combines, by taking their customers into partnership and with their assistance organizing consumption and thus controlling distribution for the equal benefit of all. This would have been in exact accordance with the ideal that had been handed down in their system of religion, that, we should always do unto others as we would have them do unto us."

"The entire history of Altruria as an independent republic belongs to the Transition Period in the progress of the world and in a larger, but not so well defined a sense it extends to the discovery of the continent, and even to an earlier period, distinguished by the breaking up of the ancient religious hierarchy and the introduction of a constantly increasing number of warring sects. These were the evolutionary forces developed under the operations of natural law, in strict accordance with the constitution of the human mind, which always tends towards the utmost possible development of the race, physically, mentally and morally. These forces in the early stages of human development, work so slowly, that even the best trained intellects do not discover their existence and hence have no power to intelligently cooperate with them, with a view to accelerating their own progress upward toward the highest possible planes of development. But, it was during the last fifty years of this Transition Period, that all these forces became more apparent to the careful historian, and it is these to which I have more particularly directed your attention."

"Human selfishness on the lower planes of development constitutes the first step in the development of that higher selfhood, which is the predominating characteristic on the higher planes. During the last fifty years of the 'Transition Period, human selfishness, in the baser sense, was making its last struggle for existence as the controlling factor in human affairs. All classes of people were inspired to action by selfish interests, and these interests could not fail to clash. Out of this clashing between forces they ultimately leaned that the best and highest interest of every individual could always be secured by carefully guarding the interest of every other individual. Out of this was evolved our present universal rule, which governs our relations towards each other, of 'each for all and all for each,' and hence all are equally secure in the exercise of every natural right and in the possession of absolute economic independence."

"The Gold Power sought for and secured universal dominion over all the nations of the earth and there being no other nations to conquer, in its inordinate greed, it continued to impose additional burdens upon the people. This met opposition, first from one class and then from another, but all these movements were animated by the same element of selfishness which characterized the Gold Power. The farmers organized to secure better conditions for themselves without any regard to the interests of the millions of wage workers and others upon whom they depended for a market. The workmen organized to secure better wages for the members of their unions with no regard for any other class of people, or even for other workmen who did not belong to their fraternity. At the close of the old system the small dealers and manufacturers were unanimous against the encroachments of the vast combines who could undersell them, but they ignored the interests of the great mass of consumers upon whom they depended for a market. Selfishness, in the baser sense, guaranteed the failure of all these movements. No one class of people, seeking to promote its own selfish interests was able to hold its own against the superior intelligence of the great financiers who had planned to financially conquer the world by controlling the world's supply of gold through an organized system of creating debts both actual, for borrowed money, and constructive as investments which exacted tribute from the wealth producing classes. This process of debt creating continued until in this country the entire volume of sixteen hundred millions of money of all kinds would have paid but a fraction of the annual charge for interest, dividends, etc., upon investments and all the gold in the world, about $4,000,000,000 would have paid but a fraction of the principal."

"But another, and in the end the most potent evolutionary force which was destined to emancipate the people, was the arousing of the moral sense of large numbers who had never turned their attention to the study of economic science but whose souls revolted at the conditions imposed upon vast multitudes of people. The Gold Power while still a mighty factor in the control of the religious press and a large number of the leading religious teachers of the country, was not able to still the voice of the truest disciples of Krystus, and these demanded that the spirit of the founder of their religion should be exemplified in the practical every day affairs of life. They well understood that if the people were doing to each other as they would have others do to them, there could be no such thing as poverty, with all its tendencies towards vice and crime. These pioneers of a Diviner Civilization, with nothing but a theological training, were perhaps not clear in their own minds, as to just how this Golden

Rule could be applied in business under the prevailing financial and commercial systems of the country, but they did believe that the ideal in every human relation could be realized, and they insisted that the effort should be made by every true follower of Krystus, to establish the dominion of good upon earth to the end that righteousness might prevail in human affairs."

"For this grand culmination, the operation of the evolutionary forces for the last fifty years had been a post-graduate course for the workers who were to set the machinery in motion, on the material plane, by which all the crushing burdens imposed by Greed could be easily and speedily removed. And in this course, the mistakes made by the people had been the most potent educators. The producing classes had been induced to organize because they felt that they were not getting their just share in the distribution of wealth; but to save that which was lost in the distribution, they made the strange mistake of organizing as producers. The farmer had no need of an organization, to enable him to produce more wealth. The soil would produce just as much without such organization as with it. The same thing was true of mechanics, miners and other wageworkers, who organized in their capacity of wealth producers. But as consumers they could all stand on one platform, and being the market upon which all producers must depend, they would be masters of the situation. With an equal distribution of the benefits of such organization of consumption, it would be just as easy to pay dividends to labor, and thus increase their share in the distribution, as it was to pay dividends on capitalistic investments."

"So it was; that at a time when every thing seemed hopeless, the few who never yield to disappointments, and who had made an exhaustive study of existing economic conditions reinforced the earnest followers of Krystus who were demanding the application of the Golden Rule in business by formulating methods by which this much desired result could be attained. They had studied the moral problem that confronted the religionists, from the objective side, and understood just how it must be solved along business lines. In as much as all material wealth was created by labor, and distributed by being bought and sold, it followed as a logical sequence, that there was but one way by which every useful worker could secure a just share in the distribution, and that was to take charge of the business of exchange (buying and selling) and divide the benefits equally among all who united their efforts to establish the largest possible round of exchange between producers and consumers. This was simply the organization of the market for the express purpose of establishing Equity in Distribution, by paying dividends to labor. The people had at last discovered the vital truth upon which the application of the Golden Rule depends, that ORGANIZED CONSUMPTION CONTROLS DISTRIBUTION."

"Organizations of consumers were effected with a view to concentrating their purchasing power through channels of their own, not to reduce prices, but to pool the net profits into a common fund for the equal benefit of all the members. A portion of this was set aside as an educational fund to extend the work, and the remainder was used to pay dividends to the members who, as customers, had paid the profits into the common treasury. This was known as the "Dividend to Labor," and it was always distributed equally, as it had been secured by the united purchasing power of all the members. And, in order to secure this fund, which belonged alike to all, no member had added one cent to his or her cost of living. It was all a saving, as between the new equitable system of exchange and the old and wasteful profit system. This was a PROFIT SAVING BUSINESS MACHINE of which the PRODUCERS who constituted, in the main, the great markets of the world, COULD NOT BE DEPRIVED, and WITH THIS, it became a matter of indifference as to who had immediate control of the LABOR-SAVING MACHINERY of PRODUCTION."

"This movement had its origin in the West where the people were more inclined to think for themselves, but the benefits were so decided and so easily secured, that it spread rapidly. The first exchanges demonstrated that the use of money could be very largely minimized, and banks were established as depositories for all the money that came into their hands, and to facilitate their financial relations with unorganized communities where money was still a necessity. These savings of money, were held as a sacred trust, to enable the members to pay taxes, and debts, in cases where the creditor could not be induced to take products at a fair price. Among themselves they used exchange certificates which were issued on the deposit of products or money, and for necessary labor. These certificates being issued on values which were seeking a market and redeemed in products needed for consumption and cancelled, constituted an ideal currency that was always just equal to the demand, — neither more nor less."

"The people learned by experience how easy it was to minimize the use of money, and the tendency of this decrease in the demand for money, was to relatively increase the amount in circulation. It was easy now, for the most unfamiliar with business methods, to understand how the large operators, under the old system, had enriched themselves by making their settlements through great clearing houses where one obligation cancelled another and only two or three per cent of money had been used to pay balances; and they could see how even this balance among wealth producers, could take the shape of a check against future production and money be entirely eliminated as a medium in the exchange of wealth."

"All the people who were doing their buying and selling through these exchanges were regularly supplied with carefully prepared literature on economic questions and business methods, and of general information as to the trend of current events, the progress of the new order which placed business on an ethical basis and all matters of advantage for an independent, cultured citizenship to understand. Then for the first time, the multitudes began to realize the weakness of the fragile thread by which they had been bound to the triumphal car of Capitalism. Their experience gave them confidence. They used the same business methods for the benefit of the many that had enabled the few to concentrate in their own hands four-fifths of the wealth of the country. It was therefore no untried experiment. They were only exercising the same kind of business sagacity that had been used by the money kings to financially conquer the world. Just in proportion as they decreased the demand for money, it flowed in upon them in exchange for their products at a steadily increasing price. They had established a DEBT-PAYING instead of a DEBT-CREATING system of business, and in the course of time their debts were all paid, the necessity for legal money had disappeared, the people were free from its extactions, and all they had to do was to produce what they consumed and consume what they produced, exchanging equivalent for equivalent for the equal benefit of all. And thus the world had been saved from its thralldom to Greed by the establishment of the 'Kingdom of God and His Righteousness' as had been enjoined by Krystus at the beginning of the old religious system two thousand years before. This which was enjoined at the beginning of the Dispensation was REALIZED at its close and hence the FIRST BECAME THE LAST, because the LAST was THE FIRST REDUCED TO PRACTICE IN HUMAN AFFAIRS."

Chapter XIII

BONA DEA — MATRONS' HOME — PRENATAL INFLUENCES -IMPROVING THE AIRSHIPS — BATTELL EXPLAINS — PLANS FOR THE FUTURE — MUSEUM OF UNIVERSAL HISTORY -RELICS OF THE PAST — BUILDING TOWARD OUR IDEALS -LAW OF HUMAN PROGRESS — PRESAGING THE FUTURE -PROFIT CAUSES POVERTY — EQUITABLE EXCHANGE THE REMEDY.

As I listened to Norrena's description of the financial and commercial system which had once existed in Altruria, I could not help but notice its close similarity to the system which prevailed in the outer world. As he elucidated the international and seemingly unlimited power that had been exercised by the owners of gold, and how it would take all the gold in the world to pay a small fraction of the annual interest on the obligations held against the people, my heart sank within me at the utter hopelessness of their condition.

I was expecting to hear that the people in their desperation had blotted this power from the earth with fire and sword, but the speaker finished with merely a description of a more equitable system of transacting business. Just as he had come to this most interesting place in the discussion, the Institute closed and took a recess for dinner, and MacNair began to introduce us to the superintendents of many of the large educational institutions of the country who were members.

As we were leaving the hall Oqua joined us, accompanied by a magnificent looking woman whom she introduced to me as Bona Dea, the superintendent of the Matron's home at Lake Byblis, saying:

"My dear Nequa, I want you to learn that in Altruria we commence the education of children before they are born. This is what these Matron's homes are established for, and Bona Dea is superintendent of one of the oldest, largest and most thoroughly equipped institutions of this kind in the world. I want you to make her acquaintance, and I doubt not that you will become fast friends."

"I am indeed glad to meet you," I said, "as I want to learn all that I can about these, to me, strange educational institutions."

"And I," said Bona Dea, "shall be happy to give you any information in my power. Oqua informs me that you are preparing a book descriptive of our civilization, and I am much interested as an Altrurian in what it may present to the people of the outer world."

"Yes," I said. "And by all means, I want it to contain a review of these Matron's homes, and all that can be learned in regard to their origin, and the good they are designed to accomplish for humanity."

"That, indeed," said Bona Dea, "would constitute a most important volume in a series, but it should not be the first one in a thorough treatment of the evolutionary forces which work for the development of the race toward higher and better conditions."

"Then," I said, "would you have me ignore this, to me, most singular system of commencing the education of children before they are born?"

"There is nothing singular about the system," said Bona Dea. "Even the savages of the olden time did the same thing, but they did not know it. The mothers were surrounded by the conditions of savagery, and their children were born predisposed to become savages. These pre-natal influences are in fact the commencing point in the education of every child that is born, as they predispose the child to a life of usefulness, or the reverse, according to the character of the influences. The object which our Matron's homes are designed to accomplish is to provide the best possible conditions, to start the child with a strong, healthy body and mind, with a kindly disposition and elevated aspirations toward the highest possible intellectual and moral development."

"If such results," I said, "can be secured by the establishment of these homes, you certainly would not dissuade me from an exhaustive review of the entire question ?"

"Certainly not," she said, "but as a teacher of your people I would have you follow the natural law and begin your work at the beginning. From what I can learn, your own country is now passing through its Transition Period, similar to that described in Norrena's lecture, and hence the first great duty of your people is to abolish poverty. When the fear of want is removed from every household the first effect will be to place better pre-natal conditions around the mothers, and the next generation will be placed on a higher plane physically, intellectually and morally. This is the first step that your people must take and then the Home may be introduced for the scientific adaptation of pre-natal influences to specific purposes. Then you will begin to determine in advance whether the child shall be an inventor, scientist, philosopher, poet, musician, teacher or explorer. The Homes are scientifically adapted to specific purposes, while economic independence and general education lift the entire people to a higher plane of being along every line of human effort. What your people need now, is the general, mental and moral uplifting of the victims of your present system, and to this end, my advice to you would be, to confine your first work to the solution of the problem, 'How to abolish poverty.' "

"But would you," I asked, "discourage these specific measures at this time because the masses are poor?"

"Of course not," said Bona Dea, "for those who are able to apply them, but I would first, place these advanced scientific methods within the reach of the entire people by establishing economic independence for all. This is simply following the natural law of human development."

"Will you," I asked, "please explain just what you regard as the natural law of human development?"

"It is the law of growth," said Bona Dea, " and always begins at the base and works its way upward. The plant germinates in the earth and then pushes its way upward towards the light. The growth of the animal organism from conception to maturity is along the same line of progression, from the bottom of the scale, toward the top. In the growth of human civilization and the mental, moral and spiritual elevation of the race, the same general law of evolution holds good. The elevating influence must reach the people through their environments. The real man and the real woman, is the ego or spirit. The physical body is the outermost environment of the individual being. By improving the physical conditions we stimulate the mental organism into a healthy activity, and the result is intellectual growth, and spiritual unfoldment. Such is the natural law of human progress from the physical through the mental to its culmination in the spiritual or divine, which is the very highest type to which we aspire."

"This," I said, "looks like a concise and logical statement of the natural law, but how do you apply it to the present conditions which exist in my own country? We have a civilization and many very intelligent, well meaning and well to do people who might be greatly benefited by a better understanding of the influences of pre-natal conditions."

"Doubtless that is true," she replied, "but your duty as a teacher is to take the whole people into consideration and not a part, and in your work for their enlightenment begin at the bottom of the scale. Your present civilization was developed along the lines of unconscious growth, just as the child grows from birth to maturity. But your work as a teacher and civilizer is to work along conscious lines and lay your plans with due deliberation. Having, as it were, reached the top, you are able to give instruction to those who are lower down and help them to climb higher. The place of the teacher is one which demands that you should understand the natural law of growth, so that you may work to the best advantage. Hence your work is to begin with the outer environment, the physical, and that which pertains to the higher will take care of itself. It is not the whole, but the sick, who need the physician, so it is not the wise, but the ignorant who need the teacher. For these reasons I advise you to confine your present work more to the economic, as that would prepare the field for the higher, and that, just where it is most needed, among the poor."

"I think I comprehend your meaning," I said,"and shall act accordingly in the preparation of my first volume on Altrurian civilization.

Oqua's advice was very similar, but situated as I am here, these numerous lines of thought press in upon me all at once, and there is so much to learn, that I often find it difficult to make a selection. I am sure that the people of my own native land are passing through their Transition Period, and I am anxious to give them that which will do them the most good."

"Then," interposed Norrena, who had joined us, "show them how to get rid of poverty. Without economic independence, political independence and personal liberty, under the law, are a hollow mockery. There can be no progress without freedom, and there can be no freedom as long as a people are driven to their work by the stern lash of necessity."

"But how is it," I asked, "that you have such a realizing sense of the horrors of poverty, when you have always had an abundance?"

"Because it is the one great object," said Norrena, "of our educational training and of our Altrurian Civilization to provide against want, and to relieve distress wherever found. Every student in our schools is required to make a careful study of our Transition Period, the helpless, hopeless condition of the poverty stricken masses, and the methods by which they got out, and which must be continued in order to stay out."

"But why," I asked, "do you now, after centuries of abundance, still make these lessons so prominent in your educational system?"

"Because," said Norrena, "we are still on the physical plane, and if we do not guard against them by every means in our power, these physical evils may again overtake us. We know for a fact that eternal vigilance is the price that we must pay for the preservation of our present blessings."

"But constituted as your people are," I said, "with their readiness to relieve distress under all circumstances, I should think that you have no cause to fear a return of the old systems of oppression."

"Certainly not," said Norrena, "so far as this generation is concerned, but should we neglect the education of the rising generation in regard to these matters, we would begin to go back toward those conditions. There is no danger so long as we do our duty as educators, and keep alive the finer sensibilities of the soul. We did not reach our present condition at one bound, and if we were to go back it would not be all at once; but it is the duty of our teachers, to see that we do not take a single step backwards. Hence, we educate."

We had now reached the Department of Public Comfort where we were making our home during our stay in Orbitello. After dinner, Battell informed us that he intended to start within an hour to Lake Byblis, and that before he left, he desired to have some definite understanding as to our plans for future work.

"Then," said Norrena, "you had better join me in my rooms and talk the matter over. I feel deeply interested in your plans for opening communication with the outer world. So if it is agreeable, come with me."

We accepted the invitation, and were soon discussing what was now the leading thought in our minds --the improvement of the airships with a view to forming a connection between the inner and the outer worlds. Batten explained his plans for constructing a ship that could be moved in any direction, the power to be applied instantaneously, so as to be able to meet all the contingencies of a storm and contending currents of air. Then plans were discussed for protecting the occupants from intense cold. For this purpose, I had plans of my own which I did not divulge. Several ways were proposed for making the vessel proof against cold, but I saw at a glance, that with all of them, the freezing moisture on the inside, would so obstruct the vision as to very materially interfere with the proper guidance of the vessel.

"Before I left," said Battell, "I gave plans and specifications for an entirely new ship, that I want you to test in a storm, if you can find one, and report as soon as possible. Captain Ganoe has agreed to go with me and assist in its completion. As soon as it is ready I will let you know. Will you come to Lake Byblis and start from there? or shall I send it to some other point? What will be your address?"

"I have made no arrangements for the future," I said, "that will in the least interfere with the proposed trial trip to the southern verge. I think, however, I had better remain here a few days, as there are some questions that I want to study, and to that end, I shall take a look through the Museum of Universal History. "

"Well, get your book ready," said Battell, "and we will find the means to send it where it will do the most good."

"I have sufficient material ready," I said, "for a number of books, but the question now is, How much out of the great abundance, shall I select to go with an account of our discoveries?"

"Well, I should think," said Battell, "that you could not send a very large proportion of what you can find in a single one of these exhibits, to say nothing of the libraries; but do your best. I have work that must be completed, in order to make yours available, so good-bye, and may success attend you."

Captain Ganoe, MacNair and Iola accompanied Battell to Lake Byblis, and Norrena, Oqua and myself went to the museum.

This was a most magnificent structure, situated on the river, on a point of land where the river leaves Orbitello and makes a sharp turn toward the east. The building was a hexagon, about 600 feet in diameter, and the foundation had been excavated down to the level of the water, which gave one-half the building the appearance of extending out into the river. In the center of the building was an inlet for boats for which there was a spacious landing, enclosed by broad, marble steps on three sides.

At the center, and each of the six corners, was an elevator which connected with each floor. Around what may be regarded as the main building, was a broad extension in the form of an inclined floor, that communicated at frequent intervals with the several stories, either on the level of the floors or by easy flights of steps.

On the periphery of this inclined spiral floor, was a railing. The whole of the external structure was supported by massive and highly ornamented columns of aluminum which reflected the light like burnished silver. In the center, and supported from above, was a double track electric tramway, with cars moving each way at short intervals. This arrangement gave the entire floor space to pedestrians and those using electric chairs and other small vehicles. The lower stories of this immense building, up to the level of the bluff, contained supplies of all kinds, required by those engaged in river transportation. The upper stories of the building were devoted to the preservation of relics and records commemorative of past civilizations and taken altogether, presented to the eye a complete history of man's progressive development along every line from the earliest period of recorded history. This wonderful exhibit, enabled the student to trace, by means of practical illustrations, the progress of the mechanical arts, from the original crude contrivances to the present high state of development under which drudgery was unknown, and the people were in the full enjoyment of all the comforts of life with a minimum of labor. It is no part of my intention to attempt to give more than the most cursory mention of this wonderful exhibition of industrial progress.

One feature, however, impressed me most, and that was the striking similarity in these exhibits, to the much smaller ones, which I had visited in the outer world. The methods which had prevailed in the different stages of civilization, were almost identical with those prevailing in the corresponding stage of outer world development. In water craft for instance, the raft of logs bound together with thongs and propelled by poles came first, followed by canoes hollowed out of logs. Then smaller boats with oars, and growing in dimensions until they assumed the shape of Roman galleys and the ships of the Northmen. Then sails were introduced and later, steam became the motor power. So, of the methods of land transportation. The sledge and oxcart were followed in time by the stage coach, this by the electric car, and last came the airship.

I asked Norrena to explain this remarkable similarity.

"This," said he, "only indicates that human development along every line of progress is determined by the constitution of the human mind. Knowing this, we have the key which explains all the mysteries connected with the progress of the race from lower to higher conditions. At every step it has been met by similar difficulties and hence the methods for overcoming these difficulties have been similar, because all have alike possessed the same mental constitution. This progress up to a certain point, has been along unconscious lines, and the average man and woman had no clear understanding of the influences which were impelling them forward. In every age, and in every condition of life, man has been building in the direction of his ideals, but never reaching them. In his primitive state, he felt the need of some means for crossing streams, and having observed that wood floated upon the water, he constructed a raft. From this he formed the plan of a boat, and constructed a canoe. As he improved in the direction of his ideals, these ideals became more exalted, and today we have the magnificent electric yacht. So it has been in every department of human effort. The higher the ideals which have been formed in the mind of man, the higher he has climbed in the scale of development. This is the fundamental law of human progress. Every one of these relics of past ages was at first an ideal that had been formed in the human mind before it was realized."

"A thought strikes me," I exclaimed. "If all these ideals have been realized, is it not a promise, or a prophecy, that our ideals of today, will be realized in the future? And if from the constitution of the human mind we could presage the ideals of the future, we could in a general way predict what the civilization of distant ages will develop."

"Certainly," said Norrena. "Your thought is strictly philosophical and applied to our immediate future it gives an infallible rule for presaging events where we are familiar with the forces impelling in a certain direction. If we can ascertain where we are today on any given line of progress, we can safely predict what the next step will be on the same line, for all things are possible to the human mind in its ultimate state of development. There is no such thing as actually turning back in the path of progress, much as man may seem to retrograde at times. The lessons taught by these seeming failures are essential elements in his still greater development further on. Nothing that is useful can be permanently lost to the race. What we are inclined to call evil, is fleeting and fades away, while the good, the true and the really valuable is immortal. Hence, human progress towards higher and better conditions, as applied to the race, and long periods of time, must ever be onward and upward toward the Infinite Good."

"I have always," I said, "been deeply interested in everything pertaining to the progress of the race, but I have been inclined to regard it as somewhat a matter of chance. You seem to have reduced it to an exact science. I can understand how certain influences are necessarily toward improvement, but how is it that our elevation is assured when so many are unconscious of such a tendency, and in the outer world at least, multitudes seem to be bent upon getting lower instead of higher in the scale? I feel quite sure that the masses of our ancestors in the past, were no better than the masses now, and did not consciously cooperate with nature for their own improvement. It seems, however, that by some kind of a blind chance they may have contributed something, but it certainly was not intentional. I see a different influence working here and the people are evidently co-operating with nature for the good of all, but I fear that it will be a long time before the people of my own country will reach that stage of development."

"Do not be discouraged," said Norrena. "The constitution of the human mind is a guarantee of human elevation. The history of human development presents two distinct stages, the unconscious and the conscious. All progress from the simple cell to the human being, is of course unconscious and is governed by fixed and immutable laws. These same laws control human development up to the point where knowledge enables the race to consciously participate in the work of its own elevation. As soon as the people are sufficiently developed to understand the operation of the laws which control their own unfoldment, they will enter upon an epoch of conscious progress by careful and well concerted measures. When at the close of the Transition Period our people reached that stage, the change for the better in every direction came suddenly upon the world, because the masses of mankind felt the need of something better. Unconscious development had prepared them for the wonderful change. The blind forces which had been slowly urging man upward toward a higher plane of existence, now had the aid of careful and well devised methods, and the long ages of darkness disappeared in the blaze of light which was let in upon the world."

"And from this," I said, "am I to infer that you think America is about ready for such an uplifting of the masses? Your description this forenoon of the Transition Period of this country, would pass as an accurate delineation of the present condition in my own. The belief is widespread among . thoughtful people in the United States that our country is on the eve of some great change. Persons of an optimistic turn of mind believe that we are near the beginning of a higher, nobler and purer civilization than the people have ever enjoyed before, while the pessimistic are equally sure that we are destined to go back toward barbarism, I want so very much to be able to disseminate the light that will dispel this darkness from our future. "

"I think," said Norrena, "that you have no cause for alarm. From what I can learn the optimists of your country are largely in the majority, and a general expectation of something better for humanity, is a powerful psychic force, to produce something better. If your people earnestly desire better things for the masses and at the same time believe that better things are in store for them, your future is most hopeful, as the people cannot fail to find out how to attain the object they are seeking.

"Thank you," I said. "But where is the light, and what can I do to shed it, broadcast among them? "

"The light," said Norrena, "is latent in every human soul and is manifested in the readiness with which all classes of people render assistance to those who are placed in peril or are suffering from some great affliction. This is the light that is manifested in your charitable institutions and public hospitals for the relief of the poor and the physically infirm. When those who provide these institutions for the relief of suffering humanity learn how the sufferings which now appeal to their sympathies can be avoided, this latent light will be developed into a flame that will enlighten the whole earth and the darkness will disappear as if by magic."

"But this," I said, "does not tell me how that latent light can be developed into such a flame. Human sympathy has always existed, but as yet in the outer world it has not succeeded in removing the suffering which appeals to our sympathies. By what means can this be accomplished?"

"By the discovery and application of the principles of equity in all of our relations toward each other," said Norrena. "To assist you in this, I suggested that we take a look through this Museum. In the relics of past ages which you find here, you can trace the operation of the fundamental laws of human progress. On this floor you have the works of man in his lowest condition. On the floor above, you find relics of a higher civilization. These have been classified as nearly as possible in their natural order, from the lowest to the highest, with a view to teaching the progressive development of the race in the most effective manner."

"I realize the importance," I said, "of such a collection to every student. But all this comes before your Transition Period and I do not see its bearings upon the great problem of the present day in my own country, how to secure the same conditions which I find prevailing here."

"As yet," said Norrena, "you have only seen the relics of barbarism. This museum is twenty stories high above the level of the bluff on which it stands, and each story bears its record of the onward and upward progress of the race. The first were erected soon after the Transition Period, but others have been added since that time, to make room for the evidences of our progress. We will now ascend to the one devoted to the Transition Period."

We stepped upon the elevator and in a moment more were ushered into one of the upper stories, and I found myself confronted by a display, such as would characterize a first-class exposition of the present day in the United States; with this difference, however; it resented the poverty and misery of the hovel as faithfully as it did the grandeur of the palace. Everything seemed familiar and I felt as if I had been suddenly transported to New York or London. Every feature of the competitive system of production and distribution was appropriately illustrated, together with the inevitable consequences to the people; wealth and the dreams of avarice for a favored few and hopeless poverty and degradation for the many.

The clothing of the workmen in contrast with the gorgeous apparel of the fashionable bon ton; the furnishings of the hovels of the poor and the mansions of the rich placed side by side; the coarse and homely fare of the wealth producer compared with the dainty viands of the non-producer; all told more plainly than words the story of undeserved poverty, and in millions of cases, the abject want and misery of the most useful classes of society, in striking contrast with the unearned abundance of the idle, and for all practical purposes, the useless rich. The manner in which the wealth created by the toiling millions, passed through the channels of trade, into the possession of a few wealthy speculators, was illustrated by pictures and printed explanations, in almost endless variety, so that even the most obtuse observers, could not fail to get a clear idea of the practical workings of a system of commercial exchange, under the operation of which, interest, profit and rent were always added to the market price of the product, every time it changed hands.

One of these illustrations was entitled, **"Thirteen Usuries on One Hog." It represented a hog passing from the farmer at one end of a long bridge to the workman at the other.** From the time the hog starts from the producer on the farm until it reaches its destination in the workshop of the consumer, its size (price) has become colossal. In exchange for the hog a plow starts from the shop to the farm, and the size (price) increases in the same proportion. Every time any commodity passed one of the commercial toll gates established between the producer and the consumer, the price was increased for the benefit of speculators who contributed nothing to its value. All this was of course to the manifest loss of the producers. The long bridge was labeled, THE PROFIT SYSTEM.

In contrast with this was a short bridge labeled EQUITY, over which products were passing both ways from the producer to the consumer, without changing size. Over this Equity bridge the product passed directly from the producer to the consumer by the shortest practicable route, and was only handled one time. Over the Profit bridge, goods became shelf-worn and deteriorated in value, by the frequent changing of hands. These two bridges, Profit and Equity, were given as symbolical representations of the Cause and Cure of poverty. There was no mistaking the lesson taught by them; neither could there be a doubt of their truth. Under the Profit system of exchange the managers are self-employed and it is legitimate that they should have a profit for the service rendered, and the larger the profit, the larger the number who can make a living out of it. Under Equity, the managers are employed by their customers and it is to their interest to see that the business of exchange is carried on with the smallest possible amount of work in handling the product. Hence the Profit system necessarily entails poverty upon the masses who have no interest in the exchange, while Equity secures abundance, because the exchange is effected by their own agents at the least possible expense. Hence, under Equity, the product passes from the producer to the consumer without changing size, and the cost is fixed by the amount of labor expended in its production, superintendence and transportation; and all parties to the transaction, get the exact value of their services; but under this system there is nothing for the money king, the profit-monger and the landlord.

"You see," said Oqua, who had been unusually silent and preoccupied, "that this symbol of the two bridges, tells the whole story of the difference between the profit system of exchange and the equitable; between the old system with its widespread poverty and the new with its abundance."

"I see the difference, " I said, " but it is not so clear to my mind just how the people can pass from one bridge to the other; from PROFIT to EQUITY. "

"That is very easy," said Oqua." Change the PURPOSE for which business is transacted. Instead of exacting profit from the producer and the consumer, conduct business for the purpose of establishing equitable relations between the producers and the consumers. When this is done the profit system will have been removed and equity will bring abundance to the household of every producer, and poverty will be abolished."

"I can well understand," I said, "what the effect of a change of systems would be, and it is equally clear to my mind that the money kings, trust barons and landlords could, if they would, easily introduce the change, but how could the poverty stricken people make such a change in the business system of the world? If it is done at all, it must be done by the very poor, and under the profit system the very poor are helpless."

"That, 'under the profit system,' is well put in," said Norrena, laughing. "It is undoubtedly true, that 'under the profit system,' the producers are helpless; and it is equally true that as long as they remain under this system, they will continue to be helpless. It is also true that the selfishness of the wealthy managers will never consent to the change so long as they can prevent it."

"Then, indeed," I said, "to my mind the condition of the laboring millions is hopeless. They CANNOT establish equity and the rich WILL not."

"Why hopeless?" asked Norrena. "Do you think they would refuse to make the change from profit to equity, if they had the opportunity to do so?"

"Not that," I said. "But the question is, How can they make the change while bound hand· and foot under the profit system?"

"Whatever has been done," said Norrena, "can be done, and you have only to look around you to see that the change from profit to equity has been made in this country and can be made in yours, notwithstanding the fact that the people are bound hand and foot and will continue to be so bound as long as the profit system continues."

"Please do not mock me," I said with some spirit, "How can a people who are bound hand and foot, save themselves?"

"By using their heads," said Norrena. "The hands and feet may be bound while the head is left free to think. Let this freedom to think be exercised in the right direction and their physical bonds will disappear."

"I am sure they do think," I responded, "and what is more, they have been thinking for a long time."

"Then," said Norrena, "let them continue to think and they cannot fail in due time to find out just what is the matter. "

"Oh, many of them have found that out," I said, "and realize that they are impoverished by the exorbitant profits on investments which go to the wealthy classes."

"Then, indeed," said Norrena, "the day of their deliverance is drawing near. They have already learned that it is the profit system that is pauperizing them. If they continue to think, they cannot fail to learn that the profit system could not continue without their constant support. That when they withdraw their patronage from profit-mongers, the profit system will disappear. If I read your literature correctly, your people are very near the hour of their deliverance."

"They may," I said, "be driven to the violent overthrow of the present system, but I do not see how they can speedily break their bonds in any other manner."

"They can do it," said Norrena, "by the exercise of the same spirit of manly independence, intelligently directed, that they now exercise in their worse than useless strikes. You have the competitive system which is self-destructive and hence weak. Your producing classes can organize as consumers and take advantage of the sharp competition between dealers to sell goods, and by a wise use of their combined power to purchase, introduce an **equitable system of exchange."**

"What is that?" I asked. "Would they expect any such

sweeping results from selling their trade to the firm that would give them the largest rebate on prices? Would not the tendency of such a movement be, to still further curtail the demand for labor, by depressing the price of products?"

"Yes," said Norrena, "such a system of selling their custom for a rebate, would have just such an effect. But you lose sight of the fact, that wholesale dealers are competing with each other for an opportunity to sell goods. They sell to retail dealers who can find customers for their goods. Organize your ability to purchase, select a competent business agent, and go into business for yourselves, and be sure not to undersell other dealers. Your exchange will have a decided advantage over every other dealer, because your trade will be organized and your sales will be certain. The wholesaler will be quick to see this, and will be anxious to get your trade, as his pay will be certain."

"But," I said, "where would be the inducement for the people to organize their trade, with the certainty that they would pay just as much for the goods as they did before?"

"The same inducement," said Norrena, "that people under the money system have for depositing their earnings in savings banks. Every time they purchase an article in their own exchange they are making a deposit to their own credit, where it will do them the most good in times of disaster. The profits will belong to the organized customers, and by leaving them in the exchange they will accumulate a sample stock of goods already paid for, from which any order can be filled. After such a stock of goods is secured, they might at regular intervals declare a dividend to the organized customers, leaving a percentage on deposit with the exchange to be used to educate the people into a comprehensive understanding of business methods and for the creation of a fund to purchase land and give employment to their members, in order to eliminate rent on land and save the profits on production."

"But," I said, "I do not clearly see how starting stores and saving retail profits would enable the people to escape the demands of interest and rent."

"The store by itself," said Norrena, "could not do this, but the financial power that can always be secured by wise business methods could. To the extent that the use of money can be minimized and debts paid, of course interest will be saved. And to the extent that consumption can be organized and concentrated, a smaller number of business houses will also be needed and thus rent saved to the customers who in the last analysis pay all the expenses. And just in proportion as business houses are not needed, they will be for sale to people who can use them, as landlords could not afford to pay taxes on property for which tenants could not be found. This property would all be needed by the organized consumers who, with their continually accumulating fund from pooling the savings of profit, interest and rent, even on a comparatively small scale, would always be able to buy. The profits on distribution will constitute an ample fund for socializing the land and furnishing employment for a continually increasing number of people."

"But," I said, "to be able to hold our own against the worldwide profit system, would require a worldwide organization."

"Do not be too sure of that," said Norrena. "The benefits of equitable exchange in a single locality, would be most decided. Of course it would be more effective if extended over a wider field. But the distribution of literature, such as the accumulating profits would enable you to make, added to the far-reaching effects of a successful object lesson, could not fail to make the organization world wide. All that is necessary for this purpose is a practical demonstration, that by this system, the productive laborer and not the money king is master of the situation."

"Is this the same plan that you outlined in your address?" I asked.

"Just the same," he said. "All that is required is such a business organization as will cover the entire ground demanded by absolute justice. It must look to the elimination, as rapidly as possible, of the elements of interest, profit and rent. To avoid the payment of interest it is necessary to minimize the use of money, and as soon as debts are paid, refuse to use it at all. To avoid profits, you must purchase your supplies and sell your products through your own exchanges. To get rid of rent, use the profits to socialize the land."

"This is certainly sweeping enough," I said, "but it seems to me, that it would be an almost endless task to induce the masses of the people to unite their trade to such an extent as would be necessary to secure the full measure of relief demanded by absolute justice."

"It certainly would be," said Norrena, "if you did not prosecute a vigorous educational work, and at the same time offer inducements that the profit system cannot afford."

"I fear that this would be impossible," I said. "The dealers with millions of money could beat us in offering inducements to catch the trade of the unthinking."

"Do not fear that," said Norrena. "They could not do that without abandoning the profit system, which is all that you would ask. As soon as you have organized trade and have a sufficient stock accumulated to meet its demands, you will be saving interest to the extent that you can transact business without money, and to this will be added all of the net retail profits. This will enable you to pay a little more for farm products than dealers can who are on the profit basis. You can safely continue this rise in prices until you pay as much as. you can sell for. This will give you the entire trade of the farmers, and the usual profits on all they purchase will be a net gain to your exchange, less the slight advance on the price of products, equal to the profits of the speculators. The price you receive for farm products, will be exchanged for goods on which you will make a profit, and if you can always make ONE PROFIT on the exchange you will be on the high road to success."

"But this inducement," I said, "would only reach the farmers. It would be necessary to offer some other kind of inducement to secure the trade of the city workmen."

"That is easily provided for," said Norrena. "Your farmer's trade, notwithstanding the fact that you pay as much for the product as you can sell it for, will net one profit on the goods for which you exchange it. With all this farm trade secure, you can begin to furnish employment to city workmen in various ways, converting the raw material into finished products to supply your increasing trade. This will enable you to make valuable customers out of all the workmen for whom you can find employment. Another inducement will be, to return one-half of the net profits on their trade in the shape of a check which will be good at the exchange for products. This will still leave one-half as a contribution to the educational and land purchase fund. I believe, however, that with a vigorous and comprehensive educational work, but few would ever draw anything in the shape of a dividend out of the business, but leave it as a permanent investment to enable them to secure homes, or as an insurance fund to support them in sickness and for the benefit of their families in case of death."

"You seem to have unlimited faith in this plan of organizing business," I said.

"And why should I not have?" asked Norrena. "These principles have been tried in this country and we know by experience that they cannot fail, wherever they are intelligently and honestly applied, on a scale large enough to constitute one good object lesson as to what can be accomplished. The system, in practice, will demonstrate that money is not a necessity. Money however, will still come into your hands, even more freely, and as long as you have debts that must be paid in money, you will have use for it. But when the debts are all paid, money might cease to circulate, as you would then have learned by actual experience, that you would get along better without it than with it."

"That puts me in mind," I said, "that in your lecture you stated that the people in this country, in their movement to establish equity in business, established banks to manage their money account. If the movement here was started by the very poor, how did they get money for the necessary cash capital?"

"By the accumulation from cash purchases made in their exchanges," said Norrena. "Their exchanges were a system of banking products, but they issued checks on the deposit of money as well as products. As these exchanges offered superior inducements, they received their full share of cash trade from the beginning, and nearly all of it when their exchange was complete. Hence they found no difficulty in establishing their own banks under the law, and as they never loaned their deposits, their banks could not break, and people who had money to deposit, brought it to them for safe keeping. As the tendency of this locking up of deposits was to curtail the circulation of money, the exchanges provided against any oppressive stringency, by loaning on good security, without interest, checks which were redeemable in products at the exchanges. It was estimated by the statisticians of that time, that every dollar locked up in the exchange banks, brought six dollars of trade per annum to the exchange stores on which the regular customers at these exchanges made an average of ten per cent or sixty per cent upon deposits."

"Were these exchanges incorporated as joint stock companies?" I asked.

"'They were," said Norrena, "but not always. The real object of the order was to ultimately eliminate the stock corporation and substitute the equal co-partnership. Hence when incorporated, every regular customer was a stockholder to the same amount, and the stock might be paid for by turning their dividends back into the business as a permanent investment. In other words, they might pay for their stock out of what they were able to save in their cost of living by their abandonment of the profit system. And further, in order to protect themselves from the danger of a constructive indebtedness in the shape of dividend exacting stock, no certificates were issued, and the stock paid for was always redeemable in exchange certificates payable in goods at the option of the shareholders, or by order of the directors of the corporation, for failure to patronize the exchange whenever practicable. As governments were especially friendly to corporations, it was deemed best by many, to incorporate and secure these advantages."

"This," I said, "was certainly the full measure of justice to be secured by a stock corporation, but how were others which were not incorporated, organized in order to secure the full measure of justice to members?"

"There was," said Norrena, "no patent on the application of the Golden Rule in business, and among business men there was a large number who really wanted to see equity established in human affairs. Hence there was nothing to hinder a merchant from entering into contracts with organized consumers, to sell his business to them, and retain the management at an agreed salary, under such rules and regulations for the conduct of the business as they might adopt. By this means many were enabled to exchange a precarious profit for a permanent income. In cases of this kind, the merchant was benefited by securing a guarantee against bankruptcy and the organized consumers by securing the services of the necessary business talent to establish Equity in Distribution, by paying equal dividends out of the net income to all regular customers. As contracts for a lawful purpose were held sacred by the courts a very large number held that the contract between the customers and the manager secured greater advantages than the stock corporation in obtaining equality of dividends."

"But," I asked, "why this equality of dividends? Was it fair to those who purchased large quantities of goods, to require them to share equally with those who purchased on a small scale?"

"It certainly was," said Norrena, "as it took the UNITED purchasing power of ALL to establish a business that enabled them to effect any saving at all, so that there would be something to divide. The large purchaser through these exchanges got something back, while under the profit system he would have made nothing at all. To him this equal dividend was a comparatively small item, while it was a most important increase of purchasing power to one who was barely able to procure the necessaries of life. Persons in affluent circumstances were thus enabled to help their poorer neighbors, and at the same time secure a dividend themselves. This system of organized consumption with an equal distribution of the net profits, was the first introduction of the fraternal features of our altruistic civilization. It was, in its application, a system of universal insurance against poverty for all, who, as consumers, withdrew their support from the profit system. In a peaceful, just and orderly manner, it enabled the poorest to take a seat at the table which our bounteous Mother Nature has prepared alike for all, and from which they had been excluded by human greed, which the founders of the old religious system had characterized as the "Mammon of Unrighteousness."

"Then it seems," I said, "that this was something of a religious as well as a business organization?"

"Yes," said Norrena, "it may indeed be regarded in that light as it was the practical application of the teachings of Krystus. This equality of interest in the distribution of that which had hitherto been lost to the producers of wealth under the profit system was the first recognition, on a broad scale, of the Brotherhood of Man in the business relations which existed among the people. This great business organization appealed to the enlightened self-interest of all classes of people, and drew them into closer relations with each other as one family, and cultivated feelings of fraternal regard for each other that will be imperishable. With an abundance for all, the inordinate thirst for gain had been eliminated and the application of the Golden Rule in business had at last been established to bless mankind."

"I am deeply interested in learning more about this organization," I said. "From your explanations I think that I have a tolerably clear idea of its general principles, and now I would be pleased to know more of its origin, history and experiences. As an organization it must have passed through many trying ordeals before it had accomplished its work of freeing the people from their thralldom to triumphant greed."

"It did have a history," said Norrena, "but it was a history of signal and sweeping victories. Its difficulties and trying ordeals were all in its efforts to get started right. Even the leaders of the great reform movements of that time, many of whom had given years to the study and discussion of economic questions, did not comprehend its scope. The people had been so thoroughly blinded by the universal system of doing business on a money basis, that they had never even tried to formulate plans for changing to the labor basis unless they could get money enough to purchase everything necessary to start up the work of production and distribution. This class of co-operators frequently put their means together, purchased lands and established colonies. Many of these proved quite successful, but they did not bring the benefits of co-operation to the millions who could not pay the necessary initiation fee to say nothing of the other millions who were forced into idleness."

"This reminds me," I said, "that Iola told me the district where I had been making my home, was a community or colony of this kind, but she said that 'the colonists were from among the very poor."

"That is true," said Norrena. "District Number One, was originally composed of that class of people in the great city Kroy, which the money kings regarded as dangerous, and hence they were permitted to go upon lands for which there was no market. The leaders were people of high culture and knew how to use their opportunities. But the colonies of which I speak were not founded by the submerged. These colonies demonstrated that co-operation contained elements of vital power that was irresistible, whenever it was fairly tested. The able literature sent out from these colonies, backed up by their experience, was a powerful educational influence which prepared the way for universal co-operation."

"But this organization of equitable exchange, as I understand it," I said, "was a business organization adapted to the general public, which enabled the people to get possession of the machinery of production and distribution. We have successful colonies in the outer world and I am familiar with their methods, but how to bring these benefits of united action to the whole people, is the question in which I am especially interested."

"1 have described its workings," said Norrena, "as clearly as my knowledge of your language will permit, and if there is any matter concerning which you are in doubt I will try to make it plain."

"I have no doubt of the principles," I said, "and from what I have seen, I am persuaded that the methods could be successfully applied wherever a nucleus of earnest reformers could be found who would make a careful study of the situation, and adopt the same business methods which were used so successfully in this country. I want some of the particulars concerning the history of this organization and a concise statement of its purposes and business methods that would serve as a model for a similar organization in the United States."

"The first organization," said Norrena, "was effected at this place which was then the site of one of the larger interior cities of that day. This was the center of business for a large population of farmers on one side and miners on the other. It started with the guaranteed trade of one hundred families and was a success from the start, as the result of the ample provision for educational work along the lines indicated. Every member was supplied with a paper which was devoted to the education of the people into a comprehensive understanding of business methods and commercial equation, as promulgated in theory and illustrated in practice by the Patrons of Equity. This paper contained the official reports of the business exchanges established under the auspices of the order. The educational work had been carried on for a long time by a few devoted workers, before it materialized into a self-supporting business. After that, the order spread rapidly. A percentage of the profits was used to employ organizers and every organization added to the trade and increased profits without any corresponding increase of expenses. When this movement was inaugurated, the number of commercial travelers in the country was estimated at about 250,000. These were persons of energy and business talent. They were quick to see the advantages which this system of commercial equity offered to men of ability, to establish themselves in business for which they were especially qualified, and they started out to find locations where they could organize business on these principles."

"But was there not some danger that designing people might get control and defeat the purposes of the organization?" I asked.

"Designing persons did get into positions," said Norrena, "but there could be no danger to the cause from this source, as in order to secure positions they had to adopt methods of business that could not fail to overthrow the profit system, and as fast as business was organized, the official paper of the order was sent regularly to every member. If at first they did not understand the principles well enough to protect themselves from knaves, they soon learned; and if anything was going wrong it was soon understood by the customers. As the business extended, the oppressive power of money decreased, and the power of labor increased. The enthusiasm of the people was aroused to the highest pitch, and the magnates of the old system were correspondingly depressed. The old system was essentially weak, while the new was peculiarly strong, and as the hosts of wealth producers came together, and utilized the actual values created by their labor as the medium by which exchanges were effected, prices went up as the result of the increase in the currency, and there was no use for money except to pay debts. Under this system, the purchasing power of labor and products was steadily increasing, while the purchasing power of money was decreasing. As long as money was needed to pay debts, products were exchanged for money at the increased price fixed under the labor standard, but when the debts were all paid, the purchasing power of money was gone and poverty had disappeared with it. Every debt had been paid according to contract, and in the payment of these debts the debtors had transferred their poverty to their creditors."

"We have gone over this ground," I said, "until, as I understand it, the great potency of this organization, was in the fact that all its methods were especially designed to ultimately eliminate the use of money in the transaction of business, but it occurs to me, that much could be done in this direction, without the organization of business exchanges, which issue certificates on the deposit of money and products to serve the purposes of a currency ."

"You are right," said Norrena. "And much was done along other lines when the people came to understand that the prime factor in the overthrow of the profits system was to avoid the use of money in the transaction of business, in every manner possible. In some localities, farther east, the use of what was known as New Occasion Notes was introduced to facilitate exchange without money. The shoemaker, for instance, would give his note, payable in shoes, for groceries. The physician would give his note for groceries payable in professional services. The grocery man had no personal use for either shoes or the services of a physician, but he needed coal, and the coal dealer needed both a shoemaker and a physician, and exchanged coal for the notes. The exchange enabled the shoemaker and the physician to get groceries, the grocery man to get coal, and the coal dealer to get shoes and the services of a physician, and all without the use of a cent of money. The use of these notes became so common, that to still further facilitate exchanges, clearing houses were established where persons who held notes payable in something they did not need, could exchange them for notes that were payable in something they did need. This system of exchanging New Occasion Notes grew into a general collecting agency, and it was found that among the large number of collections placed in its hands, a great percentage cancelled each other, and balances could ordinarily be put in the shape of New Occasion Notes redeemable in some kind of products or services. As a means of enabling people to get out of debt, and at the same time facilitating exchange and decreasing the demand for money, these agencies proved to be most effective. The Patrons of Equity contemplated the persistent use of every method that could be devised to minimize the demand for money with a view to its ultimate elimination as a medium of exchange, by the establishment of equity between producers and consumers. They had learned that money of any kind could be inflated and contracted for selfish purposes, and therefore it was a false measure and could not be depended upon to mete out even handed justice to the people who used it as a medium of exchange."

"I can plainly see," I said, " that the field of labor for such an organization in the outer world is practically unlimited, and I want you to furnish me with the details of its plan of organization, as a model for a similar one for use in my book."

"I have," said Norrena, "provided a translation of the Constitution and By Laws of the order, together with the rules and regulations for the government of its Exchange Department for your own use. I would advise you, however, not to publish these in your book. Only present the general principles, and let your people work out the details in their own way. Start the idea to working and I doubt not that they will discover how easy it is for them to escape from their thralldom to greed, and when they do, it will not be long until they sever the bonds that hold them."

"And how," I asked, "would you state these purposes so as to include all you have given me, in the fewest possible number of words?"

"For this purpose," said he, "I cannot do better than to quote the declaration of purposes from the preliminary constitution formulated by the founders of the *Patrons of Equity, as follows:

"'SECTION I. The primary object of this order shall be to organize exchange on the largest scale that may be practicable, with a view to the establishment of equitable relations between producers and consumers, by eliminating as rapidly as possible, every element of cost that does not go to the producers of the wealth exchanged, less an equitable compensation to the labor, physical and mental, that is necessary to an economical management of the business.

"'SECTION 2. And further, as opportunity offers, to effect such an organization of our financial relations as will enable us, as far as practicable, to hold all the money that comes into our hands, as a sacred trust, to be used only in the payment of taxes, and of debts in all cases where the creditor cannot be induced to take some other form of payment.

"'SECTION 3. To accomplish these objects, the first and leading work of the Patrons of Equity shall be to educate the people into a more comprehensive understanding of business methods, that will enable them to minimize the use of money in their business relations with each other, by an organized effort to make the largest possible number of exchanges with the smallest possible amount of money.

"'SECTION 4. The general policy of this order, in the conduct of all the business enterprises established under its auspices, shall be to utilize the net profits on distribution to procure lands and establish production, in order to provide the largest possible amount of employment to members in good standing.'

"This declaration," continued Norrena, "when fully understood, is seen to contain every element of a speedy uplifting of any people who are oppressed by the power of wealth. Any person with a fair understanding of business methods can work out the details for the application of these principles in actual business, and any fifty families who are able to purchase and pay for supplies to the extent of five dollars per week, would provide an aggregate sale of *two thousand dollars' worth of goods per month, which would be ample to start business, pay necessary expenses and have something left. Such a business properly managed, could, by a comprehensive educational movement, be made to absorb the trade of any community for the benefit of the customers, and thus create an object lesson that would be speedily adopted by other communities, and become general. The people would be masters of the situation, and the power of money to dictate terms would have passed away forever."

"I should think," I said, "that everything pertaining to the organization which won such a victory for humanity would be carefully preserved in this Museum of Universal History."

"It is," said Norrena, "but it will be found in the story above and we will hardly have time to extend this visit any further today."

"Nor tomorrow, either," interposed Oqua. "We have important work at Byblis tomorrow, or at least there may be. Huston and Dione, want to register as man and wife, and for some reason, Huston thinks that Captain Ganoe will have objections, and if so, they must be taken into account. Besides, we propose to have an excursion around the lake on the Ice King. So we had better return to our rooms, take a rest and be prepared to start early tomorrow morning."

"And I propose," said Norrena, "that we extend our excursion to Kroy and complete the object lesson that records the victory of Equity over Greed."

Chapter XIV

THROUGH THE AIR TO LAKE BYBLIS — ON THE ICE KING ONCE MORE — CAPTAIN GANOE IN COMMAND — MET BY THE VIKING, SILVER KING AND SEA ROVER — A WEDDING -HUSTON AND DIONE THE PRINCIPALS — GANOE OBJECTS — NORRENA INVESTIGATES — OBJECTION OVERRULED — EXCURSION BENEATH THE WATERS OF THE LAKE — DOWN THE COCYTAS — THE RUINS OF KROY — ABANDONED GOLD — THE LAST RELIC OF BARBARISM.

The journey by airship from Orbitello to Lake Byblis was as usual most interesting. I never tired of these aerial flights. My first was from the deck of the Ice King in the middle of the Oscan ocean to the continent, and now I was returning to the Ice King from the middle of the continent. Our course was an airline, several points south of east, over the fertile valley of the Cocytas. For a distance of twelve hundred miles, we were first on one side of the river and then on the other, with a bird's eye view of this highly improved valley.

We traveled at a speed of about three hundred miles an hour which brought us to the vicinity of Lake Byblis about 10 o'clock, A. M. From our elevated position of several thousand feet we had a full view of the surroundings. The lake is an expansion of the river, from five to ten miles in width and thirty in length surrounded by a magnificent boulevard, on which we could see numerous vehicles moving. The surface of the lake was dotted over with water craft of various sizes and descriptions.

On the north side, Oqua pointed out the hospital to which our sailors had been sent, the Matron's Home where Bona Dea presided, the home for the aged, and the crematory. On the south side, and situated back on the bluff, was the airship factory where Battell was employed superintending the completion of his improvements on the airship, and the Transportation Headquarters, in the Auditorium of which it had been announced that the World's parliament was to meet the following December, and give us a welcome to the inner world, as citizens-at-large. Anchored in front of the Transportation building I recognized the Ice King with the stars and stripes floating from the masthead.

The valley of the Cocytas had the appearance of having originally been a vast inland sea extending about twelve hundred miles from the coast range on the east to the great continental divide on the west, and from five to six hundred in width, bounded by high lands north and south. At the east end of the lake the Cocytas flows through a deep gorge on its way to the ocean, carrying the surplus waters of a vast valley of rich alluvial lands.

Such is the geographical location of this favorite gathering place for pleasure seekers. As we approached the famous lake we reduced our speed and took a little time to contemplate the magnificent scene presented to our view. But we have neither time nor space for an adequate description.

As we reached a point directly above the Ice King we began the usual spiral descent and in a few minutes were once more upon the familiar decks of the old ship, and exchanging cordial greetings with our old shipmates and many of our new found friends and associates. It was a happy reunion.

Pat and Mike gave us a most warm hearted Irish welcome. They informed us that they had been installed as custodians of the Ice King and were faring sumptuously. I asked Mike how he liked the people and he replied laconically:

"Better than I did but I don't know how much."

I pressed him for an explanation of his doubtful compliment, and he replied that he could not understand their queer ways.

At first he thought that they had bewitched Pat, as he got right up from his sick bed and declared that there was nothing the matter with him any more. As Pat had stayed well, it was perhaps all right, but it was queer. Then ever since they had been at Lake Byblis they had got everything they wanted but when they offered to pay for it, the shopmen would look at the money, turn it over as if they did not know what it was and hand it back.

"In fact," continued Mike, "I don't understand them at all. They never work to amount to anything, and yet they have an abundance, and that of the very best. They never pay for anything and they never charge for anything. Ever since we have been here, it has been one continual coming and going and merrymaking. But this free spread cannot last all the time or I miss my guess."

"Well Mike," I replied, "you seem to be doing well enough, for the present at least, and ought to be satisfied. And I can safely assure you that you need have no fears for the future. These people have learned that it only takes about two hour's labor per day to produce an abundance of everything they need. In taking care of this ship, so that they can come and see what kind of vessels we have in the outer world, you are doing all that will ever be required of you, and when you want to take a furlough, you can travel wherever you please and it will not cost you anything but the evidence that you have been serving the people by taking care of this ship."

"May be so," said Mike, "but I don't see how they can afford it."

I had no time to explain the situation to Mike, as it had been arranged that Captain Ganoe should again take his old position on the Ice King and give its visitors an excursion on this, to them, strange craft. The steam age with these people had long since given place to electricity and compressed air, as motor powers, and so a steamship in actual use was something they had never seen. Captain Ganoe entered into the spirit of the occasion and summoned all the surviving members of the Ice King crew to take their accustomed places.

When this understanding was agreed upon, Polaris and Dione came forward and invited us below for an early dinner. We found that on the same table where they had taken breakfast with us, on our first acquaintance, they had spread such a repast for us as had never before been attempted on the Ice King. A goodly number joined us in doing ample justice to the delicious viands.

After dinner, Captain Ganoe invited the company present to go with him and have a look over the Ice King while she was being made ready for the excursion. The first place to which he conducted us was the engine room, but it was so neat and clean that he did not recognize it, and turning to Huston, he said:

"What does this mean? I thought that you told me every thing was ready to get up steam on short notice. There is not an ounce of coal in sight and the bunkers are as neat as a lady's bandbox. How do you expect to get up steam without fuel?"

"We shall burn water," said Huston.

"Burn water!" exclaimed the Captain. "Have your new surroundings led you to believe that we can set aside the laws of nature?"

"Nothing of the kind," said Huston, "but I am learning much concerning the laws of nature that I never before suspected. You see this little metallic cube. I drop it into this jar of water. See it effervesce. I apply this match. See how it burns! This little cube dissolving in the water, converts it into its original gases. You see now how we can burn water. This tank, connected by these pipes with the furnace under the boiler, contains water that has been charged with these metallic cubes, the constituent elements of which have been found in coal and lime. I now turn on this prepared water and apply an electric spark. See the fierce flame! We shall soon have steam without having vitiated the atmosphere with smoke, which in this country is regarded as a nuisance not to be tolerated. Dione superintended this part of the arrangements."

"Wonderful! Wonderful!" was all that Captain Ganoe had to say, and he passed out leaving Huston at his post as engineer. I remained behind as I wanted to have a talk with Huston, concerning what Oqua had told us, that he and Dione intended to be registered as man and wife and that he expected Captain Ganoe would object. I asked him why he expected any opposition from the Captain.

" Because," said he, "Captain Ganoe, with all his good qualities, is a living personification of every popular error which forms a part of the outer world education, law and custom."

"But," I asked, "on what grounds do you expect him to object?"

"He will," said Huston, "unless I have misjudged the man, raise the question that I have a living wife, from whom I have no legal grounds for divorce. This is true so far as the law goes, but false in every feature that constitutes a true marriage. Captain Ganoe is familiar with all the particulars, and still he entirely disapproves of the course I took, in taking the law into my own hands and severing the bonds, just as soon as I discovered the fraud that had been perpetrated on me."

"Won't you give me the particulars?" I asked. "I am especially interested in learning all about it."

"I have no objections," said Huston. "It is no secret. But steam will soon be up and our time is limited."

"But please give me a brief outline," I persisted. "I am indeed vitally interested in learning the principal facts in this case." Huston regarded me for a moment with a puzzled expression of countenance and then said:

"I will for your sake, Jack, try to make a long story short. My father was a planter and supposed to be wealthy. Our family was proud and aristocratic. My father had a ward in a distant state who lived with his sister. She was heir to an immense estate. Though I had never seen her I had been encouraged to correspond with her, and we had exchanged photographs. Her letters indicated remarkable talent and the highest culture, while her photograph proclaimed to my imagination, that she was a beauty. I was but a boy and I confess that I was fascinated by her letters, and the affectionate interest by which she led me to the most ardent declaration of my admiration."

"Such was the relation that had been established between us when my father took me into his confidence and declared that he was a ruined man and our family irretrievably disgraced, unless I could prevent it by a marriage with his ward, Zeta Wild. The time was at hand when he must account for her estate, which had been lost through unfortunate speculations, and that the settlement would reveal a state of affairs that would send him to prison for a long term of years.

"I objected to the idea of marriage with a girl I had never met, no matter how favorably I had been impressed by her photograph and her letters. But my father's special pleading and the pressing nature of the danger to the family name, overcame my objections, and the day was set for the marriage.

"Everything was artfully arranged. We arrived in the evening and met the bridal party at the church. I was charmed with the appearance of my bride. We were married at once, and took carriages for the home of my aunt where a splendid wedding supper awaited us. "Within an hour, I found that I had married a beautiful idiot. I was shocked, and stole away from the guests into an upper room. I wanted to think. A lamp was burning on the table. My eyes fell upon a letter written to my father by my aunt. I recognized the handwriting. It was my aunt who had written the letters that had charmed me so much. In this one, she deplored the deception that was being practiced upon me, but justified it on the ground that it was necessary in order to save the honor of the family.

"My mind was made up. I passed out into the darkness of the night, started for the nearest seaport and found employment as a sailor. I have never returned home since. I learned that my father got his ward's fortune in my name. Captain Ganoe is personally acquainted with my father and has seen his ward at his house, who was introduced as his son's wife. I explained the situation to the Captain, but he disapproved my conduct in very emphatic terms, and I should have left the ship but for the fact that I had engaged to go with Battell on the expedition.

"I have also explained the situation to Dione and my part in this transaction meets her approval. We shall register as man and wife, and if the Captain objects, so much the better, as it will place my conduct in the correct light. The marriage was a fraud and no one ought to be bound by a fraud."

"I can most cordially sympathize with you," I said. "It is certainly a terrible wrong to compel people to associate in such an intimate relation when their entire natures are in rebellion against it. It cannot be wrong to sever such bonds regardless of the claims of church or state. A relation that is wrong, in and of itself, cannot be made right by lawmaker or priest."

"Thank you," said Huston. "I am glad that I am not alone among the crew of the Ice King. Indeed I believe that ultimately even the Captain will see this question just as I do. Our intention was to register while we were in Orbitello, but Oqua requested that we should wait until this excursion, and to please her we consented. I do not know her reasons for advising delay but I suppose it is all right."

"I think I understand it," I said, "and you may rest assured that her reasons are good, and good will come out of it."

"I hope so," said Huston. "But the steam gauge points to one hundred and here goes to all whom it may concern," and suiting the action to the word he pulled the rope and the steam whistle resounded far and wide, something entirely new to these people, in a country which had abandoned steam as a motor power so long ago.

I hurried upon deck and joined Captain Ganoe. Captain Battell was at the wheel, and all was ready. The decks were crowded with excursionists who had never been on board a steamship, and knew nothing of steam as a motor power, except as a matter of history. All were anxious to see the vessel move and Captain Ganoe did not keep them waiting. He signalled the engineer and immediately the ponderous engines began to move and the Ice King was backing out into the water and swinging around with her bow toward the head of the lake. She obeyed her helm beautifully and started off with a speed of which we were proud.

The route determined upon kept us near the larboard shore, while some miles to the starboard we could see a magnificent craft that reflected the light of the sun like burnished silver. I asked Oqua what it was.

"That," said she, "is the Silver King, an electric yacht, built of aluminum. She brings a load of excursionists and expects to take us down the river. She is remarkable for her speed and her splendid accommodations. She will meet us at the head of the lake."

I found too much to look at to take up much time in conversation, but cannot at this time indulge in descriptions. Suffice it to say that the scenes presented on the boulevard surrounding the lake, on the surface of the water and in the air were most animated, and all were moving as if to meet us at the head of the lake.

As we approached the mouth of the upper Cocytas, we met the Silver King and while the excursionists were exchanging greetings, a strange little craft with a dragon's head and propelled by oars, shot out from under the cover of the river bank. At the bow were our Norwegian sailors, Lief and Eric plying their oars most sturdily and singing a weird song, in which I distinguished the mythological names of Odin and Thor. The oarsmen were dressed in a strange, fantastic style, and were armed with spears, crossbows, swords, and long hunting knives.

This strange craft came out of the river and both the Ice King and the Silver King, as if by common impulse stopped short in their career while the Viking, for such it was, took its place between them. To say that I was astonished at the appearance of a style of vessel that had been obsolete for centuries, but feebly expresses my surprise, and I asked Norrena where it came from.

"It came from the outer world," he said, "about 2,000 years ago, and brought a warlike crew, the general appearance of which, the Superintendent of Festivities, has tried to imitate. The historians of that period could gather very little information from them concerning the country from which they came. They said that the people had to leave because it was so cold. This gave rise to the false impression that the outer world had become uninhabitable and that these were the last remnants of the people."

"These people," I said, "were known as Northmen, and their ships were called Vikings. They were the most daring of navigators, and penetrated every portion of the outer world, and it is not at all surprising that some of them found their way to the inside. This will probably explain why so many of your names are identical with those of the Scandinavian countries.

"That is correct," he said. "Many of our people are descended from this stock and still perpetuate the names. Our records preserve the language they brought with them as carefully as our chemists have preserved this little boat."

"Do you intend to say," I asked, "that this is the original boat that found its way into the inner world a thousand years ago? I thought that it was a reproduction. How was it possible to preserve it so long?"

"Yes," he said, "this is the original boat, and it has been preserved by forcing a chemical solution into the wood which makes it as durable as granite."

As we were speaking, two powerful metallic arms operated by machinery reached down from the deck of the Silver King and lifted this little Viking and its passengers into stocks that had been prepared for it, with the seeming tenderness of a mother lifting her babe to her bosom. So suggestive was the manner in which it was done that I turned to Norrena to ask the meaning, which he anticipated by saying:

"'This represents the tender care that vigorous youth ought to bestow upon age. This little boat is highly prized, as in the process of evolution, it may be regarded as the progenitor of the Silver King. If there had never been such boats as the Viking, there never would have been an Ice King or a Silver King. All things must develop from small beginnings."

The Ice King and Silver King now headed toward the mouth of the lake, were lashed together, and the excursionists on both vessels passed freely from one to the other. The Ice King attracted much the largest number, but I was more anxious to inspect the Silver King.

Norrena introduced us to Captain Thorfin, as visitors and seamen from the outer world. He conducted us first to the motor room and explained the workings of the machinery, and showed us a system of airtight compartments, which would, he claimed, absolutely keep the vessel from sinking, no matter how badly the hull might be injured. He stated that even the decks would float like cork.

When we reached the upper deck of the Silver King we found that the oarsmen on the Viking had exchanged their war-like equipments for musical instruments and as we came up they opened with strains of the most thrilling music that I had ever heard. As if in response, both the Ice King and the Silver King seemed lifted up on the crest of some mighty wave, and what appeared to be some monster marine animal arose out of the water behind us and moved to the starboard side of the Ice King. It had a resemblance to a gigantic turtle, but was fully three times as long as it was wide. As soon as the water ceased to flow from its sides, a hatchway opened in the center and MacNair and lola made their appearance, and began to wave their handkerchiefs to us. I was too much astonished at this strange apparition to even ask what it was. Norrena relieved my embarrassment by saying:

"This is the Sea Rover, a submarine boat, that came up the middle of the lake near the bottom. The three boats will be lashed together and thus proceed down the lake while the excursionists will have the freedom of the entire flotilla, and may amuse themselves in any way they choose. See there! The Sea Rovers have brought up their dancing floor. It is plain that they propose to have a ball. But I have some business that I must attend to while the crowds enjoy themselves. As this is to be a private party of invited guests, of which you are one, I shall expect you to join us in the cabin of the Silver King. "

I intuitively knew what was coming. We found the cabin as exclusive as could have been desired for a private party. Battell and Polaris, Huston and Dione, Norrena and Oqua, MacNair and lola, and Captain Ganoe and myself constituted the party on this occasion.

When we were all comfortably seated, Norrena said:

"I have invited you in here because we want our esteemed guests from the outer world to understand all of our usages. We are going to have what in their world is called a wedding. Ordinarily these events attract no especial attention in this country as there are but two persons interested. But there may be circumstances under which marriage is not permitted. In such cases we investigate. In this country, it is the duty of the educational department to keep a record of everything pertaining to birth, marriage and death, as all are supposed to be either pupils in school or graduates from school. Hence the school record is the record of the birth, educational attainments, name, occupation, marriage and death of every person.

"We have no such marriage ceremonies as I find described in the literature of the outer world, but we keep a most perfect system of records. All persons who are allowed to marry at all, are free to make their choice. No interference on the part of others is permitted. As a notice of their intentions, they send or bring the nativity cards which they receive on leaving school, to the proper office where they are registered as citizens. If there is nothing in the record which prevents, each couple so united receives an acknowledgment and a copy of the record, enclosed in two silver lockets, which are usually worn around the neck. This is all there is of it unless some one objects. In that case, there is an inquiry and the commissioner decides according to the facts.

"I have here two nativity cards. One is that of Dione of the Life Saving Service, and the other bears the name of Paul Huston, and the date of his registration on the books of the Sailor's Union of Citizens-at-large of Altruria. At the request of the applicants for registration as man and wife, I have invited you as witnesses and will ask if any one objects to their union?"

"I object," said Captain Ganoe.

"State your grounds of objection," said Norrena. "Because of my certain knowledge and his own admission, he has a living wife to whom he was lawfully married."

"Is this true?" asked Norrena, addressing Huston. "It is," responded Huston. "I was married according to the usages of the country where I was born and I do not believe that I have any legal grounds for divorce, but as a matter of fact, the entire transaction was fraudulent."

"State the facts in full," said Norrena.

"I will," said Huston, and he narrated the story of his marriage, substantially in the same language that he had related it to me.

Norrena turned to Captain Ganoe and asked: "Have you any reason to offer why this statement just made by Paul Huston, before these witnesses, should not be accepted as true?"

"I have not," said the Captain. "He admits that he was married to Zeta Wild. That he left her without any offense on her part for which a divorce could be obtained. Hence, he is today a married man. Married according to law, and he has no right to marry another woman, and Dione has no right to take him as a husband."

"That is your view of the matter, " said Norrena. "But under our usages, the girl to whom he was married was an imbecile and had no right to be married, and on this ground the marriage was null and void. Besides, he was deceived, and hence the marriage being fraudulent, could not be binding."

"A legal marriage, voluntarily entered into cannot be fraudulent, and is always binding upon the conscience of all well meaning people."

"But," said Norrena, "if she was a person he could not love and respect as a wife, was it not better that he should refuse to consummate the relation?"

"Certainly not," said the Captain. "When he was married to her, that ended it. I have no doubt that he could have lived agreeably enough with her if he had wanted to."

"I see," said Norrena, "that you ·are not likely to withdraw your objection, so we will not continue the discussion. It is my duty to decide in favor of the true and against the false, and hence I must overrule your objection to the registration of Paul Huston and Dione as husband and wife."

"Do as you please," said Captain Ganoe. "It does not change the facts in the case. It is strange to me that any woman would accept a man as a husband under such circumstances. So far as I am concerned with my present light on the subject, I could not as a conscientious man, consent to marry a woman, no matter how much I loved her, who according to law, was the wife of another man. As an honorable man I would advise her to return to her husband."

I had been listening intently to this inquiry. Here was a case almost identical with my own. I had married my guardian of my own free will, and like Huston, when I discovered the fraud by which my consent was secured, I had taken to the sea, and now the one whom I had loved more than life itself, and for whom I had searched for years, and with whom I had braved all the dangers of the frozen north in order to be near his person, had for the second time deliberately declared that he would not marry such a woman no matter how much he loved her. My entire being was aroused in revolt against such injustice and I arose and said:

"For the second time, Captain Ganoe, I have heard you express this atrocious sentiment, which ignores love, the only thing which can sanctify the union of the sexes in the marriage relation, and place above that the debasing doctrine that man made laws are superior to the laws of God, which are implanted in the human soul. Without love, marriage is a curse, unholy and impure. Love is an inspiration and cannot be transferred by the state or the church. If you have never realized what true love signifies, of course you are excusable, but those who have felt it, will never agree with you. Huston was right, to take the law into his own hands and separate from his imbecile wife. To have consummated the union, would have been a crime against her, against himself and against humanity. And now, so far as I am concerned, I shall drop this question. No good can come of the discussion, and other questions of far-reaching import to the toiling millions of the outer world, demand my undivided attention. Let us do what we can to abolish poverty by removing time honored wrongs, and when women are economically free, they will be able to select companions who will not trample love under the heel of antiquated wrong."

So saying I walked out of the cabin without waiting for reply. Oqua followed me and as she came up by my side, said:

"Do not be disturbed. Your victory is won. Captain Ganoe cannot long withstand the force of truth. And he has now placed his position so plainly before our people that the truth will reach him from all sides in a way of which he never dreamed before."

"Yes," I said, "I have won a victory, but it is over myself. He may come to me, when he has removed the clouds from his mind and the bitterness from his heart. I will never make any overtures. I can love humanity and work for it, and even if my work is not understood, I know that it will exercise an elevating influence on myself. My motto for the future will be, 'Plenty of room at the top where true love and a sterling devotion to the right, will be understood and appreciated.'"

"You talk like a philosopher," said Oqua, "and I have no doubt that your heroism of character will come out triumphant, but do not permit your resentment of a wrong to engender a feeling of bitterness toward Captain Ganoe."

"I shall not stoop to that," I said. "I cannot afford it. My love in the future shall go out to every human being and I still regard Captain Ganoe, with all of his prejudices, as one of the best. I have forgiven his weakness and want to forget. What I need now is something better to think about."

"Well," said Oqua, "the excursion beneath the waters of the lake in the Sea Rover this afternoon and the one on the Silver King down the Cocytas tomorrow will give you a great many things that will doubtless, very thoroughly engage your attention."

"That," I said, "is just what I need. Something to arouse my interest and exclude disquieting reflections. But what of this excursion beneath the waters of the lake? I had not beard of that."

"Oh yes," said Oqua, "the Superintendent of Festivities would not think of slighting the Sea Rovers who make the navigation of our shallow lakes, bays and rivers safe for such vessels as the Silver King and their numerous passengers. They wanted to entertain our visitors from the outer world on their own vessel and of course the excursion beneath the water was made a part of the program."

"Well, the arrangement," I said, " is better than I anticipated and it surely will be, to me, a novel experience to be able to see the world of marine life as the fishes see it."

"And as the Sea Rover!! see and improve it," said Oqua. "But see! They are signaling for us to come on board."

In a few minutes we had passed out upon the dancing floor of the Rovers and descended into an elegantly furnished cabin. I was the only one present who had not become acquainted with the crew, and Oqua introduced me as the Scientist of the Ice King, to Captain Doris of the Sea Rover who gave me a cordial greeting and introduced me to a number of his comrades. In answer to my inquiries, he gave me an entertaining and instructive description of the duties of the submarine service.

"Our work," he said, "is to keep a careful lookout for obstructions that might impede navigation and endanger life. This is especially necessary in rivers like the Cocytas, where huge stones are sometimes loosened from the rocky shores and fall into the channel, and sandbars form rapidly. These are discovered and removed by the submarine patrols."

"But how," I asked, "can you get at them?"

"Nothing easier," said Doris, "as I will show you."

At once I heard the water pouring into the hold and the Sea Rover sank to the bottom. The Captain and two of the crew passed into a little room at the rear of the cabin and immediately I noticed that the sides of the vessel were transparent and brilliantly lighted from the outside. Looking out I saw the men in diving suits leisurely walking around on the bottom, which looked like a smooth floor.

Oqua explained that by means of powerful arc lights and reflectors, these submarine navigators were able to see for long distances even at great depths, and that the work of removing obstructions was carried on by means of machinery, and that the stones which fell into the channel were reduced to powder by powerful explosives, and the surface smoothed down like a well cultivated field. The air was continually renewed from stores of condensed air, while the poisonous exhalations from the lungs were absorbed by sponges having a peculiar affinity for carbon.

In a few minutes Captain Doris returned and the vessel began to move rapidly through the water. I was much interested in the view of marine life which was revealed through the transparent sides, and especially in the level bottom of the lake, which, as Oqua had remarked, really looked something like a broad, smooth, cultivated field. But soon we turned toward the south and began to move slowly along the side of a brilliantly lighted boulevard on which all kinds of vehicles were passing and repassing. I was so much astonished at this unexpected scene, so realistic and seemingly uncanny, that I was utterly at a loss for words to express my feelings. Oqua seeing my embarrassment came to my relief by saying:

"This is the tunnel across the lower portion of the lake and constitutes a part of the boulevard you noticed along the shores."

"How is this?" I asked. "It is certainly not a tunnel excavated under the lake. If anything, we are a little below the roadway and well above the bottom of the lake with the water all around us."

"We do not," said Oqua, "excavate tunnels as we did in ancient times. They are constructed in our machine shops. This is a metallic tube with supports which rest on the bottom, and has many advantages over the old fashioned, dark and dismal excavations. The material used is a compound somewhat like common glass but as strong as steel. With our submarine fleets it is not difficult to put the sections in place and when completed the water is pumped out of the cavity and the roadway is ready for use. Even across small streams, where the banks are not too high, they are frequently preferred to bridges as more safe and durable, but for long distances and in very deep water they are indispensable, and in the case of deep water tunnels, they are frequently made to span submarine gorges."

"How fortunate," I exclaimed, "that this submarine excursion was on the program! I now see a most wonderful exhibition of the power of mind to overcome material difficulties, that it would have been hard for me to realize if I had received the information in some other manner."

"All things," responded Oqua, "are possible to the human mind in its ultimate state of development ---But we are now heading for the landing at the Transportation Headquarters and we will spend the night on the Silver King which takes us down to the ruins of Kroy in the morning."

"And," I asked, "what is to hinder you from telling me something about these ruins now, and what they have to do with Norrena's economic lessons?"

"They are," said Oqua, "only the relics of the great money center which held the people in bondage during the Transition Period. When Kroy was deserted by the money kings, the people determined to preserve it, subject only to the ravages of time, as a warning and a lesson to future generations."

As Oqua ceased speaking, the Sea Rover arose to the surface by the side of the Silver King, the hatches were opened, and in a few minutes we were welcomed on board the electric yacht by Captain Thorfin, and invited to an elegant supper. The day had certainly been most agreeably spent but its lessons were too suggestive and far-reaching in their character to be adequately presented in this small volume. I was fatigued by the incessant activity since early morning and was glad of an opportunity to retire to my stateroom and rest.

I was awake early next morning and after a hearty breakfast, we were soon speeding down the Cocytas between two lofty walls of granite. There was nothing to be seen but these towering cliffs for the first few miles and Captain Thorfin gave us a specimen of the speed of the Silver King. The cliffs seemed to dart past us as if we were on board of a lightning express train, and yet we could scarcely feel the motion of the vessel. I confess that I felt a little nervous at such astonishing speed, but Captain Thorfin assured us that there was no danger, as the submarine patrols removed every obstruction and preserved a uniform depth of water.

I asked the Captain what was the greatest speed of his vessel and he replied that he had never tested it. He had made one hundred miles an hour but the excursionists generally preferred to travel slowly. On this trip we would average fifty, and so reach Kroy in about three hours.

During the last two hours of our journey we were passing through a densely populated country. Great communal homes appeared on either side and large manufacturing plants at frequent intervals. But our interest was centered at the mouth of the river and our attention was chiefly directed over the bow. Soon a point of land appeared where the river seemed to part in twain. This I recognized as the island I had seen from the airship which had brought us to the continent, and here is where the city of Kroy had been situated. My interest had been aroused and as the Silver King turned into the northern channel, the island became the center of attraction. On the larboard side the same scenes of sylvan beauty, palatial buildings and groups of happy, joyous people continued, but it was now the uninhabited island that absorbed my attention.

I could see, in places, through the tangled brushwood and tall trees which lined the shore, glimpses of shattered walls and tumuli, overrun by vines and briers, such as in many parts of the outer world are so attractive to archeologists, as the ruins of some ancient civilization. At one point I noticed what appeared to have been costly monuments to the dead and I said to Norrena:

"Surely that must have been a cemetery."

"And so it was," she responded. "In those days, millions were expended in decorating the graves of the rich, while the masses of their fellow beings who had toiled to create what the few had absorbed, lived in poverty, and large numbers died in alms houses or by the wayside, and found their last resting place in a Potter's field. More was often expended on a single tomb than could possibly have been earned in any useful service to society, in a lifetime. They sought to secure a sort of immortality by polished granite columns and laudatory inscriptions. This has all been changed for centuries. We cremate the dead body in the most speedy and economical manner possible, and seek to secure longevity and happiness for all, by creating the best possible conditions for the living."

At another place I caught glimpses of monuments of another description, mingled with what had evidently been palatial structures adorned with the artistic work of the sculptor in great profusion. Obelisks of polished stone towered above the surrounding trees, giving the forest a peculiar appearance not easily forgotten, but difficult to describe. Noticing my interest in the scene Norrena remarked:

"This was once a magnificent park, and was ornamented by works of art from foreign lands representing the most ancient civilizations, as well as the most artistic products of their own sculptors and painters. One of those Obelisks dated back to prehistoric ages. It was transported from its original site in the Old World, at great expense as a monument to the wealth and munificence of the money kings. They had conquered the world then existing and held the people in subjection. To commemorate their success they sought to compel the Past to proclaim their greatness and gratify their vanity. But they had no future. They passed away. And now the descendants of the millions whom they oppressed, visit these ruins and gather lessons of wisdom from their contemplation."

We were now opposite a portion of the island where the ruins assumed something of the appearance of a city. An open roadway between buildings indicated that this had been one of the principal streets in the olden time. The Silver King rounded to and made fast to a well preserved dock which forcibly called to my mind the great docks of New York, Liverpool and other seaport cities of the outer world.

We disembarked and found the first restrictions on our movements that we had met in Altruria except the entrances to private apartments. Those who desired to visit the ruins on the island were required to register their names and accept an escort to see that nothing was displaced or carried away from the chief points of interest.

These preliminaries arranged, the gates were opened and accompanied by our escort, we proceeded up the well-worn roadway towards what had doubtless been the chief center of wealth and power. On either side were huge masses of debris, and falling walls of what had once marked the site of lofty structures. Briers and brambles grew in the accumulated dust of ages which now covered the well-paved streets and marble sidewalks. Wild vines clambered over the shattered walls and not unfrequently tall trees grew through the tops of buildings where the walls still stood firm. We were in the midst of a deep tangled wildwood, where on every side could be seen indisputable evidence that this had once been a great center of population, wealth and luxury. Ruined churches and marble halls where once had gathered the elite of a city, the opulence of which had been the wonder of the world, now afforded a nesting place for wild fowl.

My heart grew faint and my head dizzy as I pondered upon the wonderful lesson spread out before me. Here had been a city, no less magnificent in its prime than New York, the great metropolis of America, and I asked myself the question, could this ever be the fate of my native city? Captain Battell, who was walking by my side, broke in upon my meditations by asking:

"What do you think of it, Jack? I never saw you so absorbed."

And Yankee like I said:

"I reply by asking, what do you think, Captain? Surely you cannot be indifferent to scenes like this when you reflect that we are natives of New York City!"

"I am not indifferent," said Battell, "but I have had the advantage of former visits and hence am better prepared for it. The part of the city we are now approaching has been kept in a tolerable state of repair, to make the lessons taught by these ruins more impressive. This visit has been arranged for your especial benefit, as you are the recognized historian of the Ice King. Polaris and Dione showed Huston and myself through these ruins as soon as we reached the continent, which led me to infer that they had learned enough of our money system from MacNair to understand that we needed the lesson."

"Then you are not a total stranger to these scenes?" I said.

"No, I have been here several times and every time I come I get some new light which applies to our own country. These ruins teach a wonderful lesson. It does seem, as Norrena claims, that human progress always leads up through similar channels of development. Here we are in what was once a city, every feature of which indicates very clearly the existence of the same conditions which now prevail in the great cities of the outer world. It had its day and passed away because it had served its purpose, and so must all great centers of pride and fashion in which a few absorb the wealth created by the people and expend it for their own pleasure without ·regard for others."

We now entered a locality where all the buildings, pavements, etc., had been kept in a state of repair that had in a great measure withstood the ravages of time. Everywhere else the island had been left without care and was a mass of ruins which were largely concealed from view by a deep soil, composed of accumulated dust and vegetable humus from ages of luxuriant growth. Here, however, were the Sub-treasury, Stock Exchange and a number of great banking houses, still preserved, to some extent, as the money kings had left them.

"These buildings," said Norrena, "were occupied by the taskmasters of the people. Here was the headquarters of the gold power in this country, and having a monopoly of money, it bore to the people the relation of a Universal Creditor and absorbed the **ENTIRE SURPLUS** created by their labor to meet its demand for interest, etc. Here was practically determined the amount allowed to producers on one hand, and the price charged to consumers on the other. This power was the unquestioned dictator in every sphere of human activity. But we will visit the vaults of the great money kings of that time, which were the actual head-center of this oppressive oligarchy of wealth."

We entered a massive building. Its heavy bronze doors and polished granite walls gave the impression, that notwithstanding its artistic finish, the chief object in its erection had been strength and durability. The thick plate glass windows could be at once protected by heavily barred steel shutters. At a moment's notice this massive structure could have been converted into a fortress that would enable a small number to hold it against a multitude.

The front room was perfectly equipped as a bank, but with a strange, and seemingly reckless display of gold coins, giving one the impression that a time had come when the owners were utterly indifferent as to what became of their accumulated hoard. Large safes were standing open literally crammed with stacks of glittering coins. Tables and shelves were crowded with the yellow metal, which the custodian informed us, was kept just as it had been left, as a relic of the ages of mental darkness, when the wealth producing millions foolishly believed that they were dependent upon this golden hoard for the privilege of converting their labor into the means of subsistence.

From the public office of the bank we descended a flight of marble steps into the basement which we found brilliantly lighted by electricity. Huge steel vaults were standing open, piles of gold bricks rested upon the floors and packages of gold coins met our sight in every direction.

"You see," said Norrena, "how the gold flowed in upon the creditors when the people were making their exchanges without its use. Among the people, it was only used to pay debts, and as the money kings owned, to such a large extent, the indebtedness, the gold supply of the country flowed in upon them until it was difficult to find storage for it. Additional vaults were built and these were soon filled. At first they sought to turn this glut of gold to profit by making improvements which gave employment to labor. Great trunk lines of railroad were built and the government borrowed vast sums which were expended on country roads, waterways, harbors and so forth. But the people, now fully established in business for themselves, continued, by their system of paying dividends to consumption, to increase the price of labor and its products. When these millions were paid out as wages and entered into circulation they speedily found their way into the people's banks and were returned to these vaults to pay debts. All this time the price of labor and its products was increasing, and the purchasing power of gold was decreasing, until in time all the debts were paid and the people ceased to exchange their products for money altogether. The purchasing power of gold was gone, and the money kings, who held on to the system to the last, were poor indeed. They found starvation staring them in the face. Then, they abandoned these useless hoards, went out among the people and found plenty of employment for their really valuable talents."

From the gold vaults we passed into others where bonds, mortgages, stocks etc., had been kept.

"Here," continued Norrena, "at regular intervals, clerks were locked in and kept close prisoners while they clipped coupons for their masters. You see by the labels, the kind of securities which each compartment contained. These vaults held a legal lien upon the great bulk of the wealth of the country, the interest, dividends, etc., on which, if paid in cash, would require each year a sum equal to, at least, one and one-half times the entire circulating medium of the country, and the principal if converted into cash would have required ten times the entire volume of gold in the world. Here, in potency, was held a lien sufficient to take every acre of land and personal property in the country."

"That," I said, "calls to my mind a phase of the question which I would like to have you explain. How did the multitudes, especially in this city and on this coast, escape the grasp of these money-kings who also owned the real estate? The people had no land to go upon, and hence could not procure a subsistence by cultivating the soil without paying tribute in the shape of rent."

"Your question," said Norrena, "is far-reaching and I can only hint at the reply which it naturally calls forth. The money kings overreached themselves by encouraging people to secure loans and pledge their real estate for interest and principal, and then by contracting the circulation in order to increase the purchasing power of the money which they received as interest. As long as only a minor fraction of the land was mortgaged the interest was promptly paid, but a time came when nearly all of the lands were mortgaged and the people were compelled to force their products on the markets all at once to get money to pay interest. More and more of the debtors gave up the struggle and abandoned their farms. These lands were useless to the money — kings when no longer cultivated by a sturdy yeomanry. All along this eastern seaboard, where agriculture ought to have been most profitable, farms were abandoned because they would not pay interest on the investment. The money value of lands for actual use to producers, declined to zero, and the people crowded into the city and were regarded, in their impoverished condition, as a dangerous class. Under these circumstances the tendency of the ruling class was to encourage the homeless poor to go upon the lands and dig a subsistence out of the soil, for which there was no market."

"Iola explained this to me," I said, "but I have never quite understood why it was that these colonists were not charged a rental that would keep them in perpetual poverty."

"That," said Norrena, "would certainly have been the result, if there had been no great Central West, with a widespread tendency to agitate the money question and its relation to the economic condition of the wealth producing millions. When the people began to organize as consumers with a view to minimizing the demand for money, and to equalize distribution by paying dividends to labor, the money kings were forced to change their policy in regard to labor, and many producers got a firm hold on enough land to furnish a subsistence. The unused lands had no value and the Equitists continued to increase the price of products in the west. The money kings who were not able to sell their lands could avail themselves of opportunities to exchange them for products. The leaders of the cooperative movement here in the east knew how to take advantage of these changing conditions, and by their communal system of co-operation, were able to keep the movement on peaceful lines, and thus avoid violent collisions which might have, locally, at least, set the work of industrial emancipation back for years."

"Then it appears," I said, "that it was not the western organization of Equitable Exchange, singly and alone, that compelled the Gold Power to relax its grasp; but this eastern cooperative movement was also a factor in securing better conditions for labor."

"That is true," said Norrena. "In the west, the people had one great advantage over the east, plenty of land. But it was the organization of equity in the west that flooded this eastern financial center with money, not as interest, but because the western people were using less money and paying debts. This made times better for the eastern workmen. Both the western and eastern co-operators were working on the same principles. They were all accumulating funds to purchase land, and just in proportion as the people acquired control over business they had more influence on legislation, and the power of money was correspondingly decreased."

"So it seems," I said, "that your business organization did at last get into politics!"

"Yes," said Norrena, "it did get into politics as a business influence and what may seem strange to you, its object was to prevent the repeal of laws which had been enacted in the interest of the money monopolists. These shrewd financiers; raised a great outcry against combinations among producers to increase the price of products by using interchangeable certificates of deposit instead of money, in the transaction of business. The people were using the same methods for the improvement of their own financial condition that had been used so successfully by monopolists for their impoverishment, and the Patrons demanded that all the laws that had been enacted in favor of monopoly should remain on the statute books. They further demanded that all debts should be payable in legal tender money at the option of the debtor."

"I should have thought," I said, "that the people would be glad to welcome the repeal of laws from which they had suffered so much."

"There was a time when they would," said Norrena, "but not after they had adjusted their business relations to the operation of monopoly laws. Their debts were legally payable in money, and as the purchasing power of money was continually decreasing, it was to their interest to pay in money, and when all their debts were paid and the people refused any longer to take money for their products, the money kings who owned these vaults and their hoards of gold had to go in search of food. Many found homes in the cooperative communities and became valuable citizens, while a larger number had taken the alarm and emigrated to the Old World, only to meet a worse fate a little later on, for in the less enlightened parts of the world, the Reign of Gold wound up in a Reign of Terror."

The lesson taught by these ruins would fill volumes. Norrena's accurate historical knowledge and ever ready explanations, with the not less forcible comments of Oqua and others, covered every phase of this wonderful, speedy and peaceful evolution from the Era of Money Despotism to the Era of Man and Universal Freedom, Equality and Fraternity. No wonder, I thought, that these people had preserved the ruins of Kroy as a relic of their Dark Ages and a warning to humanity for all time to come. Here, human selfishness reigned supreme and the people of an entire continent had suffered in order to pour into this greedy maw the wealth which it had no power to consume. And now, this once great center of wealth, pride and fashion, was a solitude. Its aristocratic "four hundred" had actually been starved out by the refusal of the "clodhoppers," "greasy mechanics" and "mudsills," whom they had held in such contempt, to feed and clothe them any longer. Surely this was an object lesson well worthy of the care that had been taken to preserve it from the refining and civilizing hand of labor. Time was slowly obliterating these foot prints of a tyranny from which the people had been emancipated for ages, but it was still important that it should not be entirely forgotten, and there could be no better reminder of the evil that had impoverished and degraded the millions, as well as of the means by which it had been removed, than these ruins and the abandoned heaps of useless gold.

After a day among the ruins, and full of serious reflections, we returned to the Silver King and were soon speeding down the bay. We landed at the tower, and from this point the electric cars soon transported us to our great communal home. I was fatigued and retired to my own apartment at once, to think and rest.

Chapter XV

HOME AGAIN — LETTER FROM BONA DEA — ELECTRIC GARMENTS — REPORTER'S PHONOGRAPH — TESTING THE NEW AIRSHIP — *A* WORLD'S COUNCIL — WALLAROO ON EVOLUTION — THE IDEALS PLANTED BY MISSIONARIES — THE EOLUS — PREPARING FOR RETURN TO AMERICA — EXCURSION TO THE FAR NORTH — THE WATCH TOWER — SYMBOLIC REPRESENTATIONS — THE FAREWELL — THE REVELATION TO GANOE — "CASSIE! CASSIE! COME BACK! COME BACK !"

Next morning at the breakfast table Oqua informed me that a package and letter from Bona Dea to my address, had arrived at an early hour but that it had not been delivered, as they did not wish to disturb my rest. It had been retained in the office subject to my order when I was ready to receive it.

This recalled to my mind a private conversation I had with BonaDea at Orbitello, and I surmised that her communication might have reference to that; but I was at a loss to form any opinion in regard to the package. She had told me that one of the inmates of the Home at Lake Byblis was paying especial attention to the formation of an ideal mental picture of life and its conditions in the frozen regions. And to that end her apartments had been fitted up to represent winter scenery, and to make the impression more realistic she was provided with a refrigerator room where she subjected herself to low temperatures and was testing the heat conserving powers of various qualities of clothing.

When breakfast was over I called at the office and received a large bundle, neatly wrapped and securely sealed. The address was "Jack Adams, No. 1, care Nequa." This was a poser. The communication was in the official envelope of the Home and I hastened to my room, so that if need be I could have the aid of a lexicon in the translation. But when I opened it, somewhat to my surprise, I found it was written in English. Being appropriate as a part of this narrative, I insert it in full.

MATRONS' HOME, LAKE BYBLIS,
March 1, 1894, A. M.

My Dear Nequa:

On returning to the Home, I related to Meidra, the "Arctic pupil" of whom I told you, the substance of our conversation, and explained to her what you suggested in regard to electric garments as a means of conserving the natural heat of the body when exposed to severe cold.

She informed me that she had been experimenting on that line and had succeeded in making a suit that proved to be an ample protection from the greatest cold that her refrigerator is capable of producing. She sends you this electric suit, with the request that you test it in your proposed voyage to the southern verge.

She further requests me to tell you that she does not intend to permit you to deprive this inner world of the honor of having a Jack Adams among its great navigators and explorers by your simply taking advantage of one of our customs to change your name to such a feminine cognomen as Nequa. Both she and Tanqua are anxious to make your acquaintance. Meidra says that your image is indelibly impressed on her mind by your photograph. She has an enlarged reproduction of your picture as a prominent feature in her room, and from this she reads a most admirable character.

The people of the entire concave are aroused to the importance of your efforts to open up a channel of communication with the outer world. All the Grand Divisions want to participate in the honor and to that end each one has appointed a member to act with a representative from Altruria, and constitute an Inner-World Council to assist in every way possible.

It has been agreed that Norrena shall represent this country and I am authorized to request you to make a date for the first meeting of the Council, as soon as possible after your trial voyage "in search of a storm," as Battell expressed it. Please advise me as soon as you return, when it will suit you best to have these Inner World Representatives call upon you, and oblige

Your many friends,
Bona Dea.

I opened the bundle and found a beautifully quilted silk suit, soft and pliable, but of firm texture, with sandals, gloves, headdress and visor to match. It also contained a small inlaid jewel case with a key in the lock. I opened this and found, as I supposed a beautiful locket in which I expected to see a picture of the donor, but it proved to be a delicate piece of machinery with printed instructions, which informed me that it was a phonograph for the especial use of reporters. When wound up it recorded on silver foil every word spoken. This was something new and I recalled to mind that I had frequently talked to people who wore similar lockets. Now I had found out that they probably preserved a record of every word I said, and I wondered if I had said anything that I would not like to have repeated. With people wearing lockets of this description, I realized how important it was for all to be very careful what they said; and certainly the people of this country are the most circumspect and exact in their statements, of any people with whom I have ever met.

Just as I had finished the examination of the phonograph, the bell called my attention to my private telephone, and I was requested to meet Battell at the boatyard on the roof, prepared for a flight through the air on his new airship and to take some lessons in its management. This was just what I wanted, and in a minute the elevator had landed me on the roof. I found Battell, Huston, Polaris and Dione, together with lola, MacNair and Oqua, ready for a ride in the new airship.

It was beautifully finished but much more substantial than the light airy vessels to which I had become accustomed. I complimented Battell upon its appearance, but he was too matter-of-fact to appreciate anything that might look like flattery and said with his usual honest bluntness:

"It is not the appearance that we care anything about, but the sailing qualities. And so far as this climate is concerned we have made decided improvements in this particular. The sailing qualities are such, that everyone wants an improved airship, all at the same time. The demand is so pressing that Captain Ganoe and myself are in honor bound to these people, to give our entire attention to supplying the world with these improvements for at least a year to come. So we have concluded to turn the whole matter over to you, of constructing a vessel that will meet the requirements of an Arctic storm."

"But," I asked, "why should you give up this work, now that you have it so far completed, into my inexperienced hands? I should think that your improvements could be duplicated by native mechanics."

"So they might," said Battell, "but they want all their factories readjusted, and the same improved methods of manufacture which have been introduced at Lake Byblis. Besides we could not have completed the work without your assistance. It was just as important that you should test our improvements in the conditions existing at the verges, as it was for us to manufacture them. These EXTERNAL WORLD METHODS of testing everything by ACTUAL EXPERIMENT are absolutely necessary when we come to deal with EXTERNAL WORLD CONDITIONS. A department of the factory at Byblis has been set apart for you, where your plans and specifications will be speedily worked out."

"But," I asked, "how can they be worked out as they should be by mechanics who know absolutely nothing about EXTERNAL WORLD CONDITIONS, such as Polar waves, Arctic storms, hurricanes and cyclones which are produced by EXTERNAL influences not existing in this INTERNAL WORLD? Will Captain Ganoe and yourself, with your external world experience and observation be there to superintend the work?"

"Yes, I will be there," said Battell, "but I want to thank you now for so forcibly presenting the reasons why the people of the inner world are anxious to avail themselves of our outer world experience in adapting their airships to outer world conditions. You certainly would not deprive them of this when they have given us so much that is indispensable to the physical, mental and moral uplifting of the people who live in the external world? It is these considerations which have influenced our decision to yield to their wishes. Whenever these people who live in this Internal World of Truth, as MacNair calls it, where an Altruistic love for humanity is the controlling impulse, see an improvement, they all want it immediately because it will enable them to do more good to others and of course we could not honorably refuse to assist them to the fullest extent of our ability."

"Certainly not," I said. "That puts the matter in an entirely new light; but it also leaves to me, with my comparative inexperience, the whole responsibility of constructing a storm and cold proof ship. For this, I have no experience as a mechanic, and am but poorly qualified. My duties on shipboard have always been in some capacity that did not stimulate my mechanical faculties, if I have any. As an assistant to Captain Ganoe and yourself I thought there might be a place for me, but as to my ability to take the lead, I have my doubts. I do not see how I am to get along without your co-operation and counsel."

"You will certainly have that," said Battell. "This is a country of rapid transit and we shall get together at regular intervals to compare notes. Besides, we will have the assistance of an Inner-World Association, whose representatives will constitute an Inner-World Council of the most earnest spirits, who are anxious to unite the INTERNAL and EXTERNAL worlds by opening a channel of INTER-COMMUNICATION and cultivating a mutual spirit of fraternal regard and co-operation between the two. I have thought much along these lines and realize how necessary these two great worlds are to each other and how important that the leading spirits of both should come together and work with one accord for the highest possible development of both."

"And that is just what they must do," said Oqua. "But let us test your new ship at once and confer in regard to the work we have in hand at the same time."

Thus prompted, we embarked, Battell applied the power and we began to ascend. Every required motion of the vessel had its appropriate propelling power which was under perfect control. No turning around was necessary. The new ship could dart in any given direction, at the will of the operator.

I took my place at the helm with Battell and after a little practice found that I could handle it without difficulty. To me its management was much more simple than the old style which could only move in one direction. This facility with which the direction could be changed was the essential feature in order to be able to ride the storms and nullify the influence of the contending air currents which would be a constant source of danger in the outer world. In fancy, I pictured myself in a storm with sudden changes in the direction of the wind, and suiting the action to the thought I set the vessel to dodging and gyrating in every direction to the no little alarm of our Altrurian friends who had no conception of the conditions of an external world bluster.

"Hold on Jack!" exclaimed Battell. "Don't shake the life out of us. Wait until you get into an actual storm and then dodge as rapidly as may be necessary, but there is no need of it here."

"I was just thinking," I said, "what motions might be necessary in a regular bluster, to hold the ship steady on her course. I really feel anxious to try it, and believe that I can literally ride the storm like the petrel in such a ship as I fully believe can be made."

"Well, you can try as soon as you like," said Battell. "I see you understand the management and I leave you to test it to your heart's content. Find all the deficiencies you can and let us know what changes may be needed, and they will be made to the best of our ability. We will now return to your home, borrow one of your old fashioned ships and return to our work at Byblis."

"Well, do not send it back," said Oqua, " until it is remodeled according to the latest improvements."

"Your Department of Exchange," said Battell, "has already sent in a general order for improved airships to replace those of the old style, which in effect means, that they shall all be remodeled on application. So we will send you an improved ship as soon as it can be made."

It was now the second day of March and I had set my heart on getting ready to start for the outer world by the latter part of May or the first of June, so there was no time to be wasted. I determined to leave at once on my experimental voyage to the southern verge and announced my intentions to Oqua, requesting her to represent me during my absence and any arrangements that she made in my name would be satisfactory.

"What!" she exclaimed. "Do you propose to go alone? I thought Battell intended that two of your sailors should go with you?"

"So he did," I replied, "and at that time I thought I would need them, but since I have tried the vessel, I have come to the conclusion that I had better go alone. As Battell left without referring to the matter, I shall act upon the presumption that he had changed his mind, just as he did in regard to completing a storm and cold proof airship."

"But," said Oqua, "your journey will take a week or ten day's travel at the least, and how can you stand the constant attention to the helm without rest?"

"No fears on that score," I said. "Very much of the time will be spent in this serene atmosphere. I need only set the helm in the right direction and I can rest until I find stormy conditions.

Then I will surely be able to experiment with the ship for a few hours." Oqua, seeing that I was determined, helped me to get ready. I took sufficient supplies for three weeks, although I did not expect to be gone half of that time. The trip was most interesting but I have no room to describe the voyage. Sufficient to say that I found storm conditions and intense cold much sooner than I expected. My electric garments proved to be a perfect success, but I discovered a number of deficiencies in the ship. I returned in just eight days and presented a written report, and specifications for necessary changes. Battell assured me that the new vessel should be ready for another trial journey as soon as possible.

I had notified Norrena, that I would be pleased to meet the World Council at my own apartments on the fifteenth, and I was back from the southern verge on the tenth, ready to place my discoveries before them. Promptly at the time indicated, Captains Ganoe and Battell with our usual circle of Altrurian friends were present in the Council Chamber of the home, ready to receive our guests, and in a few minutes Norrena arrived with the representatives from the other Grand Divisions. He introduced them as Hylas of Atlan, Lal Roy of Budistan, Wallaroo of Noxuania and LeFroy of the Austral Isles. Coming as they did from all the Grand Divisions of the world, I expected to see people of widely different physical appearance and mental characteristics, but in this I was mistaken. While they showed marked differences, there were no such contrasts as we find between different races in the outer world. In complexion they ranged from blonde to a dark brunette, all spoke the same language, expressed similar sentiments and in features and general deportment seemed to be building toward a common type.

I made a report of my trial trip to the southern verge and also of our plans and specifications for the further improvement of the airship, that we believed would make it storm and cold proof. As these people knew practically nothing of the conditions of the frigid zones they accepted what we had to offer without criticism. They expressed themselves as highly gratified that they had with them experienced navigators who were familiar with the frozen regions and who knew what was needed in order to open up a channel of communication.

At this meeting it was definitely determined that we should meet again on April 15th, which interval Battell assured us would give me an opportunity to report on another trial trip, to test the additional improvements which had been found desirable. That I should go ahead with the work of preparation in my own way, and when I was satisfied that the time had come to cross the Ice Barriers I should fix the date, so that the Council could arrange for an excursion to the most northern point of the continent of Altruria where the Life Saving Service had a signal station at an ancient watch tower that had been erected in prehistoric times.

After our business meeting had closed, the representatives from the Old World plied us with questions concerning the outer world which we answered to the best of our ability. Finding that they were not a bit backward about questioning I was emboldened to ask, how it was that all the representatives from the different countries seemed to have been selected from the same race of people, while I had learned from Altrurian history that the same races of men had existed here that existed in the outer world.

"That was the case in ancient times," said Wallaroo of Noxuania, "but at this time we have practically only one race of people in the inner world."

"Here is a mystery," I said, "that I would like very much to have explained. How is it that they have all merged into one type, ranging in complexion from blonde to brunette?"

"My own explanation," said Wallaroo, "is, that identity of ideals and similarity of conditions naturally lead to similarity of development, as in accordance with natural law the race is always building in the direction of its ideals."

"'That is certainly," I said, "a scientific proposition, but it does not explain why blonde, for instance, should ever become an ideal complexion among the dark races. How do you account for it?"

"Your question," said Wallaroo, "is one that should be carefully studied in the light of science and history, in order to be understood. One thing is certain, that the early inhabitants of my own country, Noxuania, were very dark, ranging from brown to black, while at present, brunette is the rule and blonde is not uncommon. "

"But how," I asked, "do you account for the change?"

"My opinion," said Wallaroo, "is that the influence of the white missionaries created a new ideal in the minds of the people and especially in the minds of the mothers, who almost worshiped them."

"But how is this?" I asked. "In the outer world, the dark races very often persecute and destroy the white missionaries."

"And so they did here," said Wallaroo, "before Equity was established in Altruria among white people, and another class of white missionaries were sent to the dark races. These came not to promulgate metaphysical creeds, but to bring material blessings, and establish freedom, equality and fraternity. They practiced just what they preached and wherever they went, they bestowed blessings. The people, especially the women, soon came to worship them as Saviors because they sought only to do them good on the material plane which they could appreciate, and left them to free their minds from superstition in the natural way by increasing their knowledge. It is not strange, under these circumstances, that with these children of nature, white became the ideal color. Improved material conditions, together with a scientific education, higher ideals and ample time for development have produced all the changes which have been wrought out."

I found the members of the Council from the other Grand Divisions to be highly cultured people and I looked forward to meeting them in the future with pleasure. I was especially interested in Wallaroo and LeFroy because they represented peoples which at the introduction of the present Altruistic civilization would correspond to the people now occupying Central Africa and the South Sea Islands. Wallaroo had attributed their remarkable development as physical, mental and moral beings to the higher civilization derived from the religion of humanity regardless of creeds, that had been brought to them by the Altrurian missionaries. The more I thought of these things the more I was impressed that I must visit these countries, mingle with the people and make a close study of their history. Le Froy told me that their written history commenced with the work of the missionaries of the new civilization, but much additional knowledge had been gained from archeological and ethnological researches in the light of such prehistoric traditions as had been preserved. These missionaries did not come to promulgate doctrines of a FUTURE life but to establish conditions which would confer blessings in THIS life, such as could be appreciated on the animal plane. For this reason they were welcomed as superior beings to lead them morally and spiritually.

By these glimpses of a new field of discovery that was opening up before me, I was more than ever stimulated to complete the work I had in hand, which was directly applicable to the solution of the great economic problem confronting the people of the outer world. As had been promised by Battell, at the Council which met on April 15th, I was able to report the deficiencies that had been discovered in the air ship by my second trial trip to the southern verge during its winter season. At this meeting it was determined to name the new vessel the Eolus, though I preferred to call it the Petrel because I had demonstrated that it could ride the storm. The time for the excursion to the Watch Tower at the northern extremity of the continent and my departure for the outer world was fixed for the twentieth of May and the next meeting of the Council on board the Silver King on the fifteenth, while en route. This gave me really less than one month to complete my manuscript and get everything in readiness for what I regarded as the most momentous voyage of my life.

While I was enrolled as a teacher of English, and the geography, history and institutions of the outer world, I had really given all of my attention to the study of the Altrurian language, and of the manner in which the great problems now confronting my own country had been solved. Every day revealed something new or presented the old in a new light. The arts and sciences had been developed to a degree that had scarcely been dreamed of in the outer world. Psychic powers such as clairvoyance, clairaudience and telepathy, which in the outer world were classed as occult by believers, and as baseless assumptions by the multitudes, were here well understood by the many, as revealed in the fact that my disguise had been so readily penetrated by native Altrurians. But at the same time they respected my right to conceal my identity. This was a marked peculiarity of these people. The right of persons to keep a secret in their own bosoms was never questioned, and when it was discovered, as I take it for granted was usually the case, it was never alluded to. Here, my assumed character of Jack Adams, the sailor, was held in the highest esteem by the few to whom I had explained the reason for it, because it had been necessary, in order to enable me to be true to my own higher sense of right. In the outer world this would have branded me as disreputable and I would have been ostracized as something vile by the so called better classes ot society.

After years of wandering, exposed to the perils and hardships of a sailor's life, I had found my lost lover, only to learn from his oft expressed sentiments, that he regarded such a course of life as I had pursued as so grossly disreputable that no honorable man could afford to contract a matrimonial alliance with such a woman. For this reason I had not revealed myself to him, and now that I was soon to leave him, the question often presented itself to my mind as to whether I ought to let him remain any longer in ignorance of the fact that Cassie VanNess had stood by his side in so many dangers.

The time was at hand when this question must be decided and I determined to confer with my most intimate Altrurian friends of my own sex. Bona Dea had arrived at our Home at my invitation and Oqua and lola were present to assist in making out a program for the excursion and my departure for the outer world. My proposed journey was of course the subject of conversation, but I wanted to draw them out in regard to the personal matter that was uppermost in my mind. I wanted their advice but did not want to be too abrupt in raising a question that was calculated to call the attention of these public spirited people away from an important public question in which they were deeply interested, to the consideration of my own private affairs.

Oqua, however, soon gave me the opportunity I wanted by asking:

"What does Captain Ganoe think of the decision of the Council and the general consensus of the opinions of those most interested, that you should have your own way about the journey and go alone if you thought best? While he did not object, I felt quite sure that he did not approve."

"His heart," I said, "was very much set on going himself and he expresses grave fears as to my safety, notwithstanding my excursions into the stormy regions in the vicinity of the southern verge. He knows however that it was with his consent and advice that the entire matter of opening communication with the outer world was placed in my hands and I accepted the responsibility under protest. The Council regarded my proposed expedition as too perilous to risk more than one life in the attempt. But this you know is just what I wanted for reasons of my own. As a matter of fact there is less danger than in my excursions to the southern verge. I wonder sometimes what the Captain would think if he knew that it was the little girl playmate of his boyhood days and the affianced bride of his early manhood who was bidding him adieu!"

"And do you not intend," asked Oqua, "to reveal your identity to him in some way so that when you return, no concealment's will be necessary? You know that we penetrated your disguise at once but we respected your natural right to conceal your identity, and we shall continue to do so until you are willing for us to do otherwise. But I would suggest, as an act of justice to Captain Ganoe as well as to yourself, that you ought to let him know who you are. It will doubtless awaken in his mind a train of thought that will be very beneficial to him, while it will protect you from the deteriorating effects of leading a double life."

"But," I said, "this double life was forced upon me by causes over which I had no control and hence I do not see how it can have any deteriorating effects."

"That was no doubt true," interrupted Bona Dea, "in the present stage of your outer world civilization, but there is no necessity for it here. And the necessity being past, the continuance of the deception might be interpreted to mean that deep down in your soul you doubted the propriety of your conduct. Disguise is perfectly legitimate as a means of self protection, but when it is unnecessary, its tendency is to cultivate duplicity, a characteristic to be carefully avoided. Hence I would advise you to adopt some method of revealing your identity to Captain Ganoe at the moment of your departure; and the more open and frank you are about it, the better will be the effect on him as well as yourself. Better not wait until he penetrates your disguise for himself, something he would have done long ago, but for the fact that from his education, he is guided by external appearances instead of those more subtle impressions from which there can be no concealment's."

I saw the force of this kind of reasoning and determined to act accordingly, and the more I thought of it, the more determined I became to be frank, honest and kind, but strong, independent and inflexible in the assertion of my natural right to think and act for myself without having my integrity and purity of character called in question, because I preferred truth to falsehood. At first I dreaded the denouement; but the more I reflected upon it, the more" necessary it appeared, and the better I was prepared for the ordeal.

The hour of my departure was near. It had been arranged that the Silver King with the delegations from the other Grand Divisions should meet the Altrurian delegation at the ruins of Kroy, and I had agreed to give Pat and Mike a ride on the Eolus, from the Ice King on Lake Byblis, and land them on the Silver King while en route for the northern extremity of the continent. I started to the Lake early on the morning of May 15th and within an hour from my departure I was on the deck of the Ice King. I found Lief and Eric, as well as Pat and Mike, ready for the journey. As soon as I had secured some scientific instruments I wanted from the equipment of the Ice King and some personal belongings which I regarded as important,

I invited the sailors ON BOARD THE EOLUS, and in a moment more we were mounting into the air. We sailed around the lake and gave the people an opportunity of seeing the airship that was destined for the outer world. The Eolus was not built with a view to seeming greater speed but for holding its course regardless of contrary winds. In speed, however, it was capable of making considerable progress against a head wind of two hundred miles an hour. I put the ship through the various movements that it was capable of making, such as stopping suddenly, moving backward, moving sidewise and suddenly rising and falling, for the benefit of the sailors and of the numerous spectators.

Mike was quick to see the advantage that the Eo!us had over other airships and he remarked with enthusiasm:

"Well Jack, it will take a lively hurricane to drive you much from your course, but how in the world will you keep from freezing?"

"Nothing easier," I said, "as I touched a button and lighted the electric burners that were placed between the inner and outer walls. In a minute the walls were hot to the touch and the air inside became sultry."

"Gracious!" exclaimed Mike. "You can never stand this. It will roast you."

"Then we will cool it," I said, as I shut off part of the burners, "or if this is not enough, I will shut them all off."

"But," said Mike, "you have it so hot now that it will take an hour to cool off ."

"Not so," I replied. "I will open the doors and start the electric fans," and suiting the action to the word, a cool breeze took the place of the sultry air. "But if you want it cooler," I continued, "I will bring the temperature down a point or two more," and closing the doors, I opened the refrigerator compartment and in a moment we were shivering with the cold.

"Well!" exclaimed Mike, "I never knew climate to change so rapidly. I think you have not been dodging up to the Pole and back for nothing. You seem to have provided for every emergency but one, and that is the freezing of the moisture which.

is already obscuring your lookouts by this manufactured dose of winter."

"That is provided for," I said, as I started the circular lookout glasses into motion under a specially prepared brush which absorbed the moisture. Mike noticed the disappearance of the clouds on the lookouts but did not observe the cause and looked at me inquiringly.

"Put your hand on the glass," I said, "and it will explain itself."

"Well I should think it would!" he exclaimed as he jerked back his hand. "The whole window is just a whizzing; and now I see that the cross bar is a brush that seems to have drank up the moisture."

"I have tried to provide for every contingency," I said, as I turned the prow of the Eolus down the valley of the Cocytas, and put her at full speed. "I regard it as a matter of the first importance that a full account of our discoveries shall be transmitted to our own country. We must join the excursion on board the Silver King as soon as we can. I want to interview as many of the representatives from other countries as possible. I must gather all the useful knowledge I can for the benefit of the external world."

"That is right," said Mike, "and I would be far from stopping you, but I want you to be after going slow a bit."

"Why what is the matter?" I asked, as I checked our speed.

"Just this," said Mike, producing a box, "it will take money in the outer world to secure the publication of your book and here is our wages from the Ice King. It is of no use to us in this country, and we want it to be used to send your book broadcast. You will see that it is divided into two parcels, one belongs to Lief and Eric and the other to Pat and myself."

Here Lief broke into our conversation, speaking the Altrurian language like a native, saying:

"We want your book to be translated into all languages, and it will be, just as soon as our wonderful discoveries are known in any civilized country. We particularly want our own people to hear about this country, and that we are not the first Norsemen who came here. Tell them about the old Viking, and also of the Norwegian names which are found everywhere."

"I have noted these things," I said, "as well as the part you have taken in the expedition. How you saved the Ice King by your prompt action when we were caught in the ice, and how your ability as seamen enabled us to get through after the larger part of the crew had deserted."

"Oh! we ask no credit for that," said Eric. "We shipped for a purpose, and have in a measure found what we were looking for. When the right time comes our people will hear from us, and when they do, we may be able to add something of value to the great work for humanity which you have undertaken. All we ask for now is, that your account of our discoveries shall be given to the outside world."

"And I promise you," I said, "that your money shall be used for that purpose, and I fully believe that what we have learned, will be the greatest boon that could be conferred upon the people of the outer world. In the name of humanity I accept the trust you place in my hands and I shall see that your gold shall be used to emancipate your fellow workmen from the tyranny now imposed upon them by human greed."

As we sped down the valley a glass of small magnifying power brought the Silver King into view gliding northward on the bay like a thing of life. I timed the Eolus so as to join the excursion on this floating crystal palace when it passed out upon the ocean. As we slowly settled in the place that had been set apart for us, the crowds gathered around and I was kept busy answering questions and explaining the use of the various attachments which experience had demonstrated to be essential to the successful navigation of the air in the external world.

This was an excursion long to be remembered. The crowds of elegantly dressed people who thronged the decks of the Silver King had gathered from every part of the concave to accompany us to the northern extremity of Altruria, a distance of about 7,000 miles from the mouth of the Cocytas. It was intended that we should cover this distance in seven days, which would make the actual time of my departure on my aerial voyage, the morning of the twenty-third of May.

As the excursion was to last one full week a series of entertainments was provided to make the time pass pleasantly and profitably. Music, dancing and theatrical performances were interspersed with lectures and social converse touching upon leading subjects of thought and action. The program made this journey one ceaseless round of enjoyment. The records of the conversation; preserved by my locket phonograph, I regard as the most instructive and valuable historical, scientific and ethical lessons I have ever listened to, and which I hope to be able to give to the world when the occasion requires.

On the evening of the twenty-second, Oqua called my attention to the kaleidoscopic lights on the Watch Tower which was to be the point where I would bid farewell to my Altrurian friends as well as my comrades of the Ice King. In the pitch dark nights of the outer world such an exhibition would have been beautiful and grand beyond description but even here, with the reflected light which made the darkest nights comparatively light, the scene through our glasses, of the ever changing views was such, that I never tired of observing them. These lights presented all the prismatic hues of the rainbow with the intermediate shades, continually changing from one geometrical figure to another, but always coming around to a five pointed star which is the symbol and sign manual of the material civilization of this inner world; the changing colors kept pace with the changing geometrical figures, always returning to the five pointed star, until it had been reproduced in each of the seven prismatic colors.

This seemed to be the regular order, but suddenly it was broken, by giving only the stars in the seven different colors in a rapid succession, until they resolved themselves into a circle, revolving swiftly on its axis. Seeing my interest in this change, Oqua said: "The keeper has just noticed our approach and is operating the keys to send us a welcome in the name of the entire concave.

This welcome will be repeated by every signal station on

this parallel around the world. The principal use of these lights is to send messages by means of the changing figures, which are well understood by the people of this country, and especially those who navigate these northern waters. The one great drawback to their use, is, that they must be observed through glasses which are especially adapted to this purpose. Here in this inner world where it is never absolutely dark we cannot take the full advantage of these light signals, without the use of external appliances."

As she spoke she set the great telescope through which I was looking to revolving so as to take in a zone all around the concave, and I observed other signal lights responding in regular order along this zone.

"These signal stations," continued Oqua, "are under the control of the Life Saving Service, and the keepers with these glasses are always on the lookout for mariners who may be in danger, and their signal messages notify any patrols that may observe them of the nature of the danger as well as the locality of the endangered. Had the Ice King come within the radius of any of these Signal Stations at almost any other time, you would certainly have been discovered and rescued. But at the time you came into these waters the fog had effectually checkmated our observations. For this reason we are agitating for the extension of this system to medial and equatorial latitudes, as a time has come when it seems likely that other ships like the Ice King, may drift into these placid waters where sails are useless, and hence be powerless to save themselves from certain destruction by being carried into the southern verge on ocean currents which never touch the land. "

On the morning of the twenty-third when I awoke, the Silver King was lying at the wharf and I had a close view of the Watch Tower and its ever changing signal lights. It was more like a lofty building than a mere tower. It was a hexagon in shape, two hundred and fifty feet in height with a large platform on top, in the center of which was a huge column like the body of a tall tree branching out into numerous arms, each supporting a series of electric lights. The mechanical contrivance by which these lights were controlled was automatic; but as occasion required could be changed by the watchman in the observatory to signal any message required to all whom it might concern. This building from outside to outside was one hundred feet at the base and fifty feet at the top, while the inside diameter was the same from top to bottom. On the outside was a spiral stairway reaching from the ground to the platform at the top and in the center was an electric elevator, connected with each of the twenty stories.

The hour of my departure had come. According to the program I was to bid farewell to the members of the Inner World Council and my old comrades of the Ice King and some personal friends at the top of the tower where they had already assembled. The crew of the Silver King and her throngs of excursionists had gathered on the deck and the wharf to see me take my flight. When all was ready, I took my place on the Eolus and rising a few feet sailed slowly around this magnificent ship, coming to a halt on the starboard quarter where Captain Thorfin, acting as spokesman, said:

"In the name of the people here assembled from all parts of the world who have accompanied you thus far on your daring expedition, I am requested to express to you our exalted opinion of your courage, your ability and worth, and to thank you for the inestimable service which you have undertaken to render to our people, by extending their sphere of knowledge in regard to the external world. You are now engaged in a work for which our people are powerless. We realize that we are to profit by your perils. You will ever occupy a warm place in our affections. Accept our thanks for your heroic efforts to open a channel of communication with our fellow beings of the external world. Hoping for your speedy return we bid you a loving farewell."

"And through you," I responded, "I desire to extend my heartfelt thanks to those who are beyond the reach of my voice, for this demonstration of their interest, and may the channel of communication, which we hope to establish between the internal and the external worlds never again be closed. But as yet I have not accomplished anything to merit your thanks. I am the one who ought to be grateful to your people. I came among you a stranger and you received me as a brother. Everywhere I have met the kindest consideration and all my wants have been supplied without even the formality of asking. I have here found the living soul of humanity developed as it has never been believed to be possible in the external world. I carry with me to my own native land **THE PEARL OF GREAT PRICE**, the knowledge that **HUMANITY CAN BE REDEEMED FROM SELFISHNESS AND ALL OF IT'S CONSEQUENCES**. In the external world, from whence I came, we have only cultivated the external, and hence have developed physical hardihood while you have developed the finer attributes of the soul which we have neglected. My ambition is to bring these two worlds together. You need our physical hardihood while we need your higher development of soul. When the leading characteristics of both are united into one common brotherhood, both worlds will have a perfected humanity. If I can help humanity to reach this grand culmination, where both soul and body shall be developed to their utmost capacity. I shall be happy. To me, with my training, it does not seem like a daring undertaking now that I am enabled to utilize your grand discovery of the means by which the air can be navigated. Thanking you for this mark of your consideration, and promising to return as soon as possible, I bid you adieu."

As I ceased speaking, I set the Eolus to moving directly to the top of the tower. This demonstrated at once to the multitudes, its superiority over the old style of airship and they gave a cheer, which was the more expressive and significant as these people are not given to anything like loud demonstrations of applause.

At the platform I received cordial words of cheer from the committee, my old comrades of the Ice King and my most intimate Altrurian friends. Speaking for the committee, Lal Roy, of Budistan said:

"On behalf of the members of this committee, and especially of the members from the eastern hemisphere, I congratulate you upon the marked improvements you have made in our methods of aerial navigation. The construction of the Eolus marks an era in our progress that will be a monument to your memory. You will be honored and appreciated for generations to come."

"Excuse me," I responded. "I am not entitled to the honor you would bestow upon me. Captain Battell made the first move toward the improvements that were consummated in the Eolus, and Captain Ganoe and Huston have both contributed their mechanical skill. Without them there would have been no Eolus."

"Hold on Jack," said Battell. "In the consummation, we only carried out your suggestions. The improvements I started, were completed in accordance with your plans."

"Yes," said Captain Ganoe, as he clasped my hand. "You were the first person I ever heard suggest the construction of an airship that could ride the storm, and but for your suggestions every one of which was tested in your experimental journeys to the verges, we never could have succeeded. And but for your intimate knowledge of the difficulties to be overcome, I never would have consented for you to go alone. Even as it is, notwithstanding the unanimous decision of the committee, I find it very hard to reconcile myself to the thought that you are to be exposed all alone, to the cold and the storms of the polar regions. Such dangers ought to be reserved for those who have nothing to live for, and not for the young, the refined and the educated who have a bright future before them."

"Have no fears for me," I said. "You must not forget that it is now warm weather in the north frigid zone and I will not be exposed to intense cold, and the probability is that I will have no severe storms to contend with. But I will promise this: To be careful, and if I discover any defect in the Eolus that would make the journey too hazardous, I will return at once, rather than take any chances of defeating our purpose of communicating with the outer world when we have mastered the problem of riding the storm. No doubt my observations on this voyage, will open the way for other improvements. Keep up your courage. This is but the beginning of our work. We must have airships that will enable the most sensitive, to visit the outer world, and teach our countrymen the importance of cultivating the higher attributes of the soul, which can only be developed in their fullness under the benign influences of an Altruistic civilization."

Oqua here stepped forward and took me by the hand, saying:

"Nequa, my more than friend, go, and the blessings of our people go with you. May you reach your native land in safety and accomplish your mission. By so doing you will leave footprints on the sands of time that can never be effaced. As soon as your work is placed in the proper hands return with all speed to the many loving hearts which await you."

Scarcely had she ceased speaking when Polaris, as if to continue her remarks, raising her hand and pointing to the north, said:

"Yes, loving hearts will await you. And when your form has faded from our vision, in yonder deep cerulean blue, the mystic symbol of purity and truth, remember that in spirit we are with you. And I will continue to keep watch over these waters, patiently awaiting your return, as in the past I have kept watch for any of your people that might drift in here, and be left to the mercy of the currents which never touch the land. I hope to be the first to greet you on your return, but if perchance you should be lost in your perilous undertaking, I will still be flitting, to and fro, over these northern seas, awaiting the coming of your people, to assist and welcome them in the true spirit of our civilization."

MacNair gave a new turn and spirit to this closing interview, by saying in his usual cheery manner:

"In the name of humanity I protest against preparing for the funeral before the corpse is ready. Neither am I willing to contemplate the possibility of Jack Adams ever requiring any such a service at our hands. You do not understand the kind of material of which he is composed. I know that Jack is going to make the round trip, no matter what we may be doing, and so far as I am concerned, I do not intend to give myself any uneasiness about him; and instead of bobbing around up here in this chilly atmosphere, I will go home and be ready to give Jack the cordial greeting of a fellow countryman, when he returns from this last polar expedition."

"MacNair is right," I said. "I am not starting out to fall by the wayside, and do not forget that the Eolus will sail far above the ice-fields, and that during the high noon of the long arctic day of six months duration. I apprehend no danger, but anticipate a pleasant excursion to my native land. But I will not go any further this time, than is absolutely necessary. I hope to meet the right persons at some of the many stations in Alaska, and if so I will return several days earlier than I have promised. I shall return as soon as possible. My life work is here, for it will take a life-time to complete the work that I have laid out for myself to do for the benefit of my countrymen who live in the external world."

As I was speaking, Captain Ganoe stood with his hand on the door of the Eolus, as if it was by right his place to have the last parting word. Captain Battell and the other comrades of the Ice King drew near. Upon their faces, I read the affectionate regard they had for me. It was a trying moment. I wanted a last word with Captain Ganoe. I wanted it impressive, kind but inflexible. I shook hands with all who stood near, and then as I held Captain Ganoe's hand I said to Oqua:

"Step on board, I want you to assist me a moment," and to the Captain, "Wait here a moment, I have something to say to you."

Oqua did as directed, and we ascended and made the circuit of the lights, while I prepared myself for the revelation I intended. Oqua handled the ship while I hastily donned the attire which characterized my sex in the outer world. I arrayed myself in the same rich satin dress that I had worn on the last evening I had spent with Raphael, at his uncle's home in New York. My golden locks made into a neat fitting wig, and put up in the same style which he had so much admired, now covered my short cropped hair. Around my neck I had the same gold chain and locket of peculiar workmanship, and the same ring on my hand, which had been his parting presents to his affianced bride. Over all I wore a cloak that came down to my, feet.

My toilet complete, we dropped to the level of the platform, but just outside, and Oqua with a parting pressure of the hand,

and with a last injunction: "Nequa, be strong, be true, but do not forget to be kind and considerate," passed from the Eolus to the platform, and moving back a few feet, I stepped to the door and throwing aside my cloak, stood arrayed before Captain Ganoe, just as I had been when I bade him adieu at our guardian's home just fifteen years ago.

The crowd stood spellbound. None but Oqua, MacNair and the crew of the Ice King had ever seen any one dressed in the costume which is peculiar to the women in the outer world. Captain Ganoe stood rooted to the spot, and gazed at me with a look of consternation as if I was one who had just arisen from the grave, as I said:

"Captain Ganoe, you doubtless recognize me and I ask your attention for a moment. You will probably remember, that on the Ice King you confidently related to your scientist Jack Adams, the story of your engagement to Cassie VanNess, and asked him if he had ever loved. He made an evasive reply. If you care to have an explicit answer to that question, ask my trusted friend Oqua. I do not wish to have that story again pass my lips. I have done with it forever. I have now taken up a new life and henceforth I am wedded to a new lover, and the wealth of my affections shall be bestowed upon humanity.

"The memory of the old life, and the old love, carries with it the martyrdom of all that is noblest, purest and most sacred in the soul of woman, her devotion to the chosen idol of her girlhood days. These outer world conditions so foreign to all that is good and true, make me wonder that I should ever have been so weak as to be victimized by them. But such are the consequences of a false education, which belongs to a benighted past and cannot be helped. For many long years in my assumed character of Jack Adams, the sailor, I roamed over the high seas to find you, and during all of our perils in the ice, I stood by your side. I worshipped you with an idolatrous devotion. And all this, only to hear again and again from your lips, the expression of sentiments, that condemned all that I had done, as disreputable, unworthy and immoral. You have repeatedly declared that as an honorable man, you could never unite yourself with such a woman in the holy bonds of matrimony, no matter how much you loved her."

"It was for this reason, that my own self respect forbade that I should reveal my identity to you. The case of Huston was almost identical with my own, and in condemning the course which he had taken you condemned me. I took it for granted that as an honorable man, you expressed your honest sentiments, and there was nothing for me to do but to submit to your verdict —"

The Captain raised his hand as if to speak, but I checked him, saying;

"Hear me through. It is in no spirit of unkindness that I speak. I have waited patiently for you to so modify your views, that I could make myself known to you in the full assurance of your approval of my fidelity to our plighted troth. But you gave me no such opportunity. Oqua penetrated my disguise at the first sight and many others of my inner world friends with whom I have been associated, intuitively understood that Jack Adams, the sailor, was an assumed character and why it had been adopted; but you blinded by the crystallized errors of a false education, were ignorant of my identity."

"I now reveal myself to you, because I do not wish to continue this assumed character, even to escape the pain that would be inflicted by your disapproval. I do not regret the course I have taken. Under the same circumstances I would be compelled to do the same thing again, rather than be false to the higher laws of my own nature. It is true that I repudiated, and still repudiate, any legal obligation that may be secured by fraud, misrepresentation or coercion. I know that human laws, human customs and legal ceremonies may be the cover for the violation of God's laws which are implanted in the human soul. I have been true to these higher, God made laws of my own being, and disregard all man made laws and customs which violate the most sacred rights of the human soul."

"If I can not meet you as an equal, free to think and act for myself, regardless of the arbitrary rulings of either the church or state, then it will be far better for both of us, that we remain apart. I will never be bound by any ceremony that does not meet my own approval. When it comes to matters of this kind, I, Cassie Van Ness, am the lawmaker."

"You have repeatedly expressed sentiments, which could have no other meaning, than that you regarded legal and popular ceremonies as of more worth in your estimation, than the 'unpurchased, and unpurchasable devotion of a loving woman.' If you prefer a companion who cares more for what Mother Grundy might say, than she does for Captain Ganoe, than I could not possibly be that companion. When I return, let all this be forgotten. Let us meet as friends, forget if we can the past, and let each of us live our own life, true to our own convictions of what is noble, good and true. I have had one lover and lost him because I loved him so devotedly. I shall never make that mistake again. But as the widow of such a lover. I shall henceforth continue to labor for the upbuilding of all humanity, as I would gladly have lived for him, and him only."

"And now, farewell Raphael. I regret, not that I have loved you so devotedly, but that I did not learn sooner, that it was only love with certain restrictions, and within certain specific bounds, that you wanted. Excuse my mistake and farewell."

While I maintained my equilibrium, I felt that my heart would break. With my hand I waved a farewell to all, and set the Eolus in motion. As I closed the door, Captain Ganoe sprang forward and would have dashed himself from the tower but for those who stood by him. His last words have been ringing in my ears ever since as they wafted to me on the balmy air. In a voice of agonizing entreaty, he cried out:

"Oh Cassie ! Cassie! For God's sake. Come back! Come back!"

THE END

Epilogue

As you've noticed the author of the original edition is listed as Jack Adams. On page vi of the first edition was the explanation that the original work was by Mary P. Lowe's deceased husband Dr. T. A. H. Lowe.

The reading public, when looking for background information on Nequa, has been at the mercy of the experts, many of whom seemed to have never even looked at an actual copy of the book, which they write about in their compilations.

Barbara Quissell's *New World That Eve Made: Feminist Utopias Written by Nineteen-Century Women* found in Roemers *America as Utopia* discusses A. O. Grigsby as a woman writer.

Science Fiction & Fantasy Literature 1700 - 1974 written by R. Reginald and published by Gale Research lists Jack Adams as a pseudonym for A. O. Grigsby.

The 1991 edition of *Unveiling a Parallel: A Romance,* in the introduction by Carol A. Kolmerten, gives A.O. a lot of credit when stating on page xii, "a few of the male writers also questioned their culture's prevailing gender ideology in the pages of their utopian novels. The most obvious example is Alcanoan O. Grigsby whose 1900 novel Nequa describes a world where both sexes are equal after women put an end to war and demand freedom from domination of man-made laws."

In *Science-Fiction, the early years: A full description of more than 3000 stories* Evert Franklin Bleiler gives a synopsis and lists the authors as Alcanoan O. Grigsby, a male and Mary P. Lowe, a female.

No one seems to have read the "Explanatory Note" in the front of the book, which states that Dr. T. A. H. Lowe is the author. At the Kansas State Historical Archives, there is a note, written in pencil on a card in the card catalog, which says that Mr. Lowe's son also stated to a member of the society that his father T.A.H. Lowe was the actual author.

Of course there could be truth in the actual writer being of either gender or maybe even a shared endeavor. The historical times would have required that a man's name be listed as the author, since the culture of the time tended to not support female authors. Using the pseudonym of Jack Adams, but putting the copyright in A.O. and Mary's name accomplished a sufficient amount of "cover" regardless of what the actual situation might be. The explanatory note in the front of the book, listing the original work as being produced by Mary P. Lowe's deceased husband, might have also just been additional cover for various inheritance reasons or because Mary P. Lowe didn't completely trust A. O. Grigsby.

If you get a chance to read some of the speeches that A. O. Grigsby made, you will see exceptional similarities between his expositions to political audiences and the explanations of economic situations and suggestions as laid out in Nequa. He definitely provided a lot of the passages.

There also seems to be a more gentle, flowery description of certain concepts such as "Mother-love" and its ability to change a whole society if given a chance. Some of the phrasing and word usage in the interaction between Cassie and the women of Altruria, seems to be gentle, more conciliatory, more feminine. So I believe that Mary P. Lowe also contributed much of the actual writing.

There may have been others who helped with suggestions. Some one had a great sense of humor with the names for the leaders of the four distinct areas of Altruria. Mr. Wallaroo (a kangaroo) of Noxuania, LeFroy of the Austral Isles (Tahiti), Lal-Roy of Budistan (in Poland), and Hyas of Atlan (son of Atlas).

Together their personal names and country origins bring me a dazzling vision of four men in outrageous costumes.

It just seems to me that the book might have been a cooperative effort, with more than just one writer. First there is the adventure story of almost dying in the ice. Then meetings with the inhabitants of the interior, which reads like a travel story where the culture of the people is explained in historical and philosophical terms. Woven throughout are the soap operas of two couples united under less than scrupulous means and the unrequited love of Cassie and Ganoe. The characters and place names are very diverse from several literary and cultural sources. There are Irish, Scandinavians, Greek, Roman and Italian surnames or place names. I have looked up most all of the names in Nequa with varying amounts of success.

The internet is not a perfect research tool. You get strange combinations and false web sites but it allows a person in a matter of days to find things that might take years. Then after you have acquired a lot of information you have to try to sort it all out.

Here is a list of the names I looked up, followed by the notations I found. The following are in order of appearance in the book.

Leo Vincennes — Leo XIII appointed Bishop Chatard the Bishop of Vincennes, U.S.A. in 1878

"Jack Adams, Mutineer" written by Captain Chamier published in 1838 after Adams is found with his progeny on Pitcairn Island. Jack states "Look around me: from murderers and mutineers have sprung up a people who hold the christian law in veneration — who never rise without thanksgiving — who never lay their heads upon their pillows without prayer.

Janes MacNair — The McNair family are of Scottish origin belonging to the gathering of clans of whom the Earls of Lenox were the hereditary chieftains. The gathering place was near the head of Loch Lomond. Pioneers in the Presby-

terian Kirk of Scotland, resettled in Ireland and then in 1732 emigrated to Pennsylvania

Oqua — there is a town in Illinois named Oquawka Oquawka was originally an Indian word Oquawkiek changed to Oquawka. The town was the location of a strange event during the Blackhawk War. A man named S. S. Phelps refused to turn over his friend Tama, and Tama's wife and children. Tama was a Fox Indian, who had been friendly with the white population even during the Blackhawk war. 50 drunken soldiers came to the house and tried under threat of death to get Phelps to turn over his friend. Phelps said NO and averted the death of his Indian family friends and averted a full scale war of retribution by the Fox and their comrades.

Cocytas — Cocytus is the river of wailing, an underground river in Greek mythology
Thorfinn Karlsefni (Old Norse surname signifies "Makings of a man" an icelandic explorer in 1010 AD

Bona Dea — goddess of Agriculture and fertility also chastity and healing. represented by the cornucopia and the snake, especially honored by the lower classes. Public festival on May first, private rituals in homes of Romans Details of the rituals are unknown.

Polaris is the north star

Dione is a moon of Saturn. she is a Greek, her name is a title — "The Goddess" mother of Aphrodite

Byblis is a Greek mythological woman who cry's herself to death and turns into a spring. The City of Byblos named after her.

Orbetillo is a city in Italy

Oscan is a linguistic group in south central Italy

Eolus was the ruler of the winds a servant of Juno

Zeta wild — "Ancient Zeta's wild and rocky core, called Crna Gora by the Serbs and Montenegro by the rest of Europe" — from the history of the Balkan Peninsula by Schevill

Hyas is son of the Titan Atlas. He was an archer who was killed by his prey. Greek Mythology

Wallaroo is a type of kangaroo

Austral Isles are 9 islands including Tahiti and Polynesia

Lal Roy — The first Indian flying ace was Indra Lal Roy which was too recent for this book but may indicate that the name is traditionally a Surname from India. It is a bit of a stretch but, but there was also a LaRoy Moore who was in charge of the Divine Science Association in Topeka located at 623 Quincy who advertised in the "New Woman" newspaper.

LeFroy was the name of an Australian family. Anthony O'Grady LeFroy moved from Ireland to Australia at age 27 and explored Western Australia. He died in 1897.

Altruria was a utopian commune near Santa Rosa California. It was based on Christian Socialist principals, but was defunct by 1896 Led by a Unitarian pastor Edward Biron Payne Wikipedia said "Altruria" derives from the Latin alter "the other". As opposed to egotism, altruism — a word coined during the first half of the 19th century by Auguste Comte — is unselfish concern for the welfare of others. Thus, Altruria is a Utopian country inhabited exclusively by altruists, by people who believe that they have a moral obligation to help, serve, or benefit others.

Spitzbetgen is a Norwegian Island

Umbrian Sea — Umbrian is an extinct language from a region of Italy

Minerva — Roman goddess of wisdom

Behring is a sometime spelling of Bering

Lief & Eric the Norwegians Eric the red had a son Lief

I did not find notations on the following — Meidra, Tanqua, Mike Gallager, Tom Brown, Richard Sage, Cassie VanNess Captain Battell, Kroy, Paul Huston, Pat O'brien, James Van Ness

I also looked up a lot of words that I thought were misspelled but they turned out to be British spellings or archaic spellings through out the book.

If one reads this book with a critical eye watching the way that ideas are sort of rolled out it seems written for reading and discussion at a group meeting. There is a statement in one of the sales pitches in *"Equity"* suggesting that a person get five people together to buy a book. There is also a notation on page 253 about the Patrons of Equity, an organized group which actually existed in Topeka, Kansas. In the *New Woman* newspaper, it is mentioned that Matilda Gillmore is the head of the women's section of the Patrons of Equity. Did the Patrons of Equity help edit and then also use the book to help its members with the explanations necessary to explain what they were trying to accomplish?

So what contribution did Dr. T.A.H. Lowe make? Probably he laid out an idea that was reworked to fit the requirements of those who published the book. He acquired a plot into which, an explanation of what was wrong in America and what would correct it could be plugged in. Where did he get the hollow earth idea?

One of the census records said that Dr. Lowe was an eclectic doctor. In my attempts to validated Tilghman's profession, I finally got some great help from a web site listed as http://brianaltonenmph.com. Brian pointed me in the direction of where to find the listing of graduates of the Eclectic Medical Institute in Cincinnati.

Cincinnati opened a container of worms. Brian Altonen also told me about one of the professors at the Eclectic Medical Institute.

According to Brian, "John Uri Lloyd wrote a book "Etidorhpa", (Aphrodite backwards), dated about 1898-1903, in which a character tells of his travels to the center of the earth — somewhere up by the north pole. There is found the Father of time, and a character with a face without a mouth, another I think that lacked eyes. Lloyd reflected on his writings and claimed it to be an attempt to sell to "fiction readers". Based on his eclectic history, I don't fully believe that his initial reason was to compose fiction." wrote Brian.

John Uri Lloyd was a leader in the Eclectic Herbal Medical movement; his library still exists in Cincinnati. He was an early pharmacologist who made quite a bit of money with a chemical company he started. It was sort of a compounding pharmacy. He also did a lot of testing of various compounds and vegetal material. He taught at the Eclectic Medical Institute from 1878 to 1895.

Looking at Lloyd's life, introduced me to Cyrus Reed Teed (head of Koreshanity) who was also an Eclectic Physician trained at the Eclectic School in New York. Cyrus practiced eclectic medicine and started a commune in Florida which is now a State Historical site. Teed also told about a passage in a cave which led into the middle of the earth.

But most importantly, I found the novel "Mizora, A Prophecy" another feminist hollow earth writing which was serialized in a newspaper, the *Cincinnati Commercial*, in the winter of 1880-1881. It was published anonymously.

Tilghman A. H. Lowe was attending Medical school at the Eclectic Medical Institute in Cincinnati in 1880. "Mizora" was written by Mary E. Bradley Lane who tried to keep her husband from finding out about her writing, but finally put it into book form in 1881.

While the Altrurians in Nequa overthrew the man made laws and political intrigues of the male gender, Mizoraians got rid of men and all people of color permanently. Only beautiful blond women atheists and their test tube babies inhabited the Mizoraian inner earth.

Dr. Tilghman A. H. Lowe probably brought home to Kansas the outline of a hollow earth plot found in the *Cincinnati Commercial*, but he and others instilled a plot with a better heart then what became "Mizora".

With Tilghman's death in 1894, his idea of presenting a political message to the Populists and Socialists was taken over by his widow the former editor of the *New Woman* newspaper and A.O. Grigsby who had been the manager of that newspaper. Tilghman's book was launched with a serialization in *"Equity"* and the editors and copywriters were Dr. T.A.H. Lowe's widow and A. O. one of the political operatives in the Topeka area.

Dr. Lowe's book was a much more kind attempt at installing a more egalitarian society. There is an emphasis on the idea of Mother-love, as the potential salvation for our planet. It is one of the reasons given for the Altururian Utopian vision seemly "feeling" more normal to the adventurers from the surface society. Many of the Altrurian systems of economic equality seem like common sense. The explanations given for how the distribution of goods and services takes place, sound so correct that it is hard to understand why we have evolved into a convoluted capitalist system of requiring unemployment and providing scarcity.

Mother-love didn't require the removal of all men, only the removal of the "Me first" doctrine from the culture of men. Values then emphasized mankind's efforts being placed on education and the careful nurturing of children, emphasis was placed on the future, on building a very stable environment where the crystallization of a child's impressions are in the realm of correct habits of cognition, rather than immediate satiation of desires, or the instant provision of pleasure.

Mother-love refers to the transformation that takes place in most women who give birth to a child. The protection and providing for the newborn child is not a logically thought out scheme. It is the result of a transformation that takes place. A new mother will feed her new born at the expense of her own sustenance. It is observable on every nature show on television. A matriarchal society would require sustenance for all, it would allow mothers to exempt their children from the wars, to require a government that was egalitarian rather than based on the accumulation of gold to exchange for necessities. The assumption is that this personal interior change would call present accepted practices into account, eventually removing the present system and its predatory practices. The greatest assumption is that the males of our specie would slowly learn the value of Mother-love and undergo some internal change themselves.

The term Mother-love sounds sort of twerpey, sort of nerdy, but it is the law which kicks in when a woman becomes a mother. It is the self sacrifice which emphasizes the superior position of the child when the mother as a full grown human being, is physically larger and capable of very violent acts. Being bigger and badder are macho conclusions, they underlay a lot of the reasons why our present system penalizes those who aren't big, bad and full of political bullshit. Our societal systems definitely penalize those who don't wish to take the pathway of the me first mentality.

The concept that an emphasis on ones personal perspective is all that needs to change in order for the sexist, greedy systems of the world to collapse is nothing short of amazing. If it will work it is Miraculous. Generation after generation have schemed, dreamed, fought and died to change the world, and here Nequa tells us the answer is subjugation of the ego? It is as simple, as adopting an attitude of ME SECOND. Spending each day for the rest of your life trying to put yourself next in line after one less fortunate.

This answers the call of Social Justice, it is the offering of a system loosely termed Christian Socialism. It is not a call to over throw the government, it is not the sound of reveille being played to gather the troops for a conflict, rather it is a call to the reader to notice that perhaps there is a revolution possible through the evolution of certain practices that people who are committed to selflessness can personally participate in, that will cause a collapse of certain non egalitarian systems which have never dealt with institutionalized poverty.

The explanation of Mother-Love, is a call to those who personally feel a need to involve themselves in potential change through their very being, through personal choices that will, with sufficient participation elevate the people of the world.

The existence of Mother-Love is one of those whispered about transformational states, alluded to in old spiritual texts, but because we are usually only translating ideas through the intellect, with an ego spin to the information, we reject these age old suggestions for transforming the self. True mother-love requires a bit of pondering. The reality of understanding Mother-Love probably also requires the spoken perspective of a woman. Preferably a mother?

Reviews from other publications spoke of Nequa as an "occult romance" The manner in which the concept of "Mother-love" is presented does have some aspects found in occult literature. G. I. Gurdjieff spoke about a transformation that was possible with a woman's preparation to become a mother. The woman did not have to have a child only make the personal preparation.

A presentation at the 18th International Humanities Conference in 2013, given by Kristina Turner revisited Gurdjieff's statements with new commentary.

A major mystery in Nequa exists in the romance of Canoe and Cassie. Being a hopeless romantic I think a real love story probably exists behind the story book version. The story in the last few pages of Nequa, might actually carry a lot of fictionalized truth, about the private life of the copyright holders. Does Nequa actually carry a hidden truth about a real love affair that was to be fictionalized, where there was a reconciliation and it was to be revealed in Volume #2 ? The notes I've found say that A. O. and Mary lived in the same building and they worked together four or five years on *The New Woman* and on *Equity* newspapers. Stranger things have happened in our world.

It just seems to me that Captain Ganoe sounds a lot like Alcanoan. Ganoe who is left in agony by Jack Adams revealing himself/herself as Cassie Van Ness on the next to the last page. Agony which exists because of his lack of understanding of the difference between man's laws and the situation that Cassie found herself coerced into accepting. Ganoe is a victim of his education which includes a lack of acceptance of total equality. He is wrapped in ideas which prevent his desired liaison.

This story written when a new awakening was taking place might have included a lot of the real theater that obviously had taken place in the two copyright holder's lives. A. O. was seemly a man with several marriages and no divorce records for the first marriage. Mary was a woman business owner, first married at age 16 and widowed at age 32. Maybe the total acceptance of this new equality of the sexes was to appear at the end of Volume #2 where Ganoe and Cassie would be reconciled. At any rate the reality of their lives will most probably never be known. Without the appearance of Volume #2 there is nothing but wild guesses.

The individual lives of A.O., Mary P., and T.A.H. are stories in themselves, abet ones that are hard to put together, there are unexplained situations and lost years, but here follows all of the notations that I have found. Judge for yourself.

A. O. Grigsby

Albert, Alcanoan, Alcanaan, Alkanon, Alcanon, or just A. O. Grigsby was born probably in 1837 in Kentucky, to Milding or Mildon or Milden Grigsby from Virginia and Elizabeth Fulks, from Maryland.

A.O.'s mothers father was John Fulks or Foulks

A.O.'s fathers parents, were Horatio Grigsby, 1750-1794 and Susannah Owens. Horatio died at Ft. Meigs of small pox, after being wounded at the Battle of Fallen Timbers on the Maumee

River in Ohio. The family moved to Kentucky about 1808. A.O.'s fathers grandparents were William Grigsby and Sarah Owens.

By age 13, A.O. and two brothers were living with two aunts and an uncle according to the 1850 census for Fleming County Kentucky. Both parents were dead.

There is the matter of a piece of land covered by an October 1, 1860 land warrant for 160 acres in the southwest quarter of section 13, township 1 of range 15 in the district of lands subject to sale at Kickapoo Kansas. The warrant was issued to Milden Grigsby (A. O's father) for service in the War of 1812. The warrant lists minor children as John, Alcanaan O. and James H. The land was deeded because Milden had served as a private in Captain Gregg's Company of the Kentucky Militia. Kickapoo Kansas was near Leavenworth, KS.

The Kickapoo were required to sell land in an exchange required by the United States government with the new treaty signed after the War of 1812. The Kickapoo were on the side of the British. Many of the parcels of land in the area were purchased by pro slavery persons attempting to keep Kansas moving towards being a slave state.

Alcanoan spent 37 months in the 14 Illinois Infantry, company E. He probably started out in Jacksonville IL. on May 1861. The 14 Illinois was at Battle of Hatchie, Vicksburg Siege, helped capture Fort Beauregard, Battle of Bentonville, North Carolina, marched through the Carolinas participated in the surrender of Johnston and his Army. The 14 Illinois marched to Washington D.C. then was moved to St. Louis,MO., Fort Leavenworth, KS., Ft. Kearny for duty on the plains, until being mustered out June 24, 1864 in Springfield IL.. He entered as a private and left the Union Army as a private. His description is 5'10", fair complexion, blue eyes, brown hair

A. O. married S. E. Yarbrough (Susan) in DeWitt County Illinois February 6, 1866 .

The 1870 Greenup, Cumberland Co. Illinois census lists A. O. as 33 yrs. old working as a dry goods clerk married to Susan E. from North Carolina. There are two male children Aleck 4 years of age and Willie one year of age. Also listed in the same household are A.O.'s maiden aunt, Margaret Grigsby 84 and Bettie Yorbrough 18. Was Bettie a sister or daughter of Susan's??

Susan and Alcanoan had a child named Dawn, born May 16, 1873.

The report of the Soldiers Orphans Home in Normal Il. records that Dawn is admitted on November 4, 1880, listing her former residence as in the city of Bloomington in McLean County. It is noted that A.O. Grigsby "deserted family"

A.O. marries Miz J. Pierce in Decatur County Ks. in September 29, 1883.

A.O. is listed in N. W. Ayer & Sons Newspaper Annual in 1884 as the editor of the *Weekly Herald* in Mantor or Manter, Minnesota, "a large eight page independent newspaper, published every Thursday. It is a reliable guide to those who contemplate removal to Northern Minnesota"

Three years later in 1887, according to the "Proceedings of the General Assembly of the Knights of Labor of America", Alcanoan is appointed at the Mankato Session in Minnesota and gives the address as the chairman of the special committee on cooperation.

Alcanoan's second wife dies on February 24 of 1888 in Hubbard also known as Manter, a city north of St. Paul. A correspondent from that city provided the tribute, "In the death of Mrs. Grigsby, a husband has lost a faithful and loving wife and the community a noble Christian woman, whose only aim was to do good. Mr. Grigsby has our most sincere sympathy in this hour of his deep affliction."

The Minnesota Historical Society Archives do not have any copies of the Manter *Weekly Herald* and they do not have any cross reference listing of newspapers by political perspective.

In July of 1888 Grigsby from Hubbard County is elected to succeed Chairman Buel, chairman of the United Labor party.

A month later it is noted in the *St. Paul Globe* that A.O. acts as chairman of the United Labor Party Convention on August 29 1888. The platform stated "we, the farm and labor party recognize only two parties, labor and capital and the only issue at stake between those parties is: Shall the people keep the fruits of their industry or shall capital enslave the many by it's extractions?" Ignatius Donnelly is listed as their candidate for Governor of Minnesota.

The *Saint Paul Daily Globe* on November 11, 1888 carried an anouncement of an Anarchist Anniversary. Describing the event as a "Festival of Sorrow"..."To commemorate and fittingly do honor to the nobel lives and heroic deaths of these shining lights on the plan of human emancipation and to unite in greatful recognition of their service as the vanguards of the great cause they loved so well and died so bravely for. "

It was the first anniversay of the death of Spies, Parsons, Fischer, Engel and Lingg and the "judical murder of these noble and heroic men in the city of Chicago." These men came to be known as the martyers of Haymarket Square. A. O. Grigsby is listed as a speaker in St. Paul at the Anniversary Commemeration.

On November 13, 1888, *The Saint Paul Daily Globe* reports that, "Industrial Times Publishing company, incorporated yesterday, is backed by the following leaders of the working classes: J.M. Paul, J.B. Dukes, J. Lamb, J. Swift, Minneapolis; E. Olson Lake Tremont, A. O. Grigsby Hubbard. The capital stock is $1500 in shares of $10 each. Publishing newspapers, books and pamplets will be the business of the company."

Six months later on May 19, 1889 *The Saint Paul Daily Globe* reports "a new merchantile co-operative association filed articles of incorporation last Tuesday. The plan is to establish a depot of exchange in this city and provide for a direct exchange of commodities between the different classes of producers and consumers. Among the incorporators are James Doran, J. B. Gardiner, Florence Sears, Peter Paul and A. O. Grigsby."

Grigsby spoke to the Ladies Labor Lyceum in North Minneapolis that same year, and is listed as the editor of the *Industrial Age of Duluth*, a newspaper. It is noted that he was a recent resident of Hubbard County

In 1889, Mrs. Susan E. Grigsby is living at 503 West Grove in the Bloomington, IL. city directory with William L. a printer.

St. Paul Daily Globe on March 9, of 1890 lists Grigsby

as the editor of the *Industrial Age* still being published in Duluth, Minnesota.

The City directory for Duluth MN. in 1890-1891 lists A. O. Grigsby as Sec. and Editor of The Age Publishing Asso-ciation, located in Room 21 in the Fargusson Building. J.H. Baker and A. McLean are at the same residence.

In April 1891, a meeting of the executive committee of the Farmers Aliance listened to the Zenith City Knights of Labor, who claimed that they put up $1500 "into the quondam *Industrial Age,* which upon the assurance of the receipt of $200 per month from sources not stated, was removed to this city (St. Paul) where it was edited by A. O. Grigsby." The property was purchased by John Lamb, Rev. George Mueller and others, and the name of the publication changed to *The State* The Duluth parties claim that they have nothing but the debts of the old regime." Mr. Muller and others were questioned to-day and Mr. Grigsby is booked to appear before the committee."

The *Northfield News Almanac* listed the Democrat, Republican and Alliance political party representatives for 1890-1892. A. O. is the Alliance party, At large Representative from Duluth.

At some point A.O. moved to Kansas. The *Emporia Daily Gazette* for May 14, 1892 , states that *The Topics* a small daily paper published by Chesney & Fluke became the state organ of the People's Party. "The paper will be edited by A. O. Grigsby, who is the editor of the *New Era* another People's Party paper."

The 9th Biennial Report of the Board of Directors of the Kansas State Historical Society dated Nov. 18 1890 — Nov. 15, 1892 lists A. O. Grigsby as editor and J.F. Petrik as business manager of the *Shawnee Drum-Beat* a reform newspaper. The ownership of the paper was in the name of The Peoples Publishing Association of Topeka, Kansas.

In the December 21 1892 issue of *The Advocate and Topeka Tribune* it is noted that Mr. and Mrs. A. O. Grigsby are part of the reception committee for the Inauguration of the Governor of Kansas. (I have found NO notation of this marriage.)

On December 8, 1892, Grigsby takes charge of the *Wabaunsee County News*. He retires on November 23, 1893 leaving L.H.

Gregory as the manager. A little over a year later, on January 11, 1894 the *Wabaunsee County News* suspends publication and ships its materials to Topeka and the subscription list is sold to the *Alma Enterprise* in Alma, Kansas.

A.O is listed on the muster roll of the Grand Army of the Republic in 1894 -Ed Lines Post #29 in Alma, Wabaunsee, Kansas. He is 57 years of age.

Grigsby shows up working for the *Alma Enterprise* which is owned by the Peoples Publishing Company.

The census of 1895 lists A. O. Grigsby as living in Topeka, in Ward 2 with two other men in the same household as his "family" J.F. Petrik, 41 years of age from Austria, and Jas Voydk, 38 years of age from Moravia.

A "Co-Operative Congress" was held in Topeka on April 9, 10, 11, 1896. The Governor of Kansas, E. N. Morrill welcomed the Co-Operative Congress delegates to Topeka, Kansas. A. O. Grigsby gives a rousing presentation titled "Labor Exchange" at this convention.

"The Nequa" a "magazine" publication that only publishes four issues publishes the speeches and reports on the convention at length. John C. Gish is listed as the publisher of Nequa, with offices at 117 West Fifth street in Topeka, Kansas, which happens to be next door to A.O. Grigsby's future residence in 1902.

The Co-Operative Congress presentations include the concept of profit sharing for employees. Specific examples of Co-Operative companies, most of whom sent delegates to the Congress were Proctor and Gamble, Pillsbury Flour Mills , Bourne Cotton Mills, and the N. O. Nelson Manufacturing Co. of Leclaire, Illinois.

It was noted by one speaker that, "In Rockford, Illinois, there are twenty furniture factories and several for the manufacture of agricultural implements, largely under Swedish management that are called Co-operative, but are such only in the large ownership of stock among employees."

There were presentations on German Co-operative Banks and Danish Co-operative Dairying. Mention is made of the Johnson County Kansas Co-Operative Fair Association with the quote "The Society owns its own grounds and are not in debt"

In 1897, S. E. Yarbrough (Susan), A. O. 's first wife is listed in the Bloomington , Illinois city directory. She is living in the same household as the city directory recorded in 1889. She is with her daughter Dawn Grigsby and a son William L. Grigsby. William L. was born in 1869, so is most probably the "Willie" noted in the 1870 census. Susan is listed as the widow of A. O. Her residence is at 507 West Grove. William L. works at The Pantagraph, a printing establishment.

A.O. Grigsby is listed as the manager of the *New Woman* newspaper in Topeka, Kansas.

The *"Equity"* newspaper starts being published in April 15, 1899.

The census of 1900 records Susan and Dawn Grigsby living with Dock Long 41 years old, born in 1859 in the state of Georgia, a son of Susan's. They are living in Duncan Town, Chickasaw Nation, Indian Territory. Duncan is in Oklahoma west of Paul's Valley. It is noted that Susan had 9 children 6 of whom are living in 1900. She is 73 years old and Dawn is 27 which does not match with her birth or age at the time of placement in an Orphans home. Susan the mother of Dock Long is listed as widowed. Dock Long's father was noted as from North Carolina. Dock Long is a Doctor who is memorialized in the Duncan area years later.

The next notation I could find was from the *The Co-Operative Journal* for May 1901, Vol.1 No. 6 which carried a news item " A cooperative store with a large number of members, was opened in Topeka Kansas May 13. A. O. Grigsby is one of the leaders in the movement."

Another notation on a store called the Equitable Exchange located at 111 East Sixth Street in Topeka. "organized on a basis by which the customers who purchased goods furnish all capital, pay the expenses and distribute the net income equally among themselves. Page 244 mentions the **equitable system of exchange"**

The opening of this store was also covered in *The Plaindealer* on May 24th. Owned by Nick Chiles *The Plaindealer* was one of the longest running African-American papers.

It was suggested by one informant that Nick Chiles might have been the printer that was used by Grigsby. There is also the possibility of Gish Bros. being the printer as John Gish was deeply involved in Populist causes and he became the business manager at one point for *The Equity* newspaper. Perhaps he was attempting to get his money first.

In 1902 the city directory for Topeka, Kansas lists A.O. Grigsby as editor of *"Equity"*, a newspaper published by The Equity Publishing Company. His residence is at 115 W. Fifth Street. This is the same address as the home where Mary P. Lowe died. Equity Publishing was also listed as having offices at 110 Kansas Ave.

An anomaly shows up next in the life of A. O. Grigsby. *The Palestine Daily Herald* of Palestine Texas on December 19 1903 records the following.

> Chicago Dec. 18 While working on a salary of 9 a week, A. O. Grigsby robbed his employers of 200 per day according to Manager David L Roso of M. L. Bartlett Co. When arrested he is said to have had S250 worth of costly vanilla beans concealed in his clothes. In the few months that Grigsbya meager salary kept him attached to the Arm it is believed be has stolen between 12000 and S1Cooo worth of stock I needed a little ready money was the only explanation he deigned to make. Another report of the same incident says that he was quoted as excusing the act by stating "The exchange needs money" (Typographical mistakes are as found)

A.O. receives a pension per month of $30. His application for pension is 383678 Certificate # 852137 the date of his admission to the National Home for Disabled Soldiers is 9/12/1904, he is 67. Also appearing on the page is a date of Feb. 17, 1917 listed as his death from acute Nephritis. His name is spelled Alcanaan O. Grigsby. His nearest relative is listed as J. H. Grigsby of Sardis Kentucky, a brother. In attendance at his death is a black woman named Fannie Brent, whose husband died in the same National Home for Disabled Volunteer Soldiers.

In 1907 he is listed as the State Secretary of the Socialist Party of Kansas from Leavenworth.

On October 19, 1908 the Grigsby family held their first annual reunion in Tollesboro, Ky. on the centennial anniversary of Horatio and Susanna Grigsby's arrival in Kentucky. Fifty members of the family attended including A.O. from Leavenworth, Ks.

In 1914 there is a notation in the Biennial Report of the Secretary of State of the State of Texas that he is the Delta County Justice of the Peace for Precinct #1 Cooper Post Office. This may be another A.O. Grigsby as I also found an A.O. Grigsby that applied for a Confederate pension.

The Breckenridge News on October 27, 1915 from Cloverport, Kentucky shows an A. O. Grigsby running for Secetary of State.

The *Interior Journal* of Stanford Kentucky on November 3, 1916, carries a sample ballot listing A. O. Grigsby in Lincoln County as a Socialist Presidential Elector.

The *Daily Register* of Richmond, Madison County, Kentucky on October 23, 1920 and on November 1, 1920, carry sample ballots again listing A, O. Grigsby of Tolesboro, Kentucky as a Presidential Elector on the Socialist ticket.

A. O. Grigsby is listed as a contributor and subscriber to the pamphlet service in the annual report of the American Civil Liberties Union in 1920.

Alcanoan is listed as widowed in the 1910 and the 1920 Fleming County,Kentucky census. He is living with the Teager's. He had been living with a niece Eliza Grigsby Teager and her husband Robert L. Teager. The Teager's names appear on his death certificate.

Alcanoan Grigsby dies on October 3, 1925 at 87 years of age, buried in the Tollesboro Cemetery, Lewis, Kentucky. The Certificate of Death states that he died of carcinoma of the jaw and that he functioned as his own doctor. His grave stone is available to view at findagrave.com.

Mary P. Lowe

Mary's maiden name was Mary Amanda Prather. She was born August 13 1858 in Kentucky. She married Tilghman A. Howard Lowe at Ellison in Labette County on September 2, 1874. She had just turned 16, he was 24.

Mary's father was William Prather 1820-1863 and her mother was Susan Huttsell, 1822-1880

The 1880 Federal Census lists Mary A. as living in McPherson, Kansas with her husband Tilman age 30. There are two children, Viola A. 4 years old, and Walter L. 3 years old. They are living with Tilman's brother Paris V. Lowe 27, and his wife Julia 16 years old. Julia is from Galva, Ks. her maiden name was Langshaw her mother was Bridget Divine from Ireland. Bridget and her husband Alfred are buried in unmarked graves in Empire cemetery in Galva.

In 1882 a girl Nina A. was born to Mary and T.A.H.

At some point Mary quit using her middle initial A, for Amanda and started using P. the first initial of her maiden name Prather.

Mary was listed as an editor along with **Mrs. M. C. Gillmore** of a news paper titled *"The New Woman"* which published two volumes from 1897 to 1898, in Topeka Kansas.

The *Kansas Agitator* published in Garnett, Kansas carries a news item on June 18, 1897, which states that "*The New Woman* is the name of a new paper published in Topeka by Mrs. M. P. Lowe and Mrs. Matilda C. Gillmore. It is published "in the interest of woman's advancement in all lines, and it should be in the hands of every woman in the country. It is one of the best papers in its class. Send a dollar and get it a year."

Mrs. M.C. Gillmore was born in Sweden in 1855 and grew up in Lawrence, Kansas in her parents', Hotel Pacific on Vermont Street. She had a son named Jessie R. A. Gilmore who became a printer. Mrs. M. C. Gillmore is referred to as Mathilda Gilmore in one edition of the paper. In 1894 she is living at 110 West E. St. listed as a journalist. In 1896-1897 she is listed as a widow residing at the Union Pacific Hotel and later at 1224 Jackson with Jessie R. A. Gillmore, a printer. They both move to Virginia in1900 with Matilda's step-father John Anderson and mother Johanna "Jennie" Carolina Anderson. Jessie owned a Print Shop in Virginia Beach, Virginia. Matilda C. Gillmore was listed as a journalist in 1930 census. Matilda died in 1936. She is buried in Virginia Beach, Virginia.

A.O. Grigsby is listed as the manager of the *New Woman* newspaper with offices at 211 West 6th Ave.

There is an ad in the paper from J.H. Heller, "I will sell at cost for 30 days only, meat and groceries." Location of the store is at 117 East Fifth St. J. H. Heller is also mentioned as a member of the Patrons of Equity.

Later J.C. Gish printing Co. is located at 117 West Fifth

The Patrons of Equity are written about and notice of their meetings are printed in the *New Woman*. Matilda Gillmore is in charge of the women's branch of the Patrons of Equity organization.

The *New Woman* newspaper has advertisements from C. Hoffman Milling in Enterprise Kansas. but also carries advertisements for Madam Bogar Chiropodist and Masseurs. Mrs. S, V, Searing at 424 Madison Street who is a Clairvoyant & Business Medium. J.S. Kelly a Psychic Healer at 310 Harrison Street. Dr. Mary McKinstry a Magnetic Healer.

News is printed about the Kaw Valley Spiritualist Association which will have a giant outdoor meeting on Sept 4--19 and they are getting special rates from the railroad. The opening address is to be given by Mrs. Cora V. Richmond and Dr. Adah Sheehan. There is also a notice about the Brockaway family arriving for a stay in Topeka with possibilities of meeting with them privately.

There is a very interesting article on the "strange cases of healing" by a "colored woman" Mrs. Thompson who lives in "Pleasant Valley a forlorn looking settlement east of the Santa Fe Shops". She is said to have healed members of some of the very rich and powerful of Topeka with colored liquid in bottles and strange lights.

Columns notify the reader of the *New Woman* that *Nequa* will soon be published and made available. There is also a column which explains that a new publication, a newspaper, named *Equity* will be happy to take a subscription.

The office and residence at 115 West 5th was situated on the south side of fifth street. The building faced north. The property was owned by L. H. Pounds and wife and was transferred to A. W. Knowles in 1891. It stayed in the Knowles family until 1953.

The commercial area of fifth and forth streets in Topeka was a highly integrated district with African-American and Anglo businesses. The building at 115 West 5th Street had residential quarters with a black doctor, a white lawyer, and two oriental residents. There is a twenty foot alley on the east of the building. The property consisted of a 36 foot vacant lot on the west with 120 foot covered by two buildings. Today it is a vacant lot thanks to the "urban renewal" of the 1950's.

115 West 5th later became the home of Langston Hughes when he was seven years old. Langston's mother was sepa-

Office of Equity Publishing and Mary P. Lowes residence.

rated from his father. She was working for an attorney, whose office was one block away.

In the 1900 census Mary P. was listed as born in 1858 and 41 years old. She is listed as having 5 children, 3 were still living. Alma V. Lowe was living in the same home. Alma was born June 1875 and is 25 years old. They are living at 115 West 5th Street.

Mary's obituary appeared in the *Topeka State Journal* on Wed. January 22 1902, she died on the preceding Monday:

> Mrs. Mary P. Lowe died at her home, 115 West fifth Street Monday evening at 9:10 o'clock. The deceased was the surviving wife of Dr. T. A. H. Lowe, whose death occurred in this city in 1894. She was favorably known to many residents of Topeka in connection with the Equity Publishing company. Her most striking characteristic was the desire to assist others. Three children survive her. Mrs. Ola Morrison, wife of A.R. Morrison of the *Kit Carson County (Colo.) Record*: Mrs. Nina Randall, of Los Angles, Cal., and Walter H. Funeral will be held at the residence tomorrow (Thursday) morning at 10 o'clock. She was 43 years old

Dr. Tilghman Answorth Howard Lowe

I found four Tilghman Howard's. One was from Indiana and was probably the person the other three were named after.

A Tilghman Howard Hunt attend the Eclectic Medical Institute in Cincinnati at the same time as David C. Lowe's son.

I found two Tilghman Howard Lowe's which caused me a little bit of a problem, but led me to inquire as to where the name came from. One Tilghman Howard was the son of Jessie and Sophia Lowe of Omaha Nebraska. He attended Williston

Seminary from which he was expelled for intoxication. Eventually moving to California.

The other was the son of David C. Lowe's 1827-1874. David C. is buried in Springfield Cemetery in Labette County. David C. was married to Mary Catherine Evans, 1830 — 1881. There son carried a third name A. for Andrew or Arthur or maybe Ashworth. He married Mary Amanda Prather, listed above and is the Dr. T.A.H. Lowe that I was looking for.

Born in Morgan County, Indiana in May of 1850.

Tilghman served as the administrator of his father's estate. After the death of his mother, Tilghman applied for and was given guardianship of his 13-year-old sister, Ida Lowe.

He is credited with finding some petroglyphs in Labette County in 1860's.

In the summer and fall of 1880, while living in McPherson, McPherson Co., Kansas, Tilghman treated his mother, his brother Paris and his brother-in-law Franklin Higgins, and charged them all for his services. It appears he also delivered his sister Adelaide's second child, Nellie Maude.

Tilghman was an eclectic doctor, listed in the "Eclectic Medical Institute, Cincinnati, Ohio." list of graduates. The listing states that he is practicing in McPherson and Sherman Kansas.

Tilghman's proctor was George Washington HULL, b 4 Feb. 1820; probably born in Ohio; Graduated Eclectic College of Medicine, Cincinnati; Ohio in 1861. Listed as from Renick's Mill up river from Lexington, Missouri. He practiced medicine in Lexington, but was run out due to his Union sympathies; returned to Newville, Indiana for a while with his uncle Henry HULL; went to Labette Co., KS after Civil War to practice medicine.

In September of 1880, T.A.H. retires from some branch of the military.

In Jan 1880, T.A.H. and Mary Lowe are present in the home of the bride Jessie Lowe, in McPherson, Ks. She was marrying Charles Simmons. Jessie was born March 1860 and is a sister of Tilghman's.

Tilghman moves to Cherokee Co., Kansas in 1881.

In October of 1885, Dr. T. A. H. Lowe is listed as a coroner in Labette County, Kansas.

He started the *Everest Enterprise,* a newspaper in Everest Kansas on March 9 1888. It was a weekly paper with a large and influential circulation in its section of Brown County.

On 4 Jan 1888, the *Altamont Sentinel,* of Altamont, Labette Co., Kansas, states: "Dr. Lowe was down from Everest last week eating Christmas pie with the folks. Doc tips the beam at 175 pounds. Pretty good for a small man." (Everest is in Brown)

He was active in politics, running for probate judge of Brown Co., in 1888, on the Union Labor party ticket.

From *The Everest Enterprise,* dated 29 Nov. 1889, "Dr. T.A.H. LOWE spent Thanksgiving with his family. The Doctor is building up a splendid practice in Atchison." (Atchison is in Atchison Co., Kansas.)

He died in Topeka January 3, 1894. Mention is made of Mastoiditis.

Mary P. and Tilghman A. Howard Lowe are buried in unmarked graves in Topeka Kansas.

Tilghman is listed as the author of *Nequa* in the Vol. 1 # 1 April 1896 issue of the newspaper *Nequa.* The first printing is a serialization, which runs from page 1 through page 14.

Equity Newspaper

Equity starts publishing April 15 1899. The newspaper is priced at 50 cents a year and was published weekly.

The largest advertiser was always C. Hoffman & Sons owners of The Old Reliable Enterprise Mills with a capacity of 1000 barrels, a flour mill located in Enterprise Kansas. C. Hoffman & Sons made a "specialty of supplying Co-Operative and Alliance stores with a full line of Mill products" Alliance stores were those that were started by the Farmers Alliance.

I spent an enjoyable day visiting with Reed Hoffman, the grandson of C. Hoffman. His father was Walter, part of C. Hoffman's second family.

Reed told of his uncle C. B. Hoffman's Populist viewpoints. He put books in my hands that covered several of the projects C.B. was envolved in, such as the Cat's Paw Utopia which outlined the Topolobampo Bay utopian community in Mexico.

Reed talked about the *Anti-Monopolist*, a newspaper printed in Enterprise. We also discussed the C. Hoffman and Sons advertisments that appeared in other Populist papers, which was one reason that small Populist newspapers could keep printing. I was introduced to the stories about Populist notables who came through Enterprise, Kansas. Reed talked about his great uncle Michael Senn, a Kansas state senator who held Populist views. It seems that these viewpoints resulted in Enterprise being a little bit different than most Kansas towns. Enterprise was the location of the second Bahai community in America, and the first Kindergarten west of the Mississippi. The people of Enterprise built a college, and hosted an interesting list of visitors among whom were Horace Greely, poet Bayard Taylor, Susan B. Anthony, Jane Adams, Annie Diggs, even Carrie Nation visited and tore up two saloons. All contributed to the development of "The community (which) was willing to accept what was by standards elsewhere and at other times irregular behavior. It produced a "millionaire socialist" in C. B. Hoffman, and an active leader in the fight for "women's rights" in Catherine America Hoffman, his wife."

Reed explained how hard work and a waterfall were parlayed into a woolen mill, flour mill, lumber mill and became a source of funds for Populist causes., eventually reverting to a Republican perspective.

Reed provided me with several other works on the Hoffman influences such as *Populism and Silo Tech* about Kansas State University and the Populist regents and the President William E. Will who is still not mentioned very much by the educational historians. I borrowed *The Company and the Community* about the development of Enterprise, its mills and the

Ersham Shops and noted that after C. B. Hoffman moved to Kansas City, "he was one of a number of prominent citizens arrested in Kansas City at a street meeting of the I.W.W.'s in the interests of free speech."

Other advertisers in *Equity* of a minor nature were The Equity Rule and Novelty Co located in Chicago, which actually sold rulers, and several periodicals such as,*"The Altruist"* which was "Devoted to industry and social reform" from St. Louis. *The Oracle* from Boston Mass. and *"The Adept"* an occult monthly magazine published in Minneapolis, Minnesota, available for 50 cents a year.

The columns in *"Equity"* include essays on social justice themes and egalitarian measures that would alleviate the suffering of the poor. Some columns were reprinted from other newspapers around the country.

An **Abby Anderson** listed on the mast head of *"Equity"* newspaper as the Department editor. What was that position? So far I have struck out on finding any of her story, except that she authored a piece for the *New Republic*, published in Topeka, titled, *Thou shalt — thou shalt not*.

The *New Republic Magazine* published at 610 Kansas Avenue in North Topeka, *The Kansas City Star, Tribune* or *Times,* and the *New York Weekly Tribune* could be subscribed to in combination with *Equity* or *The Nequa Magazine,* paying only one price.

Before the actual publication of the book, *Nequa,* there were a lot of column inches devoted to advertising the book in various ways. Soon after the first few issues of *"Equity"* newspaper which contained the serialization of *Nequa* were sold, press notices from publications in other cities singing the praises of this first feminist hollow earth science fiction book begin to appear in the letters section.

The Philosophical Journal from San Francisco stated, "The political economy of an ideal age is outlined, and the tendency of its teachings is in the right direction."

The Journal of the Knights of Labor in Washington D.C. wrote that "Nequa is especially recommended to all, who have a kindly interest in the welfare of the human race."

The Star of the Magi from Chicago Illinois felt that, "The lesson taught is the practical application of the Golden Rule to the economic social state."

The New Republic in Topeka states that "It gives courage to every lover of humanity by demonstrating how easy it would be for a small minority of the people who possess business talent, to establish economic independence for the great masses who only know how to labor with their hands in the production of wealth."

Freedom published in Sea Breeze, Florida recommended that "Students in economics and sociology will be interested in reading Nequa."

Appeal to Reason Press in Girard Kansas , "likened it to *Looking Backward* as it brings present-day people in contact with an ideal system, but it is more complete as far as it goes than Bellamy's work and at the same time offers a practical plan for the immediate introduction of Socialism."

The Free Man in Bangor Maine thought "It is a thoroughly interesting book without a dull line in it, and we shall look with interest for another volume from the pen of "Jack Adams." It seems to be a more practical work than Bellamy's *Looking Backward*, and should have a large sale. It should be in the library of every student of advanced thought."

Now printed in San Jose, California felt it "pictures an ideal but possible society where all the New Thought and all the Sociological principals of advanced thinkers are applied to life. It improves on *Looking Backward* in the leaving of the individual perfectly free at all times to follow his or her inclinations."

The Altruist of St. Louis , Missouri found that *Nequa* "contains a description of the ideal conditions which would prevail under the practical application of freedom, equality, and fraternity in human affairs, and proposes a system of equitable exchange as a remedy for poverty."

The New Abolition also printed in Topeka found "Interwoven with the tale are economic principles not taught nor expounded with the heavyness of the pedagogue, but pictured and beautified with the skill of an artist."

Obviously those who were politically aligned with the *Equity* Newspaper publishers and editors sang its praises and encouraged readers to buy the book.

Copies of the *Nequa* newspaper were conveyed to the Kansas State Historical Society by A. O. Grigsby in 1900.

So what happened? I've seen a paper edition of *Nequa* in a Kansas library which also notes that it is the second edition. But what happened to all the rest of the books that were printed and sold? Were the economic times such that each volume was passed from reader to reader and read until it fell apart? Was the paper of such poor quality, that they just did not last? Did some catastrophe befall the books before they were distributed and there wasn't any money to start over?

What happened to the newspaper *Equity*? The serialization of *Nequa* started in Volume 1, issue No. 31. The last issue of *Equity* Vol.II #35 is published in September 1901 and four months later Mary P. Lowe dies.

The publishing of *"Equity"* ceased on Sept. 7, 1901, effectively closing off this voice from the midwest. The war for *"Equity"*, for equality, for social justice and economic stability isn't over, just this particular battle by these people. They used the power of the pen. They used the power of the word. They produced a very valid attempt to mold minds using a little feminist science fiction. The interwoven nature of *"The New Woman" "Equity"* and the feminist perspective of the book *Nequa* reminds one of the saying about the hand that rocks the cradle.

Their efforts need additional documentation. There needs to be a review and revitalization, a new attempt which encompasses the perspective and passion we find in the hundred year old pronouncement from C. W. Searing editor of the *Osage County Republican,* (a Republican paper). Searing caught the fever of Grigsby and the Lowe's efforts and explains it with great gusto, as printed in *Equity,* the newspaper.

"Whoever reads *NEQUA* will find a wonderfully fascinating book. Though simple in style, it is clear in statement, and sets forth its strange narration with marvelous power. Full of startling facts, bewitching fancies and ideal realism's, it resembles the high-born novel, but it is more than a novel. It awakens the imagination, puzzles the understanding and forces the reader to exclaim: "Are these things true?" It introduces the reader anew to his brother and sister denizens of earth, exhibiting them in a newer and a diviner light: it bears him away to the newly discovered nether world, whose inhabitants sail ambient airy seas in ponderous air ships, argosies of commerce, and practice the only government of perfect equity."

The Word Nequa

First I looked at Latin. There was the phrase nequam quidem es! — you are really no good!

There were also some Latin words that were close.

nequam :worthless,good for nothing,
nequaquam : by no means, not at all.
neque ... neque : neither ... nor.
neque nec : and not, nor.
nequeo : not to be able, to be impossible.
nequitia nequities : worthlessness, bad-ness, wicked

— but, naming a book full of positive attitudes, a book which espouses a better day that exists, just around the corner or bestowing the title "Nequa, meaning the teacher" on Cassie, are not derivitive of a negative. Assuming that a negative Latin term is the origin of the word NEQUA is all wrong. Cassie was getting ready for a better future as outlined in the story line. Nequa is a book full of promise.

With dictionary, encyclopedia, or internet searches, I personally didn't find anything for the word Nequa except Neuqua Valley and a Neuqua Valley High School near Naperville Il. the suburbs of Chicago.

I found that "Nunquam" was the pen name of socialist writer Robert Blatchford.

At first I guessed from the sound of the word that it's origin was probably to be found in a Central Asia or Native American language. One source on the internet said Nequa was a Lakota word but never provided any explanation. I found that the term qua meant woman in Potowatami.

Then on the 24th of June 2012, as I was doodling the word Nequa. On the forth or fifth lettering of the word, I placed a fancy flourish on the down stroke of the N which looked like placing a U in front of the N and my mind saw that an L at the end of Nequa spelled the word Unequal.

I knew that was the origin of the book title. A very creative way to name a book, which is presenting a culture inside the earth, where the woman is equal, where the commerce is equal and where the main objective is for the community to grow in equality and lose the thought patterns that have kept the above ground, rich and powerful, in charge of the citizenry.

A society that has kept the great unwashed masses who are living on the surface of the earth UnequaL. And in a somewhat semiotic sense, when we go inside, there she is "Nequa, the teacher", equality personified, she exists, she can be found living inside the middle of the word Unequal, she is found inside — in the middle of the earth, hidden underneath the Unequal societies that live on the earths surface, and as is occasionally suggested through out the book, there is something that suggests equality, that can be found already existing inside of every human being. We just have to go inside and get it and bring it outside, make equality part of our everyday world.

So that is all of the story that I have found, about a group of people, dead over a hundred years. A crazy quilt story sewn together from bits and pieces found in several historical collections. I have included everything I could find on the written page. But a bit of reflection brought me the question, What if greater weight is given to the negative information I found? The abandonment of a child, deserting a wife, stealing from an employer, staying only a couple of years at each place of employment tends to make a person look like a wastrel or a con man. Without a wider understanding of what exactly they lived through, our intellectual musings could fall, way short of any reality. We need a good idea of the times, the situations that existed for these writers, these newspaper people. Fairness requires a greater amount of additional information and we need to answer a lot of questions, such as:

How much could a penny per issue paper provide
in the way of living expenses for three families?

Were there a lot of Civil War veterans who had to
abandon wives and children because at least
the orphanages had warmth and food?

Were negative news reports trumped up "Bad Publicity"
to slow up the spread of ideas that certain
big business interests did not want proliferating?

How could a medical doctor and an editor
of a newspaper, both end up in unmarked graves?

Unity Publishing in Kansas City, Mo. carried advertisements for *Looking Backward* by Bellamy, why didn't they help to push the Topeka publication of *Nequa*?

There are a lot of other questions that could be answered more conclusively if one gathered additional documentation of the times and the alternatives, that were available to our authors. A more well rounded picture of A.O., Mary P., Dr. T.A.H., Mrs. M. C. Gillmore and Abby Anderson would most assuredly come to past if a comprehensive investigation were done. For me the importance is the message they put into print. What is still needed is that their message be reviewed and renewed, not forgotten.

So I hope that these people who have no other existence at present might live in a few hearts, where we keep our feelings. Hopefully, perhaps our hearts will provide a new existence, our hands will accomplish what *NEQUA* and those involved in it's production, didn't get finished, while they were alive — some of us will develop a conscience and compassion for all fellow human beings, and seek ways to implement a more compassionate age on the outside of the globe.

Bibliography

Blacks in Topeka Kansas 1865-1915 A Social History, Thomas C. Cox Louisiana State University Press1982

The Company and the Community, Edward G. Nelson Bureau of Business Research, School of Business University of Kansas Lawrence 1956

Mizora: A World of Women, Mary E. Bradley Lane, Bison Books 1999

"The American Utopian Anti-Novel" Ray B. Browne found in Frontiers of American Culture, Perdue University Studies 1968

The Tolerant Populist, Walter T. K. Nugent University of Chicago Press 1963

"Prairie Radicals: A Common Pietism." Bicha, Karel D. Journal of Church and State 1976 18(1): 79-94.

Proceedings of the 18th International Humanities Conference All & Everything 2013 "The Initiation of Motherhood" Turner, Kristina

Populism and Silo Tech, Sparks, Ralph V., Manuscript in Progress

Appreciation is extended to —

Dr. G.W. Kleihege

Staff of the Kansas Historical Archives
Topeka, Kansas

Staff and volunteers of the
Shawnee County Room, Topeka, Kansas
especially Sherrita Camp

Staff at the Minnesota Historical Society
Minneapolis, MN.

Staff and volunteers at the National Archives,
Kansas City, MO
especially Evelyn Brissette

Mary Wallace at Watkins Museum
Lawrence, Kansas

Eric Page, Unity Archives
Unity Village, Missouri

David Boutros, State Hist. Society
of Missouri-Kansas City, MO.

Twyla Jackson, Dickenson County Hist. Society
Abilene, Ks.

Reed Hoffman

Relatives of A.O. Grigsby, Jeanne and John Scott

Relatives of Dr T.A.H. Lowe, Ernest Ittner,
Thelma Gamble, Cynthia Powers

Relative of M.C. Gillmore, Charlotte Hollingsworth

David Cox, InterLibrary Loan
Kansas City Mo. Public Library

Librarians, Jeremy Drouin, Jeanne Mithen,

Staff of VisionTek
Lindsborg, Kansas
especially Marla Elmquist and Cody Whetstone

Lenora Lynam, Old Mill Museum
Lindsborg, Kansas

Mardel Esping of Green Snake Press

and that part of the internet which is not pay per view